Maggie Craig was brought up in Clydebank and Glasgow, the youngest of four children of a railwayman father and a mother who worked in the typing pool of John Brown Land Boilers. Maggie was working as a medical secretary when she met her Welsh husband, Will, when he was doing part of his apprenticeship in a Clydeside shipyard, and she and Will subsequently sailed the world on oil tankers before settling in Glasgow and starting a family.

Maggie now lives in an old blacksmith's house in rural Aberdeenshire with Will and their two children. She is the author of DAMN' REBEL BITCHES, which tells the story of the women of the Jacobite rebellion. Her four earlier novels, THE RIVER FLOWS ON, WHEN THE LIGHTS COME ON AGAIN, THE STATIONMASTER'S DAUGHTER and THE BIRD FLIES HIGH are also available from Headline.

Also by Maggie Craig

A Star To Steer By

Maggie Craig

headline

First published in 2003
by HEADLINE BOOK PUBLISHING

First published in paperback in 2003
by HEADLINE BOOK PUBLISHING

10 9 8 7 6 5 4 3 2 1

ISBN 0 7472 6526 7

Typeset in Plantin by Avon DataSet Ltd,
Bidford-on-Avon, Warwickshire

Printed and bound in Great Britain by
Mackays of Chatham plc, Chatham, Kent

Papers and cover board used by Headline are natural, recyclable products made from wood grown in sustainable forests.
The manufacturing processes conform to the environmental regulations of the country of origin.

HEADLINE BOOK PUBLISHING
A division of Hodder Headline
338 Euston Road
London NW1 3BH

www.headline.co.uk
www.hodderheadline.com

To all those who have worked so hard to keep the Forth & Clyde Canal alive.

And to Will, Sandy and Tammy,
all three of them stars,
all three of them my own personal guiding lights.

Acknowledgements

My sincere thanks to the following:

Robert Russell for sharing with me memories of his childhood in Canal Street, Port Dundas, Glasgow.

Carole McCallum, Glasgow Caledonian University Archivist, for being so welcoming and helpful and providing me with much fascinating information about the Glasgow and West of Scotland College of Domestic Science, aka The Dough School.

The Auld Kirk Museum and the William Patrick Library, both in Kirkintilloch. Published by the Museum, A. I. Bowman's *The Gipsy O'Kirky* provided details of the SS *Gipsy Queen* and her pleasure cruises between Port Dundas and Craigmarloch. The library's extensive collection of photographs of the Forth & Clyde canal was enormously helpful.

The National Library of Scotland Map Library in Causewayside, Edinburgh, for being so friendly and efficient when supplying me with maps of old Glasgow.

Guthrie Hutton for his *Forth and Clyde: The Comeback Canal* which was both informative and inspirational.

Eileen Ramsay for guidance on matters spiritual/ linguistic.

Sheila Livingstone, in particular for the poems about Craigmarloch.

My mother-in-law Lillian for the black cat.

My husband Will for tramping so many miles of the towpath with me and helping me revisit my own childhood memories of the nolly.

My sister Kathleen for her unstinting support. Likewise to Jude (the man's a saint.)

And above all to Sarah Keen at Headline for being such a brilliant editor.

Prologue

Ellie pressed herself against the rough stone of the tenement close, trying to become as small and unobtrusive as possible. Exploding into the warm stillness of the May evening, the violence had seemed to come out of nowhere.

Her own home lay two streets away. She could reach it in as many minutes if the escape route through the back court of the building in which she was sheltering hadn't been blocked by two members of the Rafferty clan. Trouble in Temple on a Saturday night and the Raffertys involved? What a surprise.

The family formed the rotten core of one of the notorious local gangs: the Bruce Street Boys. Shoulder to shoulder like sentries on watch, the two men stood with their legs apart, completely filling the building's rear exit. They exuded an air of chilling and watchful menace: like cats waiting to pounce on an unsuspecting rat.

Ellie had been playing with a group of girls much younger than herself, holding one end of a long skipping rope while they took it in turns to jump through it. At the first sight and sound of trouble their mothers had swept down into the cobbled street, scooping up their offspring and retreating to the safety of their homes. Around and above Ellie's head a succession of deafening bangs indicated that solid wooden doors were being flung shut. Neither the most persistent knocking nor the most frantic of pleas would get those defensive barriers opened again. Not till it was all over.

One of the men standing a few feet away from her pushed back his dark jacket, hooking his thumbs into his waistcoat pockets. Each held a cut-throat razor. The man had himself been on the receiving end of punishment with such weapons on some previous occasion. Following the curve of his chin, a deep and ragged line stretched from below his ear lobe to the side of his mouth. It was a well-known fact that exasperated casualty surgeons at Glasgow's hospitals saw little need to do fine stitching on patients who had brought their injuries upon themselves. Men like this one bore the resulting scars as a badge of pride.

His companion upended the beer he held, pouring the foaming brown liquid over the stone floor of the close. Adjusting his grip, he took the bottle by the neck and smashed it against the wall of the passageway. As he lifted his hand and surveyed the deadly spears of jagged glass, a chilling gleam of pleasure stole into his eyes.

Try as she might, Ellie couldn't suppress a whimper of fear. Two pairs of eyes travelled to where she stood doing her best to disappear into the wall. She saw them rest briefly on her dishevelled auburn waves.

'Alan Douglas's girl?' asked the man with the marked face. She knew who he was. His son Frank was her friend.

'A-a-aye,' she stuttered.

'Well,' observed Francis Rafferty senior, 'your daddy might be a God-cursed Protestant but I'd have to admit that he was a good man in a fight in his day.' He sounded like someone extending polite compliments on a sporting achievement.

A barrage of shouting and yelling rushed in from the street outside. Amidst the cacophony of foul language, insults and challenges Ellie picked out a familiar war cry. Sworn enemies of Catholics in general and the Rafferty family in particular, the Wallace Street Warriors had joined the fray.

Swivelling her head towards the noise, she saw one man lose his footing and fall on to the roadway, his arms flailing out in a fruitless attempt to save himself. Four other men shouted in triumph, arranged themselves around his body and began administering a savage kicking.

The man with the broken beer bottle growled, 'That's our Gerry down!'

'Sure, and won't we be repaying the compliment in about two minutes flat? We'll be able to give the black-hearted sons of bitches a much better battering if we can entice them in here.'

Francis Rafferty broke off from his discussion on tactics long enough to wave Ellie over, standing back to allow her the space to walk through between himself and the other man. 'On your way, pet. My brother and I have some business to attend to here but there's no need at all for innocent bystanders like yourself to get hurt.' The awful scar creased grotesquely as he grinned at her.

Ellie sped out into the back court and past the dog-fouled square of grass the tenants of this building called a drying green.

Like an arrow seeking its target, a question whizzed through the close behind her. 'Would there be any Fenian bastards in there?'

Frank's uncle roared out a reply. 'Sure, and why don't you bold lads come in here and find out?'

Ellie didn't wait to hear any more, swinging breathlessly into the muddy and uneven lane that snaked between the two high and long rows of grey stone tenements. But she was forced to skid to an abrupt and ungainly halt before she had gone twenty yards along it. Men and boys were coming through the closes on either side, running battles erupting all around her.

She took a hasty step back to avoid being struck by a young man retreating rapidly in front of two others. Cold steel flashed. There was an unearthly scream of pain and the lad fell backwards at her feet. Red and sticky, blood oozed up over his ripped face. As Ellie stared down at him in horror, a hand gripped her elbow. And pulled hard.

PART I

Chapter 1

1927

'What the hell are you doing here, Ellie? Come through this way. There's nane o' them in here yet.' His father might still retain the Irish brogue to which he'd been born but Frank Rafferty junior was as much a Glaswegian as Ellie herself.

As he dragged her into an unoccupied back court, her fear-filled eyes drifted to the lane. The man who'd been slashed was struggling to his feet. He got a boot in the face and went down again.

'Ellie! Get a move on!' Frank half pulled and half pushed her through a close and out into the street beyond. It was empty, all of the action taking place on the other side of the building. 'Away hame now, hen,' he said, giving her a shove in the right direction. 'Ah wouldnae like tae see ye hurt.'

'Will ye no' come wi' me, Frank?'

Poised to dive back through the passageway, he flashed her a roguish grin. 'And miss all the fun? No' bloody likely.'

'Oh, Frank! I thought you were never gonnae get involved in all o' this. You used to say it was a mug's game.'

'No' so easy when you're a Rafferty, Ellie. Certain things are expected o' you.'

'Oh, Frank,' she said again. 'Come away wi' me now. Before *you* get hurt.'

He shook his shaggy head. He was a redhead like Ellie, with thick wavy hair the same shade as boiling toffee. She had always thought it gave them a kind of bond.

'Cannae do it, hen.'

The regret sounded completely genuine. Then he vanished, swallowed up by the close. Consumed by the erupting violence.

'Where's the fire, lassie?'

'Oh, hello, Mr Anderson.' Wrenching her key out of the lock, Ellie made an unsuccessful grab for the edge of the door. In her haste to reach the safety of her top-floor home she had thrust it open with some force. As it banged and juddered against the wall, her father lifted his head and swore viciously at her.

He was sitting opposite Willie Anderson, both of them on upright wooden chairs pulled out from the table in the centre of the kitchen. The comfortable armchairs that had once flanked the fire had disappeared years ago, sold off for a few shillings so Alan Douglas could buy drink.

Still shod in their working boots, both men had their feet propped up on the rusty cast-iron of the range, which dominated one wall of the small and shabby room. Empty bottles littered the torn and scuffed oilcloth covering the floor, and the whole place reeked of red biddy, that poisonous blend of rough wine and methylated spirits.

'Were the hounds o' hell after ye or what?' Alan Douglas was in his shirtsleeves, his jacket lying in a crumpled heap on the floor beside his chair. 'Come here and explain yourself, ye wee hure.'

Sticks and stones may break my bones, but names will never hurt me. Not true, Ellie thought dully. Names did hurt. They made you feel small and mean and dirty and worthless.

'Wallace Street is fighting Bruce Street,' she explained tersely.

Her father's eyes lit up. 'Oh-ho! What d'ye say tae that, Willie? Shall we go out and lend a hand?' He grinned widely, exposing his stained and yellow teeth. 'Once we can decide whose side we're on.'

'We're a bit past that,' his friend said, winking at Ellie. 'And no' only on account o' the bevy we've sunk the night.'

Placing the heels of his hands on the edge of the chair, Alan attempted to push himself upright. 'That's shite, William Anderson. Me and you are in the prime o' life.'

As he slumped back down again, Ellie walked forward, stooping to pick up the garment he'd so carelessly discarded. When he grabbed her by the loose material at the front of her dress she yelped and dropped his jacket back on to the floor.

'Something tae eat, then,' he spat out as he yanked her to her feet. 'Make me and my pal here something tae eat. There's men in here starving tae death while you're out gallivanting, ye wee bitch.' He gulped and swallowed, opened his mouth wide and belched into her face.

Ellie recoiled in disgust. The grip he had on her bodice didn't allow her to go very far. He was a powerful man, with the strong build required for the hard physical labour of loading and unloading the coal lighters and grain scows that plied the nearby canal. Not that he did too much of that any more. It was casual work, paid by the day. He worked only enough to earn his drink money, with precious little left over for housekeeping.

'I made you your tea a couple of hours ago,' she said, despising herself for the fact that her voice had sunk to a thin and nervous whisper. Malcolm maintained she needed to stand up to their father. That was easy for him to say. Since her brother had grown taller and broader and, in theory at least, more capable of retaliation, Alan Douglas had been noticeably more reluctant to strike him. He had no such inhibitions when it came to his daughter.

Doing her best to turn her face away from his sour breath, Ellie spotted what was on the table: the remains of the packet of oatcakes and chunk of mousetrap she thought she'd hidden so carefully away. 'Och,' she said, 'why did you have to go and eat those? I was saving them for tomorrow night's tea!'

'Answer me back, would ye?' her father roared. He lifted his hand from her arm and slapped her hard on the side of the head.

'Alan, man!' protested Willie Anderson, half-rising in his chair. 'Dinna hit the lassie!'

Ellie was already at the front door. Within seconds her feet were clattering on the stone staircase of the tenement. Eyes stinging with tears of pain, rage and humiliation, she hurtled downwards.

As she rounded the wooden banister at the top of the last flight before the ground floor she stumbled. Unable to check her momentum, she careered down the final stairs with the panicky awareness that her feet were barely touching them. Oh God, she was probably going to go her length and split her head open or break her ankle or something!

Two warm and capable hands grabbed her in the nick of time. The perilous descent was over.

'Michty me!' said the comfortably built woman

standing in the open doorway at the foot of the staircase. 'What's the trouble, lass?'

'Oh, Granny Mitchell,' Ellie said, choosing one of her troubles over the other, 'I nearly got caught in the middle of a fight!'

'Which misbegotten crew are up to their tricks tonight?'

The old lady shook her head when Ellie told her. 'Both sides using religion as an excuse to bash each other over the head. Most o' them havenae seen the inside of a church for years.' Her kind face settled into unusually grim lines. 'I mind when Wallace Street was a fine respectable place; Bruce Street too. When the Raffertys moved in they dragged it down to the gutter.'

'Well,' came a sharp voice from the mouth of the close, 'it doesn't take a whole heap of folk to bring a street down. One family can give a whole close a bad name. I must say it's hard when decent people have to live cheek by jowl with thieves, drunkards and ne'er-do-wells.'

Ellie raised mutinous eyes to the newcomer's face. It was Granny's snooty daughter-in-law, Rosalie. Like a large percentage of the population of Temple, including Ellie's brother, Malcolm, young Mrs Mitchell worked for the Tait family, in her case at Bellevue, their magnificent new villa on the north bank of the canal. Beforc her marriage she had been a live-in parlourmaid in the old house, now demolished.

Once her children were up a bit Rosalie had begun working for the Taits again, going into Bellevue on a daily basis and also helping out at the parties the family often threw in the evenings and at weekends. She was aye telling people she did so only 'to help dear Mrs Tait out. There's *such* a problem getting good staff these days, you know.' Ellie knew damn fine the Mitchells needed the money the same as everyone else did.

Her employers had obviously been entertaining guests this Saturday evening. Carrying her frilly white apron and cap, Rosalie, Ellie had to admit, looked very professional in her low-waisted black dress, her uniform both smart and fashionable. It must be grand to have nice clothes, especially when someone else bought them for you. Seemingly the Taits were real generous about that kind of thing.

Smiling a little wistfully at Granny, Ellie wondered how she could fill the hours till Malcolm came home from the dancing in Partick. She wasn't going back upstairs until he did.

'D'ye want to come in tae me for a wee cup o' tea and some gingerbread, pet?'

'For goodness' sake!' spluttered Rosalie, glaring at her mother-in-law. 'D'you really think you can afford to keep on feeding the waifs and strays of the district? Not to mention tiring yourself out doing all the baking in the first place. You're not getting any younger, you know.'

Sadie Mitchell's pepper-and-salt brows knitted ominously. Not content with having buried two husbands, raised six children and helping to raise her grandchildren, she had always managed to find the time and the energy to look out for every wean in the neighbourhood who needed a bit of love and attention and didn't always get it at home. All of the local children called her Granny.

'It's all right,' Ellie said hastily, not wanting to be the cause of any trouble between the two Mrs Mitchells. 'I think I'll go for a walk along the nolly. It's a fine night and it's still light. Don't worry, I'll steer clear o' any trouble.'

The old lady's mouth settled into a firm line. 'You'll take a piece o' gingerbread up to the canal with you.'

Rosalie flounced up the stairs to her own first-floor home, closing its door firmly behind her. Looking unusually fierce, Sadie folded her arms across her generous bosom. 'I'm no' ready for my box yet!'

'No' by a long chalk,' Ellie agreed.

'I suppose she's right, though. I am getting older.' A question lurked in the tired eyes.

Ellie folded her own arms. 'Oh aye?' she queried. 'So that wasnae you I saw stoating a couple of balls off the wall in the back court the other day?'

Granny's grim expression relaxed. 'Well, the wee lassie had no one else to play with.' She chuckled. 'I damn near gave myself a seizure, mind! Come on in for a minute, hen. I'll cut you a piece o' yon ginger-bread.'

Swallowing the last morsel of Granny's home-baking as she walked past the Bay Horse – if her father wasn't drinking at home he was usually drinking in there – Ellie emerged on to the canal bank, stepping up to the nolly bridge. When its two halves weren't being laboriously raised so boats could pass between them the creaky wooden arch allowed pedestrians, livestock and the occasional motorist to cross the canal heading for Bellevue or the big house at Garscube and its surrounding farms.

Leaning forward over the handrail, she gazed down into the treacly water slapping gently against the stone walls of the lock chamber. She was thinking about Frank Rafferty.

They'd been friends for as long as either of them could remember. Even in the last couple of years, in the sort of neighbourhood where boys and girls all too quickly became men and women, their friendship had remained exactly that – nothing more, and most certainly nothing less. The bond between them was strong, and it was about more than their merely having the same colour of hair.

Like herself, Frank had been very young when he had lost his mother. Even as small children running wild together along the banks of the canal, that shared and sad experience had cemented their friendship into something special.

As he and Ellie matured, she was increasingly finding herself turning to him whenever she had a problem she needed to talk over. She loved her brother dearly but Malcolm was a wee bit inclined to think his opinion was the only one that mattered. Frank wasn't like that at all. He always listened before he spoke.

Now it seemed that funny, kind and clever Frank had allowed himself to be sucked into the stupid and pointless violence in which so many members of his family indulged. Ellie sighed, and continued to stare morosely down into the darkening waters of the canal.

If he kept doing what he'd been doing tonight, sooner or later his face would be marked in the same way his father's was. Then he'd have absolutely no chance of getting a decent job – one that would allow him to make something of himself. It was hard enough for a Catholic like Frank to get a start, especially with an Irish surname.

It wasn't easy even for a Protestant to find work, especially a not-very-clever lassie who'd never seen much point in going to school. If only she'd been brainy like Malcolm it might have been different.

He worked as a junior clerk in the offices of Tait's Boatyard. Straddling both sides of the canal a few hundred yards west of where she stood on the bridge, on the other side of the sawmill and timber yard, it built mainly puffers. Acquiring their nickname from the characteristic noise they made when steam puffed out through their funnels, the compact little boats carried coal, timber and whatever else was required along the canal and to the islands and coastal communities of the Firth of Clyde and beyond.

James Tait had taken a chance on Malcolm. Those were the exact words he'd used when he'd given him a job two years before. 'I'm going to take a chance on you, young Malcolm. Other people might say your family background isn't all it should be, but you strike me as a keen lad, willing to work hard and learn all there is to know about the expanding Tait empire. In fact,' Mr Tait had said, a comment Malcolm never tired of repeating to anyone who cared to listen, 'you remind me of myself at your age.'

Determined to do his best for Ellie, Malcolm had recently paid a visit to her teacher. Nervous but determined, he had extracted a grudging promise from the woman that some sort of written reference might be possible if his troublesome wee sister at least stopped dogging school and maintained perfect attendance until the end of the summer term.

Malcolm had rejected Ellie's suggestion that, having turned fourteen before Easter, she should simply have left school there and then. It would be hard to find a job with a reference, well nigh impossible without one. As the days lengthened and the weather grew warmer she hadn't found it easy to turn her back on the canal, which fascinated her so much, in favour of hours spent in a stuffy classroom that smelled of chalk and over-polished squeaky wooden floors, especially when that stuffy classroom was ruled by a teacher who wielded sarcasm as savagely and as frequently as she applied the punishing leather straps of the tawse.

Ellie would escape all of that in six weeks' time in exchange for a much longer day slaving away in one of the local factories. If she was lucky.

She'd still be expected to do all of the housework at home. She knew also that her father was already planning on appropriating most of whatever meagre wage she could earn with the sole aim of pouring it down his already overlubricated gullet.

'If he thinks that, he's got another think coming,' Ellie muttered, acknowledging the emptiness of the threat even as she said the words out loud. If Alan Douglas wanted to take her money off her there was no way she could stop him. Laying her forearms along the handrail of the bridge, she sank her tousled head down on to them.

Somebody laughed.

Chapter 2

Fizzing through the twilight, the laughter could only have come from Bellevue. Garscube House lay some distance to the north and there weren't any other buildings in the immediate vicinity. Drawn to the happy sound, Ellie walked off the bridge and stepped down on to the north bank of the canal.

There was no towpath on this side. Much less frequented as a result, the vegetation was free to run riot. Ellie threaded her way past the huge clump of hawthorn trees that had been her den when she was little. Then she walked between rosehip bushes, broom and whin, heading for the wooden gate in the old stone wall which was the last remnant of Gowanlea, the house that had been demolished to make way for Bellevue. When she got there she put her face to the knot-hole in the middle of it.

The new house was as impressive as its professionally landscaped gardens, both of them replacing Gowanlea and its policies so dramatically it was hard to remember what either of those had looked like. Standing out now against the increasing darkness of the surrounding trees and bushes, the flat-roofed white building – its colour had been the talk of the steamie for weeks – was startlingly modern.

Looking for all the world like one of the great ocean

liners built down the river at Clydebank, Bellevue gave the impression of sailing along the top of the airy hill on which it was built. Like a ship, the Taits' home had long sweeping lines, and curves where you might have expected sharp corners. There were even windows that looked exactly like portholes, one under each corner of the roof. This house had windows in all shapes and sizes.

French ones opened out on to the series of terraces that descended the hill to the red blaes tennis court and the small pagoda-like summerhouse, painted white, which stood at its south-west corner. There were two especially remarkable things about Bellevue's gardens: they contained only white flowers; and dotted among those flowers were small bronze statues of dainty female figures. One was an archer, bow poised to fire the arrow she held between her fingers. Another danced on the tips of her toes, pirouetting elegantly on one leg. Yet another held a hoop in front of her, tiny arms gracefully extended.

Mingling with their guests, all four members of the Tait family were currently standing or sitting in front of the French windows. One man stood up and took his leave of the party. Mr Tait shook him warmly by the hand, while Mrs Tait reached up and kissed him on the cheek. A woman in a plain black dress like Rosalie Mitchell's came out on to the terrace. That would be Mrs Drummond the cook-housekeeper, the only resident member of staff at Bellevue, ready to show the departing guest out.

Tall and broad-shouldered, James Tait was as dark as his wife was fair and as handsome as she was beautiful. It wasn't hard to believe that he had been a war hero. There was some story about him having run forward under a hail of enemy bullets to save a wounded comrade. Malcolm knew all the details, as he could also recount how his boss had entered the army a humble tommy and come out of it a captain, promoted several times on the battlefield itself for both gallantry and coolness under fire.

According to Malcolm, James Tait was now a *captain of industry*, owner not only of the boatyard but of several other companies in the district. He had snapped them up at bargain prices last year when the confusion, bitterness and financial disaster of the General Strike had proved one crisis too many for their previous owners.

His wife Angela was wearing red tonight, those wide-legged trousers that looked like a long skirt when the wearer was standing still. Three narrow stripes in the same colour trimmed the large square-cut collar of her white boat-necked blouse.

She lifted her cocktail from the glossy white-painted wrought-iron table in front of her. Ellie had only the haziest idea of what a cocktail actually was, but she knew it was what rich folk drank – women and men. No red biddy for them. Mrs Tait tilted her fashionably cropped head and put her glass to her lips.

The outside electric lights, one of the many things for which Bellevue was famous, came on, the illumination bouncing off the sparkling bracelet that dangled from Angela Tait's slim wrist and freezing her for a few seconds in the pose she had adopted to drink her cocktail. She looked as graceful as one of the small bronze ladies in her garden.

Behind her, her son Evander sat perched on the low stone wall that ran round the topmost terrace, a little distant from the rest of the group. He was fifteen, his sister Phoebe a year older. Clearly destined to become a beauty like her mother, she had the most wonderful blonde hair. Reaching to her waist, tonight it was tied back off her face with a ribbon that matched her simple but stylish blue frock. As Ellie watched, James Tait reached out towards his daughter and drew his hand down the glorious yellow fall.

Even from this distance you could see the affection in his face, could understand that some sort of teasing was going on as Phoebe turned and playfully slapped her father's hand away. He called across to his wife, saying something that made her laugh and smile at both him and their daughter.

Ellie drew back from the knot-hole, pushed herself off the gate and made her way back through the bushes to stand by the edge of the canal. She was experiencing a pang of the most intense envy.

How strange it was that Bellevue and the golden life its occupants enjoyed were separated from the violence she had witnessed tonight and the poverty she lived with every day by nothing more than this narrow strip of water in front of her. Yet in another way the distance was as great as the millions of miles that a puffer captain had once told her separated the Earth from those stars that twinkled in the night sky.

Revealing itself as this long May evening drew to its close, one of those was reflected in the black depths of the canal. Ellie looked up and fixed her eyes on it, a familiar rhyme creeping into her head.

Star light, star bright,
First star I see tonight,
I wish I may,
I wish I might,
Have the wish I wish tonight.

She had no idea how and where she had learned the little poem. She liked to think her mother had taught her. In her more honest moments she questioned that. She'd been a mere two years old when Cathy Douglas had died, the child she'd struggled to bring into the world outliving her by a few short hours.

Wondering if she should wish to be as beautiful as Phoebe Tait and live in a house like Bellevue, with lots of lovely clothes and plenty of food, Ellie's mouth curved in a wry smile. That would be like wishing for the stars themselves, thinking you could pluck them out of the sky to wear round your wrist like Mrs Tait's jewels.

In any case, her envy wasn't really directed at Phoebe's wealth and beautiful clothes. What Ellie longed for was a loving family: one with two parents who loved each other and their children.

'Too late for that now anyway,' she murmured sadly. 'I'm nearly grown up and out in the world.'

Glancing up from the star's reflection, she looked across the canal towards the Bay Horse and the tenements that huddled around it. Most of the folk who lived on that side of the canal knew what it was like to go hungry when the week's money had run out too soon. Practically nobody over there could afford to buy nice clothes. Yet lots of them knew what love was, and a happy home. You didn't have to be rich to have those two things.

That's what she would wish for, then. Love and a happy home. One where nobody got drunk and nobody got hit. It didn't have to be grand like Bellevuc, only clean and comfortable. She'd like enough money to be able to buy nice food, share it with a loving family and good friends.

Determinedly stamping on the thought that such simple dreams were as far out of her reach as the hopeless fantasy of living the same kind of life as Phoebe Tait, Ellie raised her face once more to the heavens. She split her wish down the middle, assigning half of it to Frank. 'Let him have all these things too,' she whispered, 'and let him find a decent job. A respectable one where he can earn good money honestly.'

She squeezed her eyes tightly shut and wished hard.

'It's no use, Ellie. We're completely skint. And it's only Thursday.'

Having rummaged comprehensively through his pockets, Malcolm placed the two big round pennies he had found there in the middle of the bare and stained kitchen table. He was surveying them now as though he could conjure up more money if he only stared hard enough. Lifting his head at last, he transferred his gaze to his sister. 'You havenae got anything?'

'No,' Ellie said. Perched on the edge of one of the upright chairs, she was watching him like a large bright-eyed mouse. 'D'you think maybe you shouldn't have put so much down on your suit last Saturday? Or decided to buy one of the cheaper ones?'

Well-brushed and pressed though he always ensured it was, Malcolm's broadening shoulders were going to split the jacket of the suit he'd been wearing to his work for the past two years sooner rather than later. Before he'd gone to the dancing the previous weekend he'd called in at the gentleman's outfitters in Partick that allowed its customers to pay a little money each week until they'd accumulated enough to make a purchase.

Malcolm shook his head. 'Buying cheap clothes is a false economy, Ellie. And I've told you what store Mr

Tait sets by his employees looking smart. Especially those of us who work in the office,' he added, a tinge of pride creeping into his voice.

He turned and looked in disgust at the large and anything but smart figure lying snoring in the box bed in the kitchen. Having worked three whole days this week, Alan Douglas had rewarded himself last night with a wee refreshment. He had staggered home from the Bay Horse at midnight.

Light on his feet, Malcolm stepped over to the bed and scooped up the jacket and waistcoat their father had as usual flung on to the floor, crumpled on top of his working boots. As he carried them back to the table he smiled at Ellie. 'We'll be needing to get you a new outfit or two soon. You'll have to be smartly turned out when you go looking for a job.'

A moment later his fruitless search through their father's pockets had wiped the smile off his face. 'He cannae have spent it all, surely!'

'Maybe it's in the pockets of his trousers,' Ellie suggested. Alan Douglas was still wearing those.

Malcolm walked back to the bed and tossed the clothes gently on to the foot of it. 'We'd better no' risk it, Ellie. He'll be like a bear wi' a sore head if we wake him up now.'

He came to stand beside her, checking the time on the battered old mantel clock above the range. 'You've got an hour before you leave for school. Let him sleep as long as you can but see if you can get something out o' him before you go. We cannae leave it till we come home. He'll probably have spent it all by then.'

'I'll do my best, Malcolm.'

He nodded. 'Aye. You do your best. If he gives you enough dough you and me'll go to the chip shop tonight. We deserve a wee treat. You'll go to the school today?'

Ellie bristled. 'Have I no' been every day since Easter?'

'Keep it up, then,' he responded, grinning at her indignation. 'It'll be worth it in the end.'

After he had left Ellie slid off her chair and began to clear up the breakfast things, moving around the kitchen as quietly as she could. She had made porridge for Malcolm with the last of the oatmeal, denying herself a bowl so there would be something left for her father when he eventually surfaced. Volatile at the best of times, his temper was always worse if there was nothing for him to eat.

At twenty to nine, every household chore she could think of done, she knew she couldn't wait any longer. Even if her father woke up in a reasonable mood it would take time to get the money out of him. He never parted with it easily.

At least the box bed was high off the ground. She didn't need to bend over him. The reek of alcohol and unwashed male body was bad enough as it was. Laying her hand reluctantly on his shoulder, she gave him a shake. She jumped back as if she'd been stung when the noisy inhalation of air ceased halfway through an indrawn breath. He let out a huge rattling snore, and slept on. Ellie tried a more vigorous shake. No response. She would have to call his name.

'Father' sounded awful posh. The affection inherent in the word 'Daddy' reminded her painfully how unlike a loving father Alan Douglas was. She couldn't remember when she'd last called him that. In the end she settled for two simple words, clearly and distinctly articulated.

'Wake up.'

Alan Douglas's eyes snapped open.

Ellie's heart was pounding like a steam hammer and her skin was slick with sweat. She needed to stop and pull several deep breaths into her lungs but she couldn't afford to halt her pell-mell dash towards the canal. Decked out like a bride and her bridesmaids in lacy white finery, the clump of hawthorns at the foot of Bellevue's gardens was within sight.

Grasping fingers clawed at the skimpy cotton of her frock. It took every ounce of courage she possessed to turn and face him, raising her arms in a gesture both of plea and defence. It hurt to do it. Her shoulders were throbbing, reeling from the blows he'd rained down on them seconds before.

She let out a great ragged sob of relief. He wasn't there. He wasn't far behind her, though. She could hear his laboured breathing and heavy footfalls as he toiled up the steep path of beaten earth that led to the locks. He'd delayed his pursuit of her only long enough to pull on his boots.

Eyes darting in every direction, Ellie saw that her dress hadn't been caught by her father's huge hands but had snagged on the thorns of a rose-hip bush. She yanked the material free. It tore with a horrible rasping sound, making a hole in the fabric and ripping out the stitches that secured the hem. Damn, damn, damn. It was the only halfway-decent garment she possessed.

She hauled herself up on to the narrow walkway that topped the lockgate. Nimble as a cat, she crossed to the northern bank of the canal, heading straight for the hawthorns. As she dived in under the extravagant foliage her nostrils filled up with their heady perfume.

Energy and determination spent now she had reached her goal, she staggered forward and sank down on to the beaten earth, as dry and level as a floor. It was like a cave in here. Like a huge natural umbrella, the dense and closely woven branches protected the space beneath them from wind, rain and the outside world. Ellie's eyes drifted back to the spot where she had dived in under the trees.

'Och, ye bloody fool,' she muttered, one hand flying to her mouth. The hawthorn branches were swaying wildly from her headlong burst through them. She rose to her feet, wincing as she was gripped by a vicious stitch in her side. She managed to stumble forward, lifting her hands to still the movement of the boughs.

Her father was standing on the other bank of the canal. Would he spot her when he looked in this direction? Her hair might give her away, an incongruous flash of gleaming red amidst the white of the hawthorn blossom. He was gazing up the locks at the moment, following the rise of the land that made the watery man-made staircase necessary here and at so many other places along the canal.

Eyes fixed on his profile, Ellie took one careful step back. Without warning, Alan Douglas's head swivelled round to focus on his immediate surroundings. Watching him across the lapping water, she jumped when he roared out his frustration at not being able to find her.

'Where are ye, ye wee cow? Come out and show yourself!'

She listened as he tore through his vocabulary of insult and abuse, and waited for him to get tired of looking for her and go off in search of some more alcohol. It might only be nine o'clock in the morning but hostelries like the Bay Horse, squatting malevolently on the street corner behind him, didn't have much truck with new-fangled inventions like licensing hours.

He threw one final disgusting obscenity into the air, turned on his heel and stomped off. Once he was out of sight Ellie sank down on to the beaten earth. She'd take a moment to catch her breath. It had to be after nine now anyway. She was already late for school and she'd get the belt for it. That was a foregone conclusion; as was the fact that her teacher would take enormous pleasure in administering the punishment.

She glanced down at her torn hem, thinking how the old cow would make fun of that too. She was always coming out with sarcastic comments about Ellie's outmoded and washed-out clothes, all of the prim and proper teacher's pets laughing along with her. It was hard to be either smart or fashionable when your wardrobe consisted entirely of hand-me-downs passed on by neighbours who felt sorry for you.

Ellie sighed philosophically, stood up and walked forward to part the hawthorn branches. She emerged cautiously into the open air, eyes blinking as she adjusted to the brightness of the sunny morning.

Not knowing whether her father was in the back room of the Bay Horse or had staggered back to bed, she crossed the canal by the bridge, keeping her distance from both the pub and her home. She skirted the timber yard and sawmill that lay between the bridge and the boatyard and made her way through cobbled streets towards her school.

As she drew closer to it, her pace slowed. About to turn into the street in which it stood, she came to a complete halt. 'I don't want to go,' she muttered to herself. 'Och, I really don't want to go!'

Hidden by the blank gable end of a row of tall

tenements, she stood and considered her options. If she didn't go she could spend today out of doors, have a leisurely wander along the canal, chat with the men on the barges and puffers. Many of them were rare talkers, with the ability to wax eloquent about every subject under the sun. Politics, history, geography, the names of the flowers and plants that grew alongside the canal – they knew it all. She had learned much more from them than she ever had in school.

When they tired of talking and she of listening she could walk alongside the Clydesdales which pulled most of the traffic crossing this narrow waist of Scotland, eastward to the Forth or westward to the Clyde. She loved spending time with the big gentle horses. There was something so peaceful about them, so solid and calm and dependable.

But if she didn't go in today she stood absolutely no chance of getting the all-important reference. Groaning in frustration, Ellie started towards the corner. She hadn't gone three steps before she changed her mind again. 'I can't do it,' she muttered. 'Have I no' had enough punishment for one day?'

Oh, but Malcolm would be so disappointed in her . . . She walked forward to the gable end and placed the palms of her hands against it before bowing her head to stare down at the pavement. She was so hungry too. Her stomach was already making peculiar noises. That would be something else for the teacher to make fun of.

She lifted her head again. She had to go. There was no choice about it. She needed that reference. Removing her hands from the wall, she squared her shoulders, took a deep breath and turned round. She marched purposefully to the corner of the building, turned the corner – and walked straight into the Rafferty girls.

Chapter 3

As they swept her back against the gable end and arranged themselves in a neat semi-circle around her, Ellie counted eight of them. A windowless wall behind her and a pack of Raffertys in front of her. Could this day get any worse?

Her darting eyes flickered over the hard young faces staring back at her and met those of Marie, Frank's older sister. She was the uncrowned queen of the younger generation of Raffertys. Two things gave her that position: her tawdry glamour and her ferocity in a fight. Swallowing hard, Ellie placed her hands behind her back. That way none of them would see how much they were trembling.

'Well, well, well,' Marie drawled, 'if isn't wee Ellie Douglas late for the school. Whatever will your big brother say when he finds out?' Without taking her eyes off Ellie, she stuck out a hand whose fingernails were painted the same vivid scarlet as her mouth. They had always put Ellie in mind of talons. 'Gie us a fag, somebody.'

Two girls leaped forward to do her bidding, one proffering the cigarette, the other supplying the match. Senses heightened by her rising fear, Ellie heard the rasp as it was struck, was aware of the precise second when the thin whiff of sulphur merged into the denser aroma of tobacco. Marie's painted mouth closed around the cigarette, sucking greedily to get it to draw.

She adjusted her stance, cupping her elbow in her free hand. Removing the cigarette from her mouth, she allowed the fingers and arm that held it to fall forward in a graceful arc. She'd probably practised the move in front of a mirror, aping some film star. Ellie didn't think it made her look any less cheap.

Even by the racy standards of current fashion her skirt was far too short. Her pink blouse was at least one size too small for her, emphasising her bust. She'd never had any truck with the flat-chested look. Ellie supposed it didn't do in her business. Everyone knew how Marie Rafferty earned her daily bread.

She drew some more nicotine into her lungs before repeating the long-drawn-out gesture of withdrawal, her arm once more descending slowly from her face. Ellie knew fine the whole palaver was designed to crank up her own anxiety, making her wait for whatever it was Marie was planning on doing to her.

And d'you know what, Marie? It's working. Congratulations. She'd never understood why the older girl hated her so much. It might have been jealousy of her friendship with Frank. Perhaps Ellie had simply looked at her the wrong way on some forgotten occasion. There were plenty of folk in Temple who had lived to rue the day they'd done that to a Rafferty.

At this precise moment it wasn't much consolation to think about all those other folk who spent half their lives dodging Marie Rafferty and her kind, especially when Ellie's brain was filling up with memories of previous occasions when she herself hadn't been quick enough to take evasive action.

It had started with hair-pulling and pinching

whenever Marie had passed her in the street. Then had come the January evening when the other girl had lain in wait for Ellie around a foggy street corner. She had stuck her foot out and sent her sprawling on to the icy pavement. Bruised, bleeding and stiff with pain, Ellie had dragged herself to her feet to the accompaniment of Marie's braying laughter.

Last summer, unable to keep hold of her temper after weeks of sustained verbal taunting, Ellie had turned and answered back. Marie and the two girls with her had set about her, scratching and punching and screaming abuse. Ellie had emerged from that encounter with a black eye, saved from worse injuries only by Willie Anderson's fortuitous arrival on the scene. He had angrily chased the girls away and taken Ellie to Granny Mitchell to be patched up.

Ellie flexed her sweaty hands, tucked out of sight behind her back. Willie Anderson wasn't here now. She was on her own.

Well, she could fall to her knees and whimper for mercy. She dismissed that idea immediately. They'd move in for the kill, none of them having any compunction about giving her a good kicking. She had recognised two of the girls as Frank and Marie's cousins, as hard a pair of nuts as any of the Raffertys.

Her only alternative was to brazen it out. Face up to them. *Aye, right. One of me and eight of them.* The flash of wry humour sliced through Ellie's fear, enabling her to string a few words together without stuttering over each and every syllable and betraying just how terrified she really was. She lifted her chin and squared her shoulders.

'Whatever I'm doing, it's nobody's concern but my own. So I'd be obliged if you'd let me proceed about my lawful business.'

Wondering where the hell she'd got that last grandiose phrase from, Ellie saw one of Frank's cousins twist her mouth in a sneer of derision. 'Ooh! Get her! Miss La-di-bloody-dah!'

Marie raised her eyebrows. They were thin hard lines, plucked into near invisibility and drawn back in with a make-up pencil. 'Aren't you the bold girl?' she drawled. Her eyes drifted over Ellie, resting on the gentle swell of her developing breasts. 'You're getting too big for the school, anyway. You'll be looking for a job soon, eh?'

'Aye,' Ellie said. 'And I'm no' likely to get one from you, am I?' She folded her arms, returning Marie's insolent stare. She couldn't afford to give her the satisfaction of knowing how much that long and lingering scrutiny of her chest had embarrassed her. The girl would pounce on any sign of weakness.

'As it happens,' Marie said, curling the fingers of her free hand and dropping her eyes briefly to check her scarlet nail polish, 'I could gie ye a great job. Short hours and big money. All you have to do is lie on your back and open your legs. Now, I know you're no' very clever, Ellie Douglas, but you could manage that, surely?' She smiled, a cruel little curve of her painted lips. 'You might be a bit of a novelty in my trade, pet. Especially if you're ginger all over.'

It took a few seconds. When the penny dropped, Ellie's face burst into flames. Marie let out a great dirty laugh and her pack of slavish followers sniggered. Like a dash of cold water on her burning cheeks, a wave of cold grey anger broke over Ellie. She'd had enough of this. She stomped forward. As one, the Rafferty girls took three steps towards her, the menacing circle tightening around her.

Marie moved closer too, not stopping until she was

standing with her face mere inches away from her victim's own. Anger allowed Ellie to conquer her fear. Gritting her teeth, she spat out three short words. 'Let me by.'

Marie dropped her cigarette, deliberately allowing it to skim down Ellie's dress and over her bare legs on its way to the pavement. 'Naw,' she said, smiling as the younger girl winced and took a hasty sideways step to avoid a more serious burn. 'I'm no' finished wi' you yet.'

'Jings, Marie,' Ellie said flatly. 'You're scaring me to death.'

'Aye,' Marie said, her smile growing, 'I know.' She cocked her head to one side, subjecting Ellie to another slow and insulting scrutiny. 'Can I no' persuade ye to join me and make your fortune, hen? You'd need to smarten yourself up a wee bit, mind.'

'Quite a big bit, Marie! She's no' exactly a beauty, is she?'

Marie threw a laugh over her shoulder, acknowledging the shouted comment. 'You are dead right there. And powder and paint can only do so much.'

Unbidden and unconsidered, a retort leaped to Ellie's lips. 'You should know. You've got enough clarted on your face.'

The face in question twisted into a ugly and threatening mask. With no time to brace herself for the blow, Ellie gasped as Marie seized her shoulders, those red talons digging painfully through the short sleeves of her cotton dress.

'All o' youse!' she bellowed. 'Move out a bit!'

She shoved Ellie hard, sending her spinning across the suddenly expanded circle of girls. Like a knife being drawn across a china plate, a shriek of laughter assaulted

Ellie's ears. A punch in the middle of the back sent her out again, birling round the laughing girls like a child's top. A succession of hands shot out, speeding her on her way. Pitiless young faces jeered at her as she passed, her speed increasing with each circuit.

She had to resist the growing dizziness. She had to keep her balance and stay upright. She knew her tormentors would make sure that effort would fail, and as soon as she was down they would move in and administer that kicking.

Someone had caught her. She was still standing. Breathless relief evaporated into panic and outrage. There were hands on her breasts, squeezing them hard. 'Would some o' our boys no' love a wee feel o' these?'

'We'll need to arrange that, eh? They could tell us if she's a natural redhead!'

More laughter. It echoed obscenely in her head as they tossed her between them. She was back with Marie again. The girl seized her wrist, spinning her round to twist her arm behind her back. She pushed it up hard, her mouth close to Ellie's ear. 'Would you like that?' she queried. 'A bit o' fun wi' a few o' my cousins? Somewhere along the nolly one dark night where there's nobody close enough to hear ye scream?'

Ellie groaned. The nausea was overwhelming now. Marie jerked their linked arms up and cut right through it, making her yell with pain. It was like a red-hot wire burning from her wrist to her shoulder.

'Let her go. Let her go NOW!'

'Why the hell should I?'

But the punishing pressure relaxed even as Marie said the words. Head swimming, Ellie watched as the circle of girls fell back to allow Frank to walk through.

He came up to stand in front of Marie and Ellie,

thrusting his hands into the pockets of his moleskin trousers. He wore a buttoned-up waistcoat on top of them, the sleeves of his collarless blue shirt rolled up to the elbows. 'For one thing,' he said, eyes as blue as his shirt fixed on his sister's face, 'it might no' be a bad idea to remember who the lassie's father is.'

'Alan Douglas?' Marie snorted in derision. 'When was he last sober enough to scare anybody?'

Yet Ellie felt the girl release her arm completely and move away. The idea of her father rushing to her defence was so unlikely as to be ludicrous, yet if his fearsome reputation afforded her some protection from the Rafferty girls she could only be grateful for it.

A firm masculine arm came round her waist. For a moment, its solid support only emphasised how unsteady on her feet she was. She focused with difficulty on Marie's face. Red lips were pursed in fury; hard eyes brimmed with naked rage.

'I'd really like to know what my wee brother thinks he's up to. And how he proposes to stop us from doing *exactly* –' Marie repeated the word, savouring it – '*exactly* what we want wi' Ellie Douglas. He's no' so big I cannae gie him a belt round the lug or a punch in the mouth. Done both o' those more times than I can remember.'

'Aye,' Frank agreed bitterly. 'That you have. A right wee mother to me, that's what you always were.'

'Maybe I should tan his arse for him.' When, all too predictably, more giggles greeted that statement, Marie smiled her hard little smile. 'Want to help me get his strides off, lassies?'

The giggles became whoops of laughter and raucous shouts of assent. There's only one of Frank too, Ellie thought despairingly, and all of these girls are as rough as hell, and most of them are older than he is . . .

She felt him lift the hand that wasn't clasping her waist. Squinting down, she watched as the hairs on his bare forearm caught the sun, glinting like fine copper wires. She saw his fingers dip into his waistcoat pocket. She saw them come out holding a cut-throat razor. Somebody gasped.

Ellie lifted her head, watching in disbelief as Frank put his thumb on the hook that opened the razor. Once it was fully extended he drew it through the warm air in a graceful figure of eight. Sunlight bounced off the gleaming blade. His voice was cool and detached. 'A scarred face wouldnae exactly help in your line o' work, would it, Marie?'

Everybody gasped. Around the circle eyes met, seeking confirmation that what they were witnessing was actually happening. They slid away again to rest on Marie and Frank. Within seconds no one was looking anywhere else.

'You wouldnae dare!' his sister breathed.

'Wouldn't I?' His voice was hard as granite. Aware instinctively that he needed some space, Ellie took a step or two away from him. His eyes never once leaving Marie's face, he let her go. 'You all right?' he queried.

'Fine.' Ellie moved back towards the gable end. She was horrified, fascinated and appalled. She wasn't at all surprised. This confrontation had been a long time coming.

Marie was three years older than Frank, eighteen to his fifteen. She had always knocked him about, apparently seeing it as her God-given right to treat her younger brother as she pleased. Was she about to reap what she had sowed?

Ellie watched as he balanced himself, legs slightly apart and both hands extended. His hair was as untidy as ever, his clothes threadbare. He had an air about him all the same – some indefinable quality that had stopped everyone gathered on this sunny street corner in their tracks. It wasn't merely the deadly blade he held so delicately in his right hand, nor the awful damage it could do if he chose to unleash it. It was something about Frank himself. He might not yet be a man. It was clear that he was no longer a boy.

A series of emotions washed over Marie's face: anger, disbelief, a dawning realisation that the ground beneath her feet was shifting. Ellie felt a tug of reluctant admiration when she still managed to work up a sneer.

'Come on, then,' she challenged. 'If you're hard enough.' When Frank didn't move, she laughed. 'Cannae do it, ye wee nyaff, can ye?'

Two strides and he was there, lifting the razor to her face. Ellie saw the surprise in Marie's eyes. Then the fear.

Frank brought his free hand up to grasp the pink frills at his sister's neck. 'You and your pals will leave Ellie Douglas alone.' When Marie didn't answer him immediately, he renewed his hold on the blouse, crushing the soft material between his fingers. 'You'll leave her alone, Marie. Have ye got that?'

For a few seconds it hung in the balance, brother and sister staring each other out. Then Frank angled the blade of the razor, laying it gently against Marie's cheek. She tilted her head back no more than half an inch. Half an inch was enough.

Behind her, nervous and uncertain eyes met again, acknowledging that the unbelievable had happened. The wee brother had won the war of nerves. As far as Marie's followers were concerned, the world had tilted on its axis.

'I've got it,' she said sullenly.

Frank lowered the razor and stepped back, thrusting her away from him. 'Good,' he said crisply. Spinning round on the balls of his feet, he extended the razor towards the other girls, tracing an arc through the air in front of them. 'That goes for all o' youse. Understood?'

They tripped over their tongues to assure him that they did. He gave them all one final steady look before folding the razor and putting it back in his pocket. Then he swung round to Ellie. 'Are you for the nolly, hen?'

As the other girls studied their feet, Marie lifted her head and looked at Ellie. She heard the words as clearly as if they'd been spoken aloud. *He'll not always be around to protect you. Watch your back, Ellie Douglas.*

She went up to the canal with him, not speaking till they had reached the towpath and were out of sight and earshot. She knew full well how much he detested what his sister did for a living. She knew how much he hated the stories that periodically resurfaced that in so doing she was merely following in their dead mother's footsteps. None of that helped Ellie keep her temper. Defeating his long stride by several swift steps of her own, she overtook him and planted herself in front of him.

'Answer me one question, Frank Rafferty,' she demanded, her eyes blazing with fury. 'Would you have cut your sister wi' that horrible thing?' She pointed to his pocket with a finger that shook.

He drew his breath in on a hiss. 'D'ye not know me better than that, Ellie?'

'I thought I did. But I didn't think the Frank Rafferty I knew would ever carry a razor!'

He folded his arms across his chest, giving her a look

from beneath his russet brows that mixed regret with exasperation at her refusal to understand. 'I don't have a choice, Ellie. I've aye got to be ready to defend myself. Simply because of who I am.'

'There's always a choice, Frank,' she said stubbornly.

The auburn brows went up. 'What choices do I have, Ellie? Or you, for that matter?'

'You're clever, Frank! You've got a brain!'

'I've never passed an exam in my life!'

'That doesnae mean you're no' clever.'

'Same goes for you. Why do you always think you're a daftie?'

'Because every teacher who's ever tried to knock anything into my head has told me so,' she said impatiently, brushing the question aside. 'But you could do any job you set your mind to; make something of yourself like you always said you wanted to.'

He raised one shoulder, indicating the tall redbrick building towering over the boatyard behind him. With its fourth storey projecting out over the lower floors like the bridge of a ship, it was as modern as everything else connected with the Tait empire.

'Along there, like?' Frank queried derisively. 'Where they pride themselves on never taking on any Catholics or Irish?'

Ellie shifted uncomfortably. Tait's didn't go so far as to put up those horrible signs you saw at other works and factories or where there was a room to let – No Irish – but everyone knew you had to be a Protestant to get a start at the boatyard.

'No Catholics or Irish,' Frank repeated angrily. 'Which amounts to the same thing anyway. It'll be like that in every other business Malcolm's precious Mr Tait has taken over.'

'There are still some places where they don't mind if you're a Catholic,' Ellie insisted.

Frank tossed his toffee-coloured head and bellowed his protest. 'Well, and isn't that helluva bloody big of them! They still care if you're a Rafferty. Have you no' heard that expression about giving a dog a bad name? You talk about choices, Ellie.' He unfolded his arms, his hands shooting out to grab her by the shoulders. 'Folk like us have precious few choices—'

'Oh!' she cried, wincing.

Eyes widening in alarm at her reaction to his touch, his hands flew upwards. 'Bloody hell, lassie, what else did that bitch of a sister of mine do to you?'

'N-not M-Marie,' Ellie managed. 'M-my f-father.'

Frank's eyes opened still further. 'He's given you a doing this morning already? Jesus, Mary and Joseph, ye're no' having a very good day, Ellie, are ye?'

They stared at each other. Within seconds the two of them were howling with mirth. 'And n-now I'm really l-late for sch-school,' Ellie spluttered. 'So I'll pr-probably get six o' the b-best for that! Which will put the tin lid on this wonderful morning I'm having!'

Frank's face was alight with amusement. There was an edge to his voice all the same. 'You could choose not to go, Ellie.'

She shook her head. 'I need that reference—' She grimaced, realising too late that she had fallen into the trap he had set for her. 'All right, Frank. You've made your point. I've got precious few choices either.'

Taking no satisfaction in his victory, Francis Rafferty junior let out a long breath and drew a hand through his already untidy hair. 'Do you really think some crummy wee piece o' paper is gonnae make much difference as to whether or not some boss graciously decides to exploit you, Ellie?'

'Maybe.' She glanced up at him. 'I don't know.'

He laid a hand on her shoulder, gently this time. 'See if you did have a choice, hen, what would you do today?'

She didn't even have to think about it. 'I'd be wee again,' she said. 'No' have to worry about things like references and jobs and people I care about getting themselves into trouble.'

He made a face at her. She mirrored it back to him. Then her expression grew wistful. 'D'you mind those days when we used to spend hours playing beside the canal—'

'—lying on our bellies to study the wee insects on the surface o' the water—'

'—wandering along to Knightswood Rows—'

'—daring each other to sneak right up to the Fever Hospital and then being feart we'd caught some terrible disease—'

'—climbing up the hill at Westerton and walking through Cairnhill Woods to the home farm at Garscube—'

'—pinching apples from their orchard—' Frank supplied with a grin.

The thought of those apples reminded Ellie how hungry she was. Her stomach registered its own protest. 'Oh, excuse me,' she said. 'I've had nothing but a cup of tea this morning.'

'I've a wee drop money,' Frank said. 'Come on and we'll go and buy a couple o' gammon rolls and a pint o' milk.'

Ellie narrowed her eyes at him. 'And where did you get that money? I thought you still hadnae got a job yet.'

She'd suspected for some time that he had joined his father and uncles in what was more or less the Rafferty family business: thieving from the shops and businesses that had sprung up in recent years between Temple and nearby Anniesland.

'Choices,' he said sadly. 'When you don't have many you do what you have to do.' He smiled at her, a wide-mouthed, generous and regretful curve of the lips. 'Come on, Ellie! Let me buy ye something tae eat.'

She ran a hand through her hair. 'I should go to school.'

'Want me to walk you there?'

When she hesitated, Frank pressed his advantage. 'If you don't go you and me could spend the day together. We could see how they're getting on wi' the houses they're building at Knightswood. Have ye heard what they're calling the new road down there? The Great Western Boulevard. That's got a real ring to it, don't you think?'

'Aye,' Ellie agreed, smiling up at him. 'It has. They're putting up new houses across the canal too,' she offered. 'In the fields round Westerton Farm.'

'We could go there too,' he said eagerly, 'climb up to Cairnhill Woods like we used to do. Oh, hold on, lassie,' he said, hunkering down into a crouch and stretching out a cautionary hand. 'What's that moving along there?'

They waited till the nervous hare that had crept out from the undergrowth ahead of them had summoned up the courage to lollop off into the deeper foliage on the opposite side of the path. Admiring the sleek and fluid lines of the animal's long body and the strength of its back feet, Ellie stood with Frank, both of them entranced by the sight.

'On ye go then, wee man,' he whispered, 'we'll no' hurt you.' Suddenly his head swivelled round towards Ellie. 'Why are you smiling at me like I'm soft in the heid?'

'I'm not,' she said, shaking her own head in denial. She surveyed him solemnly as he straightened up, hair sticking out all over the place, shirtsleeves rolled up and his trousers worn and threadbare. On impulse she leaned over and pressed a swift kiss on his cheek.

He looked startled. 'What did you do that for?'

'Because we're friends.'

He gave her an old-fashioned look. 'It's usually people who're a wee bit more than friends who kiss each other.'

'No' if you're rich. I saw Mrs Tait saying cheerio to a man like that the other night.'

'Aye, but we're not rich.'

She contradicted him. 'We are rich. In ways that have nothing to do wi' money.'

'Because we both like to stand looking at hares?'

'See what I mean about the brains? You were always quick on the uptake, Frank Rafferty.'

'So were you, Ellie Douglas.' He was grinning again. She had always thought it was the expression his face was designed to bear. 'So what d'ye say?' he asked cheerfully. 'Are you going to the school to get belted or shall we spend the day pretending we're wee bairns again?'

Chapter 4

'Are you two not a bit old for that?'

'More than likely,' Frank agreed, glancing up at the skinny youth standing on the nolly bridge. Ellie's vibrant head also snapped up. Responding to her jerky movement, the plank beneath her bare feet dipped violently to one side. Slippery as ink, canal water lapped over her grubby toes. She stretched out her arms and swiftly regained her balance.

'Is it not a daft thing to do anyway?' Evander Tait cocked one dismissive eyebrow. It was as dark as the thick and wavy hair that flopped forward over his pale forehead, that shade of dark brown so close to black as to make no difference. He had inherited his father's colouring, if not his charm.

'Oh, aye,' Frank said. 'But good fun all the same. Except that I'm getting a bit cold now.' He leaped between the planks bobbing in the timber basin to season and hauled himself up on to the bridge, calling back down to Ellie as he stuffed his feet back into his boots. 'Malcolm'll not be long now.'

'No,' she agreed. 'You go on home if you like.'

'And see if my sister's got my tea on the table?'

She laughed. 'Something like that.'

'If you're sure you're all right, then . . . Probably see you tomorrow sometime.' He raised a hand in cheerful farewell, nodding to Evander as he passed him.

'Are you not going to come out of there?' Evander had walked off the bridge, was standing now by the timber basin.

'Why should I?' Ellie demanded, working her feet so the plank rocked gently from side to side. 'Does your father own the sawmill too? I didnae think so.'

'My concern was for your safety,' Evander said loftily. 'Now that Frank Rafferty's gone who's going to rescue you if you fall in? There's nobody else about at this time of day.'

With the sawmill having shut up shop for the night their surroundings were eerily silent, the dull rasp of handsaws and the high-pitched whine of heavy-duty cutting equipment oddly absent. The men in the neighbouring boatyard had also downed tools for the day. Frank had been waiting with Ellie until Malcolm came out of Tait's offices, where work finished half an hour later than in the yard. He'd be here any moment now.

Ellie had encountered Evander Tait more than once during this lull when the afternoon slowly gave way to the evening. She tended to be out at this time because she had no mother calling her in for her tea or, as today, because she was waiting for Malcolm before she dared go home. She presumed Evander liked it because of its unusual quietness.

He only ever came on to the canal bank when no one else was around and would sit for ages propped against the end of one of the lock-gates, reading a book or staring moodily into the waters of the canal, as dark and impenetrable as his own eyes. There had been times when Ellie had been aware of feeling sorry for him: pretty daft when you considered who he was. Despite that, she'd felt compelled to talk to him. She'd never got more than a grunt in response. Sometimes it was a snarl.

'Eleanor Douglas! Come off those planks right now! And I mean right now!' Malcolm's face was as thunderous as that of any mature sixteen-year-old male's might be when surveying a wee toerag of a younger sister. Striding along to join Evander, he mimicked his posture, folding his arms across his own rather broader chest, the better to gaze disapprovingly at his errant sibling. 'Look at the state of you!'

Ellie suppressed a shiver as the water lapped once more over her toes. It might be a warm May afternoon but the canal was still cold. The chill was travelling up her bare legs, through her chest to her shoulders. They were beginning to ache again – and she *was* far too old to be playing on these stupid logs.

'Would you explain something to me, Ellie?' Malcolm asked archly. 'How is it that however you start the day off you always manage to end up looking as if you've been dragged through a hedge backwards?'

Tired, sore and unable to explain in front of Evander Tait the circumstances that had led to her ripped hem and her dishevelled appearance, Ellie resorted to sticking her tongue out at her brother.

'Oh, very sophisticated,' Evander said witheringly.

She wasn't entirely sure what the word meant but she got the disdain loud and clear. Forgetting all about the need to keep her balance, she placed indignant hands on her slim hips. The wood beneath her feet rocked wildly. It and her feet were about to part company.

Muttering under his breath, Evander whirled round and snatched up a branch that had broken off a nearby tree. 'Hold on to that, you wee fool. And jump!'

Breathless with a mixture of excitement and fear, Ellie did as she was bid, using another plank as a stepping stone to reach the canal bank. Light though she was, she felt it glide away from her, propelled by the speed and force of her foot. As soon as she was within range, Malcolm reached out and grabbed her, lifting her to stand on the path in front of him. He was squeezing her arms against her body, compressing her sore shoulders. She yelped in pain, but her brother was too exasperated with her to notice.

'Honestly, Ellie,' he said as he released her and allowed Evander to yank the branch out of her grasp and throw it into the undergrowth, 'grow up, would you?' He shot her a suspicious glance. 'Did you go to school today?'

'Don't you like school?'

Brother and sister turned together at the question. 'Does anybody?' Ellie asked.

'Me,' Evander said. 'I love it.' He shrugged. 'Then again, maybe I'm just odd.'

If the cap fits, Ellie thought, sliding her feet into her own boots.

A familiar sound split the evening air: the high-pitched shriek of a steam whistle. All three young people turned towards it.

'It's the *Torosay*,' Evander murmured.

Alerted by that blast of sound, the lock-keeper was coming out of his cottage, slipping into his jacket as he headed up the towpath to open the top gate. The three young people followed in his wake, crossing Crow Road and walking along the short stretch of water between the two lock chambers.

Malcolm allowed Evander to go on ahead, addressing a low-voiced question to his sister. 'If you didn't go to school, did you at least get some money to buy the tea?'

'No,' she said guiltily. 'I'm awful sorry, Malcolm.'

'Och, Ellie,' he said, 'I've been dreaming about fish suppers all day.'

There was no time to explain further. The puffer was chugging into the upper lock chamber, the cabin boy flinging the ropes in turn to the two lads. Once his boat was tied up, the top gate closed behind him and the sluices open to bring the water level down to that of the next section of the two-part lock, the captain of the *Torosay* stuck his head out of the small wheelhouse that rode on top of the puffer's stern.

'And how is everyone in Temple this fine summer's evening?' he asked, his Hebridean accent imbuing the words with a musical lilt.

Ellie beamed at him. 'We're all fine.' Captain Ewen MacLean invariably enquired after your wellbeing as though he really cared what the answer was.

'Man,' he said, rotating his shoulders in a gesture of relaxation, 'it's grand to be on a nice calm canal for a day or two!'

'Are you tying up overnight, Captain MacLean?' Evander asked politely.

'Aye, laddie,' the captain responded. 'We've some Scandinavian timber for the sawmill. We'll unload first thing in the morning.' Removing his cap with one hand and wiping his brow with the back of the other, his next words were uttered with considerable feeling. 'Opening and closing that blasted bridge will be enough work for tonight, I'm thinking.' He replaced his cap. 'Best get on with it,' he added, piercing pale blue eyes on the almost equalised water levels. 'Tomorrow we're along to Clydebank to pick up some coal and then it'll be Bowling and the river and the open sea. And after that

Mull,' he concluded happily, delighted as always at the prospect of returning to his home island.

'The open sea,' Evander repeated, his voice soft.

Ellie looked at him curiously. Bookish as he was, she had never thought of him as the kind of boy who dreamed of running away to sea.

'Aye,' Captain MacLean agreed. 'The open sea is a great place. Although tonight I'll be happy to sleep like a baby in Temple.' He glanced in the direction of the Bay Horse. 'After I've had a wee dram.'

'Captain MacLean,' Ellie said quickly, 'see when you go into the pub, could you maybe check if my father's in there and ask him to step out for a wee minute? I'm needing a word with him.' That her father was in the Bay Horse was a pretty safe bet. He usually was at this hour, fooling himself he was still a hard-working man slaking his thirst at the end of a day's labour.

'No bother at all, lass,' Ewen said. 'I'll do that for you as soon as we're through and tied up.'

As the lock-keeper opened the gates, the captain disappeared back into the wheelhouse to steer the *Torosay* through into the next lock chamber.

'I'm off home, Ellie,' Malcolm said roughly. 'I'll start the tea.'

He was gone before she could say anything, leaving her staring after him in incredulous dismay. Leaving aside the fact that she couldn't remember when he'd last cooked a meal, there wasn't a slice of bread or a mouldy old tattie in the house, and he knew that as well as she did. If he was going to start the tea he'd have to be a miracle worker.

The brilliant plan that had leaped into her head thirty seconds before had one basic flaw. It hinged on Captain MacLean accompanying Alan Douglas out of the Bay

Horse. If the captain didn't do that, Ellie would be left to face her father's rage on her own. She could hardly count on Evander Tait coming to her rescue.

He put his hand up to his mouth, covering an odd little cough. 'Isn't your father going to be in a bad mood at being dragged out of the pub?'

'Maybe,' she said shortly. 'But I need to get some money off him so I can buy tea for Malcolm and me.'

'But Malcolm said—'

'I know what he said.'

'Oh,' Evander said. 'I see.'

All too aware that he probably did, Ellie snapped back at him. 'What is it to you?' She raised one arm in a gesture indicating the sweeping hill that led up to Bellevue. 'You're probably just about to have a lovely tea with your mammy and daddy who love you,' she said furiously. 'What do you know about anything?'

Evander flushed. As the angry red tide stained his pale cheeks, his mouth narrowed into a tight line. When he spoke, his voice was flat and dull, with almost no expression in it at all. 'We eat late,' he said. 'We have dinner at eight o'clock.'

Ellie tossed her untidy head. 'So you were gonnae invite me and Malcolm home wi' ye?'

He was staring at her, gazing down into her face. Something flashed in the very depths of his dark eyes, like sparks leaping out from a log crackling in the middle of the fire. She was wondering how much longer she could hold his intense gaze when he spoke, his voice clipped and terse. 'I don't know what I was going to do.'

She stood and watched him go, prey to a confusing mix of emotions. Perhaps he had been trying to help, had maybe even been on the point of offering her some money. She gave herself a shake, dismissing him from her mind. Pride wouldn't have allowed her to take that from him anyway and right now she had more to worry about than Evander Tait and his feelings.

In all too short a time she found herself walking across to the Bay Horse with the captain of the *Torosay* and his engineer. The cabin boy was too young to visit the pub and the mate was a fearsomely religious man who never touched strong drink. Captain MacLean touched the brim of his cap to her as he pushed open the pub's scarred and battered door. 'If your father's here I'll send him out right away, lass.'

Her father was there. Ellie took one look at his face and retreated from him as fast as her legs could carry her.

She didn't even think about it, running back to the canal and across the catwalk in a flight that owed everything to instinct. Or maybe experience. Yet when she got there some other instinct made her turn to face him.

He came up and placed himself foursquare on the other side of the lock, being refilled now after the passage of the *Torosay*. 'Nag, bloody, nag.' Coarsened and thickened by years of heavy drinking and smoking, his voice was as rough as sandpaper. He didn't have to shout to make himself heard above the water splashing noisily from the sluices. 'Is it no' enough that ye roused me from my sleep this morning?'

Captain MacLean must have seen the look on her father's face too. He had come up behind him, was laying a hand on his arm.

'Malcolm and me are only wanting a couple of bob,' Ellie said, forcing herself to use the quiet tone of voice she had learned could sometimes defuse his anger and save herself a wallop. 'So we can go to the chip shop.'

Alan Douglas's eyes narrowed. 'The chip shop, is it? On a Thursday night? Why have ye no' cooked a meal for your menfolk, ye lazy wee hure?'

'Alan,' the Captain remonstrated, grizzly brows knitted in disapproval, 'there's no call to be using that kind of language to your daughter. Come on now, man. Give the lassie the money and then you and me will have a dram together.'

'Money she wants.' Alan thrust his hand into the pocket of his trousers. When he drew it out again Ellie saw the flash of silver and the dull gleam of copper glinting through his thick fingers. 'Come over and get it then.'

She blinked. Her father was smiling at her. It was an awful long time since that had happened. She imagined it was for Captain MacLean's benefit but what did that matter? She started towards the catwalk.

Still smiling, Alan Douglas thrust his arm skywards. Then he opened his fingers, splaying them as wide as they could go.

Ellie's distress was so acute that she cried out, fruitlessly reaching towards the coins he had sent spinning. They seemed to hover there for a moment, tantalisingly close, their shining surfaces glinting as they tumbled and turned through the air. She could make out each individual piece: one shilling, two silver threepennies, ten shining copper pennies. Mesmerised, she watched them slide below the water, inky-black now in the deepening shadows cast by the stone walls of the lock.

She added it up in her head. Mental arithmetic was one subject she'd never had any difficulty with. Two and fourpence. Almost half a crown.

Her father's smile had become triumphant. Gloating.

'Swim for them if ye want them. Ye'll get no more from me tonight.' He was already turning away, heading back to the Bay Horse.

It was the waste, the sheer bloody waste of it. He'd thrown away almost half a crown and now he was going back to the pub to drink whatever else was left in his pockets.

Eyes glittering like emeralds, Ellie raised her head to look at her father. Her young voice was as clear as tinkling bell. 'You're a drunken fool and I hate you.'

'What did you say, ye wee bitch?' With a great growl of anger, her father spun round and strode towards the catwalk. Fear slammed into Ellie's body, the anticipation of pain to come stabbing like a hundred steel needles.

'Alan!' Captain MacLean grabbed his arm. 'You're in no fit state to manage a catwalk, man.'

Alan threw him off, hauling himself up on to the narrow walkway. He took one step, then another two. Pausing, he looked over his shoulder at the captain. 'I'm mair than capable of walking over a catwalk. I've been doing it all my life, have I no'?'

That was gey strange. If you hadn't seen what had led up to this, you'd have sworn from that oddly dignified wee speech that he was stone-cold sober. Blood whooshing through her ears, Ellie watched him edge towards the middle of the lock-gate.

Halfway over, eyes fixed on his daughter's pale and sombre face, his mood changed again. He began to sway, bending at the waist and waving his arms about like a windmill. 'Help! Help! Ah cannae keep ma balance!'

Ellie hated it when he acted like this. It hurt all the more because somewhere, dimly remembered, she'd had a quite different father: the man he had been before he had allowed the drink to get him. Glimpses of that Alan Douglas had become as rare as hen's teeth. Ellie could still see him, though – if she closed her eyes and thought very hard.

He was tall and straight, smiling as he came through the door at the end of the day. Sliding an arm about his wife's waist, he stooped to kiss her. It was Ellie's only concrete memory of Cathy Douglas.

She could never see her face, only a cloud of fluffy blonde hair the same shade as Malcolm's smooth cap, but she knew that her mother was smiling too. Then her father sat down in the big comfortable armchair that had once stood next to the range, and inveigled her and Malcolm into looking through the pockets of his jacket, pretending to be surprised when they found the wee paper twists of sweeties he himself had put there.

The memory was so faded with time and tarnished with the violence he had meted out to them over the years Ellie often wondered if she had invented it.

'Stop acting the fool, Alan,' snapped Captain MacLean. 'For God's sake, man!'

The movement of the swirling arms grew wilder. The wolfish grin on her father's face metamorphosed, almost comically, into one of faint surprise. Like a tree being felled in the forest, his body leaned suddenly to one side. So slowly that Ellie saw it happen, his feet peeled off from the wood beneath them.

But the catwalk's not floating, she thought stupidly. It's easy to balance on. Even as the thought flitted through her brain, her father began to fall. Like the coins he had sent flying, he was tumbling and spinning through the air, heading inexorably towards the churning waters of the canal.

Chapter 5

Someone screamed. The sound was shriller than any blast ever produced by a puffer's whistle. 'Daddy!'

Barely aware that it was she herself who had uttered that anguished cry, Ellie ran forward. Arms and legs outstretched, her father lay on his back, his entire body in contact with the water. For a few seconds it looked as if the oily surface might hold him there, like a baby safely cradled in the soft folds of a thick quilt. Then his support fell away.

He went down like a stone, murky waves rushing to close the gap where he had lain. The shape of his body remained, the water displaced as he sank rising all around it. The bubbling fountain flew up the stone walls of the chamber and splashed over Ellie's feet and legs.

She let out a cry as her father broke the surface again, pushed upright by the powerful currents swirling beneath him. His dark hair was plastered to his head. Opening his mouth wide to take in great gulps of air, he shook it out of his eyes like a dog drying itself after a swim.

He tried to say something but the turbulence stirred up by the water pouring in from the sluice gates knocked the wind out of him. The strength of that turbulence bore him aloft, carrying him the full length of the lock.

Passing under one of the foaming white columns gushing through the sluices, he coughed and spluttered as water gushed over his face. He slid behind the man-made waterfall and disappeared from view. There was a sickening crack.

'Struck his head on the lock-gate,' growled Captain MacLean. Jacket and cap already discarded, he was tugging off his sea boots. 'Come over,' he commanded, reinforcing his words with an urgent sweep of his arm. He slid it round Ellie's waist before she reached the end of the catwalk, the instant the water beneath her feet gave way to the stones surrounding the lock chamber. Swinging her down to stand in front of him, he issued some more soft commands. 'Go for help – the lock-keeper, the *Torosay* and the pub. Tell Angus and Donald John to bring some rope. And run like the wind, lass. There's no time to lose!'

The lock-keeper had reversed the flow of the sluices. The chamber was growing calmer by the second, enabling Captain MacLean to tread water while the mate fashioned a secure loop out of the length of rope the *Torosay*'s cabin boy had handed him.

'Is Alan caught on something?'

Willie Anderson was standing at the front of the knot of men who had tumbled out of the Bay Horse a moment before, streaming across Crow Road and on to the canal bank to see if there was anything they could do to help. A car driver heading towards Anniesland had stopped too. He'd been dispatched to the nearby police station to ask them to call an ambulance.

'Aye,' piped up Donald John, the cabin boy, eager to supply information. 'His clothes have got tangled up wi' some lever at the bottom o' the lock-gate. The captain canna manage to get them off down there, but he thinks we can maybe pull him clear from up here.' Donald John grimaced. 'If a good few o' us get behind this rope.'

'Nae bother, son. There's plenty o' strong men here.' Willie Anderson threw a glance over his shoulder. 'Is that no' right, lads?'

There was a deep-voiced rumble of assent. Willie Anderson looked at Ellie, standing near one of the capstans with her arms wrapped about herself. 'Never you worry, hen, we'll get your daddy back for ye.'

'H-he's b-been in the w-water an aw-awful long time.' She shivered. Cooling down after the exertion of her run, a terrible chill was creeping through her body. Even her bones felt cold.

Willie Anderson walked over to her. 'You're freezing, pet,' he said gruffly. He raised his head and his voice, warm whisky-laden breath skimming over her tousled hair. 'Can we get the lassie a blanket frae somewhere?'

Ellie clutched at his dark waistcoat. 'Could somebody maybe go for Malcolm too?'

'Aye,' came another male voice in immediate response, 'I'll away and fetch the laddie.'

Willie Anderson sent Ellie down a wry smile, indicating the lock chamber with a lift of his unshaven chin. 'A wee mishap like this cannae put paid to Alan Douglas, hen. The Devil looks after his own, eh? Now,' he said, 'if you can wait for that blanket, I'd best be putting myself on the end o' this rope.'

'I'm fine, Mr Anderson,' she assured him. 'On ye go.'

Captain MacLean dived again, the looped end of the rope slung round his chest bandolier-style. Thirty seconds later he gave the prearranged signal of three sharp tugs.

'Right, lads!' yelled the *Torosay*'s engineer. 'Put your backs into it!'

They did that and more, working together to exert their combined strength on the task in hand. They pulled as one, like some sort of human engine, and they staggered back as one when their efforts resulted in an abrupt slackening of the rope.

There was a subdued cheer as the body broke the surface, Ewen MacLean guiding it towards many willing arms. Willie Anderson was one of those who pulled Alan Douglas up on to dry land, laying him gently on his front and turning his head to one side. Sombre-faced, the men stood back to allow the *Torosay*'s mate and engineer to work on the prone figure, pressing on Alan's back to expel canal water from his sodden lungs.

Exhausted, his face and hands covered in oily grime, Ewen MacLean sat leaning against a capstan, his legs stretched out before him. Donald John stooped to retrieve his captain's jacket from the ground where he had thrown it earlier and swung it around the older man's shoulders. Hotfoot from the Bay Horse, another man pressed a glass of whisky into the captain's hands. Ewen took a grateful sip of the spirit before leaning back and closing his eyes.

Someone draped a tartan blanket over Ellie's shoulders. She turned and saw Granny Mitchell. Crisscrossed by the lines age and experience had put there, her kindly face was etched with concern. Thinking how odd it was that she herself was now as tall as the old lady, Ellie gave her a wan little smile.

She was feeling strangely detached from her surroundings, removed in some odd way from all of the frantic activity going on around her. At the same time she was acutely aware of the tiniest things, even those on the very edge of her vision.

Captain MacLean had opened his eyes and raised his head again. Willie Anderson had moved so as to give himself a better view through the forest of dark-trousered legs that encircled his friend. An ambulance had parked on Crow Road and its two-man crew was running towards the canal, carrying a stretcher between them. The policeman who'd got here ten minutes ago was waving people back to allow them through. Malcolm was behind them.

'Ellie?' He looked completely bewildered. 'Is it true, Ellie?'

'Aye,' she managed, reaching for his hand. The ambulance men were turning their father over now. Ellie's breath caught in her throat. It was the way they were handling him. Every touch was so gentle, almost tender . . .

Malcolm made as if to dash forward.

'No,' Ellie said, grabbing his hand and lacing her fingers through his.

Her brother looked down at her, fair brows knotted in perplexity. 'No?' he queried.

'They've still got things to do, Malcolm,' she explained, not quite sure how she knew that.

Brother and sister stood hand in hand, watching as the final checks were made: a pulse sought, the faintest of breaths listened for. At last one of the ambulance men looked up at the policeman and slowly shook his head.

Granny Mitchell was behind Malcolm and Ellie, one hand on each young shoulder. 'Come on,' she said gently. 'There's no point in the two o' youse lingering here now.'

Malcolm muttered an incoherent protest. Ellie reached up and placed her fingers over his mouth.

'She's right, Malcolm,' she said. She took one last look round before they turned to leave.

The policeman and ambulance men were standing together at a discreet distance, waiting. They must have often witnessed scenes like these. Every so often the Forth and Clyde claimed its forfeit. On dark winter nights drunks stumbled out of places like the Bay Horse and took a wrong turning. On the sunniest of summer days people at the end of their tether saw the canal as their only way out.

Those who picked up the pieces would know it took time for other folk to pull themselves together. All eyes directed at one spot, the men and women gathered on the canal bank were still too shocked even to speak.

Ellie's own clear eyes picked out Willie Anderson. He was weeping openly, wiping the tears away with the heels of his big hands. Her gaze flickered back to her father's body.

The Devil looks after his own. Only this time he hadn't. Numb with shock, Ellie allowed Granny Mitchell to lead her and Malcolm away from the canal.

The minister was choosing his words with care, measuring each one before he allowed it to leave his mouth. 'It would seem, therefore, that your father will have to be buried in common ground. Without too much ceremony beforehand, I'm afraid.' He shifted uneasily in his chair. 'I shall, of course, conduct a brief service at the graveside. You'll want to be at that, Malcolm, but there's no need for Eleanor to attend.'

Eric Hunter smiled encouragingly at her. She was sitting across the kitchen table from him, Malcolm and

Rosalie Mitchell occupying the other sides of it. Ellie wasn't quite sure what Granny's daughter-in-law was doing there, except that since her father's death the house had never been empty of people. Meeting the minister on his way up the stairs, Rosalie had taken it upon herself to give him an escort.

Concerned that Mr Hunter might find the room uncomfortably hot, Ellie had placed him as far from the range as possible. She'd lit it first thing this morning so she could keep a kettle permanently on the boil to make tea for all the visitors.

The minister turned to Malcolm. 'There's no other money or insurance policy?'

'There's nothing,' the young man replied. One hand flew up in a jerky gesture that indicated and simultaneously condemned their dingy home. He was tight-lipped, embarrassed to be having this conversation here rather than at the manse. He had called there the previous afternoon to enquire about arranging their father's funeral but the minister had been engaged elsewhere.

'Look about you, Mr Hunter,' Malcolm said bitterly. 'We don't exactly have any family silver to sell off, do we? He got rid of anything of the slightest value years ago. In exchange for drink.' His voice grew shaky. 'Even our mother's clothes and things.'

Ellie glanced at her brother's face. She looked quickly away again, her eyes focusing on the small pile of coins in the middle of the table. Captain MacLean had started that off. 'To help see the two of you through,' he'd murmured, laying a quelling hand on Malcolm's shoulder when the lad tried to refuse the money.

Still visibly distressed, Willie Anderson had called past the previous evening to offer his condolences and hand over a jingling handkerchief full of money raised by a whip-round at the Bay Horse. Malcolm hadn't been too happy about accepting that either. He'd been even less keen on the envelope Frank Rafferty had brought round on behalf of his father and a few other members of his family.

Malcolm hadn't actually refused either contribution, although he had left it up to Ellie to express their gratitude. She had done that also to the individual callers who had contributed a coin or two.

Sadie Mitchell had taken it upon herself to wash, dress and keep Alan Douglas's body until the funeral. Her kindness had left Ellie speechless with relief. Over the last two days she had discovered it was possible to have nightmares not only when you were asleep but also while you were wide awake. You didn't even have to close your eyes for them to leap out and ambush you.

She had relived her father's death over and over again, the intensity of the experience leaving her breathless, sweaty and dizzy with fear. More times than she could count, those coins he had tossed so contemptuously at her fell through the air. Rage contorted his features as he strode towards her. The foul names he had called her still echoed in her head.

It seemed horribly possible that he could storm through the door at any moment and subject her to a beating. Lifeless though it was, to have lived with his body until the funeral on Monday afternoon would have been unbearable. It was bad enough to think of it lying there in Granny's house, three floors beneath her feet.

So many of the neighbours were being kind to them. The community was rallying round, looking after its own. Yesterday Mrs O'Donnell on the other side of the landing had passed over a pot of soup in time for their dinner at midday. Mrs Wintergreen from two closes along had supplied their evening meal: a generous serving each of beef stew and floury dumplings.

'Och,' the old lady had said, dismissing Malcolm's stiff words of thanks. 'It's a rare treat for me to cook a proper meal for young folk wi' hearty appetites!'

A downstairs neighbour and her young daughter had come up an hour ago, the mother bearing a tray of shortbread and the daughter a plate piled high with pancakes. The generosity of those who had so little themselves made Ellie want to cry. The money they'd accumulated still fell pathetically short of the cost of a decent burial.

'It'll be a pauper's funeral, then?' Malcolm's words were clipped.

'Well . . . that's a very harsh term—'

'It's an honest one,' came the savage response, 'isn't it?'

Ellie swallowed hard, and kept her eyes firmly on the piles of coins. A pauper's funeral was a dreadful thing. Even the poorest of families scrimped and saved so as to be able to put some money by for that awful day when they had to bury one of their own. Failure to do so meant you were feckless and uncaring – failing in your Christian duty too. Allowing a relative to be buried in common ground was a burning shame, one that would hang about you and yours for ever afterwards.

'Have you thought of approaching your employer for help?' Eric Hunter asked delicately.

Malcolm's face flooded with colour. He opened his mouth to speak, but Rosalie Mitchell got there before him. 'You couldn't do that! We all know Mr Tait is generosity itself, but there are limits!' She glared at Malcolm.

He shot to his feet, the force of the movement sending his chair crashing on to the hard floor. 'I wouldn't dream of asking Mr Tait for more help,' he bit out. 'He's been kind enough to me already, told me not to come back to work until after the funeral and until I get Ellie settled. He's even going to pay me while I'm off.'

Eric Hunter made a game attempt to pour oil on troubled waters. 'Sit down, lad. We understand this is a very difficult time—'

'So why don't I make us all a nice cup of tea?' asked Rosalie, dividing an unconvincing smile between Ellie and Malcolm. 'I brought some milk and sugar up with me in case you two didn't have any.'

'We've plenty o' milk and sugar,' Malcolm snapped. 'No' tae mention enough home-baking tae feed an army.'

A wave of anxiety surged up in Ellie's chest and throat. Since he'd started working for Mr Tait her brother had become so careful about how he spoke. His accent slipping was a sure sign that he was really upset.

'Maybe we cannae afford tae give our father a decent funeral, but we're no' needing charity to buy milk and sugar. We've got a' this money here, have we no'?' His voice had risen to a shout. Bending forward, he swept his arm across the piles of coins. They flew off the table, skiting off the edge of it on to the floor.

'Malcolm!'

Ellie's impassioned plea was being made to her brother's rigid and retreating back. He was out of the door within seconds, slamming it shut behind him.

As the crash reverberated up and down the stone stairwell of the tenement, Rosalie Mitchell pursed her lips in disapproval. 'Well! I'm sure there was no need for that!'

Any shyness Ellie felt at being left to cope with the minister and snooty young Mrs Mitchell on her own evaporated, superseded by the need to defend her brother. Leaping to her feet, she righted the chair he had toppled and crouched down to gather up the scattered coins. 'He's upset,' she said sharply. 'I seem to remember you were gey upset when your father died.'

'My father was an elder of the Kirk and a pillar of this community. Your father was a drunken wastrel. I should have thought you and Malcolm ought to regard his death as a blessed release!'

Ellie stood up, placing a handful of coins on the table. The rest would have to wait a while. What she had thought of her father was one thing. Having this horrible woman say it was a different matter entirely. Poised to retaliate, she was beaten to it by Mr Hunter.

'Mrs Mitchell,' he said, 'we must remember that Eleanor and her brother are newly bereaved, and that their late father was one of God's children – of exactly the same worth and value to our Lord as the rest of us.'

Judging by the expression on her face, the horrible Rosalie had her doubts about that, but she was wise enough to keep them to herself. Mr Hunter's intervention had also given Ellie pause for thought. Screaming and shouting wasn't going to achieve anything. Lifting her chin, she addressed herself to the minister.

'Whatever our father might have been, he was our father. You said I don't need to be at the graveside, Mr Hunter. I know women don't usually go but I think both his children should see him off. Besides,' she said, clinching the argument as far as she herself was concerned, 'Malcolm might need me there.'

The stern expression with which the reverend gentleman had been surveying Rosalie relaxed as he leaned over to pat Ellie's hand. 'Well said, my dear. I dare say we can abandon the usual protocol this once, especially as there are likely to be so few mourners. Now then,' he said, as Ellie resumed her seat at the table, 'have you given any thought to your future? I take it you and your brother won't be staying here on your own.'

'The factor's given us notice to quit,' she agreed. 'Says we're too young to keep up the tenancy, even if we could afford the rent. It's to be transferred to Mr and Mrs Wintergreen's son and his wife.'

Rosalie Mitchell didn't comment, but the expression in her eyes spoke for her. Hers wasn't the only household on this stair delighted at the prospect of swapping the troublesome Alan Douglas for the pleasant and respectable Wintergreens.

'Malcolm's got fixed up with digs, I hear?'

'Aye. Mr Chisholm—'

'Chief clerk in the boatyard office?' Mr Hunter queried. 'Lives in Temple Gardens?'

She nodded. 'They can take Malcolm in as a lodger but it's sharing a room with the two Chisholm boys. There's no place for a girl.' Ellie bit her lip.

'Wouldn't it be ideal if you could get a job in service, Eleanor? Somewhere you could live in?'

She frowned. Going into service had never appealed to her. She'd heard too many horror stories from older girls about it. They generally featured long hours, low wages and terrible homesickness. All too often battle-axes of cooks and housekeepers played a role in these reminiscences, and the tales of overamorous young gentlemen who thought the maids employed by their parents were fair game could make your hair stand on end.

Ellie had never forgotten the story of one girl who'd

been turned out from the big house on Partickhill where her employers' son had taken advantage of her. Pregnant, alone and friendless, she'd ended up walking the streets to earn enough money to keep herself and her child.

'I'd been thinking I might get a start in a shop. Or a factory.' The creases on Ellie's creamy forehead deepened as she gave that idea some thought, running down a mental list of those local businesses where female labour was required. 'Are there no' a lot o' lassies helping make the telescopes and things at Barr & Stroud's? They say women are really good at that sort o' work.'

'Don't be ridiculous, Ellie,' snapped Rosalie. 'Barr & Stroud's only take on clever girls.'

The minister stepped in to soften that. 'Those who can bring a good school record with them. You can't exactly do that, Eleanor, can you now?' He leaned forward over the table with the air of a man about to impart a hugely important piece of news. 'On the other hand, cooking and cleaning requires no qualifications. It's easy too. Anybody can do it. And young though you are, you've been doing it for several years.'

'Aye,' Ellie said doubtfully. 'I suppose.'

The rickety wooden chair on which Mr Hunter was sitting creaked its protest as he settled back into it, his face now bearing an expression of triumphant satisfaction. 'So,' he enquired, 'why don't you apply to Bellevue?'

'Bellevue?' Ellie repeated. Something bubbled up inside her. Disbelief. Hope. Excitement.

'They're chronically short of staff,' he pointed out. 'Mrs Tait has her cook and her daily woman, and the estimable Mrs Mitchell here, of course—'

The reverend gentleman had performed a minor miracle. The estimable Mrs Mitchell had been struck dumb.

'—but Mrs Tait was telling my wife recently that Mrs Drummond really is in dire need of help in the kitchen, especially with the garden party they're planning for the next puffer launch at the end of July.' He was human enough to allow himself a little smile at his foreknowledge of this great event.

Ellie stared at him, taking in what he was suggesting. Working for the Taits would give her a job and a home. She'd still be in Temple, close to the canal and able to see Malcolm and Frank and her other friends. None of her objections to going into service applied. She suppressed a gurgle of laughter. The thought of Evander Tait backing her into a corner and having his wicked way with her defied even her vivid imagination.

'It's the answer,' she breathed. 'The answer to everything.'

Eric Hunter beamed at her, delighted by her reaction to his idea. 'Now then,' he began, 'Mrs Hunter and I have been invited up to Bellevue for luncheon on Sunday. Would you like us to put in a good word for you?'

Ellie's eyes were shining, her spirits soaring. 'Oh, yes, Mr Hunter! Oh, yes please! Should I come up the road on Sunday afternoon too?'

The minister nodded. 'Yes. I've already discussed this with Mrs Hunter and she thinks you should present yourself at about half-past two—'

'Minister! Please!'

Like two conspirators caught red-handed in the carrying-out of their plot, Eric Hunter and Ellie turned towards Rosalie Mitchell. She looked as if a week-old haddock was slowly decomposing under her nose. 'You can't think this girl would fit in at Bellevue?'

Overdoing the horror, Ellie thought cynically. Any minute now the stupid bisom would slap the back of her hand against her forehead and fall over in a faint like they did in the pictures when something awful was about to happen.

'But it's the ideal solution, Mrs Mitchell,' Mr Hunter said. 'For everybody. The Taits' cook really does need help in the kitchen. You must know that.'

'Experienced help,' Rosalie countered. 'Professional help. Someone sent along by one of the reputable domestic registries. I mean, a family like the Taits can't employ simply *anybody*.' She waved a dismissive hand. 'Take it from one who knows, Mr Hunter,' she darted a venomous glance at Ellie, 'this girl isn't suitable for Bellevue. She's simply not the right calibre.'

Chapter 6

'*Not the right calibre?*' Frank spluttered. 'Did you ask the cheeky bloody bitch to pick a window?'

'I was sorely tempted,' Ellie said, pouring him another cup of tea. He was her second visitor since the minister and Rosalie Mitchell had left.

'What did your Mr Hunter say?'

Ellie sighed. 'He kind of backed down.'

'That's Proddy ministers for you,' Frank said blithely. 'Heretics with nae backbone.'

'That's men for you,' Ellie retorted. 'No match for a sharp-tongued woman.'

'Some of us are.' He gave her a smug smile, buttered his fourth pancake and took a healthy bite out of it.

'Maybe the horrible Rosalie's right, though,' Ellie said gloomily. 'Bellevue is awful grand. How on earth would someone like me fit in there?' Her lips twisted in a wry grimace. 'How on earth would I get on working alongside someone like her?'

'The way I understand it, you'd be working directly under the cook,' Frank pointed out. 'You'd probably no' have very much to do wi' Mrs Toffee Nose. Help in the kitchen, isn't that's what needed? You'd be ideal for that. The minister's right enough there. You've been cooking and cleaning and looking after Malcolm and your father for years.'

Ellie glanced round her shabby home, thought of the simple and very basic meals she had learned how to prepare and cook. She shook her head. 'It's no' quite the same, Frank.'

'It's no' that different,' he insisted. 'You can learn all the other things you need to know. Yon Mrs Drummond'll probably be happy to get someone young she can train up in her own ways.'

Wondering if he might possibly be right, Ellie watched him polish off the pancake. 'I was so excited when the minister suggested it. It seemed like the answer to everything.'

'It is the answer to everything. Have faith in yourself.'

Ellie gazed doubtfully at him. 'And if one member of Bellevue's staff thinks I'm no' up to the job and wouldnae be backwards about coming forward and saying that to Mr and Mrs Tait and their cook?'

'It's all about strategy. Steal a march on her. She's no' up at Bellevue all the time, is she?'

'I think she's usually off on a Sunday afternoon —'

'That's tomorrow afternoon, like? When your Proddy minister and his wife are gonnae be up there too and have offered to speak for you? And cannae be scared out o' that by the presence of the horrible Rosalie?'

The excitement was bubbling up inside Ellie again. 'So I swan in and ask for a job?'

'Nothing wrong with the direct approach. They can only say no. Maybe they'll say yes.' His eyes went to her tousled head. 'I'd go and ask Granny Mitchell for some help smartening yourself up, though.'

'Would *you* like to pick a window?'

He grinned at her. 'Can I have a piece o' that shortbread now?'

'You'll get fat,' she said, passing the plate over to him.

'Naw,' he said cheerfully. 'I've got hollow legs.' His own less-than-tidy head swivelled towards the door. 'That's Malcolm back, I think.'

According Frank the stiffest of nods, Malcolm shrugged out of his jacket and walked forward to place it carefully over the back of a chair.

Shortbread in hand, the other young man rose to his feet. 'I'll leave youse to it.'

As her brother sat down, pointedly turning his back on the departing Frank, Ellie got up to see her visitor out. 'Sorry,' she murmured as they stepped out on to the landing.

'Nae bother, hen,' he said easily. 'He's never been overfond o' left-footers like myself. Don't worry about it,' he urged, reacting to the embarrassment and regret suffusing her face. 'When you're a Catholic you get used to it. Perish the thought folk might try to get to know you before they decide they hate your guts, eh?'

'It's not right, Frank,' she said, leaning over the heavy wooden banister and watching him saunter down the stone stairs to the half-landing.

'Lots o' things in this world arenae right, Ellie.' The grim expression accompanying those words relaxed as he looked up at her. 'Lots o' other things are. Like you working at Bellevue, for instance.'

'You think so?'

'I know so. Away and talk it over with your brother.' As he disappeared down the stairs, Ellie walked back into the house.

'He's made some inroads into the home-baking.'

Angry with Malcolm, both for his attitude to Frank and for his stiff-necked inability to express his gratitude for that home-baking and everything else their neighbours were doing for them, a sharp comment sprang to her lips. Something about her brother's posture made her stifle it.

He invariably sat up straight, shoulders back and chin up, ready to take on the world. At the moment, hunched forward with his forearms resting on the table, it looked as if that world had defeated him.

'Did you go for a walk?'

'Aye. Along to the Buttney at Maryhill. Mr Tait spotted me on the way back and asked me into the house. Gave me a brandy.'

'That was kind of him,' Ellie responded, watching as he rubbed a hand over his face. He had to shave every day now and as the evening approached she had noticed that golden stubble began to appear on his jawline. That must be gey itchy.

She was feeling her way, trying to work out what kind of a mood he was in. Most folk seemed to think Malcolm was a placid person, unmoved by much of what went on around him. She knew differently.

As a rule, brother and sister didn't go in very much for physical displays of affection but now Ellie reached across the table for his hand. He allowed her to take it. Despite the warmth of the day outside and the heat of the fire burning in the grate, his fingers felt stiff and cold. She recalled the bone-deep chill she had felt two days ago, knowing in her heart of hearts that her father wasn't going to be brought out of the canal alive.

Malcolm's eyes were fixed on her face. They were slate grey, the same colour Alan Douglas's had been. Ellie had always assumed her own green eyes must be an inheritance from Cathy Douglas, her red hair a throwback to some more distant relative. She couldn't know for sure. Apart from that memory of a woman with a cloud of fair hair, she had absolutely no idea what her mother had looked like.

It wasn't a question she would ever have put to her father. He had kept nothing that had belonged to his wife: no clothes, no mementos, not even a wedding photograph. Even Granny Mitchell, a mine of information about everything that had ever happened in Temple or Netherton in the whole of either community's history, never seemed willing to satisfy Ellie's curiosity on the subject of her mother.

'Och, Ellie,' Malcolm wailed, 'Mr Tait got it out of me that we can't afford to pay for the funeral and now he's going to do it. He says he won't take no for an answer! He's buying a plot and arranging for a headstone and everything! How are we ever going to repay him?'

Ellie redoubled her grip on her brother's cold fingers. 'Malcolm,' she said urgently, 'there is a way for us to pay Mr Tait back—'

'Don't be ridiculous, Ellie,' he said dully, 'have you any idea how much a funeral costs?'

'Aye, but I've got an idea, Malcolm—'

That brought a wan smile to his face. 'And what sort of an idea could you have, you wee numpty?'

Stung, Ellie dropped his hand. 'You might be surprised,' she said.

Malcolm sat back in his chair. 'I'm starving,' he said. 'Is there any of that Scotch broth left?'

She had washed, mended and pressed her blue dress, and brushed her exuberant red waves into some semblance of neatness. Granny Mitchell had loaned her a navy jacket and a smart pair of shoes that one of her older granddaughters had grown out of and the next one down the line hadn't yet grown into.

Businesslike, Ellie thought hopefully. Suitable for someone who's standing in the middle of the pristine white stone chips of Bellevue's driveway and is about to march boldly up to the front door and ask for a job. She had woken up this morning more than ever convinced it was the only answer.

Hurt by his lack of faith in her, she had told Malcolm nothing about her plans. He had unwittingly co-operated with them, making a date to call at Mrs Chisholm's this afternoon to discuss the arrangements for him moving in. She was a motherly soul, and a famous gossip. She was bound to offer her new lodger a cup of tea, both out of kindness and the desire to know the exact details of Alan Douglas's death and what was to become of his orphaned children.

With luck, Malcolm's hard-won good manners and sense of proper etiquette would keep him there long enough to satisfy Mrs Chisholm's curiosity and, more importantly, for Ellie to carry out her mission. Her brother would be singing a different song when she returned in triumph with a job, a new home and the opportunity for her as well as him to pay Mr Tait back for his kindness to them.

That had been the idea, at any rate. Now Ellie was actually at Bellevue the reality was proving a little daunting. Heavily screened by trees and bushes, and turning its back on the canal as it did, the front of the house had never been visible to her. It had a huge wooden door, painted a glossy and dazzling white. Recessed under a curving veranda that rounded the corner of the building, it was flanked on either side by floor-length windows, each exactly the same height and exactly half the width of the door. Their crossbars were also painted white.

Once Ellie had summoned up the courage to walk in under the veranda she saw that the door was adorned with a long brass knocker in the shape of a sleek and sinuous cat. It looked like no mouser she had ever stroked. Swallowing hard, she lifted her hand towards it.

Halfway there she changed her mind, bringing the hand back to smooth down her hair. It had probably reverted to its normal windswept state by now. She hadn't worn a hat. She didn't own one herself and any of those Granny had tried on her head had seemed ridiculously old for her. Now she was wondering if it might have been better to look ridiculous than cheap.

The lack of a hat signalled a girl's social status. If you couldn't even afford that small accessory of formal dress you were clearly as common as muck, referred to disparagingly as 'a wee hairy'. Ellie's hand fell to her side. What the hell was she doing here?

It wasn't too late to cut and run. None of the occupants of the house had spotted her yet, and if she hurried home she'd get there long before Malcolm came back from Mrs Chisholm's. Nobody need ever know that wee Ellie Douglas had had the cheek to think she might be good enough to work in a house like Bellevue. She could hear Rosalie Mitchell's voice in her head, see the sneering contempt on the woman's face as she dismissed her as 'not the right calibre'.

Then, as clearly as if its owner were standing next to her, she heard a different voice, a rough but warm masculine one that drowned Rosalie Mitchell out completely. *Why do you always think you're a daftie? Have faith in yourself.* Ellie placed her hand on the cat's head and tapped out three smart raps on the white door.

A fire-breathing dragon flung it open it to her. 'And who might you be?'

'I'm l-looking for w-work, m-missus.' Ellie's well-rehearsed speech of introduction flew out of her head as Bellevue's cook-housekeeper loomed over her. Aileen Drummond was what folk called 'a handsome woman', tall and statuesque. Having glimpsed her from a distance in the street or over the pews of Mr Hunter's church, Ellie had always thought that despite her size she seemed a rather gentle person. She didn't look at all gentle at the moment.

'Who is it, Mrs Drummond?'

As Aileen Drummond turned to answer her mistress's question both her face and her voice became expressionless. 'It's a young person looking for work, madam.'

Angela Tait came forward. She seemed to be bathed in light. It was all those windows, of course, spilling sunshine into an entrance hall that seemed to Ellie about the size of a football pitch. 'Do I know you, my dear?'

'M-my b-brother, Malcolm, w-works for your man, m-missus.' Damn, damn, damn. She should have said 'husband', not 'man', and she should have addressed the lady of the house as 'madam'.

Angela Tait didn't appear to notice her unexpected visitor's lack of social graces. Her lovely face took on a sombre expression. 'The poor lad who lost his father last Thursday night?'

'Aye,' Ellie said. 'I'm Malcolm's sister, Eleanor. Ellie for short,' she offered.

'Oh, I didn't know Malcolm Douglas had a sister!' Half-blinded by the dazzling brightness of the hall, Ellie peered behind Mrs Tait and saw Phoebe. 'I'm so glad!' the girl exclaimed, quick tears starting to her eyes. 'I thought he was all alone now!'

'You're looking for work, Eleanor?' Mrs Tait asked. She extended her arm in a graceful gesture of invitation. 'Why don't you come in and tell us all about it?'

Overawed by the warmth of the welcome the Tait women – if not their fearsome cook – were extending to her, Ellie stepped into the lobby. It was not only vast, it also had an enormously high ceiling. Behind Mrs Tait and Phoebe's golden heads a white-painted wooden staircase with open treads led up to a landing that appeared to run all the way round the first floor of the house.

'Mrs Drummond,' Angela Tait said, 'will you come through with us, please? Now, then,' she said as Ellie followed her across the hall and into what she supposed you would call a sitting room, 'you stand here in front of the fireplace where we can all see you.'

Nervously aware that she was walking over a pale green carpet and hoping she hadn't picked up anything nasty on her borrowed shoes that might mark it, Ellie turned and found herself looking the great Mr James Tait straight in the eye. The expression on his face wasn't what you would have called encouraging.

Perhaps he was annoyed at having his Sunday afternoon disturbed. Should she have gone to see him at the boatyard tomorrow morning instead, asked for an appointment to come up to Bellevue after the funeral? No, she thought, returning Mr and Mrs Hunter's surprised but enthusiastic smiles, she had come today because they would be here to speak for her.

There were two other guests present. From their resemblance to one another they had to be mother and daughter. Ellie's eyes widened as she registered the sleek greyhound sitting on the floor next to the older lady, the colour of its coat exactly matching the silk of its mistress's outfit. She wondered whether it was the dog or the dress that had come first.

Mr Tait was sitting between the minister and his wife, in one of three large armchairs set facing the fire but a long way back from it. At right angles to those chairs and the fire itself were two matching settees, both of them long enough to seat four people comfortably. A long and low table, set with cups, saucers and a tall coffee pot, stood in the centre of the room.

Angela Tait sat down next to the older of the two ladies on one of the settees. Like the rest of the furniture, it resembled nothing Ellie had ever seen before. Its wooden back and side panels were painted a dark forest green. The colour was so deep and rich she itched to touch it, as she might have trailed her fingers over some velvety-soft moss on the canal bank.

All three pieces of the settee's framework tilted out at the top. They were crowned by carved wooden acorns lashed together with lengths of ship's rope – although no ship had ever had rope that clean. There was one long upholstered cushion to sit on, covered in shimmery green and silver brocade, and the back of the sofa was piled high with a profusion of small cushions in the same fabric.

Phoebe Tait walked over and perched on the edge of her father's chair. At least her brother and his sarcastic tongue weren't in evidence.

'Now, then,' Mrs Tait said, 'this is Eleanor Douglas. Her brother, Malcolm, works for James and,' her voice dropped in sympathy, 'their father passed away last Thursday afternoon due to a most unfortunate accident.'

'Oh gosh!' said the younger lady. 'What happened to him, you poor thing?' When she spoke, Ellie realised she could be only a year or two older than Phoebe Tait. At first sight her sophisticated clothes had made her look older. She wore a very short black skirt a couple of inches above her knee, a matching long tunic top in black, red and white stripes and a jaunty little red beret set on her bobbed chestnut-brown hair.

'He was crossing the catwalk, miss,' Ellie explained, 'and he fell in.'

The girl leaned forward, an expression of sympathetic interest on her attractive features. 'Did nobody try to get him out?'

'A puffer captain did,' Phoebe Tait said. As all eyes turned towards her, the colour rose in her cheeks. 'I was in the boatyard office on Friday,' she explained. 'Malcolm told me what had happened.'

Ellie acknowledged Phoebe's contribution with a swift nod in her direction. 'Captain MacLean of the *Torosay*, miss. He tried real hard.' She paused as the pictures flashed once more through her head. 'But my father's clothes got caught on something and by the time they pulled him free and brought him out he was dead.'

'How dreadful,' murmured the elegant young lady. 'How absolutely dreadful. Can I hazard a guess that your father's death leaves you personally in a bit of a pickle, Miss Douglas?'

'Aye, miss,' Ellie said, grateful to her for raising the subject. 'I need to find a job and somewhere to stay and I need to do both of those real soon.'

Mrs Tait was gazing sympathetically at her. That was all well and good but Ellie sensed it was her husband she had to convince. The expression on his face hadn't grown any more encouraging.

'Please sir,' she said, addressing him directly, 'you've helped us a lot already and me and Malcolm really appreciate it. We've been trying to think of some way we could pay you back. I know you and Mrs Tait are aye short o' help in the house and I wondered maybe if I could work for you. And live in,' she added, anxious he should realise exactly what she was asking for.

Every head in the room turned towards James Tait, deferring to him as the head of the household. An unhelpful thought slithered into Ellie's head. Phoebe Tait might not have known she existed but her father certainly did. Hadn't he told Malcolm not to come back to work until he got his sister settled? If Mr Tait hadn't thought to offer that sister a position in his house then, why should he do so now?

Her stomach churned. Probably, like Rosalie Mitchell, he didn't think someone like her would be the right calibre for Bellevue. Maybe the horrible Rosalie had even said something to her employer about the inadvisability of taking Ellie on.

Frank stomped back into her head, an expression of exasperation on his good-natured face. *They can only say no. They might say yes*. James Tait hadn't said no yet. This was her last chance to convince him to say the opposite.

'I think I'm no' a bad cook. I cannae make fancy things like you and Mrs Tait probably like but I could learn how to do them, I know I could. And you wouldnae have to pay me very much. I'd work cheap because I'd be grateful for the job and somewhere to stay, and because me and Malcolm are very grateful to you for everything you've done to help us.'

The greyhound's mistress burst out laughing. 'Oh, James, you absolutely have to take this young person on.' She looked up at Bellevue's cook. 'Mrs Drummond, is she not exactly what you need? Especially with the launch party we've been hearing is planned for the end of July?'

Aileen Drummond's voice was wooden. 'I hardly think she is trained, Lady Matheson.'

Lady Matheson? Ellie tried not to let her mouth fall open at the realisation that she was mixing with the aristocracy.

Lady Matheson chuckled. 'My goodness me, Mrs Drummond, I'm sure you know as well as I do that it's much better to have someone untrained you can bring up in your own ways. Raw, so to speak.'

Must tell Frank he was right about that . . . Ellie was feeling a little dazed, hardly daring to hope success might be within her grasp. Lady Matheson smiled graciously at Aileen Drummond. 'Like yourself,' she pronounced, 'Miss Douglas is clearly an *original*.'

Unseen by her mother, the young lady in the red beret winked at Ellie.

Then Eric Hunter sent her a smile. 'I'm sure Eleanor won't mind my saying that she hasn't exactly done very well at school. She is, however, a very honest and trustworthy girl. Mrs Hunter and I would both be delighted to recommend her for any position here.' He turned to his wife. 'My dear?'

'Indeed,' Mrs Hunter agreed. 'Eleanor has cooked and cleaned for her father and brother from a very young age. She's no stranger to hard work.'

'What more do you need, Angela?' Lady Matheson asked. 'You have to give this girl a position. James, you absolutely *must* agree!'

No, Ellie thought, glancing nervously across at him, he doesn't agree. He doesn't want to take me on and he is the master of the house and it is up to him. Well, she thought, her heart sinking, she had tried.

James Tait smiled. It was like the sun emerging from behind a cloud on the greyest of days, warming and brightening everything it touched. 'If you say so, my dear Lady Matheson.' His voice was a charming and amused murmur.

The lady in question blushed. 'Oh, James,' she laughed. 'I've told you before. You must call me Monica.'

'They gave you a job?' Malcolm asked in amazement.

'Aye. Why wouldn't they?' Ellie wasn't quite sure how she'd got back from Bellevue. She suspected she had floated down the hill and over the nolly without her feet touching the ground at all, elated by her success. 'I've to start on Tuesday morning.'

'Lady Matheson,' Malcolm repeated. 'Wife of Lord Matheson, who owns one of the biggest shipyards on the Clyde. It was her who spoke up for you?'

Ellie nodded smugly. The impact of her news on her brother was all she had hoped for and more. 'She said I was "an original". I think that means something the same as numpty.' She grinned hugely. 'Her daughter was very nice too. She gave me a wink.'

Malcolm was shaking his head. 'Who'd have thought it? My wee sister bold enough to walk into Bellevue and ask for a job in front of some of the most prominent folk in Glasgow.' He looked thoughtful. 'Probably you being my sister helped you get the job. Don't show me up when you go to work there, now. Don't give any cheek to their cook, either. Or Mrs Mitchell.'

'Of course I won't. I'm no' that daft.'

Her brother wagged an admonishing finger at her. 'Don't think you can skive off for hours on end, either. It's not like the school.'

'I know that too, Malcolm.' Ellie rolled her eyes at

him, stepping down hard both on the less-than-enticing prospect of having to work alongside Rosalie Mitchell, and her strong suspicion that it might take quite some time to get Mrs Aileen Drummond on her side. Ach, if she could talk herself into a job at Bellevue, she could do anything.

'Come on,' she said, 'let's have our tea and get to bed early. We've a big day tomorrow with the funeral and we'll need to clear up when we come back so everything's ready for the Wintergreens.'

She looked at her brother, her words bringing home the reality of the change about to affect both their lives. 'I'll miss you, Malcolm,' she said, shy about putting her feelings for him into words.

He tweaked her nose, but his voice was husky. 'I'll miss you too, wee sister. We'll no' be faraway from one another, though.'

Ellie brightened. 'Aye, that's right. When I've got some time off we can go for a walk together. Or maybe I'll get sent down to the boatyard with a message now and again.'

'But only come down if you are sent, Ellie. You and I are both going to work really hard, remember, to pay Mr Tait back *and* to make something o' ourselves. I,' he announced loftily, 'intend to work my way up. One day I'll be Mr Tait's right-hand man.'

'What about me?' she asked eagerly. 'What will I be one day?'

'Married to some rich and handsome man. Maybe you'll meet one serving cocktails up at Bellevue.'

'I don't think I'll be doing that for a while.' Her eyes slid to the coins that had been collected for them, now once more stacked up in neat piles in the centre of the table. 'If you took all of that you could get your suit tomorrow morning,' she suggested. 'Wear it at the funeral.'

'I'd been thinking that myself, Ellie. Are you sure you wouldn't mind? By rights, half of it should be yours.'

'Och,' she said, 'I'll be earning money myself soon. You take this. Then I'll get the table set for our tea.'

The minister's prediction that very few people would bother to attend Alan Douglas's funeral turned out to be spectacularly wrong. The church was stowed out.

'I expect there's quite a few folk want to make sure he's really dead,' Ellie murmured, earning herself a reproving glance from Malcolm. None of the supposed mourners had brought any flowers to lay on top of the coffin. Wondering if she and Malcolm should have spared some of the money given to them for that, Ellie's eyes travelled up past the minister in his pulpit to the beautiful stained-glass window above his head.

She had always loved the glowing blue and white depiction of St Andrew, glad that Scotland's patron saint stood tall and proud beside his distinctive cross rather than being cruelly nailed to it. Unbidden and unwanted, the image of the holy man spread-eagled against the wooden spars pushed its way into her mind's eye. Arms and legs outstretched, it was how her father had looked when he had first fallen into the canal.

The pictures and sensations surrounding Alan Douglas's last moments on earth flooded her brain once more. They were overtaken by other sensations and memories, far too many of them. She could still feel a dull ache in her shoulders from that final beating he had given her.

Lowering her head, Ellie mentally addressed the occupant of the coffin. You don't deserve flowers, you old bugger. You're in that box and soon you're going to be in the ground and you're never going to hit me again. Nobody's ever going to hit me again. I'm not letting you stay inside my head, either. This is goodbye, Daddy.

As the organist came to the end of the first two lines of 'The Lord's my Shepherd', the congregation rose to its feet. Ellie stood up straight and added her own clear voice to the singing.

Chapter 7

'May I show Ellie her room now, Mother?'

'Darling, shouldn't you be setting off for school? Evander left for the station hours ago.'

'Oh,' Phoebe said, 'he always gets in far too early! Pa did say at breakfast I was to help you get Ellie settled in, what with Mrs Drummond being too busy to do it.'

Angela Tait frowned. 'You know your father doesn't like us going into the servants' quarters. Everyone in their own place, that's what he always says.'

'Servants' quarters?' Phoebe repeated scornfully. 'Honestly, Mother, that expression is positively out of the ark! And she can't find her room herself, can she?' She flashed Ellie a conspiratorial grin. 'It's a bit of a trek, I'm afraid. Right at the top of the house.'

'All right,' sighed her mother. 'Take Ellie up the front stairs and give her a quick tour on the way up but don't take too long. She and I have an appointment at the dressmaker's at ninc fifteen.'

'Oh, please let me come too, Mother!'

Angela Tait tried to look stern. 'We've already had this discussion, Phoebe.'

'Oh, Ma, I'm nearly finished at school anyway. What does it matter if I take today off?'

Angela pointed an accusing finger at her daughter.

'You,' she said, 'are a spoiled brat. Back down here in twenty minutes, then.'

Phoebe led Ellie up to the landing, suspended above the entrance hallway like a minstrels' gallery. The white-painted stair banister continued all the way round it.

'The family bedrooms are on this floor,' Phoebe explained, pointing to the doors they were passing. 'My room, my mother's room, my father's room.'

Ellie was startled into speech. 'Your parents have separate rooms?'

'Of course,' Phoebe said, apparently seeing nothing odd in this arrangement. 'Round this way, Ellie. The guest bedrooms and bathrooms are all here.' She rounded a third corner, bringing them to the section of the landing opposite her own and her parents' bedrooms. As they reached the end of it, she indicated an alcove in the corner. 'The back stairs come up there and carry on up to the attic and this is Evander's room here, at the back of the house.'

Ellie dared another comment. 'He must have a great view.'

Phoebe turned her pretty mouth down. 'Only if you want to look out at the canal and streets full of gloomy tenements and factories. Mother and I would prefer to be in Bearsden, where most of our friends are. But Father likes to be close to the boatyard—' She clapped her hand to her forehead. 'Oh, I'm *so* sorry, Ellie! I've just remembered you and Malcolm live – *lived* – in one of those tenements. What a faux pas. That's French for false step, you know.' She groaned and smacked her brow for a second time. 'That's a second one I've taken. You probably studied French at school and I'm being dreadfully patronising.'

Ellie laughed at the very idea. 'I didn't study anything

very much at school. To tell you the truth, I'm real glad to be out of the place.'

'Oh,' Phoebe said. 'That's how I feel too! I can't wait to leave! Get out into the world and start living! And,' she continued, obviously feeling she still had to make amends for her previous comment, 'Evander likes the view over the canal, he really does. It was him who chose the name for this house. That's French too.'

'Beautiful view,' Ellie said. 'I know that one.' She smiled reassuringly at Phoebe. 'I know what you mean about it being gloomy. I did wonder if the name might be a bit of a joke.'

'So did Father,' Phoebe said ruefully. 'Thought Evander was making fun of him when he suggested it but my dear little brother swears it's a tribute to the old house. Apparently when it was first built it had "a fine vista across verdant fields and the river Clyde, and a grand prospect of the hills of Renfrewshire".' She dropped the high-falutin tones she had used for the quote. 'Evander got that out of some old book, I expect. He's awfully studious. Come and see his room. It's the absolute end.'

To say Evander's bedroom was cluttered would have been an understatement. It was stuffed to the gunwales. Books overflowed from shelves on to the floor. More had been tossed on to the colourful patchwork quilt that covered the single bed in the corner.

A battered old buttoned leather armchair stood in the opposite corner of the room, a worn tartan travelling rug flung over its back. In front of the window stood a scarred but solid wooden writing desk. Schoolbooks, sketchpads and notebooks were strewn all over it, higgledy-piggedly.

'Isn't it completely dire?' Phoebe asked in accents of

horror. 'The daily woman refuses to come in here any more. Evander has to clean it himself.'

'His walls are covered too,' Ellie observed. 'Lots of pictures.'

Phoebe sighed in sisterly disapproval. 'Such a mixture of styles too! This is a Jazz Style house. Mother and Father and I agreed that everything we put into it should be in the same style, so it would have artistic integrity.'

Wondering what that might be when it was at home, Ellie posed a question. 'Your brother didn't agree?'

Phoebe frowned. 'I'm afraid not. Him being so stubborn about it caused quite an argument with Father.'

Ellie tilted her head back and surveyed the pictures. 'I like that black cat. It looks gey fierce and bristly but it's got a twinkle in its eye too. More like a real Temple cat than your door knocker.'

'I suppose,' Phoebe allowed, glancing up at it. 'But that print's definitely art nouveau, and that's so *passé* now. That's French too,' she explained. 'It means outmoded.'

Ellie was still studying the cat picture. 'What do the words mean?'

'Oh, it was an advertising poster for a theatre in Paris,' Phoebe explained. 'The Black Cat Cabaret.'

Following her out of the room, Ellie thought that whether the black cat was art nouveau or Jazz Style she still liked it – whatever the hell either of those two terms meant.

Beginning to relax in Phoebe's warm and effusive company, she asked another question. 'Are you going to study French when you leave school?'

'I'd love to do what Lesley Matheson did last year,' Phoebe confided. 'She spent the winter with a French family and they have to not speak any English to you and take you out to places and introduce you to their friends and relations and everything. Miss Matheson said she had such a good time but Father says I can't do it until I'm older. He's awfully old-fashioned sometimes. I mean, he won't even let me get my hair bobbed for the launch party, can you imagine?' She paused at last for breath, looking at Ellie with an expectant air.

'Your hair is real bonnie,' she responded shyly. 'I can see why your father wouldn't want you to cut it short.'

'You're so sweet, Ellie! You don't mind if I call you Ellie, do you?'

'You're my employers' daughter. I expect you can call me anything you like.'

Phoebe laughed. 'I thought you might prefer Eleanor.'

'Ellie's fine. What should I call you, though?'

'Well, it'll have to be "Miss Phoebe" when anybody's about,' Phoebe rolled her eyes, 'especially my father and Mrs Drummond. She's as much a stickler as he is for that sort of thing.'

'I'm no' really looking forward to working for her,' Ellie confessed.

'Och,' the other girl said airily, 'she'll be all right. She ought to be grateful you've come to help her. Right then, we're nearly at your room. Up this way.'

Steeper and narrower than the main staircase, the treads of these stairs were nevertheless also carpeted. Ellie commented on this unexpected luxury.

'Oh yes, Father pretends to have all these ante-diluvian ideas about people knowing their place but it was him who insisted on having carpet here as well as in the rest of the house. Personally, I think we should call this "the staff wing". Sounds more modern and efficient, don't you think?'

She went on without waiting for an answer: 'Mrs Drummond's suite is on the right. She has her own bedroom, sitting room and bathroom. Mother thought that was a terrible extravagance but Pa said she would up sticks and leave if we didn't offer her really high-quality accommodation. She's a great cook, you know. People are always trying to poach her for their own houses. Oh, that's quite good, isn't it? *Poach the cook.* Right then, she said you were to have the room along at the end.'

'What are these other doors that we're passing?'

'Four more bedrooms. We're always supposed to be engaging more staff. The trouble is that no one who's sent along from any of the domestic registries ever meets my father's exacting standards.'

'I hope I will,' Ellie said nervously. 'I got the feeling he wasnae too happy about taking me on.'

'He's never happy about there being strangers in the house. Likes to run a tight ship, be able to trust everyone who sleeps beneath his roof. That's what he always says.' She turned a handle and pushed open a door. 'This is the bathroom. It's supposed to be shared but since you're the only other resident member of staff you'll have it all to yourself.'

Ellie stared dumbly into a room, which was as big as the kitchen of her old home. An inside lavvy, bath and sink, all for her and only for her?

'Your bedroom's next door,' Phoebe said, leading the way to it and throwing open that door too. 'Oh, Ellie, what's the matter? Don't you like it?'

For Ellie's eyes were glittering with unshed tears. She looked round the spacious and comfortable room, took in the bed with its neat white counterpane and plump pillows, saw the comfortable armchair set in another corner of it, spotted the modern and obviously brand-new small desk and upright chair set against the wall opposite the bed.

'Nothing's wrong. It's wonderful. Oh, I've even got one of the porthole windows!' She raised a trembling hand to her mouth.

Phoebe looked puzzled. 'So that's good, isn't it?'

Ellie sniffed back the tears. 'It's more than good.' She studied the other girl's concerned face. She was an odd mixture, this Miss Phoebe Tait. Though she was two years older than herself and had a veneer of sophistication she herself lacked, in some ways Ellie felt much more mature. She decided to take a chance on her.

'I watched you,' she confessed, 'last Saturday night.' She pointed through the porthole window to the world outside. 'You and your family had visitors and you were out on the terrace with them. I was down on the towpath, on the other side of the fence. I looked up here and I really envied you, wished I could live in a house like this. And now I do,' she finished, emotion once more overtaking her, 'and it's a bit much to take in!'

Phoebe flung her arms around Ellie's neck. 'I'm so glad you're happy to be here, Ellie,' she whispered. 'I really hope you and I can be friends.'

Ellie looked doubtfully at her. 'But you're the daughter of the house and I'm only a skivvy. How can we be friends?'

Phoebe's sombre expression relaxed into one of amusement. 'Do you always say exactly what you think?'

'Is that bad?'

'No,' Phoebe said with a laugh. 'It's refreshing.' She seized Ellie's hand and pulled her to the door. 'Come on, let's go and buy you some clothes!'

* * *

Blushing at the washed-out state of her tattered underwear, Ellie stood on a little platform as the dressmaker and the Tait women twittered around her like a flock of brightly coloured birds. Periodically they held swatches of material up against her, each one setting them off on a long and involved conversation as to whether or not that particular fabric and colour suited her. Feeling rather like a life-size doll, Ellie listened in amazement as all three women went off into raptures over the colour of her hair.

An order having eventually been placed for four blouses, two skirts and two afternoon frocks, Angela Tait drove them from the dressmaker's at Anniesland Cross along to Byres Road. Awe-struck by the whole experience, Ellie had added a new wish to her list of impossible dreams by the time they got there. How wonderful it must be to be able to take yourself somewhere, whenever you wanted to go, not have to wait in the cold for a tram or a train.

They went to a specialist shop to buy her uniforms: two black frocks and frilly white pinnies for serving meals in the dining room and two smart wraparound navy-blue overalls and neat little matching caps for kitchen work.

They visited several more shops after that one. By the time Mrs Tait had bought her two pairs of shoes – one black and one navy – and a ready-made dark blue print frock with a fashionably low waist and a pretty little white collar, Ellie was in seventh heaven. That was before Phoebe suggested to her mother that they buy her some underwear too.

Guiltily aware how upset Malcolm would be if he knew how much money was being spent on her, Ellie was taken aback to discover just how much she wanted the pretty things the ferociously genteel saleslady laid out on the glass counter in front of her. She salved her conscience by recognising how much fun Phoebe and her mother were having.

The most wonderful and amazing day of Ellie's young life continued with what Mrs Tait called 'a light luncheon' in an Italian café, followed by a visit to the hairdresser's to neaten her mop of hair. By now completely bemused, she asked herself silently how many kitchenmaids got this kind of treatment from their employers. She had to be one of the luckiest girls in the world.

It was close to four o'clock when they turned right at Anniesland Cross and drove up Crow Road towards the canal and Bellevue. Looking out from the back seat of the car – she could get used to this, she really could – Ellie spotted Marie Rafferty walking up the street. It was hard not to feel a rush of unholy glee at the incredulous expression on her face as Ellie sailed past. It was so hard that Ellie was unable to resist giving her a regal wave.

As they got out of the car at Bellevue, she was struck by a sudden thought. 'Eh, should I no' go round to the back door?'

Having walked her up to the house this morning, Malcolm had expressed himself rather forcefully on that subject. Ellie's own initial approach to Bellevue had been quite wrong. No wonder the cook had been angry with her. There were some things that simply weren't done, and a humble kitchenmaid going in by the front door was one of them.

'Nonsense,' Phoebe said, already pushing the big white door open. 'You'll come in with us. Won't she, Mother?'

Aileen Drummond was standing next to the green baize door which led to the kitchen, her arms folded across her shapely bosom. Resting above her elbows, her large and competent hands looked startlingly white and elegant, as though an artist who planned to paint her portrait had positioned her fingers in the most graceful pose imaginable. Dark and intense, her eyes bored into Ellie.

James Tait stood a few feet away from his cook, his own pose mirroring hers. He didn't look too pleased either. You could see where Evander had acquired the ability to look down his nose at you from a very great height.

'Darling!' Mrs Tait said. 'I didn't know you were planning on coming home early today.'

'Been out spending money, Angela?'

His wife raised her discreetly plucked eyebrows. 'We agreed we had to get Ellie kitted out, dear.'

James Tait's eyes slid over the shopping bags that all three women were carrying. 'Looks like you've kitted out a whole army of Ellies.' He laughed, unfolded his arms and sauntered forward, putting a hand out to stroke his daughter's shining locks. 'Have you by any chance been plunking school, my darling daughter?'

Phoebe dimpled at him. 'Oh, Pa!' she said. 'You told me you never learned anything worth knowing when you were at school!'

He laughed again. 'So I did. All I needed to know about life I learned on the battlefield. And on the battlefield which is modern business,' he added. 'Now then, might I have the pleasure of taking afternoon tea in the charming company of my wife and daughter?' He swung round to the cook. 'I'm sure you've baked something delicious as usual, Mrs Drummond.'

'I hope it will please, sir.'

Honestly, Ellie thought, it was like the voice of doom. You'd think she could have responded a little more graciously to her master's compliment.

'I'll just help Ellie take these things up to her room—' Phoebe said.

'No you won't,' her father said. 'She'll do that herself.' He spoke directly to Ellie. 'I think Mrs Drummond would appreciate your putting these things away as quickly as possible and then coming back down to see how you might help her.'

'Y-yes, s-sir,' Ellie stuttered. It was beautifully worded, but it was a rebuke all the same.

'And Eleanor?'

'Y-yes, s-sir?'

'It's not acceptable for you to use the front door. You'll remember that from now on.'

'Yes, sir. I'll be sure to remember that, sir.'

He turned his back on her before she had finished the sentence. Realising too late that he had issued an order to be obeyed rather than a request to be agreed with, Ellie hastened to relieve Mrs Tait and Phoebe of the bags they were carrying. 'Thank you very much for all of this, Mrs Tait. Thank you very much indeed.'

Angela Tait gave her a beautiful smile. 'It was a pleasure, my dear Ellie.'

Phoebe laced her arm through her father's. 'Where's Evander, Pa?'

'Upstairs with his head stuck in a book as usual, I expect.' James Tait crooked his other arm and his wife slipped her hand through it. 'Come on, my girls! I'm famished!'

Feeling a little forlorn as she watched the three

of them sweep off, Ellie readjusted her grip on the shopping bags.

'You'll never manage them all in one go,' snapped an unforgiving voice. 'You'll have to make two trips.'

'Yes, Mrs Drummond,' Ellie said, eyes downcast and intent on carrying out the task as quickly as possible. From above her head, she heard an exasperated sigh.

'Don't leave the ones you're taking on the second trip in the middle of the hall. Put them against the wall! I'll expect you in the kitchen in ten minutes flat!'

'Yes, Mrs Drummond,' Ellie said again. She was beginning to sound like old Mr and Mrs Wintergreen's parrot. She glanced up when she heard the green baize door swing. At least the parrot usually had an admiring audience. The housekeeper had vanished. Back to her lair to munch on some coal, no doubt.

Winning Aileen Drummond round might be going to take a wee bit longer than she had anticipated. Ellie suspected she might also have her work cut out persuading James Tait that she was a valuable addition to his household. She knew fine well he'd been angry when he'd seen her coming in through the front door. She'd had years of experience in recognising the first stirrings of that emotion.

Well, his displeasure hadn't lasted long and nobody had got hit. The very thought of that happening here was laughable. Bellevue wasn't that kind of house and the Taits weren't that kind of family. Struggling to keep a firm grip on even half the shopping bags, Ellie smiled happily at the thought of all her lovely new clothes.

By the time she'd reached her room she'd worked out a plan of action. She'd do everything Mrs Drummond and the family asked her to and she'd do it with a smile. Soon they'd all be wondering how they'd ever managed without her. She'd also set herself to learning exactly how things were done at Bellevue so she would fit seamlessly into Mr Tait's tight ship. She could do that nae bother. She could do that standing on her head.

She couldn't resist a peek into her bathroom before she went downstairs for the second time. *Her bathroom*. Ellie spent thirty seconds gazing in awe-struck wonder at its chequered black-and-white-tiled splendour. The bath was practically big enough to swim in.

She lowered her head to her bunched fist, pressing her mouth against her knuckles to contain another surge of emotion. She knew she was here to work. She knew it was going to be hard to please Aileen Drummond. She could deal with all of that.

What mattered was that she had a chance to make something of herself within the golden cocoon of Bellevue, safe and secure and protected from the hazards of the world outside. No more would she have to dodge her father's slaps and punches. No more would she have to run the gauntlet of people like Marie Rafferty.

She *was* the luckiest girl in the world.

Chapter 8

'Didn't your mother teach you *anything*?'

'My mother died when I was wee.'

'That was unfortunate for both of us, then,' snapped the cook.

Ellie's fingers clutched nervously at the well-starched folds of her navy overall. She'd managed to mislay both of the matching caps into which she was supposed to tuck her hair. That crime had earned her the first ticking off of the morning. On the receiving end of the second, she wondered resignedly how many more were to come.

That nugget of information about her motherless upbringing hadn't won her any sympathy. Heavy eyebrows knitted, Aileen Drummond placed her hands on her generous hips. She wore her abundance of glossy hair up, its thick and lustrous waves framing her face like a halo.

She had a large and beautifully shaped mouth. Pity it never got any smiling to do. At the start of her third week in the Tait household, Ellie had yet to witness that particular phenomenon.

The cook struck her as both too posh and a wee bit too young for her position of command. Not much older than thirty, Aileen Drummond was very well spoken, with the faintest of Scottish accents. Ellie could tell she wasn't local but beyond that couldn't pinpoint where she might come from.

'I was promised someone who would take the routine tasks off me, leave me time to concentrate on what I do best, especially with the launch next month. We've a hundred people coming here afterwards for the garden party. *A hundred people*,' Aileen Drummond repeated. 'Do you have any idea how much work that's going to be?'

Supplying the obvious answer to that question didn't strike Ellie as advisable, not if she wanted to live. The cook's cold eyes dropped to the potatoes Ellie had been instructed to prepare. 'Do you really not know that you scrape new potatoes, *never* peel them?'

'I do know that. I thought maybe you did things differently here. What with everything being so modern,' Ellie added earnestly.

Preparing the tatties had been the first real culinary task assigned to her. Since she'd arrived at Bellevue, she'd been mainly confined to the scullery and the huge walk-in crockery cupboard, bringing dishes out, washing them up and putting them away. It was an unending task in a household where a mountain of food was served up each and every day.

First thing in the morning, Aileen Drummond prepared a cooked breakfast for the family, herself and Ellie. Once that was cleared away it was time to think about luncheon for Mrs Tait and any guests she might have, plus the more robust midday dinner provided for the staff – the cook herself, Ellie, Rosalie Mitchell, the daily cleaning woman and the gardener.

In the early afternoon Mrs Drummond baked, producing delicious cakes and pastries fresh for afternoon tea at four o'clock. After that it was time to get on with the lavish meal this family called dinner, not to mention the lighter tea Ellie and the cook herself ate beforehand.

Ellie had been astonished by the modern gadgets Bellevue's kitchen contained. Not only the vast and shiny new cooking range but a host of other weird contraptions were operated by electricity. You didn't hoist the kettle up on to the range like you did in any normal house, you stuck the plug on the end of the cord attached to it into the wall. There was a special cupboard that kept food cool, a device for making toast without going near any kind of fire and a whole heap of wee trays and stands that kept food warm.

Used to a coal range, gas mantles and paraffin lamps, Ellie found it as unfamiliar as if she were living inside one of those spaceships Malcolm loved to read about. The very *modernness* of it all made her nervous. Weren't you in danger of being blown up or something when you stuck one of the thingumajigs into the wee holes in the wall through which the electricity apparently flowed?

She'd made the mistake of asking Rosalie Mitchell that question. Laughing unpleasantly at Ellie's foolishness, she'd spent much of the last three weeks making snide comments about the qualities demanded of domestic staff in such a modern home as Bellevue. She'd made it crystal clear that Ellie lacked all of them.

Knowing the woman disliked her even more now for having had the temerity to apply to the Taits against her recommendation, Ellie might have been able to discount her nasty wee remarks. Unfortunately Aileen Drummond appeared to have the same low opinion of her capabilities.

Ellie knew fine well that you scraped new tatties. She didn't know why she'd suddenly decided to peel them, except that her confidence had taken such a battering since she'd arrived at Bellevue she was no longer sure of the correct way to do anything.

'I'll do them myself.' Aileen Drummond looked pointedly at the wall clock. It was modern and electric too. 'Mrs Tait requires her lunch promptly today. She has guests coming for afternoon tea. I've scones to bake for that, not to mention getting on with planning the food for the launch party. Then it'll be time to get dinner started!'

Ellie's emotions took another spin – into sympathy for the hard-pressed cook. She blurted out a well-meaning offer of help. 'Could I no' maybe do the scones?'

'We want them edible,' came the unforgiving response.

It all went from bad to worse after that, Rosalie Mitchell smirking at a subdued Ellie as the staff sat down to their dinner in the middle of the day. Aileen Drummond was a silent and forbidding presence at the head of the table and the daily woman barely lifted her eyes from her plate. She was the sort who scuttled in, did her work, then scuttled home again. The genial middle-aged gardener made a heroic attempt to make conversation with the new girl but he soon fell quiet too, finishing his meal and returning to his own domain as soon as politeness would allow.

A lifetime of going without had made Ellie deeply appreciative of the food she had eaten since coming to work for the Taits. Aileen Drummond was a wonderful cook. Dessert this Monday was a dish that had already become one of Ellie's favourites: rhubarb crumble and custard.

Responding to her interest in his beloved fruit and vegetables, the gardener had explained to her that the fruit was of a type known as strawberry rhubarb. It had a rich and luscious flavour. The crumble was light and crunchy, the custard smooth and aromatic. The pudding was perfectly sweetened – not too much sugar, not too little.

Today it all turned to cardboard in Ellie's mouth.

'Go and get the washing in,' snapped the cook in the late afternoon. 'You're more of a hindrance than a help to me in here.'

Biting her lip, Ellie went through to the room beyond the scullery, which was probably far too grand to be called a wash house, hoisted a large wicker basket on to her hip and stepped out into the garden. Her jerky footsteps crunched on the pebble path that skirted the kitchen garden, with its rhubarb patch and neat drills of potatoes, peas, carrots, lettuce and cabbage, and led round to the fenced-off drying green.

When she got there she dropped the basket on to the grass beneath the rope and walked along the line, reaching up to feel if the shirts, nightclothes, sheets, tablecloths and pillowcases were dry. There wasn't much of a breeze blowing but the sluggish warmth of the day had done the trick. She lowered the wooden stretcher and saw the Renfrewshire hills shimmering hazily in the distance. She could just pick out the distinctively long flat plateau of Neilston Pad.

Over to the right lay Clydebank, the cranes of its many shipyards marking the line of the river as it flowed westwards towards the sea. Transferring her gaze to the foreground, Ellie's clear green eyes followed the gleaming satin ribbon of the canal. Beyond the sawmill and the boatyard Ellie could see a sturdy Clydesdale towing a coal barge.

She turned about and surveyed Bellevue, her gaze travelling up over its stark whiteness to her own porthole window. Everyone had been mightily impressed when they'd heard about her room, astounded to learn she had her own cludgie and bath.

'Aye, hen,' Granny Mitchell had said, pleased and excited for her. 'You've fallen on your feet, all right!'

Frank Rafferty had asked if she couldnae sneak him up to the attics one night so he could soak in his own dirt like a toff for an hour or so. Ellie had told him to go away and boil his head instead. 'And make soup with it?' he'd queried, a cheeky grin creasing the band of freckles that marched across his nose.

She hadn't seen either him or Granny for nearly two weeks. She got Thursday morning and Saturday afternoon and evening off. Last Thursday she had slept late, surprised by how tired she was. Saturday afternoons had to be kept for Malcolm. It was the only time off they had in common.

Her room and bathroom were lovely, the pleasure of soaking in her own dirt, as Frank had so charmingly put it, already a much appreciated relaxation. It was a bit lonely up there, though. It would be awful nice if there were other girls like herself in the empty rooms that lined the attic corridor. They could have let off steam together, had a communal moan about Mrs Drummond and the horrible Rosalie.

Jumpy in the unfamiliar surroundings, Ellie was sure she'd heard strange noises during the wee small hours on a couple of occasions last week. Wondering if Gowanlea might have housed ghosts who were angry because their home had been demolished to make way for Bellevue, she'd been far too frightened to get up out of bed and investigate.

She remembered what her former teacher had told her, her stern voice making it clear the comment was not meant as a compliment: 'You have an overactive imagination, Eleanor Douglas.' With a sigh, Ellie turned back to the washing. Doubtless she'd get another tongue-lashing if she took too long over the job. She couldn't resist one last long, lingering look at the scene before her.

Her eyes picked out the end of Bruce Street. She hoped Frank wasn't getting himself into any trouble. Scanning over towards her own old street she saw the daily woman scurrying over the nolly bridge. Her day ended at half-past three. Rosalie Mitchell normally knocked off at five, after she'd finished serving afternoon tea.

I wish I was going home too. Dizzying in its intensity, the thought caught Ellie unawares. Unpegging a pillow-case and pulling it down from the rope, she leaned forward and buried her face in the soft and fresh smelling linen.

'What's the matter with you?' came a young male voice.

Chapter 9

Bulging leather schoolbag cradled in his arms, Evander Tait was walking across the grassy sward towards her.

'I wasnae greeting,' Ellie said belligerently.

He raised his dark eyebrows. 'So why is your face wet? Don't tell me you don't like living in Tait Towers.' He propped himself against the nearest clothes pole. 'Can't stand the place myself. I preferred the old house.'

'I can hardly remember your old house,' Ellie said shortly. Embarrassed that he had seen her crying, she was giving the folding of the pillowcase far more attention than it deserved.

Lowering the heavy briefcase and allowing it to slither to his feet, Evander stuck his hands in his pockets and tilted his head back against the clothes pole. 'Oh, it was an overgrown cottage really, rooms built on all over the place.'

Mouth open to tell him she really wasn't that interested, Ellie found herself caught by the dreamy expression on his face and the faraway look in his eyes. He wasn't simply remembering the old house, he was seeing it.

'It had lots of nooks and crannies. Narrow winding staircases with deep window seats halfway up them. Funny little corners where you might find an ancient writing desk or a battered old leather chair where you could curl up and read a good book.' He smiled. 'Knowing generations of your family before you had probably done exactly the same thing in exactly the same spot.'

'Gowanlea,' Ellie said, wondering if he was talking about the desk and chair she'd seen in his room. 'That's what the old house was called, wasn't it?'

He nodded. 'Because "gowan" is the old Scots word for "daisy" and this slope above the canal was always full of them.' He took one hand out of his pocket and gestured towards the drying green. 'Before the canal was even here, I expect. Now daisies are the one white flower no longer tolerated in this garden. As soon as they come up they get mowed down again.' His voice took on a bitter edge. 'Not grand enough.'

'Gowanlea's garden wasn't all white,' Ellie offered, beginning to remember it too as he described it.

'It had flowers in every colour of the rainbow,' he agreed. 'There were hollyhocks and hydrangeas and great clumps of purple lobelia. Oh,' he said, adjusting his position against the clothes pole, 'and yellow rambling roses and honeysuckle and peonies. I remember helping my grandmother plant the honeysuckle and the roses. She really loved her garden.'

'Did she like the daisies too?'

'She loved 'em,' he said softly, a reminiscent smile curving his mouth. 'And the poppies and the other wild flowers which come up every year. The gardener and my grandfather used to say they were weeds and she'd get so annoyed with both of them. "We have to give Mother Nature her place," ' she used to say. "Who are we to impose our rules on her?" '

'Who won the fight?' Ellie asked, fascinated despite herself by this unexpectedly nostalgic Evander Tait.

He smiled again, bringing his eyes back to focus on Ellie's face. 'Oh, she did! She was about five foot nothing in her stocking soles but she always stood up for what she believed in. My grandfather was only teasing her. He used to do that for the fun of arguing with her. They really loved one another, you see. They *cared* enough to argue. It never lasted long. They would look at one another, and laugh, and that would be it. The best of friends again.'

Ellie nodded thoughtfully. She knew folk like that down in Temple. Her own experience with her father hadn't blinded her to the fact that there were lots of families in which an argument didn't inevitably lead to violence.

'She had this lovely accent,' Evander said. 'So did my grandfather.'

'Like Captain MacLean?'

'A bit like his. Although my grandparents were from the mainland, not the islands. They'd both grown up speaking Gaelic, though, like the captain.'

'Your grandfather started the boatyard, didn't he?' she asked, vaguely remembering that the place had once been known as Cameron's.

'Yes,' Evander said. 'My father married the boss's daughter.'

Ellie jumped back to his previous answer. 'Is your first name Gaelic?'

'Greek, actually,' he said, 'but very popular in the Highlands. There were always Evanders in my grandmother's family.'

'She and your grandfather both died quite a while ago, didn't they?' Ellie had the vaguest of memories of them, although Samuel Cameron had stuck in her mind as looking not unlike her image of God, a tall gentleman with a mane of luxuriant white hair. As Ellie remembered her, his wife had been a small round lady with laughing eyes.

Evander nodded. 'I was nine when she died, and he went less than a year later. Couldn't live without her.' His voice was soft with regret.

'You miss them,' Ellie said gently.

'Every day. Although I'm glad that neither of them is here to see what became of Gowanlea and its garden.' He turned his head to study Bellevue, his mouth twisting in a sneer. 'Bloody Jazz Style inside and out. The problem with my parents is that they're slaves to fashion and they think style can be bought. Which is precisely why their house is all style and no substance. The place has no heart.'

'I don't know what you're talking about,' Ellie snapped. 'In fact, I don't understand half the words you use.'

She'd almost been feeling sorry for him. Now he was back to being his usual overbearing and sarcastic self, not to mention showing off how clever he was by using all those fancy words. Ellie was shocked too by how critical he was of his parents. He seemed happy enough to live off their money. She knew plenty of lads of his age who'd been out working for a year and more.

She put a hand up to her head, irritably shoving back a strand of hair blown forward over her brow by an unexpected little breeze. When she thought of all the advantages Evander Tait had compared to people like herself and Frank and Malcolm – and of how ungrateful he seemed to be for all of them – it made her blood boil.

'I have no idea what Jazz Style is,' she said. 'We can't all be brainy.'

'It's got nothing to do with brains,' Evander said, sounding faintly surprised. 'You have to learn what the words mean, that's all. Jazz Style is what people have started to call this sort of thing,' he explained, waving his hand in the direction of the house and the formal garden. 'Everything very modern.'

Taken aback both because he hadn't sneered at her belligerent confession of ignorance and because he was taking the trouble to explain it to her, Ellie wrinkled her nose and thought about it. 'The curves of the house, you mean, and the wee dancing ladies and everything painted white?'

'All that,' he agreed. 'Lots of other elements too: buildings and objects that look like something out of Ancient Egypt, for example.'

'That's no' very modern.'

'A lot of it isn't. That's how style works. It's like a big pot with lots of things in it. Every so often somebody stirs it all up and presents it as something new.'

'So what's art nouveau then?'

'That was the style that went before. It means new art—'

'Because it was new compared with what had gone before *it*?'

He gave her the sort of approving look a teacher might bestow on a bright pupil. 'Exactly. People in *fin-de-siècle* Paris really liked it.'

'Fandy what?'

'*Fin-de-siècle*,' he repeated gravely. 'It means end of the century, although art nouveau was popular right up until the Great War and beyond.'

'And you still like it,' Ellie said, enjoying this conversation so much she was forgetting to stay angry with him. 'But you hate Jazz Style.'

'Some of it I love. What I don't understand is how people can fling out things they've had for years simply they don't fit in with whatever the new vogue is.' His brow furrowed. 'My parents got rid of so much: pictures my grandfather had collected, ornaments my grandmother had, furniture which had been in both their families for generations, things I'd known all my life—' He stopped short, looking suspiciously at Ellie. 'How do you know that I like art nouveau?'

'Oh,' she said, her face lighting up with enthusiasm, 'I saw your picture of the black cat. I really liked it.'

'Ah,' he said, lifting his hand and tapping one long finger against his lips, 'Phoebe showed you her strange brother's bedroom, did she?'

Ellie's brows knitted. 'I did wonder if you might object to that.'

He gave her a sharp look. 'You did?'

'Aye,' she said. Her old home had been too cramped for any of its occupants to have the luxury of privacy. Now that she had acquired some, she could well understand Evander being annoyed about people going into his room when he wasn't there. 'I'm sorry if you feel I intruded.'

'Apology accepted,' he said blithely. 'Not your fault you went in there anyway. What were you upset about just now?'

The abruptness of the question surprised an unexpected answer out of her. 'Coming to live here isn't quite what I expected it to be.'

'What did you expect?'

'Oh,' she said, lifting one hand to the back of her neck and twirling her fingers round a strand of hair. 'I don't know . . .'

'Yes you do. Stop playing with your hair and tell me.'

She surprised herself by obeying that gentle command. 'I used to look in here from the towpath and see you all living this sort of golden life, and I think I thought – daft though it sounds – that I was going to be a part of that . . .'

Evander took his hands out of his pockets and put them behind his back. 'You thought you were going to be taking afternoon tea with the minister's wife and playing tennis with Phoebe and her friends? And both my sister and my mother made a big fuss of you when you first got here but now that the novelty's worn off, Phoebe's gone back to school and my mother's gone back to doing whatever it is she does all day?'

'Something like that,' Ellie said sheepishly. 'Don't tell me, I expect there's a French word for that too.'

'Naïve, maybe,' he suggested. 'When you see what you want to and not how life really is. When you don't read between the lines.'

'That sounds about right,' Ellie said ruefully. She supposed it was fair enough that Phoebe and Mrs Tait had resumed their normal routine. It was daft to have hoped that Phoebe might have sought her out occasionally in the evenings or to have expected Mrs Tait to come into the kitchen now and again to ask how she was getting on.

Ellie sighed. 'The reality is that I'm a skivvy, and no' a very good one at that. According to Mrs Drummond I'm more of a hindrance than a help. She keeps telling me off.'

'Oh,' Evander said. 'Her.'

'You don't like her either?'

He straightened up and pushed himself off the clothes pole. 'I don't even like talking about the woman.

Shall I help you bring the washing in before she gives you another row?'

Ellie laughed out loud. What a strange boy he was. The thought of Malcolm or Frank or any other lad she knew making a similar offer was unthinkable. They would bring in the coal, clean the shoes or help, if pressed, to take the curtains down for washing. Never in a million years would it occur to them to offer help with what they dismissed as 'women's work'.

This strange conversation delivered yet another surprise when Evander laid a hand briefly over his eyes – though not before she had seen a gleam of devilment in them. 'I promise not to look at your and Phoebe's scanties.'

Ellie blushed, and laughed again.

He insisted on carrying the laundry basket round to the kitchen door for her. 'Your problem with Mrs Drummond,' he asked, 'what's the nub of it?'

Ellie had worked that out by the end of her first week at Bellevue. 'She really needs help but she's got her own ways of doing things and I can't know what they are unless she shows me and she's too busy to show me.'

'Admirably succinct,' pronounced Evander. 'As my English teacher, Mr Kennedy, would say. Well then, how is the problem to be resolved?'

'I suppose,' Ellie said, thinking it out as she went along, 'that I need to get her in a good mood – which presumably happens once every hundred years or so—'

Evander grinned and finished the sentence for her. '—and persuade her that it's worth her while taking the time to teach you. Eminently logical.'

'Does Mr Kennedy say that too?' she queried, intrigued by the obvious fondness with which he had mentioned his English master.

'He does indeed.'

They had reached the kitchen door. Ellie took the laundry basket from him. 'You really do like school, don't you?'

'I love it. We break up for the summer holidays next week and I'm already looking forward to going back after them. I must be deeply disturbed,' he added, not sounding in the least worried by this admission.

Ellie's response was heartfelt. 'Nice for you that you feel that way, I'd say. I suppose it makes a big difference that you're brainy. I've often wished I was.'

'Who says you're not?' he queried. 'You've worked out how to deal with your problem, haven't you? I'd better nip back and fetch my bag. See you later.'

Blinking at the swiftness of his departure, she called after him. 'Thank you.'

He wheeled round. 'What for?'

'Helping bring in the washing. Listening to my moans.'

He extended one leg and made her an extravagant and old-fashioned courtly bow over the rows of vegetables. 'Any time, Miss Douglas,' he said, pronouncing the words with a gaiety she would never have suspected him of possessing. 'Any time.'

As he disappeared behind the fence, Ellie stood gazing for a few moments at the spot where he had stood. Help and sympathy from the most unexpected of quarters. The possibility of friendship with the most unlikely of friends. Things were looking up.

'These scones are absolutely *delicious*, Mrs Drummond.'

'I'm glad they meet with your approval.'

The cook hadn't raised her head from her book. It was half-past ten that evening and with the day's work finally ended she and Ellie were sharing a cup of tea and supper before they went to bed. Sharing wasn't perhaps the right word – not with Ellie at one end of the long kitchen table and the cook at the other.

Ellie turned her head to one side, trying to read the title of the book in which Mrs Drummond was so engrossed – *Love Has Its Reasons*.

She transferred her attention to the illustration on the dust jacket. It depicted a woman in a dramatically full-skirted midnight-blue evening gown cut low over her bosom. A man in a magnificent military uniform had his arm about her impossibly slim waist. The woman was bent back at an angle that would have played havoc with any real person's spine and the man was lowering his head to kiss her, a look of smouldering passion on his handsome features.

If the cook liked lovey-dovey stories she must surely have a soft side. Ellie cleared her throat. 'Is it a good book, Mrs Drummond?'

'Yes. That's why I'm reading it.'

Right. As an opening gambit that had been a dead bloody loss. She'd have to come up with something else. 'I can't quite make out your accent, Mrs Drummond. Where is it that you come from?'

'Nowhere you'd ever have heard of,' came the laconic reply.

Desperation gave birth to inspiration. If the cook was Mrs Drummond, then where on earth was Mr Drummond? Of course! He must have been killed in the war. Ellie's fertile imagination began supplying the sad details. If he'd marched off right at the start in 1914, Mrs Drummond herself would only have been about eighteen. Probably they'd wed shortly before he embarked for Flanders.

Ellie could picture the ceremony. Bearing a remarkable resemblance to the gentleman on the front cover of *Love Has Its Reasons*, Mr Drummond stood tall, handsome and proud in his uniform. Beside him, Mrs Drummond was a statuesque beauty in a long white gown and antique lace veil.

Then he had fallen, perhaps at the Somme in '16 when so many had died. Ellie warmed to her story. He'd likely been able to come home on leave for nothing more than the odd snatched couple of days. Their happiness had been so brief, leaving Mrs Drummond without even a wee baby to console her for the loss of her husband.

Sympathy welled up inside Ellie. If the cook had suffered such a terrible loss it was no wonder she was crabbit all the time. 'Are you a widow, Mrs Drummond?'

Aileen Drummond's head came up at last. Making allowances for her bad temper was one thing. Being on the receiving end of one of her stony glares was something else entirely. 'I've never been married,' she snapped. 'And I'd be grateful if you would keep quiet. This is the only time of day I get a chance to relax. Perhaps it's time you went to bed anyway.'

Ellie frowned in puzzlement, barely registering that last comment. 'So if you're not married, why are you called *Mrs* Drummond?'

'Cooks are always called Mrs, whether they're married or single. It's the custom in domestic service.'

'Oh. I didn't know that.'

'Don't know much, do you?' came the brutal response.

Ellie's heart didn't merely sink into her boots, it went right through them to the floor below. But she couldn't back down now.

'Mrs Drummond, I know I havenae made a very good start—'

'That's something of an understatement.'

'Please, Mrs Drummond! Hear me out. This is important for both of us!'

The cook heaved a theatrical sigh, lifted a bookmark from the table beside her and closed *Love Has Its Reasons* on it. 'I suppose I'll have to give you some credit for determination,' she said grudgingly. 'All right, then. Let's have it.'

It came out in a great rush. 'Mrs Drummond, you're quite right. At the moment I am more of a hindrance than a help.' Ellie pulled her hands out from under her knees and raised them, palms upwards, in a gesture of explanation – and perhaps supplication. 'There was nobody around to teach me how to do things properly when I was wee. I wasnae any good at the school but I can learn practical things, I know I can. It never helps if folk shout at me or tell me I'm slow or stupid. Maybe I am both those things but being told so only seems to make me worse.' Eyes dropping to the pine table, Ellie's face clouded over as she remembered all those times teachers had made fun of her for not understanding something.

She looked up again, smiling apologetically. 'This is a whole new world to me. I'll have to learn how to use all the fancy machines and I'll have to learn your ways. It'll take me some time but I'll get there in the end, I know I will. If you can just be a bit patient with me. You weren't born knowing how to cook, were you? You must have had to learn an awful lot of things in your life too.'

'Yes,' Aileen Drummond said slowly, 'I have had to learn an awful lot of things.'

'And that's always more difficult when you're no' very sure where you fit in,' Ellie said. 'When you're trying to find your place somewhere – like I am here.'

She certainly had Mrs Drummond's attention now. The cook was staring fixedly at her. Wondering what on earth she was thinking, Ellie ploughed on. 'Wouldn't it be in your interest to at least try me out? I'm sure I'll be able to help you, take some of the load off your shoulders. You never know, do you?'

Aileen Drummond was still giving her that curious look. 'All right, then,' she said at last. 'We'll see.'

Ellie let out the breath she hadn't known she'd been holding. It wasn't much. But it was a start.

Chapter 10

The unimaginable had happened. Aileen Drummond was smiling at her. Unfortunately it was because she was trying not to laugh at Ellie's first attempt at Eiffel Towers, her contribution to the array of cakes and pastries that were to be served at the launch party the following day.

'They're a bit drunk,' the cook observed.

'Aye,' Ellie said glumly, cocking her head to one side to survey the little jam and coconut cakes. They didn't look any better from that angle. 'All to one side like Gourock.'

Aileen Drummond stifled an exclamation that sounded suspiciously like a snort of mirth. 'Never mind,' she said, 'you did your best. And your cocktail sausage rolls are not bad at all.'

'Can we serve them at the party tomorrow?'

'We can indeed. If there's one thing I've learned about providing food for parties,' she said, imparting the information with the air of one handing on the torch of knowledge, 'it's that you can never have too many sausage rolls. We'll put your Eiffel Towers away in the tins to keep them fresh. They'll do us fine with our tea over the next week.'

'It's all a touch feudal, don't you think?'

'Which means?' Ellie asked, speaking out of the corner of her mouth in case Rosalie Mitchell saw her and accused her of gossiping while she was working. Acting as if she were the one in charge rather than Mrs Drummond, the horrible Rosalie had delivered that lecture several times already, both to Ellie and the waiters and waitresses hired for the day.

She'd given up repeating herself only when two of them had taken umbrage, told her in no uncertain terms that they were professionals and threatened to walk out if she didn't stop teaching them how to suck eggs. Rosalie had consoled herself by ordering Ellie to 'keep circulating. Well-brought-up people have to be persuaded to eat, you know!'

Evander was doing his best to contradict that astonishing assertion. He and Phoebe were the first members of the platform party to return from the boatyard. Ellie presumed they'd decided not to stay for the glass of celebratory champagne being served down there to the VIP guests.

Helping himself to yet another tiny sandwich from the enormous platter of mixed titbits she was holding, he explained what he'd meant by his comment. 'A few peasants being graciously permitted to tread the sacred turf of Bellevue so they can tug their forelocks to their lords and masters.'

'Honestly,' Ellie said, 'you're so sarcastic sometimes. I think it's real nice of your father to invite some of the workers who helped build the new puffer.'

'Really?' Evander queried, having dispatched the little sandwich and two more of its fellows. 'So it's only me who's the ghost at the feast?'

Ellie narrowed her eyes at him. 'My brother was very excited when he got the invitation. It's a treat for him and the others. You don't appreciate what you've got.'

'Whatever you say,' Evander said equably.

Since she had left school, Phoebe had launched into a social whirl of tennis and cocktail parties, spending a lot of time away from the house. Her brother seemed to prefer to spend his summer holidays reading, sometimes in his room but often out in the garden. Bumping into one another frequently at odd moments of the day, he and Ellie were developing an easy camaraderie. He didn't seem to mind what she said to him or how informal she was with him.

'May I have something else from your groaning trencher?'

'You're like Frank Rafferty,' she observed. 'You must have hollow legs.' She held the tray out to him. 'Help yourself. You might be interested to know that I made the sausage rolls.'

'Dare I risk it?' He popped one of the dainty little morsels into his mouth and went off into an exaggerated parody of ecstasy, chewing the sausage roll as though he were overcome by the wonderful taste of it.

'Very funny,' Ellie said, but she grinned when he helped himself to four more.

'These really are good.' He put on a broad Glasgow accent. 'You're a dab hand at the pastry, hen.' He reverted to his own well-spoken tones. 'Have you noticed that my sister is making sheep's eyes at your brother? Quite nauseating, really.'

'I've noticed.' Ellie frowned. What she had also noticed was one look that Malcolm had darted at Phoebe. There could be a problem brewing there. James Tait might well like her brother and might well have risen from humble beginnings himself, but whether he would consider a junior clerk suitable to walk out with his darling daughter was another matter entirely.

'By the way,' Evander said, 'don't mention the launch to my father when he finally gets here.'

Ellie stared at him in amazement. 'Why on earth not? Is that no' what the party's for?'

'That was the idea,' Evander said, 'but it all went horribly wrong. You know how they put the boats in the water?'

Ellie nodded. She'd seen plenty of puffer launches. Because the canal was so narrow the boats were always launched sideways, retaining ropes fixed to both bow and stern. As the boat slid down the slipway, the ropes were cut and the vessel was then free to hit the water, bobbing until it righted itself.

'Something went wrong?'

'They missed one of the ropes. So the puffer went in squint, slewed round and got stuck fast on some mud. They're still trying to float her off. Not so much a launch as a grounding.'

'Oh,' Ellie said, feeling a sharp pang of sympathy for her employer, 'your poor father must be so upset. He's been looking forward to this launch for ages.'

'He's embarrassed as hell,' Evander said calmly, 'especially because it happened in front of his new friends, Lord and Lady Matheson, and all those other very important people to whom he is currently toadying. Oh,' he said, giving himself an odd little shake. 'I love it. There's a German word which sums it up perfectly: *Schadenfreude*. Which means,' he said before Ellie could ask him, 'taking a malicious enjoyment in other people's misfortunes. Wonderful language, German. I'll have a few more sausage rolls before I proceed on my merry way.'

Ellie watched him go. Just when she'd decided he

was really rather a nice person, he came out with something like that. She couldn't understand him at all.

'Smile, girl,' hissed Rosalie Mitchell as she passed. 'And circulate!'

Ellie had slept in fits and starts last night, tossing and turning and worrying about serving at her first Bellevue party. As the afternoon wore on she began to relax into it. She hadn't, as she'd secretly feared, thrown food over any of the guests. She had dropped only one sausage roll on to the grass, watching in horror as a fashionable young lady speared it with the heel of her crocodile-skin shoe. The moment when Ellie might have alerted her to her unseen cargo had passed. The bright young thing was still transporting it around with her.

'Hello!' came a well-bred female voice. 'How are you settling in?' Lesley Matheson lowered her voice. 'That battle-axe of a cook hasn't stirred you up in a stew yet?'

'No' so far,' Ellie responded with a grin. 'Would you like a wee sandwich or a sausage roll?'

'I'd love one,' Lesley said, keeping her voice low. 'I don't know about you, Miss Douglas, but I tend to reach for food at moments of high tension. Did you hear about the disaster at the launch?'

'Aye,' Ellie said, lowering her voice to match Lesley's. 'I'm feeling really sorry for Mr Tait.'

'You'd have felt even sorrier if you'd been there.' Lesley took a dainty bite from her sausage roll. 'I'm afraid my papa and a few other so-called gentlemen didn't try too hard to suppress their sniggers. The thing is,' she confided, 'they all think he's a bit of a social climber.'

'Is that bad?' Ellie asked curiously.

'My dear, it's the absolute end. You're supposed to stay in the station you're born to. "The rich man in his castle, The poor man at his gate", all that sort of thing.'

Ellie finished the verse of the hymn. ' "God made them, high or lowly, And ordered their estate." You don't believe that?' she asked, completely forgetting the considerable difference between her own station and the rather more elevated one occupied by the girl to whom she was speaking.

The Honourable Miss Matheson seemed to have forgotten that too. 'Of course I don't,' she said scornfully. 'That sort of attitude is the ruination of this country. It's like some sort of deadly disease!' she said passionately. 'Everyone with the talent and the guts to do it should be positively encouraged to make something of themselves.'

'Mr Tait really did that, didn't he? Most folk round here admire him for it.'

'Really?' Lesley said. 'Now isn't that fascinating? There are social commentators who maintain the working classes are as conservative about that—'

'Lesley?' It was her mother, coming up behind her. 'Perhaps you shouldn't be wasting time conversing with the maid when some very eligible young men are standing no more than ten feet away from you.'

'But, Mother—'

'Enough, Lesley.' Lady Matheson moved herself and her daughter on without bestowing more than a passing glance on Ellie. There wasn't even a flicker of recognition. So much for being an *original*.

Her tray was empty. She'd get her head in her hands to play with if Rosalie Mitchell spotted her mooning over some empty paper doilies bereft of sandwiches and sausage rolls.

She walked through the cool stone wash house, thinking what an odd atmosphere a house had when its occupants had temporarily deserted it. At least two people were still indoors, though. She could hear a low hum of voices. She pushed open the kitchen door and stopped short, surprised by the scene that greeted her.

One hand shading his eyes, James Tait was sitting at the kitchen table. His fingers were curved round a crystal tumbler with an inch of amber whisky in it and Aileen Drummond was placing a small plate of sandwiches in front of him. Ellie blinked. In the weeks she'd worked for him, this was the first time she'd known him break his own rule about everyone keeping to their own side of the house. His air of dejection was palpable – so strong it had her blurting out a question. 'Are you all right, sir?'

'I'm fine, Eleanor,' he said. He raised his head, transferring his hand from his eyes to his chin. 'How's the party going?'

'Very well, sir,' she said, thinking he didn't look at all fine. 'Your guests seem to be enjoying themselves.'

Aileen thrust a fresh platter into her hands. 'Well, it's your business to make sure they don't starve to death. Look lively, girl!'

Chapter 11

Ellie was wondering if she ought to request a blindfold and a last cigarette. It was the Friday evening following the garden party and she was standing beside the sideboard in the dining room. It was the first time she had helped serve dinner, Aileen Drummond having held out the duty as a reward if she did well at the party.

Ellie had been looking forward to it, seeing it as a sign of the cook's increasing acceptance of her as a useful assistant. Now she wasn't so sure. James Tait's mood since the disastrous launch two days before had been of the blackest, casting a pall of gloom over the whole household. Ironically enough, only Evander seemed to be sunny-tempered at the moment. Already sitting at the dining table, he was reading as usual.

Her demeanour unusually subdued, Angela Tait entered the dining room and took her place at the foot of the table.

Following her in, Phoebe spoke quietly to Ellie. 'Father likes us to be formal at dinner, I'm afraid. That means not talking to the staff. All these silly rules of etiquette . . .' she murmured apologetically.

Aileen Drummond had already imparted some of those, threatening Ellie with the direst of consequences if she disobeyed any of the instructions that had been rattled out to her earlier that day. 'Speak only if and when you're spoken to. Keep watching the table to see if anything is required and be ready to provide it instantly. Don't listen to whatever it is they're talking about. If you are listening, don't react in any way. What the family do or say is none of your business.'

Surveying the table she had helped to set and wondering how folk could possibly need so many knives and forks simply to eat their tea, Ellie stood back to allow Mrs Drummond to place a large white porcelain soup tureen on the electric warming tray that stood on the sideboard.

There was an awful lot to think about: keeping that poker face, spotting if the family needed anything and remembering to serve from the right and clear away from the left was bad enough. What would she do if her hand shook while she was carrying a plate of soup to the table? Bloody hell, it could end up in one of their laps.

Mrs Tait turned her sleek blonde head towards the dining-room door. The master of the house had arrived at last. Aileen Drummond's eyes flickered to Ellie, a signal that they were about to start serving. She moved to stand next to the cook at the soup tureen, her hand reaching for the first plate.

James Tait didn't, however, take his own place at the head of the table. Instead, he surprised everybody by walking to the middle of it. Ellie caught the change in atmosphere immediately. The firing squad had arrived. Only its rifles weren't trained on her, they were aimed straight at Evander.

'Care to explain this, laddie?'

He slapped a newspaper down on the table, rattling

the array of cutlery in front of his son. Blinking as he raised his head, Evander put Ellie in mind of a mole that had left behind the safety of the dark earth to pop its head above ground and was surprised to find itself out in the light.

'Oh,' he said, 'I didn't hear you come in, Father.'

'Of course you didn't,' his father said. 'You had your head stuck in a book as usual. Nothing useful, I take it.' He plucked the volume from Evander's slim white fingers and flipped back to the title page. 'A novel,' he sneered. 'A made-up story about people who never really existed.'

Evander flushed. 'It's a new novel about the Jacobites and the 'forty-five,' he said. 'It's a marvellous story.'

James Tait snapped the book shut and hurled it across the room. He did it with considerable force, sending it skidding along the polished wooden floor to slide in under the long and low radiator beneath the room's main window.

Evander let out a little cry. 'That's Mr Kennedy's book. He loaned it to me, said I could give it back to him after the holidays—' He started up from his chair but his father's hand descended on to his shoulder.

'Leave it where it is.' Each word was spat out like a bullet. 'I'm more interested in what you've been writing than what you've been reading.' He lifted the newspaper.

> 'The crowds were there, the very important people were there, the local dignitaries were there, even the men who'd toiled to build the wee boatie were there. The sun was shining and the canal was peaceful. Then it all went downhill, quite literally in respect of the puffer that sank ignominiously

into the mud at the launch at Tait's Boatyard near Anniesland yesterday. It was all rather embarrassing for Temple and Anniesland's very own captain of industry, James Tait.'

Phoebe darted an anxious glance at her mother. Angela Tait shook her head, a tiny movement, and brought her clasped hands up to rest on the edge of the table. Her husband put one large hand on the back of Evander's chair and yanked it out from the table, swinging it round so the two of them were facing one another. 'You wrote this drivel, didn't you?'

Watching, Ellie thought that he had moved the chair and Evander as though the burden weighed no more than a bag of feathers. James Tait had to be as strong as her own father had been. Her breath coming faster, she fought against taking that thought any further.

There was a peculiar little smile on Evander's face. 'I sent a contribution to the diary section of the paper, yes. How did you find out it was me?'

'I found out,' James Tait replied, every word precisely enunciated, 'because I wondered why everyone at the Chamber of Commerce lunch today was laughing behind their hands at me. Although you weren't man enough to put your name to your pitiful little "contribution", the rumour had already spread that my son had written it.'

The strange little smile was still on Evander's face. 'I take it you're not proud of my talent with a pen then, Father? I thought I'd hit the style they require rather well.'

James Tait straightened up, jerked his arm back and struck his son a stinging blow across the face.

Unable to stifle her reaction, Ellie cried out, looking

wildly to Aileen Drummond for guidance. Face impassive, the cook was staring straight ahead of her, following her own dictum to the letter. *What the family do or say is none of your business.*

Evander's voice was shaking. 'Going to send me to bed without supper, Father? Let me save you the trouble.'

He tried to rise to his feet but his father tightened his grip, leaning forward and hissing into his face, 'Did I give you permission to leave the table? You'll move if and when I tell you to, boy. I've some things I want to say to you.' James Tait straightened up. 'Perhaps you'd care to tell me why I pay through the nose for you to attend that expensive school when you use the education you get there to mock me? Perhaps you'd care to tell me why I fought my way through the blood and mud of Flanders and worked my guts out to build this business up and give my family every comfort when my son doesn't appreciate one little bit of it? Perhaps you'd care to tell me that, sir?'

By the time he'd come to the end of this little speech, James Tait was red-faced and breathing heavily. When Evander said nothing, his father flung out one more angry statement and one more angry question. 'Brave enough to sneak behind my back but a lily-livered coward when it comes to saying it to my face. Now why doesn't that surprise me?'

When the colour rose in Evander's cheeks, his father smiled contemptuously. 'Cat got your tongue, you little pansy? No wonder you've got no friends.'

'My books are my friends,' Evander said quietly. 'Perhaps you ought to try reading sometime, Father. There are some wonderful novels inspired by the war which might help you put your own experiences into perspective.'

The spiky silence surrounding the two protagonists of this unfolding drama grew more jagged still. Oh Evander, Ellie thought, you shouldn't have said that . . . and you shouldn't have sounded so disdainful and condescending when you did.

She waited for an outraged 'What did you say?' but James Tait didn't ask his son to repeat himself. He simply hit him again. This time he struck him across the mouth with the back of his hand. It was a viciously effective blow, sending the boy's head snapping back against the high back of the dining chair. There was a crack as it made contact with the unforgiving wood.

As his son let out a yell of pain James Tait lunged forward, gripping his shoulders and thrusting him back once more against the chair. Evander moaned. Acting on pure instinct, Ellie started forward. Aileen Drummond's arms shot out. One steadied the soup plate Ellie hadn't realised she'd still been holding. The other came across in front of her like a barrier.

'No,' the cook whispered.

James Tait reached past his son to seize the newspaper he'd thrown on to the table. He twisted it and sent it flying in the same direction as the book. As he walked to the head of the table, he pointed one finger at Ellie, standing frozen in horror against the wall of the dining room. Still holding the soup plate, she was gripping its edge fiercely, trying to stop her hands from shaking.

'You'll burn that rag and that book after dinner, during which you will not serve my son any food. He'll sit here and watch us eat and that'll maybe make him mind his manners in the future.'

To her right, Ellie sensed rather than saw a movement. Evander had risen to his feet. Swaying a little, he was holding a linen napkin against his mouth. 'I will not sit here and watch you eat,' he said. 'I will NOT!'

His father caught him before he was halfway to the door, grabbing him and swinging him round to face him. The force of the punch he threw sent Evander spinning across the room. He lost his balance and fell heavily onto the polished floor, his momentum carrying him to where the book and the newspaper lay in front of the low radiator. He struck it with his shoulder and let out another yell of pain.

Watching him struggle to his feet, aching to run forward and help, Ellie looked at Mrs Tait and Phoebe. Like Aileen Drummond, their eyes were downcast, their faces completely impassive.

As Evander slunk towards the door, walking as gingerly as a wounded beast, James Tait resumed his place. 'Now then,' he said, turning to his daughter with every expression of interest on his face, 'let's see if you can twist your poor old father round your little finger and persuade him to allow you to cut your hair.' His voice took on a teasing note. 'Before you're really old enough, my girl!'

Phoebe lifted her head and gave him a shaky smile.

Aileen Drummond took the soup plate out of Ellie's trembling fingers. 'I'll serve this course,' she said quietly.

'Don't say anything about it!'

'But, Mrs Drummond, he really hurt him. Look!' Ellie thrust out the crumpled linen napkin she held. 'There's blood on this. His signet ring cut Evander's lip when he hit him on the face the second time. And to throw him across the room like that . . .' She shook her head in bewilderment. 'He must be so hungry by now, too. You know what an appetite he's got.'

She gazed at Aileen Drummond, hoping for some sort of explanation of the shocking outburst of violence they had both witnessed this evening. Her father had subjected her to beatings like that. She'd seen other men inflict worse injuries on each other in the grimy backstreets in which she'd been born and raised. She'd never expected to see anything like it in a house like this or in a family like this.

'It doesn't happen very often,' Aileen said shortly. 'And not usually at the level it did tonight.'

Ellie's green eyes opened wide. 'Not very often?'

'Not very often,' Aileen repeated stubbornly. 'Sometimes we can go for months without it happening, and it's only ever the boy he goes for. Nobody else is in any danger. You're not in any danger, if that's what's worrying you.'

'Does it make it all right that it's only Evander he goes for?' Ellie's voice rose on a note of mingled outrage and disbelief.

Aileen pursed her lips. 'Evander shouldn't have sent that story into the newspaper. Nor should he have made that smart-aleck comment about putting the war experiences into perspective. Both of them were bound to provoke his father and he knew that better than anybody.'

Aileen Drummond ran a distracted hand through her luxuriant hair. After they'd cleared away dinner she had pulled all the pins out of it, allowing it to settle about her shoulders. 'They clash with one another, that pair.'

'I didn't see Evander hitting back,' Ellie said stubbornly. 'And it wasnae exactly a fair fight, was it? His father's much bigger and stronger than he is. It wasnae right,' she said again, 'and it wasnae right that Mrs Tait and Phoebe just *sat* there. How come they didnae try to stop Mr Tait?'

Aileen raised her hands to her face, rubbing them over it. She was very pale this evening. 'He gets these rages,' she said, 'from the war. What he went through was terrible. Unimaginable.'

Ellie frowned at her. 'Then he should go and see a doctor, no' lay in to his son.'

'Oh, Ellie! There are lots of things people *should* do—' Aileen Drummond caught herself on. 'It's none of our business,' she said, her voice flat and dull. 'Let's get cleared up and off to bed.'

After they had stowed away the last of the crockery, she pulled open the door of the pantry, pointing to one of the tins that sat on the top shelf. 'Your Eiffel Towers are still in there. D'you want to take them upstairs in case you're peckish during the night? They'll be nice and soft, I imagine. Easy to eat. And I put the book and the newspaper out in the wash house. You were going to deal with them, weren't you?'

Their eyes met in perfect agreement and understanding.

After Aileen had gone upstairs, Ellie fetched the book and the newspaper and placed them on a large tray on which she'd put a plateful of the little cakes, a glass of milk, some witch hazel and a clean soft cloth. She hadn't counted on Phoebe being there as she emerged from the back stairs on to the first-floor landing.

The girl stretched out a pleading hand. 'Don't look at me that way, Ellie!'

Ellie surveyed her over the tray. 'What way, Miss Phoebe?'

'I couldn't have stopped it if I'd tried, Ellie. When Father's like that, nothing will stop him!'

'Lucky for you he only goes for your brother then, isn't it?'

'Oh, Ellie,' Phoebe said. 'You don't understand!'

'I understand your father's liable to hear us if we stand here whispering for much longer,' she said fiercely. 'Good night, Miss Phoebe.'

She left her standing and padded along to Evander's door. When there was no response to her soft knock, she put her mouth to the crack between it and the door jamb. 'It's Ellie. I've got some stuff for you. Including Mr Kennedy's book.'

Nothing happened for a few seconds. Then she heard footsteps and the sound of a key being turned. He opened the door a few inches.

'Let me in before your father catches me.'

He swung the door wide, standing back to allow her to walk forward and set the tray down on the old writing desk in front of the window.

'Put all the debris under your bed when you've finished and I'll sneak up and collect it tomorrow morning sometime.'

'I don't know if I can eat anything. My mouth's sore.'

She could hear that from his slurred speech. Burning with sympathy for him though she was, instinct told her not to express it. 'These wee cakes are very soft,' she said. 'You'll maybe manage.' When she turned round from the table and saw him properly for the first time since he'd left the dining room, she couldn't quite suppress a gasp at his battered appearance.

Hands behind his back, he stood against the coats and dressing gowns hanging on his bedroom door looking like a lost child. Both cheeks were bruised, livid red splashes against his usually pale skin. The cut on his lip was already swollen, angry as a bee-sting.

'My,' Ellie said lightly, 'your face is going to be all the colours of the rainbow come the morning.' Turning back to the desk, she lifted one of the cloths and the bottle of witch hazel. 'This might help.'

He was carefully not meeting her eyes but as she approached him he brought a hand out from behind his back. He held it palm outwards in an unmistakable gesture of rejection.

She'd already drawn the stopper from the bottle. 'Och, well,' she said, replacing it, 'you'll maybe do it yourself later. I'll leave all the doings here anyway.'

'Do what you like,' he said bitterly.

'Evander,' she said, 'I know what it's like—'

His voice was as bleak as a winter's night. 'Nobody knows what it's like, Ellie. Thank you for bringing all this stuff but would you please just go away now and leave me alone?'

Her father was coming across the canal towards her, sure-footed as a cat on the narrow walkway that topped the lock-gate. His face was florid with drink and contorted with rage. He was going to beat her senseless and there was absolutely nothing she could do to stop him. She raised her head, searching frantically for Captain MacLean. Hadn't he been here a moment ago?

The only other person in sight was Marie Rafferty. She smiled coldly at Ellie. 'Me and my friends are next in line,' she said, 'once your daddy's finished with you.'

He had reached her now, was pulling his right arm back to power the first blow. He was aiming for her mouth. Please God, she thought resignedly, let it be a slap and not a punch. Not a punch, God. Please don't let him punch me. That hurts so much more than a slap.

'But I'll have to punch you, ye wee hure,' he said calmly, as though it were the most reasonable thing in the world. 'Look.' He brought his hand up under her nose and she saw the glint of silver and the dull gleam of copper shining through his huge fingers. 'If I open my hand all this money'll fall out. That's what ye want, isn't it? Money to buy the tea for you and Malcolm? This'll feed the two o' ye for years.' The powerful fist was drawn back once more.

'No, Daddy!' she screamed. 'Don't hit me! Please don't hit me!' Ellie put up her hands to protect herself – and for the umpteenth time that night found herself wrestling with sheets and blankets tangled crazily around her legs. She came upright like the blade of a pocketknife snapping into position.

Somewhere in the house she heard a clock chime. Two o'clock. Moonlight was flooding in through her porthole window, spilling in a silvery column across the floor. She extricated herself from the bed, got out and remade it. She was on the point of climbing back in when she heard a noise out in the corridor. She tiptoed to her door and opened it the merest crack.

James Tait was standing at the open door of Aileen Drummond's room. He was in dressing-gown and slippers and his voice was a low murmur. 'Let me in, Aileen. Please let me in. Please. I need you.'

Ellie heard a long, low sigh. Then a graceful white arm emerged and crooked itself around his neck, drawing him into the room.

As the door swung shut behind the two of them, Ellie retreated into her own room, walking backwards until she bumped into her bed and sat down abruptly on it. She stared at the column of moonlight spilling across the floor. It was suddenly illuminating an awful lot of dark corners.

She understood now why James Tait never wanted to employ any live-in staff; why Aileen Drummond was so moody; why she had found the two of them alone together in the kitchen on the day of the launch; why she had so often thought she'd heard noises in the night. Oh, she understood a lot of things!

Ellie continued to stare at the shaft of moonlight. She'd thought Bellevue was a sunlit house, occupied by a family that enjoyed a golden life. Now she saw it for the sham it was.

Chapter 12

Malcolm didn't stop talking until they were nearly at Westerton. 'Mr Tait was in a lot better mood today,' he confided cheerfully. 'After all, no harm came to the puffer and what happened could have happened to anybody. Onwards and upwards, that's what he says. He called everyone in before we left at midday to thank us for our hard work and announce we've two more orders after the next one, so that's fine. Then he asked if he could have a personal word with me.'

Malcolm's face shone with pride. 'He says I could go far. He even said he wishes Evander were more like me. Says he's too much of a dreamer.'

'Really?' Ellie's tone was icy. Caught up in his own concerns, Malcolm didn't notice.

'It's a challenge to live up to what Mr Tait expects of me but I can do it, Ellie, I know I can. By the way,' he said, smiling down at her, 'he told me that you're settling in very well. He and Mrs Tait and the cook are particularly pleased by how you did at the party.'

'Oh?' Ellie enquired, finally getting a word in edgeways. 'Should I be jumping for joy because the great man deigned to mention me?'

Malcolm frowned. 'Don't be pert, Ellie, it's not becoming in a young woman in your position.'

She was so dumbfounded by that response her mouth

almost fell open. Had her brother always been this pompous and she simply hadn't noticed it? Her vision was as sharp as glass now.

She wondered what Malcolm and all those other folk who looked up to James Tait would think if they had seen what she had seen last night – either of those two events to which she had been an unwilling witness.

Her brother had launched into a lecture on how she had to behave herself at Bellevue and how important it was for both of them to do everything possible to please the Tait family. While she waited for him to finish pontificating Ellie gazed at the spectacularly steep hill on the other side of the canal. The folk who lived in the terrace of houses being built up there were going to have a wonderful view.

It must be rare to have a nice wee house of your own. She couldn't hope for that for a long time yet but she could hope to go to work for another family in theirs, a family as unlike the Taits as possible. She waited till Malcolm had finished telling her off.

'I don't want to stay at Bellevue,' she said quietly. 'Did you hear me, Malcolm? I'm not happy with the Taits. I don't like it there and I want to leave, look for a job and somewhere else to live.'

If this hadn't been so serious the fact that his mouth had quite literally fallen open would have made Ellie laugh. It took him a moment to find his voice. 'Last week you told me you were getting on great.'

'That was last week.'

'So what's happened to change things?'

Ellie opened her mouth to tell him. She closed it again without saying anything. Somehow it felt like a betrayal of Evander to talk about what he had been subjected to last night, and the prospect of telling her brother about James Tait and his housekeeper was an excruciatingly embarrassing one.

Would Malcolm even believe her? Perhaps he might put both stories down to her well-known vivid imagination. Studying the rippling circles in the canal, which indicated the presence of a fish just below the surface, Ellie wondered if she could give him some other reason for what must seem her inexplicable wish to leave Bellevue.

'I don't like living where I work,' she said at last. 'I feel locked in.' As she said the words, Ellie realised she wasn't telling any lies. She loved her room and her bathroom and she was beginning to enjoy the work but she did feel cut off from the outside world. A big house like Bellevue was its own world, one she no longer wished to inhabit.

'Are they bad to you?' Malcolm demanded.

'No.' Not to me, she thought bleakly.

'Haven't they given you a lovely room and bought you lots of clothes? Didn't you tell me that Mrs Tait and Phoebe have been really welcoming and friendly?'

'Aye,' Ellie admitted. But when Evander was being hit last night, neither his mother nor his sister lifted a finger to stop it.

One part of her brain was registering the faint blush on her brother's face when he had spoken Phoebe's name. She didn't have time to worry about that now.

'Don't they feed you well?' Malcolm asked. 'Hasn't Mrs Drummond started to teach you how to make all sorts of things?'

'Aye,' Ellie said again. 'She's a great cook . . .' A woman betraying another woman, but a great cook.

'Ellie,' he said earnestly, 'I do understand how you feel about being shut in.' He threw a glance at their surroundings. 'This is where you feel you belong, isn't it? Running wild along the canal bank with Frank Rafferty.' That name produced a grimace of distaste. 'There comes a time when we all have to grow up, Ellie. I know that's hard. I really do know that.'

'I grew up a long time ago, Malcolm—'

He interrupted her. 'Did you know that our mother had a pauper's funeral?'

Ellie stiffened. 'I know hardly anything about our mother. I didn't know that you remembered very much about her.'

'I remember lots of things about her.' He gave Ellie a sad little smile. 'I remember our wee sister too. Granny Mitchell held me up to look at her minutes after she was born, you know. She was lying in the crook of Mammy's arm and she was a miniature version of you. Red hair and everything. Mammy asked me what we should call her and I said "Ellie" because she looked so like you.'

It was hard to swallow the lump that had risen in her throat. Ellie forced herself to do it, hungry to hear more. 'What did Mammy say to that?'

'Not much. Looking back on it, I realise how much her strength must have been fading. But she laughed when I said the baby should get your name. She was aye laughing, our mother.' Like a lamp being lit on a winter's afternoon, his face glowed with a memory that caused Ellie a sharp little pang of jealousy.

' "Cannae call her Ellie," she said. "There's only one o' them. Like there's only one Malcolm. We'll need to think of something else. Stella," she said. "We'll call her Stella." '

'That's a gey fancy name.'

'She'd read it in a book, I expect. She always had her

head stuck in one of those love stories women like to read. You know.'

'Aye,' Ellie said slowly. 'I know them. You wouldn't have gone to Mammy's funeral, though, would you? You were only four years old. Did Granny Mitchell not keep both of us?'

'He made me go. Our father, I mean.' Malcolm's face hardened. 'I couldn't understand why the men were putting our mother and wee Stella into a hole in the ground. When I started screaming he grabbed me and dragged me away.'

He drew his fair brows together, revisiting one memory Ellie didn't envy at all. 'It felt like my arm was being ripped out of its socket. I was kicking and punching so he would let me go but we were nearly out of the cemetery before I managed to get away and run back to the grave. Running back to Mammy.' His voice was a husky whisper. 'By the time I got there the gravediggers had already covered her and the baby over with earth.'

Ellie placed a hand on the lapel of his jacket. 'Malcolm, don't tell me this if—'

'I need to tell you,' he said, his voice firmer. 'I sank down on to the grass and sobbed my heart out. I must have looked so pathetic. Then he caught up with me. He hit me and swore at me and stuck me under his arm. He turned to the gravediggers and made a joke about it. I can remember them laughing. They were burying our mother and our sister and they were laughing while they did it. Willie Anderson was there. He said he'd buy me a sweetie.'

His face had grown hard again. 'I'd lost my mother and that drunken sot thought he could make it right with a sweetie. You know something, Ellie? Our mother didn't even have a coffin. She and wee Stella were buried in a sheet. Tied up with rope like a bloody parcel.'

Ellie left her hand on his lapel and waited until she was sure he had nothing more to say. 'Why did our father deserve better than that?' she asked eventually. 'Should we have given a damn that he had a proper funeral when our mother and sister didn't?'

'He didn't deserve better,' Malcolm said tightly. 'We did that for us, not for him. To save us the shame of it. I'll always be grateful to Mr Tait for paying for it.' He gestured back along the canal in the direction of the boatyard. 'That's why all of this is so important to me. It's not only a matter of paying Mr Tait back for the funeral, it's the chance he's giving both of us to make something of our lives. Och, Ellie,' he cried, 'think how important that is! Think what a mess our father made of his life. Think how our mother ended hers.'

Ellie tucked a stray strand of hair behind her ear. 'You really think me working at Bellevue is so important?'

'I know it is. You said yourself that Mrs Drummond is a brilliant cook. You're going to get a really good training there, Ellie. Once you've got that you can go anywhere you like, do anything you want. I'm not asking you to stay there for ever, just for the next few years.' He smiled down at her. 'Maybe only until you marry that handsome man.'

'Maybe I want more out of life than that, Malcolm. You do, don't you?'

His answer was simplicity itself. 'I want to be James Tait.' He gave an odd little laugh. 'I want to *have* everything he has. A successful business. A beautiful wife.' As he blushed again Ellie wondered if he was thinking of James Tait's wife or James Tait's daughter. 'A lovely home and a happy family.'

Ellie gazed sadly up at him and knew she could never tell him what she now knew about James Tait's lovely home and happy family. It would have destroyed every dream her brother had. It would have destroyed him.

She went back to Bellevue and trudged up the stairs to her room, relieved to be off until the following morning. Worn out by all the emotion of the last few days, Ellie lay down on her bed and fell asleep.

Returning to her room after her evening meal she decided to have a long soak in the bath. As she started to unbutton her blouse, she gazed out of the window at the garden. It was August now and the days were beginning to shorten. In the deepening twilight a flicker of movement down by the tennis court caught her eye. Evander. Heading towards the canal.

Fear made her clumsy. When she finally got a firm grip on the big metal doorknob of the gate set into the old wall, she couldn't get it open. She tried turning it the other way, rattling it furiously when that didn't work either.

'I've always found it hard to open that gate when it's still locked,' came a voice from behind her.

She whirled round, relief flooding through her although she couldn't actually see him. Daylight had evaporated completely and the moon hadn't yet risen. 'I'm in the summerhouse,' he said.

As her eyes adjusted, Ellie picked out the shape of the little pagoda, a squat shadow denser than those that surrounded it. She walked back up to it. 'I couldn't see you in the dark.'

'That was the general idea. As you so accurately predicted, my face is somewhat colourful today. I wouldn't like to frighten the horses. What brings you down here at this time of night?'

'Oh,' she said, stepping in under the pagoda's roof, 'I saw you from my window and . . .' Still breathless after her hurtle down the back stairs, she paused to take a breath. She heard the scratch of a match and smelled the pungent aroma of tobacco. He extinguished the match almost immediately and finished her sentence for her.

'And you thought I'd gone to throw myself into the canal.' His voice was as light and sarcastic as ever. 'I appreciate your concern, but now you know I'm still in the land of the living I'd be obliged if you'd bugger off.'

'That's no' very nice,' Ellie protested.

He said it again. 'Bugger off. I want to be on my own.'

'I will in a wee minute.' She sat down next to him on the slatted wooden bench that filled this side of the summerhouse. 'There's something I want to tell you first.'

She launched into it before he could stop her. 'I know what it's like to have a father who hits you. I know how much it hurts. I know how much it keeps hurting, even after the actual pain has stopped. I know you were finding it hard to look me in the eye last night because you were feeling angry and ashamed and all mixed up. I don't know the fancy words to describe them but I do know what all the feelings are like and I know there's one question you can never find an answer to. Why?'

It was fully half a minute before he answered her. She counted the seconds.

'Did your father used to hit Malcolm too?'

'When he was wee, aye. Not once he got too big for him.'

Evander struck a match, held it between them. 'Don't scream at the horrible sight.'

Ellie cocked her head to one side, considering. 'It's no' so bad in poor light. Less colourful. Has he always done it to you?'

'Since my grandparents died. Did your father always do it to you?'

'Right up till the day he fell into the canal.'

The match went out. Evander lit another one. 'But not Malcolm.'

'No,' she agreed. She knew he was comparing himself to her brother and finding himself wanting but she wasn't prepared to be anything less than honest with him. It seemed important.

'Malcolm's a strapping lad, of course,' he said reflectively, lighting another match. 'I'm a skinny weed. And my father's quite right, I don't have any friends.'

'He shouldn't hit you,' Ellie said. 'It's wrong.'

Evander's voice was as bitter as vinegar. 'Everyone thinks he's so wonderful.'

'I don't. Not now. Do you know about . . .' She paused, embarrassed by the topic she had been about to raise.

'Him and Mrs Drummond?' Evander supplied. 'Yes, I know. It's been going on for years.'

As the second little flame he had lit flicked and went out, a curse that sent Ellie's eyebrows shooting skywards sounded in the soft darkness.

'Sorry,' he said. 'I've burned my bloody finger.'

'Don't strike another match, then. I can make you out now, anyway. Am I not your friend?'

'Why would you want to be friends with someone

like me?' came the gloomy response. 'I'm odd and I'm strange and I don't fit in anywhere.'

Ellie wrinkled her nose and thought about that. 'I don't think I fit in anywhere, either. All my brother thinks I should want to do is find a rich and handsome husband.'

'And you want more than that?'

'I do,' she said. 'Not sure what yet. I suppose that makes me odd.'

'So we're a couple of misfits?'

'Aye,' she said cheerfully. 'So what?'

'*So what?*' He laughed. It was a healthy and happy sound, as welcome as it was unexpected. 'You're an original, Eleanor Douglas, do you know that?'

'Och,' she said, laughing with him, 'call me anything but that!' She told him the story, then tilted her head back against the wood panelling of the summerhouse, gazing up at the night sky. She thought, the stars are out . . .

Evander adjusted his position on the bench, stretching his legs out in front of him. 'When I'm old enough I'm leaving this place.'

'Me too,' Ellie said. 'Shall we go together?'

'Why not? I get some money from my grandparents' will when I'm twenty-one. We'll use that to do something together. How would that be?'

'Grand,' she said. 'How shall we find our way to wherever it is we're going when we leave here?'

He was smiling now. She could hear it in his voice. 'When I was a wee boy I once asked Captain MacLean how he saw to drive the *Torosay* in the dark.'

Ellie laughed. 'What did he say?'

'He told me how he steered by the stars.' Evander tilted his head back as far as it would go, raised one arm and pointed. 'That's the crucial one. The Pole Star.'

'That's what we'll do then,' Ellie said. 'We'll steer by the stars.' She laughed again. 'Why are we sitting out here talking nonsense?'

'Because it's fun?' he suggested.

'You don't want me to go, then?'

'No,' Evander said. 'I don't want you to go.'

PART II

Chapter 13

1929

Ellie stood at the kitchen table, up to her elbows in butter and flour. These days she did all of the pastry-cooking at Bellevue. Aileen Drummond had acknowledged a long time ago that her young assistant had both cooler hands than herself and a much lighter touch.

To say that she and Aileen – as Ellie now privately thought of her – had become friends over the past two years might have been to overstate the case. The cook remained reserved and disinclined to talk very much about herself. She had told Ellie only that she came from Perthshire, where her people owned and ran a large country house hotel somewhere near Pitlochry.

From the odd comment she had let slip, Ellie suspected that the Drummonds, having fallen on hard times, had turned their own ancestral home to commercial use. She was also pretty certain that the cook was estranged from her family. There were never any letters to her from Perthshire. There were never any letters to her from anywhere.

Apart from when she escaped into her romantic novels, Aileen Drummond's life revolved around Bellevue, her work one of the two central pillars of her existence. Ellie tried not to think too often what the other pillar was.

That wasn't always easy. Adopting diplomatic deafness when she heard noises in the night was one thing. Pretending not to notice when the cook had been crying after yet another quarrel with her lover was another. After one such occasion Ellie had plucked up the courage to attempt a clumsy offer of sympathy. It had been rebuffed so fiercely she hadn't dared try again.

When it came to work the two women had developed an excellent relationship. Responding to Ellie's eagerness to learn, Aileen Drummond had taught her how to make so many dishes: mouth-watering traditional soups based on the richest of stocks and the freshest of vegetables, rich and savoury French ragoûts and casseroles, highly flavoured Indian curries and extravagant desserts for special occasions. The Taits ate well and liked their many guests to do so too.

Aileen Drummond sometimes bemoaned their tendency to favour fashionable foreign dishes at the expense of the cuisine of their native country. In another indication that she had once been much better off than she was now, she occasionally waxed lyrical about a trip she'd taken through France and Italy before the war and her enjoyment of what she called those countries' 'real food'.

'There's so much wonderful, traditional fare – peasant food, if you like. But when it's brought over here it gets all fancied up, becomes fussy and pretentious. The best food is simple food,' she often said, a look on her face that brooked no denial. 'And if you cook it well, nothing in the world can beat Scottish produce.'

Ellie knew the litany off by heart now: beef from Aberdeenshire, salmon from the Tay, shellfish from the west coast, potatoes from Ayrshire, tomatoes from the Clyde Valley, raspberries from Blairgowrie. The cook knew all the old Scottish recipes too, counting it a major victory if she could persuade her mistress to include any of them on a menu: Cullen skink, partan bree and cock-a-leekie soup to start with, clapshot and skirlie to accompany the main course, cranachan, Caledonian cream, whim-wham or Edinburgh fog for dessert, a small square of sweet tablet to accompany the coffec at thc end of the meal.

Some dishes were too humble to make the grade. Stovies, for example, that visually unexciting but hugely appetising combination of tatties and meat left over from a beef roast or stew. Ellie often thought she had brought herself and Malcolm up on them. Served to an appreciative staff, the main difference in the Bellevue version was that there was an awful lot more meat in the mixture.

Dazzled at first by all the new dishes she was learning to cook, as her experience grew Ellie found herself agreeing about the attractions of simple, well-cooked food. Aileen's light and fluffy omelettes were a case in point. Made at the table so they could be eaten immediately and at their best, savoury, or filled with jam for dessert, they had acquired a legendary status among the Taits' guests. Ellie had been initiated into the secret of how to make them so they turned out perfectly each and every time.

It was a matter of judging when the sizzling butter in which they were cooked was at exactly the right temperature, of loosening the edges of the forming omelette with the right type of round-bladed knife, allowing those parts of the mixture that were still runny to fill the resultant gaps, of knowing exactly when to fold in the sides.

Confidence came into it too: knowing and believing that you could do it. That was also part of Aileen's cooking philosophy. Be bold. There was one more article of faith. The very late but still much lamented Mrs Isabella Beeton was to be regarded as a goddess of the kitchen and her *Book of Household Management* nothing less than the culinary equivalent of the Bible.

It was undeniably true that Mrs Beeton could supply the answer to any question related to cooking, etiquette or the running of a house. Some of the ideas contained within the massive tome gave Ellie a few private chuckles all the same. Her favourite was the dictum that a young female servant like herself could and should find the time to sit down and do needlework 'for two or three hours in the summer evenings'.

Doing the cooking for a household that prided itself on its generous hospitality but continued to be chronically short of staff didn't allow for very much free time. Young and vigorous though she was, Ellie was often too tired on her half-days off to resist the lure of a good book or a long soak in the bath. Sometimes she combined the two, occasionally to the severe detriment of the book.

Evander was still going on about the state in which she'd returned his copy of *The Flight of the Heron*, the novel he'd originally borrowed from his English master. The romantic tale of days gone by had become young Mr Tait's favourite book. He'd been less than impressed with Ellie's argument that she'd taken it into the bath because she'd been enjoying it too much to put it down.

She was planning on buying him a replacement copy this afternoon when she went out for tea with Frank Rafferty. She usually reserved Saturdays for seeing Malcolm but he was setting off today on a week's camping and cycling holiday with some friends from the boatyard.

Emerging from school disinclined ever to pick up a book again, the love affair Ellie now had with reading was entirely due to Evander's encouragement. He'd gone to great lengths to convince her that books were a treasure house both of pleasure and knowledge, a mine of information she'd be daft to ignore.

When she'd arrived at Bellevue she'd been unable to read with anything approaching ease and enjoyment. Insisting that practice would indeed make perfect, Evander had invited her to ask him the meaning of any word that foxed her. If he was out she was welcome to go into his room and look it up in his big dictionary.

That volume rivalled Mrs Beeton for size. As Ellie and Phoebe had jointly discovered, either book was excellent for balancing on your head while you walked up and down perfecting your posture, trying to sway across the kitchen or Phoebe's bedroom as elegantly as one of the fashion models employed by the big stores in Sauchiehall Street and Buchanan Street.

Pastry crumbs forming between her fingertips, Ellie raised her hands high over the bowl, allowing air into the mix. It was one of the many tricks of the trade Aileen had taught her.

A strand of russet hair escaped from Ellie's blue cap, falling forward over her creamy brow. Sparing the back of one wrist to push it away, she thought about what the minister – nice man though he was – had said when it had first been mooted that she should work at Bellevue: 'Cooking's easy. Anybody can do it.' What a cheek.

She walked through to the tile-lined pantry in the scullery to fetch the jug of water she'd placed on a shelf there to cool earlier that morning, a little beaded cover on top of it as protection from any flies that might be buzzing about on this warm summer's morning. She had the jug in her hand when she heard the back door open. That would be Rosalie Mitchell starting her shift. Acknowledging her entry into the scullery with the briefest of greetings, Ellie headed back through to the kitchen.

'Heard about your friend Frank Rafferty?'

Well used to this opening gambit and knowing it always presaged some unpleasant piece of gossip about Frank or whoever else the nasty Mrs Mitchell currently had in her sights, Ellie threw a polite but dismissive response over her shoulder. 'I expect he'll tell me all his news this afternoon. We're having tea together.' She walked across the kitchen, rounded the end of the table and leaned forward to set the jug down next to the mixing bowl.

Rosalie Mitchell was right behind her. 'Oh,' she said, her voice as slippery as silk, 'I shouldn't think you'll be meeting him today.' Standing surveying Ellie from the other side of the table, there was an unpleasant gleam in the older woman's eyes.

'Perhaps if he hadn't been out and about last Saturday he might have been able to meet you this Saturday. I may be wrong, but I don't *think* they let people out of gaol so they can go for afternoon tea with their friends.'

The heavy jug slid out of Ellie's fingers. Its solid base prevented it from tipping over, but it rocked before it settled, water splashing up out of it like a small wave hitting a harbour wall. 'What did you say?'

'He's got six months,' Rosalie Mitchell said triumphantly. 'That gang he runs with started a fight at a dance hall in Partick last weekend. Frank Rafferty slashed three men with a razor.' Her mouth settled into an expression that Ellie knew she was supposed to take for righteous disapproval. She could see all too clearly the real emotion her tormentor was experiencing.

What was that German word Evander liked so much – *Schadenfreude*? That's what this was. Rosalie Mitchell was squeezing all the malicious pleasure possible out of this particular piece of bad news. She leaned forward across the table, hissing her next words into Ellie's face. 'Apparently he slashed one girl too, cut right through her top and bottom lip. Nice sort of people you're friendly with, Eleanor Douglas.'

Ellie's groping fingers found the back of one of the kitchen chairs. She was shaking her head as she sank down on to it, desperately trying to deny what had been said.

'Frank would never hurt a lassie.' Her voice was a horrified whisper. 'Frank Rafferty would *never* do that!'

'He's been locked up for it. He must have done it.' The taunting voice became carefully casual. 'They had to wait for him to come out of the Western Infirmary before they could bring him up before the sheriff. Once they got him there they didn't waste any time. They never do with hooligans like him.'

Ellie gasped. 'Frank's been hurt too?'

Rosalie looked like the cat that had got the cream. 'Ripped open from his mouth to his ear. Terrible mess, so they say. Apparently there was blood everywhere.'

'That's enough, Mrs Mitchell,' said an authoritative voice. Aileen's warm fingers squeezed Ellie's shoulder. 'Sit for a minute. I'll make you a cup of tea.'

'All of you!' Phoebe burst into the kitchen, laughing as the green baize door swung against the back of her legs and catapulted her still further forward. 'Father's home early and he wants everybody in the morning room now!'

'A summons from the master?' Aileen Drummond said drily. 'We'd better jump to it.'

Ellie raised her head, watching as the cook tugged off her cap. Aileen's luxuriant brown hair still framed her face, although these days she wore it shorter and in a more modern style. Unlike Phoebe's hair, now also short and permed, Aileen's sat naturally in the newly fashionable waves that had replaced the previous vogue for boyishly cut hair and simple bobs.

Picking up on spiky silences, covert glances and atmospheres you could cut with the proverbial knife, Ellie had deduced that Aileen's dramatic change of hairstyle had been some sort of punishment for James Tait after one of their quarrels. Sometimes she thought both of them got up in the morning and wondered how best to hurt one another that day. They were arguing bitterly about something at the moment, she knew that.

As the cook stepped over to the mirror to the left of the scullery door and patted her hair into place, Ellie experienced a sharp twist of emotion, a combination of resentment and sympathy. Seconds before, Aileen had been feeling genuine compassion for her. Now, even though she was clearly furious with him, all she could think of was that she was going to see her lover.

Angela Tait sat expectantly on the edge of one of the armchairs that flanked the morning-room fire. Evander stood opposite his mother, one elbow resting on the high white mantelpiece. Now seventeen, he had shot up in height over the past six months, standing well over six foot. He was stronger and broader too, convinced that the exercises he did in the privacy of his bedroom had brought about that particular transformation.

Using a large proportion of his meagre allowance – it was one of his father's petty tyrannies that Evander received a quarter of what Phoebe did – he'd sent away for a fearsome-looking contraption advertised in a Sunday newspaper, one of the scandal sheets for which Angela Tait harboured a surprising weakness. The device consisted of two wooden handles joined together by some fiendishly strong springs. Pull on the handles a hundred times a day and a manly chest was guaranteed or your money back. Ellie had helped out by intercepting the postie before anyone else saw the mysterious package and smuggling it up to Evander's bedroom.

When she entered the morning room, he smiled and tapped his cheek with one long finger. As Ellie wiped the smudge of flour from her face Evander pointed to the centre of his forehead. She rubbed that mark away too and he responded with a swift grin and a discreet thumbs-up sign.

James Tait stood in one of his favourite places, in the large bay formed by the morning room's broad, floor-length window. Lit by the noonday sunshine streaming in through it, his habit of positioning himself there had once provoked one of Evander's acerbic comments about his father: 'Thinks he looks like Jesus Christ when he does that.' Personally Ellie always thought her employer bore more than a passing resemblance to Judas Iscariot.

There was obviously an announcement in the offing. James Tait would make them wait for it, not speaking until everybody was silent, in position and hanging on his every word. Resigned to it, Ellie watched as Mrs Tait and Phoebe settled themselves. Why they always took so long to do so was beyond her. Also critically observing his womenfolk, Evander sent Ellie a grimace to show that he shared her exasperation with them.

'Perhaps my son and Eleanor might pay attention,' James Tait said sharply. 'It doesn't seem too much to ask.'

'Indeed, no,' Angela Tait said, throwing a glance of rebuke at Ellie before turning back, all attention, to her husband. 'Do tell us your news, darling. We're all *dying* to hear.'

'Actually,' he began, jovial now he had their attention, an actor on his own little stage, 'I have several pieces of news. The first is that I'll be away on Monday for a week. I'm making a business trip to Newcastle. I should be home by the following Monday.'

'Well, it's not much notice, but shall I come with you, James?'

His face softened as he looked at his wife. 'It would be frightfully boring for you, darling. A lot of wandering around boatyards and looking at obscure pieces of machinery. But,' he continued, 'I have accepted an invitation for next weekend on behalf of you and Phoebe. I hope you don't mind.' His next words took any protest out of her mouth. 'Lord and Lady Matheson have very kindly invited you and Phoebe to a party down at their house at Kilcreggan. You're asked for the whole thing,' he added proudly, 'from the Friday afternoon right through till the Monday morning.'

'Oh,' Angela Tait breathed, 'isn't that wonderful!'

The Mathesons' summer home at Kilcreggan on the Firth of Clyde was a sprawling Victorian mansion, famous for its extravagant house parties and the sparkling set that attended them.

'Is Evander invited too?' Phoebe asked, a little frown between her brows.

'I shouldn't think so. They like to have lively people

at their parties,' James Tait glanced at his son, the dark eyes they shared cold, 'not dull dogs.'

Only half listening to the conversation, her mind still working on the awful news about Frank, that cutting remark jolted Ellie back.

Over the past two years she'd seen Evander beaten by his father on five separate occasions. Each explosion of violence had left him bruised and battered, and Ellie shocked and sickened, not only by James Tait's brutality towards his son but also by the way Angela and Phoebe lowered their eyes and allowed it to happen.

Ellie had no problem understanding their reluctance to challenge James Tait's authority, especially when something Evander had said or done had sent his father spinning into one of his spirals of rage. Even if you weren't the focus of that white-hot anger – and it was unthinkable that he would ever physically assault his wife or daughter – it was terrifying to witness.

What she couldn't understand was the unwillingness of the Tait womenfolk to help Evander afterwards. Never in a million years would it occur to James Tait that any member of his household would dare disobey his orders, his arrogance so great he never thought to check they had been carried out. Who, then, was to know if a tray had been taken up to Evander's room, or if someone had helped him bathe his cuts and bruises?

Although it was one of the few subjects they never discussed, Ellie sensed how much Evander was hurt by the emotional distance his mother and sister kept from him. He had reacted by growing ever more brittle, disdainful and sarcastic, his outward air of insouciance hardening into a shell that gave people who didn't know him very well the impression that he couldn't care less about pretty much anything. Ellie knew the reverse to be true. Evander Tait cared too much about almost everything.

Knowing how much the beatings hurt and humiliated him, sometimes she thought the harsh words did as much damage. Her own experience with her father had taught her how painful those could be. The verbal belittling to which James Tait constantly subjected his son ate away like acid at the protective coat Evander had tried so hard to grow, mounting an incessant attack on his fragile and precarious self-esteem.

Ellie willed him to receive her silent sympathy. To her surprise, he appeared barely to have registered his father's cruel remark. He had stopped propping up the mantelpiece and was standing very tall and straight. The pose was the opposite of his usual casual slouch, the one specifically adopted to irritate his father.

Usually Ellie thought that if Evander were a dog he'd be some sort of soulful-looking wolfhound; right now he reminded her of an intelligent collie that had finally spotted the stray sheep it had been searching for. Suddenly she realised why his interest in this conversation had sharpened.

James Tait had been angling for an invitation to one of the Mathesons' house parties for months. Now he'd secured it he was choosing to go off on a business trip instead. Something didn't add up here.

Phoebe's frown had deepened. When her father enquired why she didn't seem very pleased about going to Kilcreggan, she hastened to reassure him.

'I'm really excited about it, Pa. It's wonderful, it really is. I was wondering about the employees' excursion to Craigmarloch, that's all. Isn't that scheduled for the week after next, on the Monday holiday?'

Oh, Phoebe, Ellie thought, be careful you don't give yourself away . . .

The mutual attraction between Phoebe and Malcolm had blossomed into a relationship about a year before. Reluctant at first to do anything of which James Tait might disapprove, Malcolm had held out for a long time against it. Caught between his frustration and Phoebe's misery, Ellie hadn't known whether to be relieved or worried when his feelings had finally got the better of him.

With her usual optimism, Phoebe was convinced that her father would come round to the idea sooner rather than later. Acutely aware of his own position and inherently more cautious, Malcolm was insisting they keep their love affair a closely guarded secret, for the foreseeable future at least.

Their favourite trysting place was the summerhouse down by the tennis court, close by the gate in the old wall where Phoebe could turn the key and unobtrusively usher Malcolm in from the canal bank. Since the occupants of the pagoda were invisible from the house, it had become one of Ellie and Evander's favourite places too.

Their liking for sitting there late in the evening setting the world to rights clashed now and again with Phoebe and Malcolm's need to be alone. Both sets of siblings were currently engaged in some vigorous negotiations over the issue.

The excursion to Craigmarloch would provide Phoebe and Malcolm with a legitimate reason to be in one another's company. If they were discreet about it they could spend a large part of the day together.

'I've decided to postpone the excursion till the Tuesday of that week,' James Tait said. 'Give the work force an extra long weekend.'

Phoebe's face cleared. 'Oh, I'm sure they'll all appreciate that, Pa!'

'They've already expressed that appreciation. I told them first thing this morning.' He beamed at Phoebe, his good humour restored.

She smiled back at him. 'Should Mother and I take Ellie with us, Pa? To do our hair and look after our clothes and things?'

'I hardly think she'd be up to that,' James Tait said dismissively. 'Better do without help than have her show you up in front of the Mathesons and their staff. Besides, Eleanor will be needed here. Mrs Drummond has asked if it might be all right for her to take a week's holiday to visit her family in Perthshire and I've said she may go.'

Beside her, Ellie felt Aileen Drummond give a start of surprise, then swiftly cover it up. 'Thank you very much, Mr Tait. If I may, I'll leave tomorrow.' She raised her eyes briefly to his face before dropping them to her hands, clasped demurely in front of her as she stood between Ellie and Rosalie Mitchell.

So that was it. He was going away on a week-long business trip and Aileen Drummond was spending the exact same week with the family she hadn't spoken to in years. Aye, Ellie thought cynically, that'll be right. She glanced across the room at Angela Tait, wondering for the umpteenth time if she really had no inkling of what was going on right under her nose.

Ellie blinked. The master of the house had been addressing her directly.

'Were you away in a dwam, my dear?' Angela Tait queried. As ever when she used a Scots word she gave it a comical emphasis. A passionate Scottish Nationalist, Evander found that one more thing to criticise about his mother. 'Mr Tait was saying he was sure you'd be able to cope with the cooking over the next week.'

'I'm in charge while Mrs Drummond is away?'

'Oh, Ellie,' Phoebe spluttered, 'you do say the funniest things!'

Angela Tait's lovely face was also alive with amusement. Wondering exactly why what she had said was so funny, Ellie felt a great wave of despair break over her.

Frank had told her nothing of his progression to a position of leadership within the Bruce Street Boys. She had known all the same. It was there in the deference other lads showed him, glimpsed in the occasional cocky comment, the way he laughed at her when she tried to persuade him to go in search of respectable employment.

'I'm doing all right,' he always said. 'In fact, I'm doing grand.' Well, he wasn't doing so grand now, was he? *Ripped open from his mouth to his ear*. Like his father before him.

James Tait's booming voice broke into her thoughts. 'Well, my darling daughter,' he said to Phoebe, 'I have one more piece of news and it specifically concerns you.'

'Me, Pa?'

'Indeed.' He was smiling broadly. 'You've finally managed to persuade me that you should go to France with your friends next winter. Miss Lesley Matheson has very kindly agreed to make the arrangements with the family with whom she stayed two years ago.'

Ellie almost felt sorry for him. He'd been so careful to leave this announcement till the end, the excitement it would engender burying everything that had gone before. It did that all right, only not quite in the way he had expected. Phoebe's face fell so far it almost reached the floor.

Chapter 14

'Oh, Ellie! What on earth am I going to do?'

'You'll only be in France for six months,' Ellie said wearily, irritated that Phoebe had ambushed her on the back stairs and hustled her into her bedroom. 'It's not exactly an eternity.'

Now sitting in front of her dressing table, Phoebe lifted her head and addressed their combined reflections in the large rectangular mirror. 'You can't ever had been in love, Ellie! If you had you'd know that six months is an eternity! Even Malcolm being away for this week seems like an eternity!'

Sighing inwardly at Phoebe's tendency to speak in exclamation marks, Ellie leaned forward and picked up a hairbrush. 'Relax,' she said. 'Let's talk about this calmly.'

'How can I be calm?' Phoebe demanded. 'Pa's so angry with me!'

'Well, do you blame him?' Ellie asked in exasperation, finding herself in the novel position of defending James Tait. 'You've been pestering him for ages about going to France and when he finally agrees to it you show about as much enthusiasm as if you were going to your execution.'

She drew the brush through the shining waves of Phoebe's hair. 'It might have helped if you'd been a wee bit more excited about Kilcreggan. After all, that's only a weekend, and Malcolm and his friends probably won't come back now till next Sunday. You'd only miss a day with him.'

'Even a day without seeing Malcolm—'

'Oh, for goodness' sake!' Ellie snapped, losing patience with her. In the right mood Phoebe could be great fun, with a beguiling charm and a highly developed sense of the ridiculous. In the wrong mood she was impossible. The most wearing aspect of her personality was her absolute conviction that her own high emotions should take precedence over every other consideration, not only in her own life but in everyone else's.

Ellie had spent so much time today worrying about Frank. No one had offered her a shoulder to cry on, allowed her to express her dismay, anger and disbelief. Malcolm must have known what had happened. He could have got a message to her before he went off on holiday, but he had no time for any of the Raffertys, and to say that he disapproved of Ellie's continuing friendship with Frank would have been putting it mildly.

It wasn't much consolation that it would never have occurred to her brother how much it would upset Ellie to get the news from a complete bitch like Rosalie Mitchell. Both he and Phoebe were too wrapped up in one another to pay much real attention to what was going on in anyone else's life.

Ellie still couldn't believe the Frank Rafferty she knew would ever deliberately hurt any woman, but what if it had happened in the heat of the moment? The fight had taken place in a dance hall, after all, a place filled with members of both sexes.

Why hadn't the stupid bampot realised he might end up cutting a girl with one of those vicious razors he carried in his waistcoat pockets? Was it really any less awful that he had slashed lads, anyway? Oh, but she was so angry with him!

At the same time she was also aching with sympathy for him. The scar he was going to be left with was bad enough: a badge of dishonour that would mark him for the rest of his life. What was even worse was thinking of him cooped up in some tiny prison cell. Like herself, Frank had always loved being outside.

A memory flooded back: her and him on the day her father had died, both of them standing motionless on the canal towpath so as not to startle the nervous hare that they had watched lollop off into the safety of the long grass. How could a boy like that have grown into the sort of man who lashed out mindlessly with a cut-throat razor?

'It's France that really worries me!' Phoebe wailed, too wrapped up in her own concerns to notice how upset Ellie was. 'If I say I don't want to go, Father will ask me why and then I'll have to tell him about Malcolm.'

Ellie let out a soft sigh and lifted the hairbrush away from the golden head. That way she might manage to resist the temptation to bash its owner senseless. Five more minutes, that was all Miss Tait was getting from her tonight.

'Don't you think Ellie's got enough to do without being your lady's maid, Phoebe?' Loose-limbed and rangy, Evander stood propped against the doorjamb of his sister's bedroom, one hand clasping the elbow of his other arm. His white shirt was open at the neck and he'd unbuttoned the cuffs of it. 'I don't suppose it ever occurs to anybody that *she* might need a bit of a break from this place?'

'The place is fine,' Ellie snapped. 'I could have a fine holiday here if I could only get rid of all of you lot for a few days.'

'Ooh,' he said, sauntering into the room, 'dipped your tongue in vinegar this evening, Miss Douglas? Heard about your boyfriend, by the way?'

'If you're referring to Frank Rafferty,' Ellie said, banging the hairbrush down on the glass top of Phoebe's dressing table, 'then yes, of course, I've heard about him.'

Phoebe perked up, swinging round to look at Evander. 'What about Frank Rafferty?'

Her brother told her. 'Bound to happen sooner or later,' he added blithely. 'He who lives by the sword dies by the sword, and all that.'

Ellie's temper had been smouldering all day. That comment put a bellows to the glowing coals. 'That's it!' she cried. 'Write Frank off, like he's been written off since the day he was born. Och, I'm going out for some fresh air!'

'Don't start,' she warned ten minutes later, alerted to Evander's presence by the smell of tobacco behind her. 'Don't go on about your father going off with Aileen Drummond either.'

'Beats me why you defend the woman.'

'You wouldn't understand.' Ellie wrapped her arms about herself. The day had been hot and sunny but it was late now and growing chilly down here by the old wall. She raised her head, studying the great swathes of light still visible in the night sky.

Evander's voice had a hard edge to it. 'This'll be the you're-so-protected-by-the-cocoon-of-Bellevue-and-your-father's-money lecture, will it? Or perhaps the well-known variation on that. The you-don't-know-anything-about-real-life lecture.'

Ellie turned. He had tucked himself in under the roof of the summerhouse, long legs stretched out on the grass in front of him. He crossed them at the ankles and put his cigarette to his lips, narrowing his eyes against the smoke.

'Don't *you* start,' he said, watching her gaze follow the narrow blue column skywards. 'I'm well aware that I only smoke in order to annoy my parents. The fact that they don't know for certain that I do it and that they themselves smoke like chimneys doesn't impinge on the twisted satisfaction the foul habit gives me. La, what a confused and troubled little boy I am.'

'Oh, stop it!' Ellie yelled, infuriated by his theatricality. She had never lied to him about anything. Aware of all he had to contend with, there had been times when she had held back, kept some of her harsher opinions to herself. Tonight she was in exactly the right mood to let rip. She bunched her hands into fists, banging them hard against her legs to vent her frustration.

'You have absolutely no idea what it's like to grow up knowing you've got hardly any choices. That because of that you can be forced into making the wrong ones, the ones that lead you into terrible places.'

'I imagine prisons are rather terrible places,' Evander mused. 'Thankfully I only know that from reading *The Ballad of Reading Gaol*.' He sighed dramatically. 'Dear old Oscar. I would read Wilde anyway but the fact that my papa disapproves of him so strongly for having been – and I quote – "a raving pansy and a raging fairy" . . .' He cocked his dark head to one side. 'I've often wondered exactly how a pansy would go about raving. Or a fairy rage, for that matter. Then again, sometimes the little people can be quite malevolent, in literature and myth, at least.' He bent his long body forward, pretending to look about him. 'Shall we find some fairies and ask them what they think? There ought to be some down here at the bottom of the garden, surely.'

Ellie folded her arms and pursed her lips.

'Ah, Miss Douglas is unwilling to play games this evening.' He put his cigarette once more to his mouth. 'Would Frank Rafferty be a poetry-reading man?'

'Why, are you going to send him a copy of *The Ballad of Reading Gaol* so he can put his prison experience into perspective?' Ellie unfolded her arms and howled out the words. 'Sometimes you can be so bloody superior, Evander Tait! You think you know it all but everything you do know comes out of books! Have you any real idea what life's like for people like Frank, for people like Aileen Drummond, for people like me?'

He sent her a look from under his brows. 'You think I have such a great life?'

'I think you've made a deal with yourself.' Ellie responded, too angry with him, Frank and the whole world to be able to measure her words. 'I think you put up with it because you're scared of finding something much worse out there. I think all those dreams you have about doing something when you get the money from your grandparents' will when you're twenty-one are only dreams. I think it's better the Devil you know and I think that most of the time you're comfortable here. Too comfortable.'

He leaned forward, head bowed as he dropped his cigarette and ground it out on the grass. Ellie watched as he drew his knees up and clasped his hands over one of them. Under his unbuttoned shirt cuff, his watch had slid down his wrist. It always did. Despite his broadening chest and shoulders, he was still skinny. Yet his fine and long-fingered hands looked strong and capable. Manly.

He looked up, his gaze direct and intense. Ellie found herself momentarily silenced by it, unable to form a coherent thought or think of anything to say. He gave her a bitter little smile.

'My, my. Isn't this a fascinating conversation we're having?' Raising one long arm to the roof, he pulled himself up and out of the summerhouse. 'But I'm afraid you'll have to excuse me. It's past my bedtime.' His voice dripped sarcasm.

Since he'd put on that growth spurt he was a full head taller than her. Ellie didn't let that stop her. Stomping up to the pagoda, she placed her hands on her hips and squared up to him. 'Can't take the truth?' she challenged. 'Doesn't that make you a coward, Evander?'

Even as she heard his sharp intake of breath more wounding words spilled out of her mouth. 'Whatever Frank Rafferty is, he's most definitely not a coward.' She looked him straight in the eye. 'You could say that about your father too. Are you sure you're not jealous of both of them?'

Evander looked at her as though she'd just crawled out from under a particularly nasty stone. 'Let me get this straight, Ellie. Are you telling me you admire Frank Rafferty for going about fighting people with whom he has no real quarrel? Presumably you also admire my father for having fought in that *stupid* bloody war.' His voice shook with emotion. 'All those lives lost so each side could gain a few muddy yards of France. Is that what you think makes a man? A willingness to kill? The ability and the desire to hurt other people?' Now he was looking down his long nose at her. 'Bit of an odd attitude coming from a girl who had a father like yours.'

Stung by the disdain in his voice, Ellie could only stare blankly at him. She opened her mouth without any clear idea of what she was going to say. 'Evander, I—

He cut her off. 'Isn't the pot calling the kettle black anyway? You've been telling me almost since you got here that you want to leave. Isn't it the case that *you* might be a bit too comfortable with the Devil you know? That you might be a coward too?'

Now it was she who was taking the outraged breath.

Evander's face and voice were once more carefully expressionless. 'I'm going back to the house. Good night, Ellie.'

She stood and watched him go, up through the white flowers and terraces still glowing dimly in the gathering darkness. By the time she walked up to the kitchen door ten minutes later the remnants of daylight had vanished completely.

Chapter 15

At half-past ten on Friday morning – one full hour after they'd planned to leave – Ellie waved Angela and Phoebe off. Both of them having got out of bed unusually early, she had spent the last three hours convincing them that the clothes bought during their marathon shopping trip to Glasgow earlier in the week really were ideal for their weekend at Kilcreggan. She'd also assured them a hundred times that it absolutely wasn't necessary to take the cases, bags and hatboxes out of the car and start all over again.

As she walked back through to the quietness of the kitchen she wondered what to do with the rest of the day. Mrs Tait had told her to take it off if she liked, suggesting she might want to go into Glasgow.

Whatever faults you could accuse the Taits of, meanness certainly wasn't one of them. They paid wages well above the going rate. Since Ellie had no living expenses to speak of, she now had a respectable sum of money tucked away. There was more than enough in her little nest egg for her to be able to afford a new dress or some other treat. It was only a pity she couldn't seem to work up much enthusiasm for going anywhere today.

Frank's fate was weighing heavily on her mind. Life in prison had to be terrible: humiliating, brutal and dangerous, more awful even than the most dreadful of the pictures her vivid imagination kept presenting to her. Would Frank come out of there cowed and broken or would he go the other way? The gentle and humorous boy she had known might emerge as a flint-eyed and fully fledged Glasgow hardman. Ellie wasn't entirely sure which of those options was the worst.

Then there was Evander. The two of them had been carefully avoiding one another all week. Ellie had no idea what to do about any of it.

Making her way down the steps of the railway station a few hours later, she decided she must be a very shallow person indeed. Having reached the conclusion that going out would at least be an improvement on sitting moping around an unusually quiet and deserted Bellevue, she had discovered that a shopping trip to Glasgow had cheered her up no end.

Her purchases didn't include a new dress – she hadn't seen any that appealed to her enough – but she was delighted with them all the same. As she walked past the shops at Anniesland Cross, she kept trying to catch a glimpse of herself in their windows.

She looked surprisingly different. The transformation was due not only to the smart little brown felt hat she'd bought but also to her investment in two of the bust bodices that were becoming fashionable now that the vogue for flat chests had passed.

The saleslady had persuaded her to keep on one of the new-style brassieres. 'You're young yet,' she'd said, surveying a blushing Ellie with a professional eye, 'but you're developing a nice womanly figure. Why not show it off?'

Standing in front of the mirror in the kitchen

admiring her new shape, Ellie was wondering if she really did look more like a woman than a child and regretfully contemplating the necessity of taking off the hat. She turned her head this way and that, happily deciding the style was much more flattering to her than cloche hats ever had been. The colour also made a lovely contrast with her yellow sprigged cotton afternoon frock.

When she heard the wash-house door open, she glanced up at the clock. Who on earth would be coming in that way at half-past five on a Saturday afternoon?

'Hello,' Evander said, one hand curling round the edge of the kitchen door. The other was clutching a book.

'Hello,' Ellie responded. 'I've been out.'

'I know. I saw you coming over the nolly bridge a few minutes ago.' His eyes went to her head. 'You suit a hat with a brim. Did you buy that today?'

'Aye. It sort of jumped out and said, "Buy me, buy me." '

'That must have been alarming,' he murmured. 'Is the frock new too?'

'No,' she said, fighting the urge to wrap her arms about her newly visible curves as his gaze drifted southwards. 'I've had it for ages.'

'Well,' he said, bringing his gaze back to her face, 'you look very nice in it, anyway.'

'Thank you,' Ellie said gravely. 'I hope you found your lunch. I put it out in the dining room before I left.'

'I found it,' he said. 'Thanks.' He came properly into the room, pushing the door to the scullery shut before leaning back against it and folding his arms across his chest, cradling his book like a baby. Clean but crumpled, his grey linen shirt fell into soft folds over his bent elbows. As ever when he could get away with it, he'd left its collar off and its cuffs unbuttoned.

Over the shirt, its mother-of-pearl buttons also undone, he wore a black velvet waistcoat that had belonged to his grandfather. A little rubbed and worn in places, it was still a magnificent garment, its narrow lapels and shallow pockets decorated with heavy black frogging. Topped by the tousled waves of his dark hair, the whole ensemble made him look like a handsome and rather dangerous gypsy. All he needed was the earring.

Made uncomfortable by the comparison she herself had just drawn, Ellie removed her hat and laid it to one side. 'Mrs Mitchell isn't in today; she's at a wedding. She's coming back after it, though – about midnight. Your mother asked her to sleep over this weekend to chaperone the two of us. Isn't that daft?'

Evander neither agreed nor disagreed that the idea of Rosalie Mitchell chaperoning them was daft. He simply stayed where he was and continued solemnly to study Ellie.

'I bought you a replacement copy of *The Flight of the Heron* to make up for the one I dropped in the bath.'

'Oh. Thanks.'

'Right,' Ellie said, wondering how much longer they were going to stand here thanking one another, 'I'll get on with preparing your dinner as soon as I've had my own tea.'

'I came in here to talk to you,' he said quietly, 'not to ask you to be my servant.' His eyes dropped to the kitchen floor, then rose to meet hers again. 'I'm sorry for how I behaved last Saturday night. I was pompous and oafish and sarcastic and unkind, and that's the worst crime of all, because you've always been so kind to me. I know how worried you must be about Frank Rafferty and I'm sorry I was so unsympathetic. You deserve better, Eleanor Douglas. You deserve an awful lot better.'

It was the handsomest of apologies. 'Evander, I said some harsh things too,' Ellie responded. 'And some stupid ones.'

He raised a hand, stopping her from going any further. 'You were quite right to take me to task. I am afraid of what's out there.' She saw his Adam's apple bob as he swallowed. 'When it comes right down to it, I'm pretty much afraid of everything.'

'Och, Evander,' she said, her voice softening as she started towards him, 'don't you think I am too?'

His expression was oddly wistful. 'I don't think you're afraid of anything, Ellie. I used to watch you and Frank Rafferty jumping about on those logs in the seasoning basin and know that even if the two of you would have let me join in, I'd have been too feart to participate.'

She smiled at the Scots word. They'd spent so much time together since she'd come to work at Bellevue that each of them had picked up a lot of the other's vocabulary and turns of phrase.

'I'm scared of a lot of things, Evander,' she assured him, 'and you were right about me too. I need to start making plans, think about what I want to do with my life. I don't want to stay here any more than you do.'

'So you're not going to tell me you never want to speak to me again?'

Without consciously thinking about it, Ellie reached for his hand. 'Of course not. We're friends, you and I.'

What might have been the makings of a smile lifted

the corners of his mouth. 'You really like me, Ellie?'

'How can someone as intelligent as you are about some things be such a numpty about others?' she asked, her exasperation as genuine as it was affectionate. Sometimes she got a searing insight into the low opinion he had of himself, despaired of ever being able to assure him of his own worth. 'Of course I like you,' she said. 'I don't know what I'd have done without you over the last two years.'

'Honestly, Ellie?'

'Honestly. You and I will always be friends.'

'Always,' he repeated. 'That's a good word.' His smile dared to grow. Ellie was returning it when she felt his warm fingers thread themselves through her own cool ones. They stood for a second or two just looking at one another.

Much shorter than him, Ellie noticed the shadow of the stubble beginning to darken his jawline. She also noticed the length and lustrous thickness of his dark eyelashes. She slid her hand out of his grasp and stepped back. Those luxuriant eyelashes quivered as he blinked in surprise. 'Something wrong?'

'Not a thing,' she said, 'but I need to get on. I've things to do.'

'What are you having for your tea?' he asked.

'Stovies.'

He smiled at her, a happy and healthy seventeen-year-old boy. 'Is there enough for two?'

'This is nice,' he said as he sat down opposite her half an hour later.

Ellie tucked a stray strand of hair behind her ear. 'I'm not sure the sainted Mrs Beeton would approve, but I like it.'

She had thrown a yellow gingham tablecloth over one end of the long kitchen table. Chunky tumblers stood at both places. He had offered to raid his father's wine cellar, but Ellie had drawn him a look and told him sternly that a glass of cool milk was the only possible accompaniment to stovies.

'Oh, and you've picked some flowers while I was upstairs.' He looked more closely at the old blue-and-white striped jug into which she had put them. 'Wild flowers too. Poppies and bluebells.'

'I've been persuading the gardener all summer to leave some of them uncut.'

'I'd noticed. Around the edges and down by the wall. A few daisies, too. Or gowans,' he said, cheerfully correcting himself.

Ellie nodded. 'In memory of Gowanlea. I asked him especially to leave some of those.'

Beaming at her, he sniffed appreciatively as she removed the lid of the large china serving dish set between them. 'That smells wonderful.'

'Pass me your plate.'

He waited politely until she had served herself before reaching for his cutlery. That was of the simplest setting possible: one fork and one spoon. Lifting the former, he indicated the latter. 'Does that imply we're having pudding too?'

Ellie laughed, happy to be treading solid and familiar ground. 'Aye, you gannet, it does. I made an apple pie yesterday. It's warming in the oven even as we speak.'

'Does it come with custard?' he asked hopefully.

When she told him it did he clapped a hand to his chest. 'The gods are smiling on me today. I haven't been allowed to eat stovies since my grandmother died, and after I've polished them off I get custard and pastry made by your own fair hand.'

'Stop talking nonsense and eat your tea.'

He wasted no time in obeying her command. After a few appreciative mouthfuls he spoke again. 'Been thinking any more about The Minister's Cat?'

Ellie's mouth quirked. 'You mean this mythical restaurant I'm going to run one day?'

'Nothing wrong with having a dream,' Evander said firmly.

It was the dream into which her ambitions of doing something with her life had coalesced and the two of them had knocked the idea about many times. The original name of Ellie's castle in the air had been *Le Chat Noir*, in honour of Evander's theatre poster, which she liked so much.

When he had later expressed himself volubly on how pretentious it was for restaurants to write their menus in French – unless they were in France, of course – Ellie had thought about it, agreed with him and extended that view to the name of her own imaginary establishment. She had come up with a name that kept the connection with Evander's poster: The Minister's Cat.

They had played the word game hundreds of times. Evander had instituted it, asserting that running through the alphabet would be a great help to Ellie in assimilating all the new words she had learned from her voracious reading.

'I've been thinking about the interior décor,' she said loftily. Cocking her head to one side, she surveyed the table she had set. 'It should be something like this: informal – a place where people would feel comfortable and not have to worry about which knife and fork to use.'

'Bright and cheerful,' Evander contributed. 'Colourful tablecloths and jugs of flowers in the middle of the table. Good, honest food. Like stovies,' he said, putting paid to the last remnants of his own.

'Aye,' she agreed. 'Somewhere folk could come in at any time of day or evening and get a proper meal if they wanted it or something a bit lighter. An omelette or Welsh rarebit or scrambled eggs on toast.'

Evander took a long swig of milk. 'That would be good in a busy place,' he said, unselfconsciously wiping his upper lip with the back of his hand. 'Near a railway station, for instance. People going on a long train journey might want something more than a sandwich and something less than a full meal. May I have some more stovies?'

'Help yourself,' Ellie said.

'See us over the dish, then. What's so funny?'

'Oh, nothing,' she said, pushing the serving dish towards him. 'You can finish those off, if you want. I've had enough. It sounds so funny sometimes, that's all.' She mimicked his well-bred tones. ' "May I have some more stovies?" Then you tell me to "see you over the dish". Your mother would be horrified.'

'Aye,' he agreed, smiling in acknowledgement of his use of another word that his mother found both too Scottish and too common for her taste, 'especially since she and my father chose an education for both their children specifically designed to eradicate any tendency to lapse into the vernacular.' He paused, serving spoon poised above the remaining stovies. 'Half the masters at my school seem to think it's their sacred mission to turn us into imitation upper-class Englishmen.'

'Aye, laddie,' Ellie said, exaggerating her own accent.

'It's as weel your mammy and daddy dinna ken that the other half are supporters of home rule for Scotland.'

'Isn't it just?' Evander murmured, provoking another laugh from Ellie. His face took on a rueful expression. 'Did I do it again?'

'You did,' she said, watching with the warm satisfaction of the cook as he applied himself to finishing off the stovies. She rose and went over to the oven to take out their dessert. 'It's like speaking two separate languages, though, isn't it? It's grand to have a guid Scots tongue in yer heid and it's grand to be able to read all the books and poems written in what you might call Oxford English.'

'Indeed it is,' he agreed cheerfully.

'Speaking of which,' Ellie said. 'You only took *The Flight of the Heron* upstairs with you. You forgot your other book. Poetry, isn't it?' Her hands being full of apple pie and the cloth with which she was protecting them from the heat of the dish, she used her head to indicate the volume in question, lying where she had placed it near the foot of the table.

'I didn't forget it. I left it here on purpose.' As she placed the pie on a cork mat in the middle of the table, Evander looked up at her. His voice held an accusing note. 'You promised me custard.'

'It's coming, it's coming. I've only got one pair of hands, you know.' She flicked the cloth at him.

'Aargh!' he yelled, raising his hands in a parody of defensive alarm. 'Dinna dae that, lassie, ye'll hae ma eye oot!'

'Numpty,' she said amiably.

After she'd had one helping of dessert and he'd polished off two, Ellie offered him tea or coffee.

'No, thanks,' he said. 'I'm fine. More than fine,' he amended. 'That was a lovely meal, Ellie.' He sat back in his chair, hooking his thumbs into the pockets of the velvet waistcoat. The easy relaxation of the pose was contradicted by the faint blush that rose in his pale cheeks. 'The company was grand too.'

Aware that she also was on the brink of a blush, Ellie cast around for a nice neutral topic of conversation. Her gaze landed on his book. 'Going to read me a poem? How about "I met a traveller from an antique land"? I love that one.'

'Maybe later.' He pushed his dessert plate abruptly away from him and half rose, stretching down the table for the book. 'Right now I want to read you a different one.'

Puzzled, Ellie gazed across the table at him. Her cheerful companion of only a few moments before had become the Evander she didn't like to see: the brooding, intense and unhappy young man. Studying his bowed head, she saw that the book had obviously fallen open at the right place.

'It's by Robert Herrick. He lived about three hundred years ago so you might have to concentrate a bit to understand the language he uses.'

'Don't mumble, then. And don't bend over the book like that. I can hardly hear you.'

He raised his head by a fraction of an inch and began to read.

> 'A sweet disorder in the dress
> Kindles in clothes a wantonness:
> A lawn about the shoulders thrown
> Into a fine distraction:
> An erring lace, which here and there

Enthrals the crimson stomacher:
A cuff neglectful, and thereby
Ribbands to flow confusedly:
A winning wave, deserving note,
In the tempestuous petticoat:
A careless shoe-string, in whose tie
I see a wild civility:
Do more bewitch me than when art
Is too precise in every part.'

There was a dog barking somewhere. It sounded like the Alsatian she knew which lived with its master at the top of Crow Road. Funny how far a noise like that could travel when your immediate surroundings were quiet enough to hear a pin drop.

'Did you understand it?'

'Most of it – although I'd have to guess what a stomacher is. Or was.' She gave him an uncertain little smile. 'I liked that bit about the "tempestuous petticoat". That's me,' she said lightly. 'Always a bit of underskirt showing or a wee hole in one of my stockings or a smudge of flour on my face.'

'That's why this poem always makes me think of you. That's why I love it so much.' He closed the book with a crack that made her jump.

'Ellie,' he said urgently, 'do you have any idea why I'm always so sarcastic about Frank Rafferty?' Pushing the book out the way, he rose suddenly to his feet and answered his own question. 'Because I'm jealous of him. Oh, Ellie, I'm so jealous of him!'

For the space of three heartbeats she did nothing but gaze up at him. Then she too stood up, trembling so badly she had to brace herself against the table top by her fingertips. 'You don't have to be,' she whispered.

'Oh, Evander, you don't have to be!'

He tasted of apples and Demerara sugar and the vanilla pod she had used to flavour the custard. When the shy and fluttering kiss was over Ellie realised that he also smelled of soap. She raised an unsteady hand to his smooth chin. 'Did you shave when you went upstairs?'

His lips moved against her cheek. 'Yes.'

'You were so sure I was going to let you kiss me?'

'Not at all sure.' She felt his smile. 'Only hopeful. What would you say if I asked if we could do it again?'

She straightened up and extended one hand to him. He took it in his. As if they were performing some old-fashioned courtly dance, they walked together to the end of the table. When they got there they came slowly together. Hands hovered like butterflies on shoulders and waists, hardly daring to settle. 'I'm not really sure how to do this,' he confessed, blushing a little. 'Do you know?'

'In the romantic novels—' She broke off, embarrassed that she might know something he didn't.

'Tell me,' he urged, daring to slide one arm around her waist.

'Well,' Ellie whispered, her eyes dropping to his mouth, 'sometimes it says, "Her lips parted under his".'

'Let's try that, then,' Evander murmured. 'I'll open mine a bit too.'

It was some time before either of them spoke again. He recovered himself first, although he had to take a deep breath before he could speak. 'Oh. That was nice. That was very, very nice. Have you done this with Frank Rafferty?'

'No,' Ellie said indignantly. 'How many times do I

have to tell you that Frank isn't my boyfriend?' She struggled against the encircling arm but Evander tightened it and kept her where she was, raising his free hand in a gesture of surrender.

'All right, all right, I believe you. Stop giving me the fishwife glare.'

'At least I'm looking at your face and not at your chest,' she pointed out, unwilling to forgive him just yet.

His eyes were bubbling with laughter. 'I have been doing that, haven't I? Why *do* your breasts look so nice all of a sudden? Oh,' he added in delight, 'now I've made the wee fishwife blush!'

Ellie buried her burning face in his shoulder. 'You used that word deliberately.'

'Of course I did. It's a lovely word. Especially when it refers to your anatomy. Answer the question.'

She mumbled it into his black velvet waistcoat.

'I'm in for a treat, then,' came his teasing voice from above her, 'when all you girls switch over to the new style.' He laughed out loud when Ellie's head snapped up. 'There's no need to glare at me again. Don't you know that I'm at the mercy of my male instincts? We men respond to visual stimuli.'

'Did you get that out of a book?' she demanded. But her indignation was already melting into the heart-stopping pleasure of thinking how happy he looked. She lifted her hands to the mother-of-pearl buttons on his waistcoat. She had always yearned to touch their shining smoothness. Now she could.

Evander glanced down at her busy fingers. The laughter left his face, replaced by a hungrier emotion. 'Put your hands underneath,' he said huskily. 'Where I can feel them.'

Ellie never knew where the question came from. It was simply there. 'Do you want to touch me in the same place?'

He answered her without words.

Completely focused on one another, neither of them was aware that the green baize door had been pushed open. Nor did they hear the sauntering footsteps. Not until it was too late.

Chapter 16

'Well, well, well,' drawled James Tait. 'I'd never have thought you had it in you.' He looked coldly at his son. 'Just don't come running to me for help when you give the little tart a fat belly.'

Ellie drew her breath in at the crudeness of his words. Evander spared her a reassuring glance. 'We haven't done anything wrong, Ellie. You and I both know that.'

His father snorted in contempt and looked pointedly at where his son's left hand was resting. Evander calmly removed it, ducked his head and planted a swift kiss on Ellie's cheek. One arm resting protectively on her shoulders, he turned them both round to stand side-by-side, facing his father.

Those cold eyes came to rest on Ellie's burning face. 'Sleeping with my son isn't going to get you anywhere in this house. Not the sharpest knife in the drawer, are you?'

She felt Evander's arm twitch. When he spoke he sounded perfectly composed. 'Ellie happens to be one of the brightest people I know. I'll thank you not to insult her morals either. In fact,' he added, each and every word precisely enunciated, 'I'd suggest you don't judge other people by your own standards, Father.'

James Tait stiffened. 'What did you say?'

'You heard me.' Carefully light though it was, his

young voice was loaded with condemnation. 'Why are you back early from your trip? Did your week away with Mrs Drummond not work out as you wanted it to?'

It took three long strides. No more. Evander hurriedly shoved Ellie towards the scullery door, out of harm's way. Spinning round as soon as she got there, she saw James Tait's arm go up and back, gathering the strength to power the first blow.

'Don't hit him!'

Even as she yelled the words, she saw Evander's arm shoot out to meet his father's. As his long fingers fastened like a manacle around his wrist, the icy fury on James Tait's face metamorphosed into a series of confused emotions. Surprise. Shock. Fear?

Evander sounded completely cool, calm and collected: in command of himself and in command of the situation. 'He's not going to hit me, Ellie. He's never going to hit me again.'

James Tait's voice was a snarl. 'Exactly how does an effete little pansy like you propose to stop me?'

'I think we've established that I'm very far from being that.' Evander tightened his fingers, his knuckles whitening with the force of his grasp. James Tait grunted.

'Surprised how strong I've grown while you weren't looking, Father? Then again,' Evander added, unable to keep the bitterness out of his voice, 'when did you ever take any interest to me? Only when you needed a whipping boy.'

As he tightened his grip yet again, Ellie saw the sheen of sweat on James Tait's forehead. His son spoke softly into his face. 'Those days are over, Father. Hit me and I'll hit back. Literally and metaphorically. If you ever attempt to strike me again I'll tell Mother and Phoebe about you and Aileen Drummond.'

'And I'll back him up.'

Ellie wasn't sure either of them had heard her. Father and son stayed locked together for an interminably long moment, staring deep into one another's eyes. It ended only when Evander loosened his grip and took a couple of steps back. His father crooked his elbow, holding his arm up in front of his chest and rubbing his wrist with the fingers of his other hand. 'Maybe there's nothing to tell.' He glanced at Ellie. 'I'll make do with sandwiches for dinner. In the smoking room as soon as possible.'

'Certainly, Mr Tait.' Staring after him as he disappeared through the green baize door, Ellie whirled round when Evander said her name. He was standing leaning against the kitchen table. 'Did I really do that?' he asked bemusedly. 'Stand up to him?'

'You did,' she said. 'You really did.'

'It's you who gave me the strength to do it, Ellie.'

'No,' she said. 'You found that by yourself.'

He gave her a slightly shaky smile. 'So what do we do now?'

'I don't know what you do,' she said brightly. 'I'm going to get on with your father's dinner.'

She began to gather what she needed: bread and breadboard, butter, cold meat, tomatoes and cheese. She got the grater out of one of the wall cupboards. When she came back to the table she saw that Evander had straightened up and was surveying her with a very perplexed air.

'Ellie, what have I done? Why are you suddenly so angry with me?'

'I'm not angry with you.' She cut off a hunk of cheese. When his hand shot out and wrapped itself around her arm, she froze.

'Please look at me, Ellie.'

'Please take your hand off my arm.'

'All right,' he said, doing that, 'but I need to know why you're angry with me. Please tell me.'

Her reluctance to meet his eyes was all too evident. 'I'm not angry with you. I'm angry at myself.' She saw him lean forward, straining to hear her softly spoken words. 'Because of what I allowed you to do before your father came home.'

'*What you allowed me to do?*' he repeated. 'Weren't you enjoying it too, Ellie? I certainly thought you were.' The expression on his face would have melted the stoniest of hearts, but she couldn't afford to allow it to melt hers.

She cleared her throat and spoke in a stronger voice. 'Your father would be perfectly within his rights to sack me, you know.'

'He won't sack you,' Evander said, with a scorn she understood wasn't directed at her. 'Not now.'

'Can you imagine what would have happened if it had been Rosalie Mitchell who had walked in on us? The story would be all round Temple in less than twenty-four hours.'

'You care so much what other people think?'

Ellie's voice hardened. 'I have to care, Evander. Once a girl like me loses her reputation she's got nothing.' She made a dismissive gesture with her hand, an angry slice through the air. 'She *is* nothing. You heard what your father called me.'

'We both know it was completely unjustified. Not to mention breathtakingly hypocritical. You must also know that I'd never do anything to damage your reputation.'

'You're doing it now,' she said. 'We both are. Simply by being here alone together. Please go away.'

'Is that what you really want?'

'Yes,' she said. 'That's what I really want.'

As the green baize door swung behind him, she began grating cheese as though her life depended on it.

Aileen Drummond arrived back at Bellevue before lunchtime on Saturday in the foulest of moods. She took her temper out on a wholesale, if slightly belated, spring-cleaning of the kitchen.

Directed to clean out cupboards, wash plates and dishes, swab floors and wipe down walls and paintwork, Ellie was drooping with tiredness by the time Angela and Phoebe returned home on Monday afternoon, full of their weekend at Kilcreggan. She was dragooned in to help them too, struggling to find wardrobe and drawer space for the clothes they had bought for their visit to the Mathesons.

In the evening Phoebe sought Ellie out, asking her to chum up with her on the bus ride into Glasgow and during the sail out to Craigmarloch. 'I need to put my parents off the scent,' she said gaily, excited at the prospect of seeing Malcolm again after the eternity of their week's separation. Ellie was so weary by then that she would have agreed to anything.

On Tuesday morning as she stood on the deck of the little steamer that was taking them out to Craigmarloch, a familiar voice penetrated the tiredness that a night's sleep hadn't quite dealt with.

'My, my, young Ellie, you've done a wheen o' growing up since the last time I saw you.'

'Captain MacLean.' Ellie turned and found herself looking on to the deck of the *Torosay*. Both it and the excursion boat were moored by Spiers Wharf at Port Dundas, high on the hill above Glasgow's city centre. Dominated by the massive cooling tower of Pinkston

Power Station and the towering chimney of a nearby whisky distillery, Port Dundas was the meeting place of two canals, and an industrial hub with a complex of locks, docks, repair yards and workshops.

Spiers Wharf itself was lined with tall warehouses and whisky bonds. All of the buildings, including a fine old Georgian house, were covered with at least a century's worth of soot and grime. Despite that, the area around the excursion boat and the cobblestone quay over which the chattering crowd was making its way to the *Gipsy Queen*'s gangway was absolutely spotless.

'Aye,' Ewen MacLean said when Ellie, bestirring herself to make conversation, commented on this apparent anomaly, 'that's because the good people taking you out for your sail today have been here since first light, making sure that everything is as clean as a new pin. They pride themselves on it. You'll be for Craigmarloch?'

'We are,' Ellie agreed. 'What about yourself, Captain? Which way are you headed?'

'We've some timber for the sawmill at Temple. But we're waiting for a part to be delivered to a factory in Clydebank and it's been delayed. I've just been informed it'll not get here till the late afternoon.' He pushed his cap back on his head in a gesture of disgust. 'At this rate we'll be unloading both our cargoes on either side of midnight.'

'So you'll be spending the night with us?'

He shook his grizzled head. 'However late we are we'll have to make tracks as soon as we unload. I've telephoned ahead to let both places know that some poor unfortunate souls will have to wait up for us. My daughter is getting married in Tobermory on Saturday and if I don't get home in plenty of time to help with the preparations she and Mrs MacLean will have my guts for garters.' He laughed and looked past Ellie. 'I was just saying what a fine grown-up young lady she is getting. D'you not think so yourself, young Mr Tait?'

Coming up behind Ellie, Evander's voice was a low growl. 'She's a very bonnie young lady getting, Captain MacLean. That's what I think. But I'm probably not allowed to say that. I'm not sure why.'

The captain looked from one unsmiling young face to the other, his own features growing thoughtful. 'Well,' he said gamely, 'have a good day.'

As he disappeared back down into the *Torosay*, Ellie spoke out of the corner of her mouth to Evander. 'Please don't embarrass me in public.'

'Ellie, we need to talk.'

She sent him a pleading look. 'Please, Evander. I don't want folk gossiping about us.'

He moved away, retreating a few paces to lean against the handrail that ran round the promenade deck. Like most of the young men on board, he was wearing light-coloured clothes today. They were in no danger of getting dirty. The *Gipsy Queen*'s rail was as clean and sparkling as everything else on board the little vessel.

An ear-splitting blast of her whistle signalled the start of the trip. As they glided away from Spiers Wharf a cheer went up. Moments later someone found the on-board piano. People began to point out landmarks to each other, enjoying seeing them from a different perspective: the Gothic spire of Glasgow University on Gilmorehill, the elegant white architecture of Trinity College up at Park Circus, the solid tower of Ruchill Hospital.

Ellie caught a glimpse of the cemetery where her father was buried. Memories of him no longer troubled her very much. She'd put them all away in a box in her head, never to be opened again if she could help it. Just as well. She had a whole new set of problems to deal with now.

It didn't take long to reach Stockingfield Junction where the Glasgow spur of the canal joined in with the main section of the waterway. 'Only a few miles to Temple that way,' one lad observed, 'but all those locks at the Buttney at Maryhill would have taken too much negotiating for the boat to come and fetch us.'

'What are those boys doing?' cried Phoebe.

As the *Gipsy Queen* slowed right down to complete the awkward manoeuvre of negotiating the right-angled turn, Ellie looked over at the far bank. Clad only in tattered underpants, two boys were diving into the canal. Treading water, they waved and gestured to the passengers on the little steamer.

'I've heard about this!' another girl shouted. 'You throw money in and they dive for it!'

That started a spate of coin-tossing. Each time one of the boys came up with his fist wrapped proudly around some money, more would be sent flying towards them. Phoebe clapped her hands in front of her like a delighted child. 'Isn't this fun?'

'Why don't you throw them a ball and see if they can balance it on the ends of their noses? Don't you think it's pretty disgusting that there are people in this city who're so poor they have to beg for coppers like this? Honestly, Phoebe, what do you have between your ears?'

The group of young people in Evander's immediate vicinity turned guiltily to look at him.

'Oh,' Phoebe faltered, 'I hadn't thought of it that way.' As her mother slid a comforting arm about her shoulders, her father glared at Evander.

'Apologise to your sister, sir! Right now!'

'No,' Evander said coolly. 'I don't apologise for telling the truth.'

Ellie heard the collective intake of breath, saw the darting eyes and felt the surprise when James Tait simply looked at his son and then turned to Phoebe and Angela and suggested a turn about the deck. Without a metaphorical shot being fired, Evander had apparently won his second battle with his father. Ellie suppressed a shiver. Somehow she knew that the war wasn't over.

They had barely stepped off the boat at Craigmarloch when a girl Ellie had been friendly with at school came running up to her. 'Hello there, Ellie. I didn't see you on board. Fancy being first on the putting green?'

'Excuse me,' Evander murmured politely, stepping between the two girls. Ellie's eyes were troubled as she watched him stride off.

'Are you friendly with him?' the other girl asked. 'I thought he was supposed to be a bit odd.'

'He's not odd at all,' Ellie said before she could stop herself. 'He's misunderstood.'

Her old schoolmate turned to her, eyes gleaming with interest. 'D'ye tell me that, Ellie Douglas?'

Groaning inwardly, Ellie steered her firmly in the direction of the putting green.

Lunch was a substantial meal, served in The Bungalow. Despite its name, Craigmarloch's restaurant occupied a two-storey building, with a tearoom on the first floor and a huge dining room on the ground. Tait's excursion filled the building to capacity. As they worked their way through the meal the din of chattering voices grew deafening.

After the lunch was finished there was a general stampede outside. Shaking her head in amazement that despite having only recently put away Scotch broth, steak pie, pears and creamed rice some folk were already queuing up for the ice creams being sold from the veranda at the front of The Bungalow, Ellie slid round a corner in the hope of finding some solitude.

'Oh!' she said. 'Sorry!'

The exclamation had been startled out of her by a girl in a capacious white apron sitting on the grass with her back to the wooden building. She looked up with a smile. 'Having a wee rest after my labours,' she offered.

'You're the chef?'

'My friend and I were indeed the perpetrators of that stodge. The menu never changes, you know. It's death to the creative cook.'

'It was beautifully prepared and presented,' Ellie protested. 'And you obviously use only the best ingredients.'

Squinting up against the bright sunshine, the girl gave her a shrewd look. 'Do I detect a compliment made from a professional standpoint?'

'I'm in service. Do you and your friend work here all year round?'

The girl shook her blonde head. It was obvious that she'd recently tugged a cap off but you could still see that her hair was beautifully cut and professionally styled. 'We're students at the Dough School. The College of Domestic Science, if you prefer our alma mater's Sunday name. Working here earns us some pennies at the weekends and during the long vac.'

'Are you training to go into service?' Ellie asked, a little puzzled. She'd always assumed cooks got their training by working under other cooks. This girl seemed a little too posh to be contemplating a life in service.

'We're going to be unleashed on some as yet blissfully unaware school pupils as domestic science teachers,' she explained. 'The College does train people to be cooks, though – for houses and restaurants and hospitals and all sorts of places. There are lots of different courses, day and evening, full and part time.' She ticked some off on her fingers. 'Cook's Certificate, Advanced Cook's Certificate, Vegetarian Cookery, Cordon Bleu Cookery . . .'

'Sounds interesting.'

'Give me your name and address,' the girl said. 'I'll ask the office to send you out the new prospectus once it's printed.'

As she handed over a piece of paper with the details on it Ellie felt a brooding presence behind her. She turned and saw Evander, standing with his dark head tilted back against the wall of The Bungalow. He was giving her a decidedly long-suffering look.

'Ooh. Tall, dark *and* handsome. Aren't you the lucky one?' The blonde scrambled to her feet. 'Back to work for me, I'm afraid.'

Evander waited until the girl had disappeared back inside The Bungalow.

'Come for a walk with me. Please. We'll go along the towpath. In full view of everybody.'

Ellie smiled wryly. 'You think that'll stop them gossiping about us?'

'Of course it will. They'll say, "There goes Ellie Douglas with that strange Evander Tait. Probably his parents made her take a walk with him and she had to go because she works for them." ' He tapped the pocket of his jacket. 'I've got some poems in here about Craigmarloch. I copied them out of an old book. We'll sit on a bench somewhere and I'll read them to you and they'll all look at you pityingly and say, "Poor girl, having to put up with that." That's what they'll say, Ellie.'

'You're mad.'

'They'll probably say that too. Please come with me.'

Ten minutes later, still walking eastwards along the towpath, Evander stopped and looked back in the direction of the little resort. There were two or three people further along the path but no boats on the canal and nobody within earshot. 'I've got some things to say.'

'Go on, then,' Ellie said, also coming reluctantly to a halt.

'I've been thinking about what happened last Friday night, trying to understand your feelings, trying to work out why you told me to go away. I need to know one thing. Did you enjoy what we were doing before my father came home? I want an honest answer.'

'Maybe I enjoyed it too much.'

'What does that mean?'

'I got carried away,' she said miserably. 'Led you on. I shouldn't have done that.'

'Didn't we lead each other on? To somewhere we both wanted to go?' His eyes narrowed. 'Are you upset because of what my father called you?'

'Maybe I deserved what your father called me. I can't believe what I asked you to do. Or the things I talked to you about.' She blushed, and folded her arms protectively across her breasts. 'When I thought about it later it made me feel cheap.'

Evander's eyes flickered down to those protective arms, then back up to her rosy face. 'Ellie,' he said gently, 'what you said and did doesn't make you cheap.

It was beautiful: as beautiful as you are. Both outside and in.'

Her face broke into a weary smile. 'I'm not beautiful. I've got freckles, for a start. Haven't you ever noticed?'

'I've noticed.' He brought his right hand up her face, his fingertips tracing a delicate line across it from one cheek to the other. For a moment they simply gazed into each other's eyes.

Then Evander spoke again: 'I love your freckles. Each and every one of them. Oh, Ellie!' he said passionately, 'I love *you*.'

Chapter 17

Her voice was an astonished whisper. 'What did you say?'

He dropped his hand and took a step back. 'I love you,' he said. 'That's what I said, Ellie.'

'Don't say those words when you don't mean them!'

'Don't tell me I don't mean them,' he said mildly. 'I do. I love you, Ellie.' When he saw her eyes well up with tears he stepped forward again, defeating her attempts to fend him off. 'Oh, Ellie! Move back with me behind that big horse chestnut over there. Then nobody will be able to see us.'

Sheltered by its huge trunk, they stood together under the spreading branches of the chestnut tree. Her face was buried in his shoulder and his arms were wrapped about her. He spared one hand to push back the little brown hat, murmuring a soft question into her hair. 'Doesn't this feel nice?'

'That's not the point.'

'What is the point?'

'You know very well what it is.'

'That I'm the son of the house and you're the kitchenmaid? What a Victorian point of view, Ellie. Where does it leave your brother and my sister?'

She pulled back a little so she could look up at him. 'Do you really think there aren't going to be ructions when your parents find out about Phoebe and Malcolm? That's different, anyway.'

'I don't see how.'

'I do. Your father sees Malcolm as a younger version of himself.'

'Probably as his successor at the boatyard,' Evander agreed. 'He certainly doesn't see me following in his footsteps.'

'Exactly. If Malcolm and Phoebe take it slowly and play their cards right your parents will come round to the idea of them being together. How d'you think your mother or your father would react if they could see us now?'

'I don't think they give a damn what I do. Especially my father.'

'You're still his son and you're still a Tait. I'm a skivvy and a nobody.'

'You most certainly are *not* a nobody,' Evander said hotly. 'You're clever and you're funny and you're kind . . . and, oh,' he said, gazing down at her, 'you're the girl I love too.'

'And you think that solves everything?' A tiny smile touched her lips. 'You're such a romantic, Evander.'

'And you're always so sensible.'

'One of us has to be,' she said sadly. 'I think we should go back now.'

'I don't.'

'Please, Evander.'

'I know, I know.' He sighed. 'You've got your reputation to consider. Will you let me kiss you first?'

She couldn't hold out any longer. She wanted this as much as he did. As the kiss became deeper and more passionate she found herself responding, clinging on to him as tightly as he was holding her. His arms slackened.

Ellie heard someone moan in protest and realised with a little start of surprise that it was her.

Those same arms began to explore her body. She should stop them. She knew she should. She didn't want to. She wanted this to go on for ever.

When it was finally over they stood for a moment with their foreheads pressed together, recovering. Both were equally excited, their breath coming fast and shallow against one another's face.

'Meet me in the summerhouse after we get back tonight.'

'I can't . . .'

'Oh, Ellie,' he moaned. 'Please. We'll just kiss. I promise!'

'Just kiss like we just kissed there?' She extricated herself from his embrace, knowing she wouldn't be able to think straight until she did.

'Will you come if I agree that you can tie my hands behind my back?'

She smiled at that, but she shook her head too. 'Come on. Let's go back to The Bungalow before anyone misses us.'

He reached for her again but she evaded his grasp and ran across to the towpath. When he caught up with her he blew his cheeks out like a fish, buried his hands in his hair and gave himself a brief but vigorous scalp massage.

'What *are* you doing?'

'Trying to feel normal again.' He scowled at her. 'When I'd rather feel like I did five minutes ago.'

'You look like a mad poet.'

'Your fault,' he said. 'If you won't let me do what I want to I'm going to behave like a mad poet and declaim verses at you all the way back to The Bungalow.'

'Don't do that. I want you to tell me something. It's something I've been curious about for a long time. Ever since the first time I saw your father hit you.' She grimaced. 'Or ever since we talked together after that event.'

He shot her a dirty look. 'Are you deliberately trying to destroy the moment? Ask away, then, if you must.'

She rattled it out before her courage could fail her. 'You could have threatened to tell your mother about your father and Mrs Drummond at any time. Why didn't you?'

'There have been times when I've wanted nothing more than to tell her – in the crudest words imaginable.' His eyes searched Ellie's face, looking for an answer. 'Does that make me a terrible person? To want to devastate my own mother? Show her that the life she's living is the most awful bloody sham?'

'She's stood by and watched your father beat you; not helped you afterwards.'

'Nobody would ever believe that, would they?' he asked bitterly. 'Everyone thinks she's so charming and kind.'

'She is,' Ellie said. 'The thing is, it doesn't cost your mother anything to be charming to her friends or kind to people like me.' She revised that. 'I suppose it's cost her some money in my case – buying me clothes. Not to mention the cost of my father's funeral.'

'But she's got plenty of money?'

'Aye,' she said, relieved that he had understood. 'It's not like someone sharing their last penny with you. I mean, I think she's quite fond of me but she doesn't really *care* about me. There's no effort involved. Does any of this make any sense?'

'All of it does. Go on.'

'I think she really cares about you but because your father's temper is so terrifying and because she hates to have anything remotely unpleasant in her life, she's always done everything she can not to face up to what he does to you, which means she's failed you time and time again. She knows that and she hates herself for it. More unpleasantness. What does she do about that? She tries to close her eyes to it.'

'See no evil, hear no evil, speak no evil,' Evander quoted softly.

'Exactly. But you cannae go through life ignoring the nasty bits, can you? Sometimes you've got to deal with them. Especially if someone's getting hurt.' She turned her mouth down, self-deprecating. 'The Eleanor Douglas philosophy of life.'

'It's a very good philosophy of life. You've given me something to think about.'

'Have I?' she asked, pleased with herself. 'Oh look, we're nearly back at The Bungalow.'

'Oh, goody,' he said sarcastically. 'Now I get to share you with hundreds of other people. Any chance you'll reconsider meeting me in the summerhouse tonight?'

She looked up at him, her eyes troubled. 'Evander, I can't afford to get into trouble.'

'I know you can't. Please, Ellie. I promise we won't go too far.'

She bit her lip. 'But what if we can't help ourselves?'

'Think about it,' he pleaded. 'I'll wait in my bedroom for you.' His face lightened. 'We could take a midnight feast down with us. Is there any of that ham and egg pie left over that you made for luncheon yesterday?'

She relaxed immediately. 'In case we haven't eaten enough by the end of today, you mean? Did you say that to make me laugh?'

'Maybe. Although that pie really was delicious.' His smile went as quickly as it had arrived. 'Please come, Ellie. Please.'

They got back to Temple shortly after eleven o'clock, climbing out of the hired buses at the boatyard gates. Waving to Captain MacLean and his crew, still busy unloading, Ellie followed the Tait family up the hill to Bellevue. When they got there, Phoebe wished her a dreamy good night and glided up the main staircase, her mother and brother following in her wake. James Tait announced his intention of having a brandy before he went to bed and disappeared into the drawing room.

As Angela Tait and Phoebe closed the doors of their respective rooms, Evander looked back down at Ellie, an unmistakable plea in his expressive eyes. She couldn't answer it. She knew she couldn't.

Fifteen minutes later she was still fully dressed, sitting on the edge of her bed staring at the wall opposite. She'd rehearsed all the arguments in her head several times already. She couldn't possibly go. She shouldn't go. His having his hands tied behind his back was all very well. What about her own?

She closed her eyes, remembering Friday evening in the kitchen, remembering how it had felt to lay her hands against his crumpled linen shirt and feel the warm body beneath it. She remembered this afternoon at Craigmarloch, when he had kissed her and held her and pulled her against him.

Ellie groaned. She wanted to be with him. She wanted to be with him right now.

She leaped up from the bed, grabbing the spare blanket lying folded at the foot of it on her way to the door. They'd be careful. She'd insist he take his own blanket, for a start. The thought of both of them under the same one was . . . something which made her blush all over. As she peered out into the corridor her blood was fizzing through her veins, all tiredness evaporated.

Halfway along it, walking on tiptoe so as to be as quiet as possible, she stopped dead. What was she doing? Taking the biggest risk of her life, that was what. She stood there racked by indecision: torn between safety and excitement. Sensible Ellie. That's what Evander had called her today. Oh, if only she didn't want to be with him so much!

I love you. Even the memory of the words sent a tremor through her body. She hadn't yet given them back to him. She had seen in his eyes how much he wanted to hear her say them.

Ellie headed for the top of the stairs.

Chapter 18

That was odd. There was a light showing under Aileen Drummond's door. She was sure it hadn't been there when she had passed on her way to her own room a quarter of an hour ago.

'Ellie? Is that you?'

She swivelled round and tossed the folded blanket back along the corridor. It landed right outside her door, hitting the carpeted floor of the corridor with the softest of thuds. With a bit of luck she'd be able to convince the cook she was on her way in instead of her way out. She pushed opened Aileen Drummond's door.

Struggling up on to her pillows, her hand still on the switch of her bedside light, the cook was as white as the sheet that covered her – except where that sheet was spotted with blood. Ellie's eyes widened in alarm.

'Aileen,' she said as she stepped hastily into the room, the cook's first name surprised out of her. 'Are you ill? Shall I run downstairs and ask the master to telephone for the doctor?'

Aileen Drummond sank back on to the pillows. 'I've already seen a doctor today.' Her big mouth curved in the travesty of a smile. 'Mind you, I believe he was struck off the medical register some time ago. Don't worry,' she said, watching as Ellie's eyes opened wider still. 'He knows his job. I'm all right. But I'd like to see the master.' She grimaced as she said that word. 'Ellie, could you please go and fetch him for me?'

Evander answered the knock on his bedroom door immediately. In a few whispered sentences Ellie told him what had happened. 'Will you come with me?' she asked, 'to get your father?'

'Try stopping me,' he said grimly.

They found James Tait still in the drawing room, sitting alone in front of the empty grate nursing his brandy. Setting down the crystal tumbler on the little high table that stood at his elbow, his response to Ellie's message came in two terse sentences. 'Wait here for me. Both of you.'

Ellie sank down on to the sofa, pulling Evander with her. All at once aware of how cold she was, she needed the warmth of his body next to her own.

'How could she?' he muttered. 'How could any woman do that to her own child?'

Ellie slid an arm round his hunched shoulders. 'Some women don't have any choice, Evander.'

She'd known a few of those women, her motherless state leaving her much less protected from such information than other girls of her age. She'd heard the malicious gossip too – more than once in the case of certain people, Frank's sister among them. An unexpected pang of sympathy for Marie Rafferty went through her. Hazy though her knowledge was, Ellie knew enough about the details of what she and Aileen Drummond had undergone. More than enough.

Evander dug his hands deep into his hair, denying what Ellie had said. 'There's always a choice. Especially in this case. My father could have given her the money to go away somewhere. She could have had the baby.'

'Maybe she had a choice,' Ellie said. 'Maybe she

didn't.' She was thinking how far gossip can travel, of James Tait's fear of scandal, of his arrogance and selfishness. He wanted his mistress where she was, conveniently under his own roof.

Back within ten minutes, he lifted his glass, strode over to the cocktail cabinet and took down two more, sloshing a generous measure of brandy into each of them. 'I think we all need this.' He set both glasses down on the low table in front of the sofa before throwing himself back into the chair beside the fireplace. 'This stays between the four of us who know about it.' He tossed back a gulp of his brandy. 'Is that understood?'

Ellie had already reached for her drink, was putting the glass to her lips to take a reviving sip. She saw too late that Evander had contemptuously pushed his away. She ought to have realised he would take nothing from his father's hand.

'How can you sit here calmly drinking brandy?' he demanded. He rose to his feet, the movement as jerky and abrupt as if he were a puppet whose strings had suddenly been pulled. '*How can you?*' he asked again. 'You've murdered an unborn child today.' His eyes were wild, filled with the horror of it. 'Caused the death of an innocent.'

'Oh, spare me your bleeding heart!' James Tait took another angry swig of brandy and surveyed his son over the crystal tumbler. His next words were spat out. 'What the hell do you know about anything? If you'd been on the Western Front you might have known something about the deaths of innocents.'

Evander tossed his untidy head. 'You expect us to accept that the carnage you witnessed there justifies what you've done today?'

'I don't expect you to understand anything of what we went through. Nobody can who wasn't there.' James Tait lifted his glass again. 'I fought alongside lads who were only seventeen years old. The same age you are now.'

It was a statement of fact. Watching as father and son stared coldly at one another, Ellie knew it was a lot more than that.

James Tait must have awful memories of that most terrible of conflicts, they had to allow him that. Ellie's imagination was at work again, furnishing her with images of unspeakable horror. She shuddered as they threatened to become overwhelming. The involuntary movement drew James Tait's attention to her.

'You can wipe that look of disapproval off your face, miss. If you keep carrying on with my son you might need the same medical attention yourself sooner rather than later.'

Evander's eyes were as hard as black diamonds. 'What did you say?'

'You heard. Drink up your brandy and then let's all get away to bed.' The handsome face set itself into a sneer. 'Our own beds.'

Evander drew himself up to his full height. 'Don't equate a girl like Ellie with your own fancy woman. My intentions towards her are strictly honourable.'

James Tait laughed harshly. 'So the two of you weren't off in the bushes at Craigmarloch this afternoon? You didn't have her buttons undone or your hand up her skirt?' He threw Ellie a look so contemptuous it took her breath away. 'A wee Temple trollop, like a hundred canalside whores before her. Now I come to think about it, I seem to remember some story about her mother—'

Ellie's head snapped up but Evander had heard only the 'wee Temple trollop'. 'Take that back!'

'Don't be tiresome.' His father finished his brandy and stood up. 'Now, if you'll excuse me, it has been rather a tiring day—'

Evander launched himself forward, roaring with anger. Catching James Tait unawares, the momentum sent both of them flying past the armchair, heading inexorably for the wall behind it. They cannoned into the cocktail cabinet, rattling the bottles and glasses.

Evander wasted no time in taking advantage of his father's surprise. He pulled his hand back, made a fist and let fly. Knees buckling under the force of the blow, James Tait stumbled backwards towards the door of the drawing room. One of his flailing arms caught the brandy bottle, stood on the edge of the cocktail cabinet. It fell, missing the carpet and striking the varnished floorboards around the edge of the room. As it shattered, the smell of the spirit wafted up from the floor, sweet and cloying.

Evander walked through the vicious shards of glass as though he didn't even see them. He hit his father again, sending him through the open drawing-room door and spinning like a child's top out into the hall.

Already on her feet, Ellie gathered her shattered wits about her and followed them, her lips shaping Evander's name. What she saw when she reached the hall silenced her.

James Tait was standing in the middle of the tiled floor as though he were about to lead the dancing off at a wedding. Stretching his arm out, he beckoned to his son. Two contemptuous flicks of the fingers. Evander's chin went up.

Ellie yelled out his name. 'No! Don't do this!'

He was past hearing her. As the two Tait men circled their way round the hallway and each other Angela and Phoebe came running out on to the gallery on the first floor, clutching the balustrade as they peered over at the scene below.

'Ellie!' Angela Tait shouted. 'Stop them!'

Already desperately trying to work out how she could do that, Ellie saw Evander land another punch. His father called him the foulest of names and responded with a sharp and vicious jab, catching him on the nose. There was a nauseating crunching sound.

It was followed by a fountain of blood. It sprayed everywhere, spattering both protagonists before falling to dot the black-and-white tiles with thick and viscous red spots the size of halfpenny bits.

Evander sank to one knee and let out a groan of exquisite pain. His father sauntered forward and stood looking down at him. His son was taking great juddering breaths through his mouth. His nose was oozing blood, his eyes bright with tears of pain. He raised his head and meet his father's gaze, using the back of one shaking hand to clear the mess away like a child wiping a runny nose.

James Tait's voice was as smooth as silk and as corrosive as acid. 'Thought you could take me on, boy? Better think again.' His hand shot out, grabbing Evander by the hair. 'So intelligent,' his father said. 'So sensitive.' He pronounced both words with infinite contempt. 'A heart that bleeds for the entire world, that's you, isn't it?'

The punishing hand shoved his head back. Evander moaned. Not knowing whether to pray the pain might make him black out, Ellie saw his father bend over the broken and bloody face. 'I think you're a pathetic excuse for a man. Nervy. Unstable. Not quite right in the head. What sort of young lad sits around all day reading poetry? What kind of unnatural son attacks his father for absolutely no reason? Or makes up scurrilous stories about him?'

Although he didn't bother to look at her, Ellie knew his next words were as much for her as for Evander. 'Who's going to believe the word of an unbalanced boy and a skivvy who's no better than she should be against that of my wife, daughter and housekeeper? Cross me again and I'll have you in a locked ward before you know what's hit you.'

Ellie caught a flash of movement out of the corner of her eye. Angela and Phoebe were hurrying down the stairs. They'd heard nothing of what had been said in the last couple of minutes. James Tait had made sure of that.

Clutching her silk kimono about her throat, Angela Tait's lovely face was a picture of panic, anxiety and confusion. Close behind her, Phoebe was still dressed, although her clothes looked crumpled, as though she'd been lying on top of her bed.

'James,' Angela Tait asked, 'what on earth is going on?'

Her husband straightened up. 'The boy went berserk,' he said shortly. 'I think we may have to call the doctor and have him restrained in some way.'

Ellie opened her mouth to deny vehemently that version of events. Then she saw that Evander was struggling painfully to his feet. She started towards him but he put a hand out, fending her off. She stopped in her tracks. If he needed to do this by himself she had to respect that.

He made it – swaying, bruised, battered and covered

in his own blood, but standing on his own two feet. The spirit that had refused to be broken by all the years of his father's cruelty had never burned so brightly.

'Berserk?' he repeated. 'I'll show you berserk.' Steadying himself, he lunged forward and swung his fist. James Tait went down.

Evander was straddling him in an instant. The crack as his fist found his father's jaw made Ellie jump. 'Five.' He was panting with exertion but otherwise his voice sounded perfectly calm. He administered another punch. 'Six.'

As he pulled his right arm back to power the next one, Phoebe screamed, 'Do something, Ellie! He'll kill him!'

Ellie ran forward, skidding to a crouch on the hard floor. She was inches from James Tait's head but her attention was completely focused on the boy seemingly intent on beating his father to a pulp.

Ignoring the risk to herself, she reached for Evander's upraised arm. Her touch reached him as her voice had not. When he looked at her and blinked, Ellie strove to speak to him in as gentle a voice as possible. 'What are you doing, Evander?'

'I'm counting the punches,' he said, explaining it to her as he might have told her the meaning of an obscure word. 'Giving back every one he's ever given me. I've counted them all up, you know. I know how many I owe him.'

'Oh, dear God in heaven,' Phoebe muttered, 'he has gone mad!'

Ellie fought to keep her voice both brisk and matter-of-fact. 'You've done enough, Evander. You can stop now.'

The child was there again, looking at her out of trusting eyes. 'Can I, Ellie?'

'Aye.' She tugged on the arm she held. 'Stand up now. Come on. I'll help you.'

He stumbled as they reached their feet. As Ellie put a hand on his chest to steady him, he glanced down at her and quite visibly became once more the Evander she knew and cared for, as though he'd just that moment stepped back inside his body.

'All right?' she murmured.

His speech was slurred with pain and blood and God knew what else, but he managed to answer her. 'In the very loosest sense of that expression.'

Ellie sent up a silent prayer of thanks. If he could still come up with a smart-aleck comment at a moment like this it looked as if he *was* going to be all right. As soon as they had moved away, James Tait pulled himself up so he was sitting with his back to one of the columns that supported the first-floor gallery. His wife kneeled down beside him.

'James, darling, are you all right?'

'I will be,' he said. He pointed a condemning finger at Evander, standing with his arm draped heavily about Ellie's shoulders. 'Once that boy has been locked up. He went for me, Angela. For no reason whatsoever. He's unstable – I've always said that.'

Evander laughed. 'I've never felt more sane than I do tonight.'

Angela Tait's face was a picture of bewildered horror. 'And can you give us any explanation for what you've done?'

Ellie could feel the solid thump of his heart, gradually slowing down to a normal speed after the exertions of the last ten minutes. She could feel more than that.

It was all there beneath her fingers: the anguish of his lonely childhood; the pain of all the beatings he'd endured; the mental torment of the constant belittling. She could feel something else too: the essential goodness of him, that goodness that meant he did have scruples about tearing the veils from Angela Tait's face.

'You'd better call the police, Mother; have me arrested.' He smiled down at Ellie. 'Maybe Frank Rafferty and I can share a cell.'

'He has gone mad!' That was Phoebe again.

'No police,' James Tait rasped. 'We need a doctor. First to sedate him and then to get him admitted to Gartnavel.'

Another layer of horror added itself to Angela Tait's face. 'Gartnavel?' she breathed. 'Not that, James, surely?'

Sitting grimly on a hill in secluded grounds above Great Western Road, few people knew what went on within the walls of the sprawling Victorian asylum. That ignorance had always bred fear.

'The doctor,' James Tait repeated. 'Send the girl for the doctor.'

'You need his attentions too, James.' Angela's face cleared with the realisation that here was something practical she could do. 'Let's get you through to the drawing room for a brandy. That's what you need, a good stiffener.'

As the thought flitted through Ellie's mind that brandy had, in a manner of speaking, started this whole thing off, Angela Tait looked across at her. 'You heard Mr Tait, Ellie. Go and fetch Dr Boyd.'

Evander still had his arm about her shoulders. There was as much of his blood on her as there was on him, and whether she was holding him up or it was the other way round was a moot point. 'Oh, for God's sake! Can't Phoebe bloody do it?'

It was a measure of how much Angela Tait's comfortable world had tilted on its axis that she didn't react to her kitchenmaid not only answering her back but also swearing at her. 'Yes,' she said vaguely, 'you go for the doctor, Phoebe. You know it's not far. Come on, James, let's get you that brandy.'

Ellie heard the front door swing shut behind Phoebe and mentally kicked herself. She had no idea how easy or hard it was to put someone in a mental hospital. She only knew that James Tait was a hugely influential local businessman and that Dr Boyd had never impressed her as having much of a backbone. She only knew that folk said once you went into Gartnavel you never came out of it. She only knew that she and Evander didn't stand a chance of being believed against everyone whom James Tait could line up on his side. As she led Evander through to the kitchen her brain was racing.

When they got there, she pulled out one of the chairs and gently pushed him down into it before moving to the refrigerator to get some ice. She grabbed a cloth, poured the ice into it and twisted it into a parcel.

'Here. Tilt your head back and hold this against your nose. I'll be back in five minutes.'

Their luck held. Leaving the house by the back door, they made it down to the timber yard in the nick of time. Ewen MacLean and his crew weren't very far away from casting off. Belying his maturity, the captain leaped nimbly from the deck of the *Torosay* when he saw them, and strode along the towpath to meet them.

'What the hell's happened to the laddie?'

'His father,' Ellie said simply. 'It's been like that for years. Captain MacLean, I'm so sorry to ask you when I know you're hurrying home for your daughter's wedding but can you please take Evander with you? It's the only way I can think of to get him away and to keep him safe. It's all right, nobody saw us leave the house.'

Ewen MacLean brushed that aside. Nor did he ask one single question. He simply reached for the holdall Ellie was carrying. 'I've to call in at Greenock the morn. We'll take him to the doctor there and see if his nose is broken and what's to be done about it. Ice externally and whisky internally should give him some comfort until then.'

'Oh, Captain MacLean!' Tears of gratitude rose in Ellie's eyes. 'Thank you! Thank you so very, very much!'

He laid a hand on her heaving shoulders. 'You'll have to say your farewells quickly, lass.' He walked back towards the *Torosay*, allowing them some privacy.

'Ellie,' Evander said brokenly, 'I can't leave you to cope with all of this on your own . . .'

As though she were handling the most delicate piece of porcelain, she took his battered face between her two hands. 'You can't stay. You heard what your father said. He'd be perfectly prepared to ruin your life. We know that.'

'What about your life?'

'My life?' A smile touched her trembling mouth. 'Don't you worry about me. I'll get out of here too.'

'I'll come back for you!' he said desperately.

'You bloody better had.' She slipped an envelope into the pocket of his jacket. She had tried to do it without him noticing but the noise of paper rustling and coins clinking was unmistakable.

'No!' he protested, trying to get his hand into his pocket while she held his forearm and prevented him from doing exactly that. 'I can't take your savings, Ellie. What if they give you the sack?'

'I'll have no trouble getting another job. There's a servant problem, hadn't you heard? I'll go to Granny Mitchell if they throw me out tonight.'

'I can't take your money—'

'Pay me back the next time we meet. Now go!'

Ellie watched until the *Torosay* rounded the bend in the canal and went out of sight, standing as still as a statue until she was absolutely certain she could no longer hear it puffing its way along to Clydebank. When she couldn't distinguish the faintest sound she sat down abruptly on one of the capstans to which the puffer had been moored. As though she no longer had the strength to remain on her feet.

Chapter 19

Looking considerably healthier than she had done six weeks before, Aileen Drummond slapped a brown envelope on to the kitchen table. 'Mail for you.'

Busy chopping vegetables for soup, Ellie looked up, one name springing to her lips. 'Evander?' she whispered.

'Not unless there's a typewriter on the *Torosay*. Glasgow postmark and official-looking.' The cook's brown eyes were soft with sympathy.

On the terrible night that had culminated in Evander's departure, Ellie and Aileen Drummond had sought and found comfort in one other. Returning to a dark and quiet Bellevue, Ellie had sat on the edge of the cook's bed and spilled out the story of what had happened downstairs and that Evander had left the house. Horribly distressed but still conscious of the need to protect him until he was safely away, she had ended her tale abruptly, offering no details of where and how he had gone.

'Tell me the rest when you're ready, Ellie,' Aileen had said. 'But only if you want to.' She had reached for Ellie's hand and they had sat together like that for ages.

In the days that followed, it had been Aileen who had persuaded Ellie not to do anything hasty, like leaving Bellevue. 'Give yourself time to think,' she'd urged.

'That's what I'm going to do.' The cook had also asked Ellie to call her by her first name. 'Nobody else does,' she'd explained sadly. 'Only *him*.'

Preparing herself to resist an interrogation the following morning – and possibly to find herself out on the pavement looking for a new job and a new home – Ellie had found herself subjected to precisely no questions at all. The Taits had dealt with their son's departure from the family home in the same way as they dealt with all unpleasant occurrences. The events of that night were simply to be swept under the carpet and never talked about again.

Stunned, relieved and disgusted all at the same time, Ellie had told Phoebe – who had at least shown some interest in her brother's fate – that Evander had gone off somewhere he would be safe. She had wondered afterwards if she knew that for a fact, or if she only hoped for it. She'd had no word either from him or from Captain MacLean.

Wiping her fingers on the cloth that lay crumpled on the table next to the chopping board, Ellie reached for the letter and for the knife that Aileen had set down beside it. *Glasgow postmark and official-looking.* Could it be something to do with Frank?

The previous week, slowly emerging from the awful numbness that had surrounded her since Evander had left, she had wondered whether she ought to write to her childhood friend and playmate. She didn't know if people in prison were allowed to receive letters.

Wondering if he might have got permission to write to her – perhaps the envelopes of such letters had to be typed by some official – Ellie inserted the knife under the flap, slit her mail open and drew out a small booklet. She read out the title printed on its front cover.

' "Glasgow and West of Scotland College of Domestic Science, Prospectus for 1929–1930." Oh aye,' she said vaguely. 'There was this girl at Craigmarloch—'

She broke off, remembering that sunlit day which seemed now as if it had happened a hundred years ago. Thinking of what Aileen Drummond had been enduring while she had been losing herself in Evander's arms, Ellie glanced across the table.

'Don't worry,' Aileen said grimly, responding to the all-too-readable expression on Ellie's face. 'I'm not that fragile. Were you thinking of going on a course, then?' She pulled out a chair and sat down.

'Och, I don't know,' Ellie said, doing the same thing. She pushed the chopping board out the way, throwing the cloth over the vegetables. 'Maybe I was dreaming. The girl I met at The Bungalow thought there were part-time courses I could go on. One day a week or evening classes or something.'

'Let's see what you could do, then. Is there an index?'

There was. It sent Ellie first to 'Training for Domestic Service'. She read it out. ' "Course for girls wishing to train for domestic service." You've got to be over sixteen, it's continuous over two terms and includes practical instruction in "cookery, laundry work, housework, serving, mending etc.".'

'No,' Aileen said, 'that's not right for you. Try something else.' She put her elbows on the table, made a steeple of her hands and tapped her fingers against her lips.

Ellie went back to the index. ' "Cookery Practice Lessons" and "Cookery Demonstration Lessons". Individual or a course of ten. Every morning from ten till one, Wednesday afternoons from two till five, Friday evenings from six till nine.'

'That's more like it. You'd want to do the practice lessons rather than attend the demonstrations, although it would have to be the daytime classes. I can't do without you on Friday evenings.'

'No,' Ellie agreed, head still bent over the prospectus. 'The practice lessons are split into different courses: "artisan cookery, vegetarian, household, high-class, confectionery lessons, cakes and scones and sickroom cookery". High-class is the most expensive, three pounds ten shillings for the course of ten.'

'Is high-class cookery what you fancy doing?'

'Maybe,' Ellie said, watching as Aileen rose from the table, picked up the kettle and walked over to the sink to fill it. 'Och, I don't know,' she said listlessly. 'Three pounds ten is a lot of money and you've probably taught me an awful lot of this already.'

'I hope I have.' Aileen came back to the table and set down two cups, saucers and side plates. 'Although,' she said, 'it wouldn't hurt you to have some sort of certificate. Do you get that with the practice lessons?'

'Don't think so,' Ellie said after a closer examination of the information.

'They must do something which gives you a qualification, though. See what else you can find.'

By the time Aileen came back from the pantry with one of the cake tins, Ellie had found the entry describing a 'Cook's Certificate'. ' "The course includes practice and demonstration lessons in artisan, household and high-class cookery, and in cooking dinners, arranging menus for luncheons, dinners, suppers, etc." '

'That sounds good. A well-rounded course and you get a certificate at the end of it.'

'It sounds great,' Ellie said, doing her best to respond to Aileen's enthusiasm. She read the small print at the head of the entry, and her voice flattened. 'But it's not going to work. You have to attend every day for three months.' Her face fell still further when another piece of information caught her eye. ' "Fee fourteen pounds." We can forget that one, then. I don't have fourteen pounds.'

Aileen proffered the cake tin. 'You might have done if you hadn't sent a certain person off with all of your savings.'

Ellie's head snapped up. 'How did you know that?'

Aileen gave her a look that recalled some of the glowers Ellie had been on the receiving end of in the past. 'Because you're a woman. And women are stupid. Especially when it comes to men. That's how I know. Tell me some more about this Cook's Certificate.'

Ellie dropped her eyes to the prospectus. 'Not much more to tell. If you pass it you can go on to do an advanced certificate or a cordon bleu certificate. That takes a mere year,' she added drily, 'and costs thirty-six pounds. Since I can't even afford the time or the money to do the Cook's Certificate, is there any point in considering the subject any further?'

Angry with herself for having almost got excited about something that was so far out of reach, Ellie closed the prospectus and tossed it on to the table. The force with which she flung it would have sent it skidding down to the foot of the smooth pine if Aileen's hand hadn't shot out and grabbed it. 'Would you like to do this?'

'I can't afford the fees. How would I get the time off anyway?'

'Both of those objections could be easily overcome. Answer my question. Would you like to do this Cook's Certificate?'

Ellie's mouth set in a firm line. 'I can't take your money, Aileen. I *won't* take your money.'

'It wouldn't be my money.'

'Oh, no,' Ellie said. 'I'll work for my wages but I'm not taking any other money from *him*.'

'Don't be daft, Ellie. Besides, having a professionally trained and qualified cook in the house will be a benefit to the family. Especially after I leave.'

'Oh,' Ellie said. 'You've made up your mind, then?'

'I'm going at Christmas. I met my family in Glasgow two weeks ago and they've graciously consented to take the black sheep of the family back into the fold.'

Ellie frowned. 'It sounds as though you're going to be there on sufferance.'

Taking her by surprise, Aileen grinned widely. 'Oh, my sister was so far up there on her high horse I was surprised she didn't get dizzy and fall off.' She raised a derisive brown eyebrow. 'My brother, on the other hand, was willing to confess that the hotel's suffered from a succession of disastrous cooks over the past couple of years. They need me to restore its reputation for good food. In return I've negotiated a good salary, a generous amount of time off and a good deal of privacy. I'm taking over the old lodge-keeper's cottage.'

'Well,' Ellie said stoutly, 'if they want to be known for their good food, you're the woman they need. There's absolutely no doubt about that. I'll miss you, though.'

'I'll miss you too. But you'll come and visit me. We'll go for healthy hikes through the hills and paint water-colours.'

Ellie laughed. She liked this new Aileen Drummond. 'Don't think I'd be any great shakes with a paintbrush.'

'You never know till you try,' came the blithe response. 'As I said, I'm not going till Christmas. That'll give you time to do this course.' Aileen tapped the prospectus with her fingertips.

Ellie gave her a reluctant smile. 'Don't give up, do you?'

The cook leaned forward over the table. 'Look, Ellie. Once you've got a qualification you'll be able to get out of this place and make your own fresh start. I know you're very upset about Evander at the moment—'

'But I'm young and I'll get over it?' Ellie suggested bitterly. 'That's what my brother says.'

'I wasn't going to say that at all. Your brother's a fool. Which is why he and Phoebe suit each other right down to the ground.' As Ellie started in surprise, Aileen gave her an old-fashioned look. 'I'm not blind, you know. Or so completely wrapped up in myself I don't notice other people.' Her voice softened. 'I also know that love can hurt. Whatever age you are. I wasn't much older than you when I first met James Tait.'

'That was during the war?'

'Yes. My parents had turned the house into a hotel before it. During it they did their patriotic duty and transformed it into a convalescent home for wounded officers. He was one of them.' Aileen's voice grew softer still. 'He was so handsome. Troubled, though. Deeply troubled. I felt so sorry for all of them but there was something about him which clutched at my heartstrings. A feeling that he needed me.' She looked across the table at Ellie. 'Much the same as you felt for Evander, I imagine.'

'Maybe,' Ellie said. Unwilling to allow any similarity between Evander and his father, she'd been unable to deny a jolt of recognition at that 'deeply troubled'.

'I'll never know what he saw in me,' Aileen continued. 'I was always the ugly duckling of my family. Too tall, too big, too clumsy. I spent my life in the kitchens with our cook. I learned everything I know from her. James Tait added another dimension to my life.' Her smile was heartbreaking. 'He made me feel loved and graceful and desired.'

'But he was married even then?' Ellie asked, thinking that he must have been not only married but also the father of a young Phoebe and Evander.

'Oh yes,' Aileen agreed, 'he was married. He'd been to hell and back but his precious wife couldn't cope with his nightmares. They disrupted the household, that's what she said.'

'Hear no evil, see no evil, speak no evil,' murmured Ellie.

'What?'

'Nothing. Go on.'

'The rest you know. I disgraced my family by running off with a married man.'

'Did you think he would marry you?'

'At first,' Aileen said. 'He said he'd divorce her once the children had grown up. I was naïve enough to believe it.' She smiled that sad smile again. 'I wanted to keep the baby, you know. I could have gone away somewhere, brought it up by myself. He could have visited us now and again. When it came down to it, that would have *inconvenienced* him.' She said the word with infinite distaste. 'Deprived him of what he wants. So I allowed him to persuade me to go through with the operation.' She looked at Ellie. 'I cannot tell you how much I regret that.'

'Oh, Aileen,' Ellie said. She reached across the table for her hand.

The cook gave it to her. She sniffed. 'I'm all right.'

'Of course you are.'

'Of course I'm not. But I will be. Once I'm on my own and independent, with no need for any man to pay for the roof over my head. Take your lesson from me, Ellie. Take your lesson from me.'

Ellie paused to check the map on the back of the prospectus. She had hopped off the tram opposite Kelvinbridge underground. So now she thought, tracing it with her finger, she had to cross Great Western Road, walk past the subway station and turn right into Park Road. So far, so good. If she managed to reach the other side of this busy thoroughfare alive she'd be fine.

It was teeming with buses, trams, horse-drawn coal and milk carts – not to mention what seemed like hundreds of pedestrians weaving erratic paths between all of those vehicles. A carter yelled a protest as two middle-aged housewives with shopping bags in the crooks of their arms stepped out in front of his slow-moving horse. The beast reared back, nostrils flaring.

'Ladies!' the man pleaded. 'Mind ma cuddy! He's a sensitive animal!'

A tram bell clanged as a young man stepped nimbly over the lines in front of it. Its driver was less polite than the carter. He leaned out of the front of his car and shook his fist at the lad. 'Ah cannae go round ye, ye great bloody gomerel! Have you no' even got the brains ye were born wi'?'

'I've enough to know that a person could grow older standing waiting to cross this road,' the young man retorted. ' "He who hesitates is lost",' he quoted cheerfully to Ellie as he took a long step on to the pavement and went on his way.

And she who doesn't hesitate ends up under the hoofs of a Clydesdale, and what a loss that would be to the culinary future of Scotland, Ellie thought, laughing. Sliding the prospectus into her roomy shoulder bag, she concentrated on finding a gap in the traffic.

A good five minutes older, she marched purposefully along Park Road, hoping she looked as if she knew where she was going. That the wee map in the prospectus indicated the College's position in Park Drive by means of a big black rectangle was fine. She wished there had been a photograph as well. She didn't want to look like a complete eejit on her first day by having no idea on which side of the building the front door was located.

She had enrolled for the Cook's Certificate by post, Aileen Drummond supplying her with a cheque signed by James Tait for her fees: fourteen pounds for the course itself and five shillings for the general registration fee. Since it was obligatory to take lunch in the college, Aileen had wanted to get the further five bob a week that would cost from him too, but Ellie had insisted she would pay for her lunch herself. She was prepared to be beholden to her employer only as much as she needed to be.

She wasn't sure if she was going to join the Students' Union, optional if you were only taking a short course. Aileen was doing her best to nag her into it. Ellie felt she would be leaving the cook to cope on her own at Bellevue for long enough each week without swanning off to play hockey and tennis with the young ladies who went to the Dough School to come out as teachers of domestic science.

Busily ironing and starching the white overall and cap Ellie was obliged to wear for her course and which were now neatly folded in her shoulder bag, Aileen had pursed her lips and said nothing. Ellie recognised the look. By hook or by crook, Aileen Drummond would see to it that her protégée got involved in the social life of the college.

Swithering briefly as to which direction to take round a large school set like a tall island in the middle of its playground, Ellie shaded her eyes against the sunshine of the warm September morning. Could the college be that large and handsome red sandstone building on the other side of Woodlands Road? It had to be. A stream of young women were heading for what was, to Ellie's considerable relief, unmistakably the front door.

The entrance hall was full of people who all seemed to know exactly where they were going. Ellie approached a middle-aged lady who was standing a few steps from the bottom of a wide staircase.

'Please, ma'am,' she began politely, 'I'm starting the Cook's Certificate this morning and I'm not sure where to go.'

'Well, young lady, you might try perusing that blackboard over there.'

'Oh,' Ellie said. 'I missed that.'

'What with everything being so new to you, I expect.'

'Yes,' she said gratefully, glad that having failed to see the rather large blackboard propped on an equally large easel didn't mean she had failed her course already.

'You're rather young to be doing the Cook's Certificate, aren't you?'

'Begging your pardon, ma'am, but nothing in the prospectus says you have to be a certain age to do it. For some of the other courses, yes. I should know,' she confided. 'I've read it from cover to cover about a hundred times!'

A smile crept into the corners of the lady's mouth. 'Indeed? But at your age might you not have been better to do our Training for Domestic Service course?'

Ellie shook her head. The force with which she did it almost loosened her little brown hat. She clutched at it to keep it on. 'I've been in service for the past two years, ma'am. As a kitchenmaid under a very good cook-housekeeper. She's taught me an awful lot already.'

'I'm delighted to hear it,' the lady said crisply. 'What we advocate here is, of course, the scientific approach.'

'I know that, ma'am. And I want to learn everything the College can teach me.'

The lady asked Ellie her name. 'Your ambitions lie within domestic service, Miss Douglas?'

Ellie took a deep breath. *Nothing wrong with having a dream* . . . 'No, ma'am,' she said firmly. 'One day I want to run my own restaurant.'

She could have laughed at her, a girl who looked no older than her sixteen years, whose accent indicated her humble origins and who was currently working as a kitchenmaid. Eyes narrowing in curiosity, she asked a question instead. 'What type of food do you intend serving at this restaurant?'

'Good food, ma'am,' Ellie said passionately.

The lady gave her the broadest of smiles, leaned past her and beckoned to a young woman walking up the staircase. 'Miss Dunlop, this young lady is starting the three months' Cook's Certificate course today. Would you show her how to proceed, please? Good luck, my dear,' she said to Ellie, 'I hope you'll have a very happy and successful time here.'

'Well, hello there!' Seeing Ellie's puzzled look, the girl who'd been instructed to act as her guide pointed at her all-encompassing white cap. 'It's this thing. Renders us completely unrecognisable to even our nearest and dearest. Pray God I don't meet any desirable men while

I look like a cross between a nurse and a nun. You and I met at Craigmarloch, remember? I'm Anne Dunlop.'

'Oh aye,' Ellie said. 'Thank you very much for getting them to send me the prospectus. Oh!' She had spotted another familiar face. It was wreathed in smiles and it belonged to the Honourable Miss Lesley Matheson.

'Well, hello, Miss Douglas! Fancy meeting you here! But I don't know your friend.'

'So you're training to be a teacher of domestic science,' Lesley Matheson said warmly after Anne Dunlop had introduced herself. 'How I envy you doing something worthwhile with your life! I'm on what the newspapers call "the Bride's Course".' She rolled her eyes at the other two girls. 'Would you believe it? It's the only thing my parents and my beloved would agree to.'

'I heard you were getting married,' Ellie said. 'A winter wedding, isn't it?'

'January of next year,' Lesley agreed. 'After that we're off to see the world. What course are you doing, Miss Douglas?' When Ellie told her, she looked thoughtful. 'That sounds interesting. I wonder if I might be able to transfer.'

Anne Dunlop indicated the lady to whom Ellie had been speaking earlier, now standing in a corner of the entrance hall. 'Go and ask Miss Melvin. She's the principal.'

'Oh,' Ellie said faintly, watching Lesley Matheson run downstairs. 'I didn't realise I was talking to the high heid yin of the whole college.'

'Well,' her companion said, her eyes also on the departing Lesley, 'you seem to mix in rarefied circles yourself. I take it she's Miss Matheson of Mathesons the shipbuilders?'

'Yes. She is.'

'Playing at it, is she?' asked Anne Dunlop. 'I mean, wanting to get her Cook's Certificate and *do something useful with her life*.' As she mimicked Lesley's cut-glass tones, Ellie frowned.

Spotting Ellie, Anne Dunlop gave her a cheerful wave and indicated a couple of empty seats at her table.

'Over there,' Ellie said to Lesley Matheson. Her hands being fully occupied by her lunch tray, she indicated the direction with a lift of her chin.

'I'm not sure the invitation extends to me.'

'Och, of course it does!' Confidently leading the way, Ellie wasn't nearly so sure about that once she had reached the table. There was definitely an uncomfortable atmosphere as she and Miss Matheson sat down. She was wondering how best to accomplish the introductions when Anne Dunlop beat her to it, surveying Lesley Matheson with a none-too-friendly air.

'How should we address you?' she asked, her voice very dry. 'Do you require us to use the "Honourable" at all times?'

The other girl looked her straight in the eye. 'I'd much prefer it if you called me Lesley. And there's absolutely no need to curtsy. My mother's still inclined to expect that sort of deference from the peasantry but personally I'm beginning to find it a little old-fashioned.'

Everyone froze. Ellie clapped her hands over her mouth. It was too late. The laugh had got out. Anne Dunlop looked at her. Then she looked at Lesley. 'I deserved that.' She reached across the table to shake hands. 'Hello, Lesley. Welcome to the Dough School. Call me Anne.'

'First names all round then?' Ellie suggested.

She saw the tiny frown between Lesley Matheson's

beautifully arched eyebrows. The privileged Miss Matheson had been scrupulous about addressing her as 'Miss Douglas' ever since they had first met. Ellie had always liked her for it but they were meeting here on a different playing field.

Tucking a strand of her bright hair under the voluminous cap, she set about reassuring the young woman whose social status was so dizzyingly high above her own. 'While we're here learning together we should all be equals, don't you agree?'

Lesley Matheson's face cleared. She stuck out her hand. 'I agree absolutely. Hello, Ellie.'

Ellie smiled into her eyes. 'Hello, Lesley.'

Chapter 20

'Tell us some more about the wedding of the year, Lesley. How many bridesmaids are you up to now?'

'About a hundred and fifty at the last count,' Lesley responded gloomily. 'Few of whom are actually known to me. It's the same with the guests. Since our family's only had a title for a mere three generations, my dear mama is mightily impressed by the fact that Lachie and his people are related to half the noble and ancient families in Scotland. She's insisted we invite all of them.' Her lovely brow furrowed as she surveyed the young women gathered in her sitting room. 'Which means I can't invite a lot of my real friends.'

'Excuses, excuses,' Anne Dunlop said blithely.

With three others, she was ensconced on a big squashy sofa draped with ancient Paisley shawls and piled high with cushions in a myriad of contrasting colours and fabrics. Lesley had invited everyone for afternoon tea at her flat in Otago Street in Hillhead, a short walk from the Dough School. Her Wednesday at-homes were becoming regular occurrences.

Both delighted and amused to hear that Ellie and the Honourable Miss Lesley Matheson were on first-name terms and fast becoming good friends, Aileen Drummond had insisted Ellie should visit Otago Street whenever she was invited. Of course she could manage without her for another couple of hours each week.

Ellie was currently sitting cross-legged on Miss Matheson's floor, on top of the jewel-bright Moroccan rug that covered the floorboards between the sofa and the cast-iron and Dutch-tiled Victorian fireplace.

Anne Dunlop danced her fingers along the top of her head. 'We know we're not up to scratch socially, don't we, Ellie?'

'Indeed we do,' Ellie said cheerfully. 'But we'll come to Glasgow Cathedral to see you in all your finery anyway.'

'And after we've watched you emerge from the great west door we'll fight all the other street urchins for the coins at the scramble!'

Watching Lesley do her best to join in with the laughter that greeted that sally, Ellie felt a pang of sympathy for her. She was obviously miserably embarrassed at not being able to invite the friends she'd made at the Dough School to dance at her wedding. Ellie couldn't imagine that was something that would worry Lesley's fiancé.

The young man had attended two of Lesley's at-homes, quite obviously because she had persuaded him to. Oh, his manners had been impeccable. He was highly intelligent and in possession of a considerable amount of charm. Well-schooled in the nuances of social behaviour after two and a half years at Bellevue, Ellie hadn't missed the hint of frost.

To say that Lachlan Hamilton-Stewart – 'a name to conjure with,' as Anne Dunlop had murmured out of Lesley's earshot – wasn't too pleased that his fiancée was mixing with young women who had to work for a living might have been a bit of an understatement. His reaction to being formally introduced to a kitchenmaid had been as clear as a newly washed window.

Nor had Ellie much cared for the way he referred to the Otago Street flat as 'the hovel'. With five spacious and high-ceilinged rooms, a huge kitchen and bathroom, its own back garden and handsome door on to the street, it was very far from being that. Since, however, it was blindingly obvious that Lesley Matheson was madly in love with her 'Lachie', Ellie had grudgingly decided that there must be some good in him.

Enjoying the fire burning in the grate – it was November now and the days were growing both shorter and colder – she slid one arm around the greyhound Lesley had inherited from her mother a few weeks before. When Ellie had enquired how Lady Matheson could bear to part with such a gentle and good-natured beast, Lesley had drily commented that greyhounds were no longer so modish a fashion accessory as they once had been.

Her mother had named the dog Diaghilev. Maintaining she would feel a complete fool calling *that* out in the middle of Kelvingrove Park, Lesley had invited her new friends to come up with a more reasonable name. So far nobody had managed to find one that everybody liked.

'Don't worry about not inviting me, Lesley,' Ellie said. 'I could hardly go to a wedding my employers are attending. Mrs Tait would have kittens.'

'Yes,' Anne Dunlop said, 'she might have to show some manners towards you and address you as *Miss* Douglas. I hate the way servants are addressed by their surnames. It always sounds so rude to me.'

'Oh,' Ellie said, sending a smile across to Lesley in acknowledgement that she had never committed that particular crime, 'the Taits have always called me by my first name. Although,' she added thoughtfully, 'I'm not sure if that's really any better.'

'Because it doesn't work the other way?' Lesley asked.

'Mmm,' Ellie replied, thinking about it. 'Mrs Tait would have a second litter of kittens if she knew I call Phoebe by her first name when we're alone together. I could hardly call her mother "Angela", though. She's older than me, for a start, and I suppose calling me Ellie is a lot friendlier than barking out "Douglas".' She turned to the dog. 'I mean, how would you like it if I barked that out at you, boy?'

'That's it!' Anne Dunlop cried. 'Douglas the Dug. It's a perfect name for him!'

Lesley looked doubtful but agreed to abide by the democratic vote which followed. The show of hands was otherwise unanimous. Ellie sent her newly christened namesake into a state of ecstasy by rubbing him gently behind his silky ears. If Douglas the Dug had been a cat, he'd have been purring.

'What's the story about Evander Tait, Ellie?' asked one of the girls. 'There seems to be a bit of a mystery there.'

Douglas growled a protest as the warm human fingers stopped moving. Glasgow's a village: the old adage was all too true. The girl who'd posed the question came from Bearsden and had been one of Phoebe's regular tennis partners when they were both at school. She wasn't the only person Ellie had met at the Dough School who was acquainted with the Tait family.

'There's no mystery. He and his father had a fight and Evander's left home.' She'd perfected that answer over the last couple of months. *A fight*. Everyone had taken that as meaning an argument, not the brutal physical contest it had really been.

'Never darken my door again, was it?' asked Anne Dunlop. 'Where did Evander go?'

Ellie shrugged. 'How would I know?'

Anne frowned. 'I thought you and he were quite close—'

Lesley reached for the book lying on the small square table that sat in her bay window. 'This is great, isn't it? All the old Scots recipes. I bet you know how to cook loads of these, Ellie.'

'Y-yes,' she said vaguely. 'I knew most of the ones that were read out earlier.'

'Let's have another one, then. Oh, girls, listen to this!' Lesley cleared her throat and began speaking in precise and careful tones. ' "Powsowdie, or Sheep's Head Broth, Meg Dod's Recipe. Choose a large, fat, young, head." '

Someone giggled. 'My intended would fit that description.'

' "When carefully singed by the blacksmith, soak it and the singed trotters for a night, if you please, in lukewarm water. Take out the glassy part of the eyes—" '

A succession of disgusted groans ran round the room.

' "—scrape the head and trotters, and brush till perfectly clean and white; then split the head with a cleaver, and lay aside the brains—" '

'Yee-uch!'

'Enough, Lesley!' called Anne.

Another girl put her hand over her mouth, miming being sick.

Miss Matheson looked up from the book, the picture of innocence. 'You don't want to hear about cleaning "the nostrils and gristly parts"? Or that some people prefer "the head of a ram to that of a wether"? Or that it's important to boil your head – if you'll pardon the expression – slowly and for about four hours?'

'No!' The word came in a chorus of young female voices.

'Fancy walking a bit of your journey?' Lesley asked as she followed Ellie out into Otago Street. 'Douglas – and I'm sure I'm going to feel just as daft calling *that* out – needs his exercise but it's getting a bit dark to go to the park.'

'All right,' Ellie said, turning the collar of her coat up against the damp chill of the November afternoon. As they turned the corner into Great Western Road Lesley slipped the gloved hand that wasn't holding the dog's leash through the crook of Ellie's arm. 'May I ask you a question?'

'That's always a dangerous question in itself,' Ellie responded, slanting her a smile.

Lesley laughed. 'You're very mature for your age, Miss Douglas. Which I say from all the lofty height of my own twenty-one years.'

'Ask your question,' Ellie said, liking her.

Lesley wasted no time. 'Everyone at the college talks all the time about what they want to do when they leave – their ambitions. You never say a word about yours. I can't believe a girl as bright and as talented as you are doesn't have any.'

They were walking past a long row of shops, their windows glowing cheerfully against the increasing darkness of the afternoon. Interspersed with swathes of artfully draped red and gold fabric, bottles of perfume and cologne were on display in a chemist's shop. At the baker's next door, a beautifully decorated Christmas cake and a carefully lettered card telling you how much it cost and how you might order it took pride of place.

'I've got ambitions,' Ellie said.

'Care to share them with Douglas and me?'

'Do you think he's really interested?'

'Trust me,' Lesley said. 'He's riveted.'

Ellie took a deep breath. 'I want to run a restaurant. And I want a home of my own. In my dreams it's beginning to look a lot like your flat.'

Lesley stopped dead, provoking a muttered curse from the man walking behind them. As he pointedly walked round the two girls, Lesley looked at Ellie. 'The world's ill-divided, isn't it? You work so hard and have very little. I do practically nothing and have so much.'

'The world is ill-divided. But I don't begrudge you having what you've got.'

'No,' Lesley agreed, 'you're not that kind of a person.' They began walking again. 'So,' she asked as they approached the tram stop, 'are you going to look for a job in a restaurant when you get your Cook's Certificate?'

'Don't you mean *if*?'

'*When*. You cook like an angel.'

'So do you.'

Lesley smiled. 'Walk to the next one?'

'Sure,' Ellie said. As they stood waiting to cross the busy junction between the top of Byres Road and the foot of Queen Margaret Drive, she glanced at a newspaper billboard. 'Financial crisis deepens. More suicides in New York and London.' She shivered. 'How awful it must be to feel such despair that you don't want to live any more. I'm glad I don't have any stocks and shares to worry about.'

'Maybe not,' Lesley said grimly, 'but the Crash is going to affect everybody in this country sooner or later.'

'You think so?' Ellie asked, surprised.

'I'm afraid that's the way our modern world works.

When one person sneezes, everyone catches the cold.'

They were walking past the elegant façade of the houses in Grosvenor Terrace before Ellie answered Lesley's previous question. 'I've been thinking about applying for work in a hotel.'

'But that's not exactly what you want to do. And I believe you told me last week that living where you work has its drawbacks.'

'Just a few,' Ellie murmured. 'But I'd pick a hotel with a good restaurant and that way I'd get my accommodation thrown in too.'

'You couldn't afford to rent a room somewhere?'

'Not yet. At my age I can't expect very much in the way of a wage.' She grimaced. 'Probably much worse than I get paid at Bellevue.'

'I could lend you some money.'

'No you couldn't. I've had enough of being beholden to people.'

'Is that a problem about leaving the Taits? They paid for your father's funeral, didn't they?'

Ellie looked at Lesley in surprise, wondering how she knew that. Then she remembered. 'Of course, you were there that day I came up to Bellevue asking for a job. I must have seemed so gauche!'

'You seemed real,' Lesley said. 'I envied that.'

'*You* envied me?'

'Don't sound so incredulous. *Is* that a problem about leaving Bellevue?'

'My brother Malcolm thinks it is. I don't. Not any more.' Uncomfortable though she was that James Tait was paying her college fees, as far as Ellie was concerned that other, larger debt had been discharged long ago.

It wasn't that she now knew how insignificant the cost of the funeral had been to the Taits. Not everything could be bought and paid for in pounds, shillings and pence. There were emotional costs too. She had paid plenty of those. As had Evander.

'Here's your stop,' Lesley said.

Ellie glanced down at the dog. 'Has Douglas had enough exercise?'

'By the time we get back to Otago Street he will have. He doesn't need as much as you might think. Greyhounds are bred for bursts of speed, not twenty-mile hikes.' Lesley looked along the road. Darkness had fallen now and the streetlights had come on. 'No sign of a tram yet.' She turned back to Ellie. 'Listen. You're not in any kind of . . . trouble, are you?'

'Trouble?' Ellie queried.

Seen in the sickly yellow glow of the lamp above their heads, Lesley's face took on a distinctly embarrassed expression. 'I wondered if it might have been you that Evander and his father fought about.'

'Oh no,' Ellie said, realising what Lesley meant, 'it wasn't anything like that.'

'You're sure? I would help you, you know. If you were in trouble.'

'I'm not,' Ellie said definitely. 'I can assure you of that.'

'But you and Evander were . . .' Once again Lesley hesitated, searching for the right word. She chose the one Anne Dunlop had used earlier. 'Close?'

'You could say that.'

'I'm sorry, Ellie. I really am.'

'I'll live.' She swallowed the lump in her throat, pushed back the ache of the loss of Evander and dropped a hand on to Douglas's smooth head. 'Not much choice, is there?'

'What *was* the argument about?'

'Don't ask me that, Lesley. Other people's secrets, you know? Not mine to tell.'

The other girl's intent expression relaxed. 'You know something, Ellie? You're a very nice person. Here's your tram coming now. Listen,' she said as it drew nearer, 'if you won't take any money from me, will you at least take my flat?'

'What?' Poised to board the tram, Ellie turned and stared at her. Had something just gone wrong with her hearing?

'Why don't you take over Otago Street while Lachie and I are on honeymoon? We're going to be away for over a year.' Lesley pulled a face. 'The Idle Rich, that's us. On you hop.'

Ellie climbed aboard, took a firm hold of the pole and turned to look back in astonishment at Lesley, standing on the pavement smiling up at her. 'You'd be doing me a favour, honestly you would. My parents have no interest in the place.' She grimaced. 'Why would they when they've got a Greek Thomson villa in Glasgow and that hideous Victorian monstrosity down at Kilcreggan?' She clapped Douglas on the neck. 'And you could look after this mutt for me. Otherwise he'll have to go back to my parents' house and my mother doesn't really want him any more. You wouldn't do that to the poor creature, would you? It might give him one of these Freudian complexes you hear so much about.'

'You've struck me dumb,' Ellie said faintly.

As the conductor rang the bell and the tramcar glided away from the stop, Lesley called after her, 'Think about it, Ellie. Think about it.'

All through a foggy November and into a sleety December Ellie did little else but think about Lesley's amazingly generous offer. Typically, she refused to consider the possibility of Ellie paying her any rent, and, of course, she would leave some money behind for the dog's food. Douglas might look like a skinny malinky long-legs but did Ellie have any idea how much a greyhound could eat?

As the year wound down towards Christmas, Ellie worked out the finances of it over and over again in her head. If she was frugal she could last a month, maybe even two, without working. Surely, armed with her Cook's Certificate from the prestigious Glasgow and West of Scotland College of Domestic Science she would be able to find a restaurant job in that time? Once she had it she would save like mad so as to be able to afford a room of her own by the time Lesley and Lachie came back from their extended honeymoon.

Her youth was against her, she knew that. She'd probably have to work as the very humblest washer-upper and floor-sweeper before she'd be allowed anywhere near food. That didn't matter. Once she got in somewhere she could work her way up.

She was indulging in a daydream about saving the day when a chef was suddenly taken ill after eating the wrong kind of mushrooms as she clanked along Great Western Road on the tram on one of the last Saturdays of 1929. There had been a special ceremony at the college that morning to present all who had successfully completed the three-month Cook's Certificate course with their awards.

A group of them had gone out to lunch afterwards, using the occasion to present Lesley with the wedding present they had clubbed together to buy. Typically, Miss Matheson had then insisted on paying the restaurant bill for everybody. Ellie's smile at the memory faded as she looked over at the gloomy spires of the asylum at Gartnavel, sharply defined against the crisp December day, above and behind the skaters on Bingham's Pond. She never passed the place without thinking that Evander might have spent his life locked up in there.

She still hadn't heard from him and kept trying to will him to write before she left Bellevue. In the haste of his departure there had been no time to discuss how they might get in touch with one another but he would surely remember that she was generally the first person to see the mail in the morning. When she left Bellevue she was going to have to rely on Phoebe to intercept the postie for her – not an ideal solution. If Evander wrote soon she would be able to write back giving him her new, if temporary, address in Otago Street.

Ellie stepped down from the tram at Anniesland Cross and walked up Crow Road. As she crossed the old nolly bridge she looked at the new one being built alongside it. You could hardly avoid it. Designed to cope with the increasing amount of road traffic heading to and from the growing suburbs of Bearsden and Milngavie, it was a huge thing. High enough above the canal that smaller craft could pass underneath it, it swung open for larger boats much more easily than the antiquated system that operated the old wooden bridge.

Ellie had a rather large bridge of her own to cross before she left Bellevue. Malcolm was going to hit the roof when he discovered what her plans were. That wouldn't only be because he continued to believe that they both owed a great debt to James Tait. The more selfish reason was that Ellie had always played a vital role as a go-between and passer of messages between him and Phoebe. Mind you, both of them were soon going to have to face up to being separated while Phoebe spent her six months in France.

Spending so much time considering her own future had set Ellie to thinking about Frank Rafferty and his. He was due to be released from prison at the end of March. With considerable relish, Rosalie Mitchell had supplied the information that an extra three months had been added to his sentence because he had taken part in a riot within the gaol.

Dismayed, and bitterly disappointed in him, Ellie had torn up the letter she'd been in the middle of writing. Two weeks ago had come the shocking news that Frank's father had been stabbed in a drunken brawl, bleeding to death on the pavement outside an illegal shebeen. Heart going out to Frank when she heard – via Granny Mitchell this time – that he had applied for but been refused permission to attend the funeral – Ellie had sat down and composed a fresh letter.

Not trusting Marie Rafferty to forward it, she had enlisted the help of the Reverend Hunter. He made enquiries for her and got exactly the right address. She had posted the letter in Glasgow this morning.

Dear Frank,
I was very sorry to hear about your father. Please accept my condolences.

I hope you are well. Since you stood me up for afternoon tea back in the spring I wonder if you'd like to meet me at the same place on my birthday in April? I'll be there at three o'clock and you can tell me all your news and your plans for the future.
With best wishes,
Your friend,
Eleanor Douglas

If he met her at the tearoom, she would spell it out for him. She needed to hear from his own lips exactly what had happened at that dance hall in Partick, and she needed to know what he intended to do with the rest of his life. For the sake of their long friendship she was prepared to give him one last chance.

If he committed himself to turn his back on the violence – and surely he would when it had killed his own father in such a horrible way – she would help him however she could. It had occurred to her that he could stay with her in Otago Street for a few months until he found his feet. That would shock people, she supposed. Daft. There had never been anything like that between her and Frank.

Besides, who would know? Hillhead had the reputation of being quite a bohemian sort of place, populated by artists and writers and folk who were prepared to live and let live. Lesley's home was also a main door flat. You didn't have to care what the people in your building thought about you if you didn't share a close and a common stair with them.

Crunching over the pebbles of Bellevue's drive, Ellie walked round to the back door. She went through the wash house and the scullery, stopping in surprise when she reached the kitchen. Aileen was sitting at the table with her hat and coat on, two suitcases and an assortment of bags on the floor beside her. An older woman, with the sort of face that could turn milk sour, was stirring something at the electric cooker. The atmosphere between her and Aileen Drummond was spiky with mutual dislike. It was the newcomer who spoke first.

'You'll be the kitchenmaid, I expect. Douglas, isn't it? I'm Mrs Rogerson, the new cook. I'd be obliged if you'd take your coat off as soon as possible and start preparing the vegetables for dinner.'

Ellie stared blankly at her. She turned to Aileen for enlightenment.

'New regime,' she said. 'Cook, parlourmaid and housemaid started this morning. I made the mistake of being considerate enough to give three weeks' notice. Funny how easy it's been to find staff after all those years of there being nobody suitable, isn't it? Now you're back I can phone for a taxi. Will you see me off the premises?'

The new cook sniffed. 'The vegetables?'

Ellie looked pityingly at her. 'Bugger the vegetables,' she said.

'I'm sorry to go so abruptly, leave you in the lurch.' They were standing in front of the house, on either side of Aileen's cases and bags. 'When he sprang all these new people on me this morning I felt I couldn't stand being under the same roof as him even for one more day.' The cook's mouth twisted in a bitter smile. 'No reason not to have a full complement of staff now he's no longer creeping up the stairs in the middle of the night.'

'Don't you worry about me,' Ellie said. 'I'll be gone soon myself. Oh, but I'll miss you!'

'You'll come and visit? As often as you like. Whenever you like.' Aileen's bottom lip was trembling. 'I'll even kick a guest out to make room for you!'

'Oh, Aileen!' The two of them embraced over the luggage, hugging each other hard and long. Ellie had to choke back tears before she could speak. 'We've become friends. I could never have imagined that when I first came to work here.'

'I was a bit of a battle-axe, wasn't I?' Aileen turned at the sound of wheels. 'Time to go. Let's not disgrace ourselves in front of the taxi driver.'

'No,' Ellie agreed, picking up one of the cases. 'Have you got everything?'

'I've left some stuff. A few books and things. Will you deal with them for me?'

'Be glad to.' Ellie smiled mechanically at the taxi driver and handed him the case she held. Aileen gave her another swift hug before she got into the cab. 'Here,' she said, holding out a small parcel. 'An early Christmas present. Open it once I'm gone.'

Ellie waited until the taxi had gone through the gates, turned and disappeared from view. Then she tore the wrapping paper from what was obviously a book. She had to wipe away tears before she could make out its title: *The Scots Kitchen: Its Traditions and Lore* by F. Marian McNeill.

It was inscribed 'To dearest Ellie, who made life bearable, from her friend Aileen. Don't forget to ask the blacksmith to be careful when he singes your sheep's heid!'

She had shared the story of that happy gathering at Lesley Matheson's with Aileen, and raved about the book that contained so many recipes they both knew. Ellie closed the book and clutched it to her before turning blindly away.

She stumbled past the kitchen door and went on down the garden, seeking the sanctuary of the summer-house.

As she got there, her brother stepped out. 'Thank goodness you're here, Ellie. Phoebe and I need to talk to you.'

'Not now, Malcolm,' she said. 'Not now!'

'Ellie!' That was Phoebe. 'Ellie,' she gasped. 'I'm in trouble!'

Something in her voice dried Ellie's tears. Narrowing her eyes, she took a step towards the other girl. 'What sort of trouble?'

Phoebe had been crying too. Her pretty face was wet and blotchy, made ugly by distress. 'Oh, Ellie!' she wailed. 'I'm in absolutely the worst sort of trouble a girl can be in!'

Chapter 21

Hugging Aileen's parting gift beneath her folded arms, Ellie retreated as far as she could into the minimal shelter offered by the roof of the summerhouse. 'How far gone are you?'

'I'm not sure . . .' Phoebe looked up at Malcolm, standing next to her where she sat on the opposite end of the bench from Ellie. 'It's hard to work out.'

'Presumably the two o' you can work out when you slept together.'

Phoebe flushed. 'It's been more than once.'

Ellie rolled her eyes heavenwards. 'Did you no' realise what a risk you were taking?' She reined in her annoyance. Recriminations would serve no purposse. What they needed to do here was sort out the practicalities. 'Right then, Phoebe. When did you have your last period?'

'Ellie!' Malcolm's voice was choked with embarrassment. 'Don't be so coarse! I don't think you're in any position to cast the first stone either after that day at Craigmarloch. Several people realised that you and Evander had disappeared off somewhere together.'

Ellie blushed faintly but held her brother's gaze. 'Neither you nor anybody else knows what Evander and me did or didn't do that day,' she said, her voice as crisp as the winter's afternoon. 'And I'd have to point out that it's no' me who's in trouble. You and Phoebe have asked me for help, Malcolm. If I'm to give you any, we have to be able to discuss this frankly. So I'm asking again. Do you have any idea at all when the baby's due, Phoebe? We need to know when you'll start to show.'

'Ellie's right, Malcolm,' Phoebe said. Her face bright red, she listed some dates.

Ellie did the sums. 'So the baby's probably due in the middle of April. Near my birthday, in fact.'

Phoebe's hand slid to her stomach. 'The baby,' she repeated. 'You know, Ellie, until you said that I hadn't thought of the baby as a real person.'

'It'll be a very real person soon,' Ellie said grimly. 'And it's way too late to stop it from becoming one. I wouldn't have helped you do that, anyway.' She pulled off her knitted tammy and ran a hand through her hair, feeling the familiar pang as she thought of Aileen Drummond's child: the one whom James Tait's selfishness had denied life. For the first time, she realised sadly that Aileen's child would have been Evander and Phoebe's half-brother or -sister.

She stuffed her tammy in her coat pocket, took a deep breath and squared her shoulders. 'Let's consider your options. You could get married straight away. Even if you're under twenty-one you don't actually *have* to get your parents' permission, do you?'

Malcolm coughed. 'Not under Scots Law, no.'

Phoebe looked hopefully up at him but he shook his fair head. When he saw her lip tremble at his negative response, he shot down on one knee in front of her, taking both of her hands between his. 'Phoebe,' he said in an impassioned whisper, 'it's not that I don't want to marry you! I want that more than anything! I'd marry you tomorrow if I could but we *have* to wait. I can't afford to keep a wife and child. Not yet. If he finds out what we've done your father might even give me my cards. What would we do then?'

'Oh, Malcolm!' Phoebe said. 'You know I'd come and live with you in the dingiest back street in Temple! Live on the dole if we had to!'

'I wouldn't ask you to do that, my love! I *couldn't* ask you to do that!'

Ellie was growing impatient with the lovebirds. There was a time and a place, and this wasn't it. Since the thought of Phoebe cooking and cleaning and raising a child without a nursemaid in some cramped single-end was something that defied even her vivid imagination, she didn't see any point in dwelling on that either.

Anticipating the likely response to her next question but knowing it had to be asked, she sidled along the bench so that she was closer to Phoebe. 'Are you going to tell your parents?'

'I can't, Ellie! I can't! My father would be so disappointed in me!'

Reminding herself that Phoebe always making such a big fuss about her feelings didn't mean she wasn't experiencing some very strong ones at the moment, Ellie slid an arm about the other girl's shoulders and consciously made her voice as calm and as gentle as possible.

'What about telling your mother, Phoebe? She loves you very much. You know that. She's not going to be disappointed in you.' Wrestling with her own innate honesty, Ellie hesitated. 'Well, she might be a wee bit disappointed to begin with—'

'Of course she will! Mother thinks anything to do with this sort of thing is disgusting, anyway!'

Just as Ellie was thinking that might explain one or two things Phoebe squirmed out from under her arm and wrested her hands from Malcolm's grasp. 'I might as well go and fling myself in the canal right now!' She was already at the gate, fumbling for the key but too distressed even to co-ordinate her fingers enough to turn it. Any minute now she'd be in the grip of full-scale hysterics.

Reaching her, Malcolm put his hands on her heaving shoulders and pulled her into his embrace. 'You don't have to tell your mother. Not if you don't want to. Ellie was wrong to say you had to.'

Forbearing to point out that she had said no such thing, Ellie joined them by the gate. Malcolm glowered at her. 'Phoebe shouldn't be upset, you know. She is going to have a baby.'

Phoebe herself stretched out a trembling hand to Ellie. 'You won't tell my mother, Ellie, will you?'

'Of course I won't, Phoebe.'

'Promise!' the girl cried. 'Promise you won't ever tell her! Or anybody else!'

'I promise never to tell a living soul that you've had a baby,' Ellie said solemnly. 'Come on back to the summerhouse now.'

When they got there, Ellie watched as Malcolm sat down next to the distressed girl and put his arm about her. 'And I promise that it'll all work out. You know I'm going to stand by you.'

Ellie exhaled an exasperated breath. Like a puff of smoke, it floated up into the chilly air. 'That's helluva bloody big of you, Malcolm. It does take two to tango, you know.' She pointed in the general direction of Phoebe's stomach. 'That's as much your fault as it is Phoebe's.'

He looked up at her. 'Ellie, would you please stop being so coarse? It isn't helping.'

Ellie's temper snapped. She gestured angrily towards the house. 'If I'm not back in the kitchen within the next five minutes, that sour-faced wifie who's going to miserably fail to fill Aileen Drummond's shoes will have my guts for garters.'

She pre-empted the words she saw rising to her brother's lips. 'Don't tell me again that I'm being coarse. Shouldn't Phoebe go back in too? Sitting outside in this cold can't be good for her or the baby.'

Malcolm swallowed. 'Don't go yet. There's something I – we – want to ask you.'

'Spit it out, Malcolm. I really do have to get in.'

He took a firmer clasp of Phoebe's hand. 'We've got a plan, Ellie.'

'I'm delighted to hear it.' She put her hands on her hips. 'Is it a secret or are you gonnae let me in on it?'

He glanced at Phoebe. When she nodded, he looked up at his sister again. 'I reckon it's going to be two or three years before I can win Mr and Mrs Tait over. To seeing me as a suitable husband for Phoebe, I mean. I've got a plan worked out for that too,' he confided. 'But it's going to take time. Until then we want you to take the baby. Look after it for us.'

Somehow Ellie found her way to the bench. 'Look after the baby for you?'

Malcolm nodded. 'It's only for a couple of years. Until I'm twenty-one and Phoebe and I can get married. We'll take the baby back when we do.'

Ellie opened her mouth and closed it again. There was so much to be said here she didn't know where to start. Malcolm launched into an explanation of how things might be arranged.

'You and Phoebe would go away together somewhere where nobody knows you, while her parents think that she's in France. She'd have the baby and come home and you would stay. We'd be able to give you living expenses out of my pay and her allowance.' He frowned, clearly stumbling over a flaw in his plan. 'Having enough money to rent a decent place is a bit of a problem, I have to admit.'

Ellie found her voice at last. '*A bit of a problem?*' she repeated incredulously. 'Malcolm, you haven't thought this through. In any case, how would Phoebe get out of her trip to France?'

'She's already told thc two friends she's supposed to be going with that she can't bear to be separated from me—'

'Which is true.'

Malcolm smiled tenderly down at his lover. She was already much calmer.

'As far as her friends are concerned she's going to stay with that dotty aunt of hers in Edinburgh – the one her parents never talk to – so that she and I can see each other.'

'What about the family in France? Aren't they expecting three girls?'

'They don't speak any English. Isn't that why people go and stay with them? The girls will explain that the third person was taken ill at the last moment and couldn't go. They've already agreed to send Phoebe a batch of blank postcards. She'll write them, send them back to France in a big envelope and they'll fire them off to her parents at regular intervals. I thought of that,' he said smugly. 'Phoebe will have to go and collect them from said dotty aunt, of course, but that shouldn't be a problem.'

'So,' Ellie said carefully, 'the only *bit of a problem* you do have is trying to persuade me to fall in with your clever wee plan. Oh no,' she added, unable to keep the sarcasm out of her voice, 'you have to come up with somewhere for Phoebe and me to stay while she has the baby and for me and the baby to live afterwards.' She stopped dead, two unwelcome words sliding into her head. *Otago Street.*

'What?' her brother asked.

'Nothing,' she said crisply. 'Nothing at all. I can't do this, Malcolm. I simply can't do it.'

'You mean you *won't* do it.' The coldness in his voice cut Ellie to the quick.

'Malcolm,' she said, 'in all this planning you did, did you give *any* thought to how this might damage my reputation? People would assume the baby was mine!'

His face was stony. 'So you won't help us? Don't you think you're being a little selfish, Ellie?'

That question took her breath away. Malcolm started to say something else but Phoebe put a hand on his sleeve and stopped him. 'Ellie's quite right,' she said sadly. 'We had no right to ask her to do this.'

Ellie's reply was flung at her brother. 'No,' she agreed, 'you had absolutely *no* right to ask me.' She pointed an accusing finger at him. 'This is your problem, Malcolm. Not mine!'

Not my problem. Not my problem. Throughout the weekend and the start of the following week the words ricocheted around Ellie's head. Outwardly calm, inwardly she was seething with anger. How could they have asked her to take their baby? *How could they have?*

The servants' corridor was suddenly full of sharp-eyed strangers. The new cook was a petty tyrant. Ellie scarcely reacted to either, going about her duties as though she were a sleepwalker.

Obeying graceless orders, she peeled potatoes and vegetables at the crack of dawn and put them to steep for the entire day without a protest that they lost so much of their goodness that way. She baked scones and gingerbread and Empire biscuits for afternoon tea and sat silently watching the new staff scoff half of them without a word of appreciation or thanks. On Tuesday afternoon she said nothing when the cook told her to go and scrub the scullery floor again because she hadn't done it properly earlier in the day. She was even glad of the monotony of that last task.

Down on her hands and knees wiping the floor clout rhythmically across the already perfectly clean red tiles, her brain kept repeating those same three words: *not my problem. Not my problem.* None of it was her problem. But, oh God, what on earth were Malcolm and Phoebe going to do?

They would have to tell Phoebe's parents. There was nothing else for it. Would they make their daughter undergo the same awful procedure that Aileen Drummond had endured? Or would they send her away somewhere to have the baby and then force her to have it adopted?

Ellie tipped the water away, wiped the bucket out and returned it to its cupboard. She stood at the deep sink to wring out the floor cloth. Whatever happened, it would be the end of Malcolm and Phoebe's love affair – not to mention Malcolm's employment at the boatyard. Everything he had achieved would go down the drain as surely as the water she herself had just poured away.

His fault, she thought as she walked back through to the kitchen. His problem.

'Stop day-dreaming, girl! There's work to be done!'

Ellie blinked, recalled abruptly to her surroundings. 'Aye,' she said. 'I'd best get on with the baking. Mrs Tait said she wanted sultana scones today.'

'I've already done them. It is my place, after all. Now that I've settled in, I'll be doing all the baking from now on.' With a sweep of her arm, the new cook gestured towards the cloth-covered wire tray lying in the middle of the kitchen table.

Ellie walked over and raised the tea towel. She lifted one of the scones, weighing it delicately between her thumb and her index finger. 'You were planning on serving these to Mrs Tait and her guests?'

'Is that any of the kitchenmaid's business?' snapped the cook. She pointed impatiently at a cardboard box that had appeared in the middle of the pine table while Ellie had been out in the scullery. 'Get rid of that rubbish,' she said curtly.

Ellie stepped over to the table and realised that she was looking down at some of the bits and bobs Aileen had left behind. 'It's not all rubbish,' she said, lifting the old and worn hairbrush that was lying on top of the box. 'There are some books here someone might like to read.'

'Penny dreadfuls,' the cook retorted. 'Silly romantic nonsense which puts daft ideas into young girls' heads.'

'Lovely books,' Ellie murmured, smiling as she riffled through them and came across *Love Has Its Reasons*. She had read and enjoyed all of these stories, revelling in the escapism of their exotic and glamorous locations. She had identified with the heroines and fallen in love with the heroes, breathlessly alongside both of them every inch of their passionate way.

Within these dramatic covers the course of true love never ran smoothly. Yet things always worked out as you wanted them to in the end. Ellie knew only too well that wasn't always what happened in real life. Probably that was why it was so nice to read about it.

As she picked up another old favourite, a scrap of

folded paper fell out of it and fluttered down on to the kitchen table. It looked like a page torn out of a notebook. Opening it up and smoothing it out, she saw two handwritten lists, one above the other. She scanned down the first one: 'James Alexander Matthew Rory'. The first of those four names had been circled.

Beneath them Ellie read another set: 'Alice Faye Eleanor Rosalind'. This time it was Ellie's own name that had been circled. Puzzled by that, it took her a moment to realise what she was looking at. When realisation struck, she felt the hairs on the back of her neck stand up.

'For pity's sake! Are you reading one of those trashy books?' Mrs Rogerson's hectoring voice was coming from an awful long way off. Ellie was lost in the two heart-breaking lists: the ones Aileen must have drawn up when she had been deciding on what to call her child. That poor wee baby who'd never had a chance.

There was another new life growing under the roof of this house that could have that chance: a new life that was Ellie's own flesh and blood. Evander's too.

A couple of years. That's what Malcolm said. I'll still only be nineteen or twenty. What's a couple of years of my life against the same in a baby's life?

She slipped the piece of paper into her apron pocket and turned to face Mrs Rogerson. 'Those scones,' she said.

'What about them?' demanded the new cook.

'They're as hard as Dumbarton Rock. They probably *taste* like Dumbarton Rock.'

She didn't wait for the penny to drop or to hear the sound of her boats burning away to one charred and blackened spar. Instead, she climbed the back stairs to the first floor.

'Well,' she said as she walked in to Phoebe's bedroom, 'you'd best apply yourself to your French, Miss Tait. You'll need to teach me enough that I can help you come back here more fluent than when you left. That's the only way we're going to get away with this.'

Phoebe had been sitting listlessly at her dressing table. At Ellie's words she spun round, her blue eyes opening wide. With a little inarticulate cry, she sprang to her feet and flung herself into Ellie's arms.

Angela Tait was peering at her as though she had grown an extra couple of heads. 'But why ever would you want to leave us, Ellie?'

She was standing where she had stood when she had first come to Bellevue, in front of the glossy white mantelpiece in the drawing room. Angela Tait was sitting on one of the long green sofas, James Tait in one of the matching armchairs. He was pretending to be engrossed in the *Glasgow Herald*, although he'd lowered it from his face the moment Ellie had announced her desire to leave Bellevue. His interest in this conversation was so sharp she could feel it.

'Things have changed, Mrs Tait. I don't really feel I have a place here now.'

Angela frowned. 'Mrs Rogerson has spoken to me about you, Ellie. She's accused you not only of dumb insolence but also of outright impertinence. That's not like you. I hope there's nothing wrong, my dear. You're not in any kind of . . . trouble?' She had paused before using that word, pronouncing it with an exquisite delicacy.

Thinking what a very specific meaning that word carried when applied to young women, Ellie answered her in a firm and definite voice. 'No, Mrs Tait, I'm not in any kind of trouble. I feel I need a change, that's all. I'd like to leave straight after the New Year, if that's all right with you.'

Angela Tait looked searchingly at her for a moment. Then she sighed. 'Well, Ellie, if that's how you feel. We'll give you a reference, of course. Won't we, James?'

'Of course,' he said.

Ellie met his eyes. 'Would you like me to make arrangements to pay you back my college fees, sir?'

'That won't be necessary,' he said smoothly. 'Take them as our parting gift to you.' He smiled and looked away, quite clearly dismissing her. He thought he'd won. He really thought he'd won. He'd got rid of Evander and now he'd got rid of her, the one person still in Bellevue who knew about his affair with Aileen.

She went upstairs, deliberately doing so by means of the main staircase and walking round the gallery to Evander's room. Two weeks after he had left on the *Torosay*, his father had given orders for the room to be gutted. It was completely bare now, repainted and waiting for the modern furniture that would turn it into another featureless spare bedroom.

She stood in the echoing room and willed him, wherever he was, to hear and understand what she was thinking.

I'm getting out of here at last. Out of this unhappy house with its nasty little secrets. I'm going to look after our nephew. It's a new beginning, Evander. It's a new beginning.

She added one more thought, rather less exalted but just as heartfelt. Please write to me. Oh, please write to me soon.

Chapter 22

Breathless with anxiety, Ellie dodged round the corner of the tall red sandstone building and into the lane at the top of Byres Road. Pressing herself back against the wall, she watched as Anne Dunlop walked past, laughing and talking with another girl. Ellie gave it thirty seconds, breathing a sigh of relief as she saw Anne and her friend disappearing round the corner into Great Western Road.

That was the second time this month she had narrowly avoided bumping into someone she knew from the Dough School. Meeting anyone she hadn't known especially well might not have been too hazardous. She could simply have said a swift hello, implied she was now living and working in Hillhead and gone on her way. Anne, however, would have been cheerfully nosy, demanding chapter and verse on Ellie's doings since they had last met.

Missing the camaraderie of the girls at the college, Ellie would have liked nothing better than a blether with Anne, but she couldn't afford to take the risk. She might occasionally have to behave like a character in a film supposedly on the run from agents of a foreign power but at least she could still get out and about. Poor Phoebe was really suffering from cabin fever.

In their first few weeks at Otago Street she had

ventured out two or three times in the late evening, going for a short walk around the neighbouring streets. Now that her pregnancy was nearing its conclusion she was restricting herself to the enclosed back garden and then only at night when it was too dark for the upstairs neighbours to see her. Explaining why Phoebe Tait wasn't in France would be bad enough. Explaining away Phoebe Tait's condition was something else entirely.

Ellie recounted her narrow escape when she got back to Otago Street, placing the day's newspaper in front of Phoebe where she sat at the kitchen table. 'Stay where you are,' she said, seeing the heavily pregnant young woman placing her hands on the solid surface to lever herself up.

Phoebe shook her head. 'I'll help you put the shopping away. Can't have you doing all the work, Ellie. So you've had a nerve-racking morning?'

'Not quite so bad as when I nearly ran into your mother two weeks ago,' Ellie said as she helped Phoebe to her feet.

The other girl heaved a weary sigh. 'Sometimes I think what I really want is to run into my mother.' She rolled her eyes. 'Confess everything and go home with her.'

Ellie looked at her sympathetically. 'You wish she could be there when you have the baby?'

'I do.' Phoebe patted her shoulder. 'I'll have you, though. And I'm so grateful to you, Ellie. I don't want you to think that I'm not.'

Ellie smiled into the blue eyes. 'I know you're grateful to me. You keep thanking me for what I'm doing. Now then, if you put the shopping away I'll get on with our lunch.'

* * *

A month later, at exactly eight a.m. on a fresh April morning, Phoebe brought her son into the world. Much later that day, when the mess had been cleared up and the midwife who'd exchanged her skills and her silence for a healthy fee had gone home, Ellie woke with a start. Still wearing the clothes she'd put on the previous morning, she couldn't have said when she'd flopped, exhausted, on to her bed. She'd delayed only long enough to phone Malcolm at Tait's and let him know he'd become a father.

Lying on the rug beside her bed, Douglas the Dug raised his head and wagged his tail hopefully. 'Sorry, pal,' Ellie said. 'You'll have to be satisfied with the back garden today. I'll make it up to you tomorrow.'

She let him out before going through to the bedroom Phoebe had been occupying for the past few months, pausing for a moment in the doorway to gaze in awe at the new occupant of the room. The amazing little scrap of humanity whose arrival had stunned and humbled her was sleeping peacefully in a bassinet set beside his mother's bed.

Phoebe was awake. She was lying on her side, one hand supporting her head, and she too was gazing in wonder at the new arrival. Looking up, she spotted Ellie in the doorway. 'Come and see,' she whispered. 'Isn't he beautiful?'

Soft-footed in her stocking soles, Ellie tiptoed forward. 'The most beautiful wee baby there's ever been in the entire history of the world,' she agreed. 'Look at his wee mouth. Oh, and his fingers too. Each one so tiny and each one so perfect.' She looked up, and the eyes of the two young women met.

'Thanks for everything, Ellie,' Phoebe said softly. 'Everything you have done and everything you're going to do. Not to mention being with me through it all.' Her smile was a little lopsided. 'Especially the last twenty-four hours.'

'You did it all, Phoebe. I thought you were really brave. I'd have been screaming the house down.'

'I had you to hold on to. You've no idea how much that helped.'

Ellie's smile was as rueful as Phoebe's. 'You didn't realise how terrified I was, then?'

'You and me both.'

Ellie grinned at her. 'Are you hungry?'

'Famished.' The new mother looked again at her son. 'I dare say this little man will feel the same when he wakes up.'

'Well, I'll feed you,' Ellie said gaily, 'but you'll have to do the honours for the wee one. After that we'll get the both of you washed and changed for Malcolm coming.'

She walked across the bedroom to the window, hoping she had sounded confident. The prospect of bathing a tiny baby was only marginally less terrifying than trying to make yourself useful while he was being born.

'Malcolm did say he was going to try to get away from work early, Ellie?'

'He did. Shall I open the window a wee bit? It's a beautiful spring day outside.'

'The baby won't get a draught?'

'He's on the wrong side of the bed for that,' Ellie reassured her.

She pulled the window down an inch or two to allow a little of the freshness of the April afternoon into the stuffy room, standing for a moment to gaze out over the rooftops and back gardens of Hillhead.

'By the way,' Phoebe said from behind her. 'I ought to wish you Happy Birthday.'

Ellie whirled round. 'It is my birthday, isn't it? I'd completely forgotten.' She started to laugh. Then, just as suddenly, her brow creased in a frown. 'Oh, damn!'

'What's the matter?'

'I was supposed to be meeting Frank Rafferty today. It was arranged ages ago and I completely forgot about it.' Ellie glanced at the small clock on Phoebe's bedside table. Twenty to four. She should have met him forty minutes ago. 'Well,' she said brightly, 'he's probably given up on me by now. Not that I could have left you anyway, Phoebe.'

Registering the other girl's concern, she hastened to reassure her. 'I'll write to him. Think up some excuse for why I wasn't there today.' She was brought up short by the quite different emotion now flitting across Phoebe's face. 'Oh,' Ellie said flatly, 'you'd rather I didn't tell Frank where I am. Or what I'm doing.'

'I have absolutely no right to ask you not to get in touch with him,' Phoebe said. She bit her lip. 'Both Malcolm and I have asked you to sacrifice so much already. Oh, Ellie, I'm so sorry! But we are so grateful to you for what you're doing!'

Ellie put on a mock-ferocious glare. 'Stop thanking me! And don't worry about Frank. I promise I won't tell him about you and the baby. Now,' she said decisively, 'I'm going to fetch some sustenance. For new mothers and new aunties. Tea and toast *tout de suite*,' she added, trying out the French she'd learned over the past few months.

'*Formidable!*' Phoebe responded. As Ellie left the room her eyes dropped once more to her son.

* * *

A mile or so away from Otago Street, Frank Rafferty was sitting in solitary splendour in the tearoom in Partick. Some stubborn instinct had made him pick a table right in the middle of the place. That way as many as possible of the respectable folk who surrounded him could get a good look at his face.

His scar wasn't as bad as it could have been. He'd caught a junior casualty surgeon not yet sickened by the Saturday night specials, that stream of more or less self-inflicted injuries. The young houseman's stitching had been neat enough. It had the effect of giving Frank a permanently wolfish grin.

Ellie's letter had reached him on Hogmanay. He'd lain on his top bunk in the cramped and stinking prison cell and read it over and over again. It had seemed a good omen for the future, a ray of light in the darkness into which his own idiocy had led him. Eleanor Douglas hadn't given up on him.

He'd been a troublemaker during the first six months of his sentence, daft enough to risk more time inside by wanting to look big in front of the other men. The combination of the shock of his father's death and the comfort he derived from Ellie's letter turned him into a model prisoner. He ignored the taunts his good behaviour provoked from his fellow inmates and set his sights on getting back out into the world and doing something with his life.

When Ellie hadn't turned up after he had waited a full hour, he rose to his feet. As he made his way to the front door he realised that he was provoking a quiver of nervousness throughout the whole tearoom. What did they think he was going to do? Challenge the woman sitting at the table near the door to a fight?

Her companion, an attractive blonde in her early twenties, who had to be her daughter, had barely taken her eyes off Frank throughout the whole of the last hour. He'd been out of prison only a few weeks but already he recognised that look. She fancied him as a bit of rough, his scar making him all the more dangerous and all the more desirable.

'You're not my type, sweetheart,' he murmured as he passed her. 'I prefer brunettes.'

He stood for a moment on the other side of the tearoom's glass door, looking up and down Dumbarton Road. Could Ellie have got the time wrong, forgotten what she'd told him in her letter?

He waited for another twenty minutes before walking slowly along to the tram stop. He'd been looking forward so much to seeing her again. Staring moodily out of the window as the tram clanked up Crow Road he wondered if she hadn't turned up because she had, after all, given up on him. He rejected the idea as soon as he thought of it. If she'd decided to do that she'd have got a message to him to say she wasn't coming. She wasn't the sort of girl who would derive any pleasure from standing him up.

By the time he jumped off the tram at Anniesland Cross he'd decided on a course of action. He'd been laying low since he'd come home a few weeks earlier, not wanting to embarrass Ellie or himself by turning up at Bellevue's kitchen door. Now he was going to have to brave it. It was either that or go round to her brother's lodgings.

Frank grimaced. Neither place was going to put out the welcome mat for him. He had to make sure Ellie was all right, though. He was beginning to worry about her.

* * *

'Say something, Malcolm.' Phoebe's voice shook a little. 'Don't you like him?'

'Like him?' Malcolm repeated, lifting his gaze at last from the baby. '*Like him?* He's the most wonderful thing I've ever seen in my life.' He had to wipe away a tear before he could speak again, his voice tinged with amazed disbelief. 'Did we really make him, Phoebe? Are we really his parents?'

Phoebe was laughing and crying at the same time. 'Yes, Malcolm, we made him. He's our son! Oh, come here!'

As Malcolm sat down on the bed and went into her arms, Ellie retreated, softly closing the door between herself and the little family. She was wiping her own eyes as she went through the big square lobby to the kitchen.

She gave them half an hour. When she went back through she was carrying a small folding card table, which she flicked open and set beside the bed. 'I thought we could all eat in here – Malcolm and I at this thing and you with a tray in bed, Phoebe. How's that?'

'It's great,' Phoebe said. 'I've been telling Malcolm what a tower of strength you've been.'

'Aye, Ellie,' her brother said. He was sitting in the upholstered chair on the opposite side of the bed now, cradling his son in his arms. Carefully adjusting his grip, he stretched out one hand and found Phoebe's lying on top of the coverlet. He interlaced his fingers with hers. 'We're both so grateful to you. I mean that from the bottom of my heart, wee sister,' he added awkwardly.

Touched, Ellie threw a cloth over the green baize of the card table and walked round to him. She laid her fingertips gently on top of the baby's head. 'Decided on a name for your boy yet, Daddy?'

Malcolm laughed and glanced across at Phoebe.

'We have, actually,' she said. 'We're going to call him James. After my father.'

'Oh,' Ellie said.

'D'you think you should maybe get up today and have a wee walk about the house, Phoebe? You'll have to take it easy to begin with, mind.'

'I think I'll probably have to take your arm as well, Ellie.'

'That's all right.' She was moving about the room, sorting out a few of the multifarious chores young Master Tait had brought with him. He'd been in the world a mere week but already his laundry was littering the house. Days of April showers had necessitated the lighting of the kitchen range and the drying of nappies and baby clothes inside.

'Ellie?'

'Yes?' she said absent-mindedly. She was holding a succession of tiny vests against her face to make sure they were perfectly dry before she stacked and put them away.

'You're not happy about the baby's name, are you?'

Ellie checked two more vests before she answered. 'If you and Malcolm like it, that's fine by me. It really isn't any of my business what you call the wee one.'

'Except that you're going to be looking after him and you've never called him by his name yet. Are you going to keep referring to him as the wee one?'

Ellie reached deeper into the woven willow laundry basket. It was all nappies now to be checked. She plucked the first one out by one of its corners.

'You really hate my father, don't you?'

She made sure the first nappy was dry. She folded it in half, then folded it again. She was paying meticulous attention to the simple task, taking pains that each side lined up with all of the others. Only when they were perfectly aligned did she look up. 'Yes,' she said. 'I really hate your father.'

'Because of what he did to Evander.'

And because of what he made Aileen do . . . but she wasn't going to share that story with a new mother.

'You think my mother and I failed Evander, don't you?'

'Phoebe,' Ellie said a little desperately, 'is this conversation going anywhere?'

'Bear with me,' Phoebe said. 'Having James has made me think about my brother. I've been remembering what a vulnerable little boy he was.'

Ellie lifted the folded nappy to her face and undid all the work she had just done.

'Oh, Ellie . . . Come and sit by me.'

Ellie stumbled to the bed, finding the edge of it more by luck than anything else.

'You still miss him?'

'I think I'll always miss him,' she managed.

Phoebe wrapped her fingers around Ellie's wrist. 'He'll come back. I'm sure he will.' The blue eyes were full of compassion. That didn't surprise Ellie as it would have done a year ago. Phoebe had changed over the months of her pregnancy, become quieter and more thoughtful. 'I wanted to explain a bit about my father and Evander. Will you hear me out?'

Ellie forced down the lump in her throat. 'Go on. Are you comfortable enough sitting up like that?'

'I'm fine.' Phoebe turned her golden head towards

the window. 'When my father came back from the war he used to have these terrible nightmares – when he was awake as much as when he was asleep, if you know what I mean.'

'I had those after my father died. I kept seeing him falling off the catwalk. Over and over again.'

Phoebe nodded. 'He would suddenly start staring into space.' She frowned in puzzlement and recollection. 'Or at the table or the curtains or something. Seeing things nobody else could. He would shout too. Awful things. Calling out men's names and yelling that they'd just had a leg shot off or taken a bullet in the head. Even worse things than that . . .' She shivered, and turned her head away from the window. 'I remember Evander and I both being really scared and I remember our grandfather trying to calm Father down and our grandmother taking us out into the garden until it had all blown over again. Mother insisted Father had to go off to a convalescent home somewhere because he was scaring us. In reality, I think she was as scared as we were.'

'Why hold it against Evander that he had to go away? Why not blame the rest of you too?'

'That's not what I'm saying. I'm trying to explain to you how my father must have felt: that he was losing his mind and terrifying his family into the bargain. Can you imagine how awful that must have been for him?'

'Possibly,' Ellie said, unwilling to feel any sympathy for James Tait. 'I still don't see how any of this justifies what he did to Evander.'

'It doesn't. Perhaps it makes it a little more understandable. I used to think,' Phoebe said painfully, 'that part of what he did to Evander was about trying to toughen him up in case he ever had to go through what Father did during the war.'

'Maybe that's what you'd like to think,' Ellie said stonily.

'Maybe,' Phoebe allowed. 'But I do think that as far as my father was concerned, looking at Evander must have been like looking in a mirror.' She swallowed hard. 'Not much liking what he saw either. Somehow mixing it all up with what he went through during the war and how scared he must have been when he thought he was going mad.'

When Ellie said nothing in response to that, Phoebe offered another softly spoken observation. 'My father and my brother are very alike, you know – physically and mentally. Sensitive and passionate and as deep as the ocean.'

Ellie shook her head, denying the comparison for all she was worth. 'Evander is nothing at all like his father.' Too angry to sit, she rose to her feet and strode back to the linen basket. 'How can you *possibly* say that your father's sensitive?'

'He *was*, Ellie. His experiences forced him to harden himself.'

'He made a bloody good job of that.' Ellie grabbed another clean nappy. 'Let's leave this subject alone, all right?'

Phoebe sat forward in the bed, her lovely face troubled. 'Ellie, I didn't mean to upset you. I'm probably talking the most absolute nonsense.' Drawing her knees up under the covers, she clasped her hands around them. 'Don't I usually? I'm not clever like you or Malcolm or Evander.'

'I'm no brainbox,' Ellie said shortly.

'People underestimate you,' Phoebe said with surprising shrewdness. 'And you're too inclined to believe them.' She bit her lip. 'I'm really sorry if I've upset you, Ellie.'

Ellie threw the nappy down, relaxing her stiff posture. 'It's me who should be sorry, Phoebe. Where did this all start, anyway?'

'A discussion about the baby's name,' Phoebe said ruefully.

'Look,' Ellie said, 'how would it be if I called him Jamie? Would you mind?'

'Jamie.' Phoebe looked at her son before slowly repeating the name, stretching out its two syllables as though she were getting the feel of it. 'Ja-mie.' She beamed at Ellie. 'I wouldn't mind at all.'

Chapter 23

'I can't do it,' Phoebe whispered. 'I just can't do it.'

Sitting on Lesley Matheson's big cushion-piled sofa clutching Jamie to her breast, she looked like an absurdly beautiful fair-haired Madonna. Ellie glanced up at Malcolm, standing in front of the fireplace. He looked despairingly back at her.

It was the end of June and time for Phoebe to go back home. Malcolm had come to Otago Street to collect her, although he would put her in a taxi to Bellevue and make his own way back to Temple by public transport. The story would be that Phoebe had decided to surprise her parents by arriving back in Glasgow from France a few days earlier than they had expected her.

Malcolm had spent the last ten minutes trying to coax Phoebe into handing Jamie over to Ellie. Now he gave his sister the silent message that she should try. Ellie crouched down in front of the sofa, remembering how bravely Phoebe had told her yesterday that she knew she mustn't cry when the moment of separation came. 'My parents will notice if I've been crying,' she'd said. Now she was battling against breaking down completely.

'You know I'll look after him for you, Phoebe. You'll visit as often as you can and I'll write up that diary we talked about – a few lines every day about what he's been doing and how he's progressing.' She glanced up once again at her brother. 'Malcolm's bought that box Brownie and taught me how to use it. I'll take loads of pictures and I'll stick those in Jamie's diary too. You know I'll look after him,' she repeated.

'I know you will, Ellie. I know you'll do all those other things too and I know I'll visit as often as I can. Oh, but Ellie,' she howled, no longer able to hold back the tears, 'this is like having my heart cut out!'

A mere six months ago Ellie would have put that statement down to dramatics. Now she knew it to be nothing but the truth.

They persuaded her eventually. As Malcolm closed the front door behind them, Ellie walked over to the big bay window with Jamie in her arms. She knew Phoebe would turn to look back at the house. Ellie smiled and waved, lifting Jamie's little arm as though he were waving too. Not to be left out, Douglas put his paws up on the windowsill and wagged his tail. Ellie made a funny face and pointed towards the dog.

Phoebe tried to laugh but her face crumpled. Malcolm pulled her in close to him and ushered her swiftly away. Ellie looked down at the baby. Now she was alone with this strange, wonderful and terrifying little creature.

Master James Tait chose that moment to smile his first smile. And Eleanor Douglas fell head over heels in love.

Ellie had absolutely refused to follow Malcolm's idea that she should buy herself a cheap wedding ring and pass herself off as a respectable widow and Jamie's mother, arguing that nobody would believe that of someone as young as she was.

Her plan was to keep herself to herself, watching what times of day she went out so as to be less likely to bump into anyone she knew. Other people in the neighbourhood would get used to seeing her and the baby, of course. She'd be friendly, but uncommunicative about personal matters. If she encouraged Jamie to call her by her first name folk would assume she was a nursemaid like any of the others you saw accompanying their charges about the area.

Besides, once the little boy grew old enough to ask questions, she felt he should be told as few lies as possible. Phoebe was wholeheartedly in agreement with that sentiment, although she'd been reluctantly persuaded to go along with Malcolm's insistence that their son also be taught to call his parents by their first names.

She visited as often as she could, usually two or three times a week. To see how her face lit up the moment she saw Jamie was something that never failed to tug at Ellie's heartstrings. As he began to develop, sit up and take an interest in the world around him, the two girls forged a deep bond in their love for the little boy.

When he was awake they played with him. While he was having his nap, Phoebe pored over the snapshots Ellie took and the notes she so religiously kept. They discussed his progress, studying the booklet on child development that Ellie had picked up at one of the local pharmacies. They agreed on the importance of good nutrition and a healthy amount of fresh air. When Jamie was two weeks old they had gone together to buy a pram and spent far too much money on the handsomest one in the shop. Malcolm had turned pale when he heard how much it had cost.

Ellie had laughed with Phoebe at his reaction. Even though it was going to cut into her monthly allowance, she had urged Phoebe to buy the high and beautifully constructed gleaming dark blue baby carriage. Nothing was too good for Jamie.

'I wish my mother could see him,' Phoebe said one afternoon in early August as she came back through to the living room. She'd arrived only ten minutes before but had already checked twice on Jamie, hoping he would soon be waking up from his nap. 'She's missing so much of his growing up.'

'You're absolutely sure she doesn't know?' Ellie asked curiously. 'That she doesn't notice anything different about you, even?'

'Sometimes I wonder,' Phoebe said, walking over to join Ellie at the small square table set in the bay window. 'She was giving me a distinctly odd look the other day. I suppose I have changed since I had Jamie.'

'Quite a lot, I'd say.'

Returning Ellie's smile, Phoebe sat down opposite her. 'I have some good news, by the way.'

Ellie's head snapped up. 'A letter for me?'

'Oh Ellie, I'm sorry,' Phoebe said, her smile evaporating. 'Not that. I'm so sorry if I raised your hopes. You haven't heard from him at all?'

Ellie's eyes dropped to the red velour cloth that covered the table. She began smoothing it with her fingers. 'How could I have? He has no idea that I'm here and I've no way of letting him know that I am. Bellevue's the only place he can write to.'

'You know that if anything comes in I'll get it to you as soon as I possibly can.'

Ellie looked up into eyes brimming with sympathy for her. 'What if he wrote while you weren't there?' she asked. 'And your father destroyed the letter? Evander will think I don't want to hear from him.'

'Why would he think that?' Phoebe curled her fingers around Ellie's wrist and gave it a gentle shake. 'If that did happen I'm sure he'd try again. He'd guess that you might not have got the letter.'

Ellie slid her hand out from under Phoebe's and held it briefly in front of her eyes. 'I suppose you're right. Cheer me up by telling me what your good news is.'

'It doesn't matter,' Phoebe said quickly.

'Of course it does. Is it something to do with you and Malcolm?'

'You're too smart, Ellie.'

'Tell me.'

'Oh, all right, then. If you insist. Mother and I are planning a tennis party for next weekend and we were checking through all of the names and realised that we were one man short. So Mother said to Father, "Why don't we invite that nice young Malcolm Douglas from the boatyard office, James? I'm sure he'd fit in very well." '

'She must know something, then!' Flung back in her chair by Phoebe's words, Ellie was alert again.

'I think she knows that I like Malcolm.'

'*Like* him?' Ellie laughed. 'That's great news, Phoebe. It really is.'

The other girl smiled at her. 'It's a start,' she said. 'It's definitely a start.'

'And how is ze wee laddie zis morning?'

Ellie smiled at the enquirer, the male half of an elderly couple she invariably met whenever she chose to take the baby to the Botanic Gardens for his daily constitutional. They were White Russians, refugees from the turmoil and devastation of the civil war that had succeeded the October Revolution back in 1917.

They spoke a wonderful English. Heavily accented and defined by the cadences of their mother tongue, it was decorated with some wonderful flourishes of pure Glaswegian.

'Sleeping fine now, the wee blighter,' Ellie said, responding to the query about Jamie. 'He kept us both up half the night. I think he's cutting his first tooth.'

The old lady nodded sagely. 'Och, it is a gey sore time for ze vee vuns. Ye vish ye could take ze pain yourself, d'ye no'?'

'Aye,' Ellie agreed. 'But all you can do is give them a cuddle and let them gnaw on your finger.'

'A vee drop of your Scottish visky should help,' the old lady advised. 'Rub zat on his gums.'

Thanking her for the tip, Ellie made straight for the licensed grocer's at the top of Byres Road. As she approached it, a frown creased her freckled brow. She might be in sole charge of a young baby but she was still a mere seventeen and a half years old. Was she old enough to buy a bottle of whisky? There was only one way to find out.

'I'm wanting a quarter-bottle of whisky,' she announced with some bravado. 'The baby's teething and he needs it. It's not for me.'

The man behind the counter grinned. 'That's what they all say, hen.'

Ellie tucked the bottle in at the foot of the pram and smiled at Jamie. Securely strapped in by means of the clips that dangled from either side of his soft blue leather harness, he was sitting up, one sturdy little arm stuck out in front of him like a general directing troops. Now six months old, he was constantly doing things that made her laugh.

Looking after him was an awesome responsibility all

the same, all-consuming and occasionally worrying and exhausting. Often afraid that she wasn't doing the right thing, particularly when the little boy was suffering from some minor ailment, Ellie longed to be able to sit down with someone like the Russian lady and talk it all over: or to be able to make friends with some of the experienced nursemaids or young mothers she saw out and about.

But she couldn't, and that was that. She had taken on the responsibility of Jamie and it looked as if she was going to be doing so for quite some time to come.

Malcolm had been invited back to Bellevue on three separate occasions now. He had so impressed one middle-aged lady he'd met there that her invitation to the Taits to a house party she was holding at her house in Fife this weekend had been extended to include Malcolm too. He and Phoebe were both elated about that.

It was still a long way from his being accepted as Phoebe's young man, let alone her husband. How he and Phoebe were going to explain away the existence of a two- or three-year-old child when and if that day ever came to pass was also something that had always rather been glossed over.

'Shall we walk a bit further?' Ellie asked the baby. When he chortled at her from beneath his knitted blue helmet she took that for a yes.

They'd already had a walk today, her increasing restlessness impelling her to leave the housework and tidying-up in favour of taking Douglas for a run round Kelvingrove Park halfway through the morning. A dog with a mind of his own, the greyhound had planted himself firmly in front of the fire when she'd tried to persuade him to come out again this afternoon.

'Up to the canal again?' she asked Jamie as they crossed over Great Western Road. That earned her a look of which a six-month-old couldn't possibly be capable. Her own guilty conscience must be fuelling her imagination. Longing to hear news of Evander, she had taken to walking up to the canal several times a week in the hope of meeting Captain MacLean. It was a fair step, especially when so far she'd had no luck.

When they reached the canal Ellie manoeuvred her way up on to the towpath, turning the pram so Jamie was looking in the same direction as her before putting the brake on. The little boy did like it here. There was always something going on at the complex of locks and basins that made up the Buttney.

They watched as a coal scow negotiated its way through. One of the men on deck kept waving to Jamie. Each time the little boy responded he laughed uproariously, his teeth a dazzling white and his tongue a startling pink against his coaly face. 'As black as the Earl of Hell's waistcoat, eh, Jamie?' Ellie murmured.

Ten minutes later she sighed and took one last look in both directions, first to the east and then to the west. Her heart began to pound. There was a puffer steaming over the Kelvin aqueduct. Her persistence had finally paid off.

'Well, hello, stranger! What in the name of the Good Being are you doing here?' Jumping off the *Torosay* with his usual agility, Ewen MacLean's remarkable blue eyes dropped to Jamie. The smile slid off his face but there was no condemnation in his voice, only pity. 'Och, lassie,' he said. 'Och, lassie.'

'He's not mine, Captain MacLean,' Ellie said quickly. 'I'm looking after him for his parents.' Her voice grew eager. 'Have you heard anything of Evander?'

Ewen frowned. 'Did you not get my letter?'

'What letter?'

'I came up to Bellevue looking for you.' He removed his cap, scratched his grizzled head and thought about it. 'Let me see now. It would have been about a month after the lad left – the very next time I was back. I came up to the kitchen door and I handed over a letter to yon Mrs Mitchell.'

'I never got it,' Ellie said breathlessly. 'Tell me what was in it.'

'There's not much to tell. The doctor at the hospital in Greenock fixed up his nose and then I took him to the Pool.'

'The Pool?' She knew what it was. Everyone who lived anywhere near the river did: the office you went to if you were looking for work on board a ship. 'He's gone to sea?' she asked incredulously.

Captain MacLean laid a sympathetic hand on her shoulder. 'He hasn't written to you, lass?'

Ellie shook her head. 'What if something's happened to him?'

'We would know,' he said reassuringly. 'He refused to put either of his parents down as his next-of-kin so I told him to list Mrs MacLean and myself.' His eyes fell once again to Jamie.

'He's not Evander's,' Ellie said. 'Or mine either.'

Ewen MacLean studied her for a moment. 'Aye, lass,' he said softly. 'Are you all right for money?'

When it comes right down to it, I'm pretty much afraid of everything. Ellie remembered Evander's words as she pushed Jamie home. He'd said them in the kitchen at Bellevue, that magical evening when they had kissed for the first time.

She wondered dully what it must be like being on board a ship in the middle of the ocean if you were pretty much afraid of everything. Most of all she wondered why the boy who was so at home with the written word had chosen to send her no letters, not even a postcard to reassure her at least that he was alive and well.

Captain MacLean had reluctantly admitted that even a ship on a long ocean-going voyage would put into some port every couple of months or so. Evander had been away for almost a year and a half. He would have had several opportunities to send a letter home.

Ellie wondered bitterly if she was fooling herself into believing that anything he might have sent had been intercepted by his father. Perhaps Evander had simply decided that she belonged to a past he would rather forget.

Confused and upset, she pushed the pram into the tiny front garden at Otago Street. She took her key out of her bag and scooped Jamie up into her arms. The door opened when her hand was still a foot away from the lock. The first thing she saw as it swung open was Douglas, wagging his tail at her as usual. The second thing she saw was the dog's mistress.

Chapter 24

Lesley Matheson looked at her. Then she looked at Jamie. 'What's been going on here, Ellie?'

Behind her, framed in the open doorway of the sitting room, her husband laughed harshly. 'Isn't it obvious, darling? The girl's duped you. God knows, I thought you were mad to let her stay here anyway.'

Ellie still hadn't said a word, her eyes fixed on Lesley's face. Pale and rather drawn, she wasn't the laughing-eyed girl who'd been her friend almost a year before.

'You'd better come in,' she said, her voice clipped.

Once she had closed the door she turned and put her back to it. 'Is the child Evander Tait's?'

'No!' Denying that accusation for the second time in one day, Ellie's vehemence hadn't done her any favours. It sent Lesley jumping immediately to the next most obvious conclusion.

'So it didn't take you very long to find someone else? I'm disappointed in you, Ellie. Has whoever it is been living here with you?' Lesley looked around the lobby as though there might be a man lurking behind the hall-stand.

'Of course not,' Ellie said indignantly. 'There isn't anybody. Lesley, I can appreciate how this must look but it's not what you think. Honestly it isn't.'

Lachlan Hamilton-Stewart sauntered forward.

Propping himself against the hall-stand with the easy and nonchalant air of a man who'd never had to question where his place was in the world, he gave Ellie the top-to-toe treatment. 'Going to try and convince us that you're the child's nursemaid?' His voice was an insulting drawl.

Desperately wondering how she could explain Jamie away without betraying Phoebe and Malcolm's secret, Ellie felt her brain seize up. When she didn't give him any answer Lachie's face set itself into a sneer.

'This is not what you think,' she repeated, unable to think of anything else to say.

Lesley pushed herself off the front door, stepped forward and peered into her face. 'Then explain to me what it *is*, Ellie. Believe me, I really want to know.'

'She *can't* explain it to you, darling. Honestly, you must resist this tendency of yours to take on charity cases. Especially when we ourselves might soon be on our uppers.'

Ellie glanced at him. 'On your uppers?'

Lesley shrugged her elegantly clad shoulders. 'The order book at my father's yard is empty. Nothing to be built after the current ship.'

Ellie nodded. Time were hard all along the river, and beyond the Clyde's banks too.

'So we had to cut our trip short because it would look bad if the hard-hearted capitalists were off enjoying themselves while the workers' hours are being cut.'

'It's about more than how it looks, Lachie,' Lesley said sharply. 'I happen to believe that it would have been wrong for us to keep gallivanting about the world when so many of father's employees are struggling to make ends meet.'

'Oh God,' he complained, 'you and your socialist

tendencies. I hope they don't run to suggesting we share the hovel with the proletariat.' He looked pointedly at Ellie.

Her chin went up. 'I'll relieve you both of my presence as soon as I possibly can.'

'Do you have somewhere else to go?'

'For God's sake, darling!' Lachie exclaimed, giving his wife a pained look. 'That's hardly our concern!'

'No,' Ellie said, wondering how someone like Lesley could have married such a horrible man. 'It's not.' At this precise moment she couldn't think whether she had somewhere to go or not. She only knew that she had to get out of here, away from the two sets of accusing and condemning eyes trained on her.

She had thought Lesley Matheson was her friend, the sort of friend who would always give you the benefit of the doubt. Then again, she had thought Evander Tait had really loved her. Perhaps she simply wasn't a very good judge of character.

Ellie squared her shoulders. 'I need a little time to pack, Lesley. And to change and feed the baby. May I do that?'

'Of course.' The two words were uttered with steely politeness before Lesley turned on her heel and walked back into her sitting room.

Forty minutes later Ellie knocked on its door. She'd already tucked a sleepy Jamie into his pram, leaving the front door slightly ajar in preparation for her final departure from Otago Street.

'I'm afraid I can't take all our things right now,' she said. 'I've put them altogether in the bedroom we were using and I'll arrange to have them collected next week.'

Sitting at the table in the window, Lesley was gazing sadly at her.

'I'm sorry if you feel that I've taken advantage of you,' Ellie said. 'Goodbye, Lesley.'

'I'll see you out,' the other girl said stiffly.

Her husband laid a hand on her shoulder. 'I'll do it, darling. You stay here.' He closed the door of the sitting room behind him, striding forward to overtake Ellie on her way to the front door. His cool smile made her shiver.

'Perhaps I should go through the bags you are taking with you.'

Ellie's head went up. 'I'm not a thief, Mr Hamilton-Stewart.'

'So what do you call what you've been doing here?' She was getting the top-to-toe treatment again. She saw his gaze linger on the swell of her breasts, the gleam in his eye as lascivious as it was contemptuous. 'It's clear to me that my wife has been harbouring an opportunistic slut as a friend.'

Ellie stepped back as though he'd struck her. Her hand found the dog's nose. He'd come to take his leave of her. She bent her head towards him, smoothing his silky coat for the last time. 'Goodbye, beautiful boy,' she whispered. 'I'll miss our walks.'

Although it meant she was going to have to walk all the way to Temple, Ellie was glad she had the big pram. She'd been able to fit quite a lot into the body of it and in the soft bags she'd tied on to its handle. Glancing at the wristwatch Phoebe had given her as a belated birthday present back in May, she saw that it was ten past five. She'd better alert Malcolm to what had happened before he left work.

She stopped outside the newsagent's, parking Jamie beneath a blue 'You May Telephone From Here' sign.

Keeping an eye on him through the window, she dialled the boatyard's number. When she asked the switchboard operator to connect her to Mr Malcolm Douglas, she gave the name she had given when she had phoned to tell him that Jamie had been born: Miss McIntyre of Baird & Co.

'Miss McIntyre. How can I help you?' Judging by the businesslike tones, her brother was expecting the real thing.

'It's Ellie,' she hissed. 'I need to talk to you, Malcolm.'

'Mr Tait is very well, Miss McIntyre, thank you for asking. He's standing a few feet away from me even as we speak.' Seconds later his voice flooded with relief. 'Thank God, he's left the office. You mustn't phone me here, Ellie—'

'Shut up and listen.' She summed it up as quickly as she could and waited for his response. A deafening silence echoed down the line. 'Malcolm? Are you still there?'

He coughed. 'You didn't tell Lesley Matheson the truth, did you?'

'Of course I didn't. Can we come to your digs in Temple Gardens?'

'No!' he said. 'You know what a gossip my landlady is. Besides, I'm not going to be there. I'm going off for that weekend in Fife with Mr and Mrs Tait and Phoebe, remember?'

'Malcolm, this is an emergency!'

'I can't not go, Ellie. What possible excuse could I give? And you of all people know how important it is that her parents start to accept me. Look,' he said, 'why don't you go to a respectable boarding house over the weekend?'

'What sort of respectable boarding house do you

think is going to take in a single girl and a baby walking in off the street, Malcolm?'

'A hotel, then,' he said. 'They'll only be interested in your money, not your morals.'

'My morals are impeccable. My money is short. We're near the end of the month and Phoebe hasn't given me my allowance for November yet.'

'Oh God,' he said. Ellie could visualise him running a hand through his hair, trying desperately to come up with a solution to the problem. 'Sudden brainwave,' he announced. 'Go to Granny Mitchell's. Try not to let anybody see you. We don't get back from Fife till late on Sunday so I'll call round on Monday night after work. Don't worry, we'll sort this out then.' He cut the connection.

' "Don't worry, we'll sort this out then. Try not to let anybody see you." ' Repeating Malcolm's words with a mixture of disgust and incredulity, Ellie tucked the blankets more snugly around a baby rapidly slipping into the land of Nod. 'Your daddy's heid is full o' mince, Jamie.'

An hour later, she pushed the pram past the shops at Anniesland Cross and wondered exactly how she might walk through Temple without anybody seeing her. As she turned into Crow Road, her lips twitched ruefully as she passed a piece of waste ground occupied by a group of young men and women sitting around a bonfire. They'd be sending the fiery cross out before she'd gone a hundred yards up the road.

She didn't think Granny Mitchell would judge her when she turned up on her doorstep with a baby in tow but the old lady might well think she was entitled to some explanation as to why Ellie had simply vanished off the face off the earth almost a year before.

However, when she opened the door of her ground floor home and saw her standing there with Jamie in her arms there was nothing in that wise face but smiling kindness.

It was such an enormous relief – like sinking into the comfort of a warm bath. 'Granny Mitchell,' Ellie breathed. 'It's so good to see you. I can't tell you how good it is to see you!'

Granny kept right on smiling. 'Come away in, lassie,' she said. 'Bring the wee bairn in out o' the cold.' As the door of the house across the lobby opened, puzzlement crept into the old eyes. 'I'm sure I know ye, hen. Though I cannae quite place ye.'

'Granny,' Ellie said, 'what are you talking about? It's me. Ellie. Ellie Douglas. You know me, surely?'

'She doesn't know anybody,' came a well-remembered voice from behind her. 'She's away with the fairies.' As Ellie turned slowly to face her, Rosalie Mitchell added, 'We're breaking up her house tomorrow and taking her to stay with my sister-in-law in Dumbarton. She'll be happier there.'

'You're making her leave her home?'

'She'd have left it months ago if I'd had my way.' Rosalie looked at Jamie. 'Evander Tait's or Frank Rafferty's?' she asked, leaving that trademark pause of hers before she delivered the punchline. 'Do you even know?'

Ellie kept hold of her temper only because she had to keep hold of Jamie too. 'You don't understand the first thing about it.'

'I understand you came here hoping my mother-in-law would take you in. And you nothing more than a slut.'

'I'm very far from being that,' Ellie said quietly. 'But

yes, I was hoping that Granny would take me in. She's always been the best Christian among us.'

'I suppose you're also hoping the Taits will give you some money. I shouldn't think that's very likely.' Rosalie looked her contemptuously up and down.

That made two people too many who had subjected her to that treatment today. Ellie took a firmer grip on the baby. 'I don't think that's any of your business.'

'They're away for the weekend, anyway.'

Wanting only to get away from her, Ellie allowed Rosalie the false triumph of thinking she had told her something she didn't know.

'Mr Hunter and his wife are away too. What a nuisance for you if they were going to be your next port of call. Don't suppose you know that your brother's going off with the Taits this weekend. How is it that he turned out so right and you turned out so wrong?' Rosalie Mitchell's face twisted into quite the most unpleasant smile Ellie had ever seen on anybody's face. Rosalie was so keen to get the words out that she forgot the pause, folding her arms over her skinny bosom in an attempt at nonchalance. 'I suppose it's a case of like mother, like daughter. She was a slut too.'

Trembling with rage, Ellie redoubled her hold on Jamie. 'You're a poison sprayer,' she said. 'If I never see you again, it'll be too soon.' She turned back to Granny, leaning forward and crooking one arm around the old woman's neck, the baby held briefly between their two bodies. It felt like a blessing. From the old soul to the new.

'Goodbye, Granny,' Ellie whispered, her voice cracking with emotion. 'Thank you for everything you ever did for me.'

Once she'd got Jamie back into the pram she stood

for a moment at the mouth of her old close and considered her options. They were diminishing by the minute. She'd have to trudge all the way back to the West End, go to the first decent-looking guesthouse she could find and hope both that they'd let her in and that her meagre funds would stretch to the cost of two nights' lodging. Night was beginning to fall and it was growing cold. She didn't want to keep Jamie out any longer than she had to.

The bonfire on the waste ground was crackling away, its flames burning a bright orangey-red against the darkness of the evening. Ellie hoped the local weans hadn't been assembling firewood for weeks in preparation for Guy Fawkes' Night only to find that these older lads had set a match to it too early. She glanced over and saw that three young women had joined the group. Her heart sank when she saw who one of them was.

'Well, well, well,' said Marie Rafferty as she sauntered over to join her on the pavement, 'if it isn't Ellie Douglas! She's got a bread-snapper wi' her too. No' a bad-looking wean,' she said, leaning forward and peering in at Jamie. 'You've got a nice pram for the wee bastard too. Did you earn the money for that on your back?'

'That's your department, Marie. No' mine. And kindly don't use that horrible word when you're talking about the baby.' Ellie surveyed her coldly, too tired, dispirited and footsore to be much bothered by the fact that the other girls and two of the lads were walking over to join Marie.

'I'll call him what I fucking like. That's what the wee brat is, am I no' right?' She gave Ellie an appraising look. 'There's a few names we could call you too. Now you're no longer little Miss Innocent.'

'Oh, shove off, Marie,' Ellie said wearily, getting ready

to push the pram away. 'I've got places to go and people to see.'

'If ye havenae seen them already.' Marie inclined her head in the general direction of Bellevue. 'Been up there to screw some money out o' the wee one's grandparents?' Her hand went down to the brake of the pram. She yanked it on. 'It's amazing what you can get in one o' these fancy big prams, isn't it?' Her voice hardened. 'Lift the wean out.'

Ellie swore at her and stooped to release the brake. Her hand was seized in a punishing masculine grip. The young man pulled her back from the pram, dragging her closer to the bonfire. She felt the sudden increase in warmth.

She yelled as he twisted her arm up behind her back. He exerted more pressure, enough to make her bones crack. Ellie was seeing stars, the ones that live behind your eyelids. By the time the rapid waves of pain had diminished to a dull ache, she found herself with both hands behind her back, pinioned at her wrists. The young man's other arm was hooked around her neck.

A slim length of cold steel flashed in front of her eyes. It blazed like a torch, reflecting the flames of the bonfire. He drew the back of the razor across her face, sliding it oh-so-slowly over her smooth cheek. 'Want to stay bonnie, hen?' he growled. 'Then you'll stay still as well.'

One of the girls was bending over the pram, lifting Jamie out of it.

'Don't hurt the baby!'

Marie Rafferty looked faintly surprised. 'We're no' gonnae touch the baby.' She began to rake through the pram, pulling back the blankets and the mattress to search the compartment beneath them. She found the quarter-bottle of whisky, still tucked in at the foot of the pram. With a cry of triumph, she tossed it to one of the lads.

When she didn't find anything else other than clean nappies and baby clothes, she made a start on Ellie's bags. She found her purse and emptied its contents into her palm, disgustedly surveying the couple of pounds it contained.

'Must be more than that,' she said, slipping the notes and coins into her own pocket. 'Got it concealed about your person?' Her eyes went to Ellie.

'There is no money. You've just taken everything I've got.' Her heart was pounding and her mouth suddenly dry as she thought of all the things this lot might do to her. She glanced at Jamie. Blissfully unconcerned by what was going on around him, he was pointing at the bonfire.

'Aye,' said the girl who was holding him. 'That's a fire, wee mannie. Hot, isn't it?'

It was like a nightmare. Something way beyond reality. Maybe the whole day had been a bad dream. Except that everything Ellie was experiencing felt only too real: the heat of the fire on her face and legs, the crackle of the burning wood in her ears, the rough fabric of her captor's jacket sleeve under her chin and the terrifying coldness of the razor he held only inches from her face. She could feel his arousal too. That terrified her.

Marie smiled. 'Why don't you lads search her, Michael? I'm sure she'd enjoy that.'

The man called Michael came forward, leering. He ran his hands over Ellie's breasts. 'Naw, Marie. There's a lot there but I think it's all her. Maybe I should check again, though. Just to make sure.'

The three girls laughed, like witches cackling.

He touched her again, deliberately rough. Then he crouched down in front of her and curled his fingers around the hem of her skirt. 'Oh,' he murmured, 'I'm really looking forward to getting my hands on what's under here.'

The man who has holding Ellie growled and pressed his body harder against her. 'My turn next, Michael.'

'Maybe the three o' you should find a wee quiet corner,' Marie suggested. 'We'll mind the wean. If she gives you lads what you want, maybe we'll even let her have him back afterwards!'

More of that witches' laughter. Ellie squeezed her eyes tightly shut and prayed. She prayed harder than she ever had done in her life before. She prayed that she would wake up from the nightmare. The hand slid up between her legs.

Someone snapped their fingers.

The greedy and invasive hand froze. She felt him withdraw it, stand up and move back from her. She felt the man who has holding her let her go. He did it so abruptly that she stumbled forward, falling on to her hands and knees. She looked up, aware that the laughter had stopped. The only noise now was the snapping of burning twigs and the whoosh of the flames that were consuming them.

They had cleared away before him like the Red Sea parting in front of the Israelites. Lit from behind by the bonfire, he looked as if he had a halo around his head. With the terrible scar glinting like a silver thread across his left cheek, he looked like a fallen angel. Lucifer must have had red hair, Ellie thought stupidly. He must have done.

More smartly dressed than she had ever seen him,

he wore a collar and tie and a fashionably cut black suit and waistcoat. *As black as the Earl of Hell's waistcoat . . .*

As she watched, Frank pushed the unbuttoned jacket back to expose one waistcoat pocket and what protruded from it. The message didn't need to be spelled out. As he walked forward, the other two young men retreated in front of him.

'Did I say you could go?' The words cracked like the lash of a whip. He turned his attention to Ellie. At first she thought he was smiling at her. Then she realised it was only a trick of the light. Or perhaps a trick of that awful scar.

'Run out of choices, Ellie?'

She looked up at him and nodded dumbly. He stepped forward, took her by the elbow and pulled her to her feet. 'Pay the forfeit,' he said. The kiss was hard and prolonged and full on the mouth.

'She's mine,' he said when he released her. 'Nobody else touches her.'

The girl who was holding Jamie spoke. 'What about me, Frank? There isnae room for two women in your hoose.'

'Correct,' he said crisply. 'I'll leave your things out on the landing and you can collect them the morn.'

'But, Frank—'

He quelled her with one look. 'Put the baby back in the pram, and beat it. You can all beat it.'

He didn't speak at all on the way back to Bruce Street. When they got there he told Ellie to take the handle and help him carry the pram up the stairs. Shaken and exhausted, she dared to ask if they couldn't take Jamie out and leave the pram in the close overnight.

'You've been away too long, Ellie. It wouldnae be

here in the morning. Or some wee shite would have taken the wheels off just for the hell o' it.'

Ellie stood rigidly in the middle of his kitchen while he gathered up some things: clothes, make-up, a hairbrush and a few women's magazines. 'She made the place untidy, anyway,' Frank muttered.

'What about Marie?'

'Plying her trade in her own place now,' he said briefly.

He threw the clothes and bits and pieces he'd gathered into a cheap cardboard suitcase, put them out on the landing and closed the door. Then he propped himself against the coats hanging on the back of it, folded his arms and looked at Ellie. She was standing next to the pram, wondering how long it would be before she had to cling on to its handle to stop herself from keeling over on to the floor.

'Wee lassie or wee laddie?'

'A boy,' she said. 'Jamie.'

'When was he born?'

'My birthday this year.'

Frank's rigid expression relaxed a little. 'That'll be why you stood me up that day. You were otherwise engaged.'

'I was real sorry I couldn't meet you.'

'Not sorry enough to get in touch with me. Jesus, Mary and Joseph, Ellie, it's been six months! Did ye no' think I might have been a wee bit worried about you?'

She looked at him, startled by his vehemence. 'It was difficult,' she said, all too aware of how inadequate her words were as an explanation of her failure to get in touch with him. She had thought about writing to him several times but hadn't managed to work out how to do that without agreeing to meet him and without letting Phoebe and Malcolm's secret out of the bag. Nor could she tell Frank the truth now. She had made a specific promise to Phoebe that she wouldn't tell him.

'I went looking for you,' he said. 'Up to Bellevue and round to Ma Chisholm's. Both the horrible Rosalie and your brother sent me off with a flea in my ear. Didnae tell me anything. Does Evander Tait know about the baby?'

'No.'

'Do his parents?'

She couldn't blame him for jumping to the obvious conclusion. She was beyond working out how to deal with that. 'Frank,' she pleaded, lifting a trembling hand to her head, 'could you maybe stop asking me questions? Right now I can't seem to think straight.' She attempted a smile. 'You might say that I'm no' having a very good day.'

'And you're expecting me to take you in?'

'I don't expect anything for nothing. I know there'll be a price to pay.'

He launched himself off the door and walked over to where she stood. 'There's always a price to pay, Ellie.' He moved closer to her. 'And I don't think you've got any choice about paying it. Folk like us seldom do.'

His face softened as he looked down at her. 'You look worn out, hen. A good night's sleep, that's what you need.'

Chapter 25

The sound of shouting dragged Ellie out of confused dreams. Pushing her hair back from her face as she raised herself up on to her elbows, she saw Frank hurrying across the room, pulling his trousers on as he went. He threw up the sash window and had a brief conversation with someone in the street below. All she could make out was his final yell: 'Send 'em up.'

He pulled his head back in and rammed the window shut. It closed with an eye-watering screech. 'Make yourself decent, Ellie,' he said, hastily buttoning up his flies. 'We've got company.'

She shot into an upright position, automatically glancing over at the big pram. Jamie was beginning to stir. Small wonder with all of this noise and activity going on around him.

'Who's visiting you this early on a Monday morning?'

Frank lifted the shirt he had thrown over a chair the previous night. He thrust his arms into it and made do with fastening two of its buttons. 'Yon proddy minister o' yours, Mrs Tait and Phoebe Tait.'

'What?' Ellie swung her legs over the high side of the box bed. 'Frank, I'll have to get dressed!'

'You don't have time. Put this on and get up and sit by the range. I'll see to the wean.' He grabbed something from among the coats on the back of the door and tossed it on to the bed. Ellie slipped on the lurid artificial silk kimono he'd presumably forgotten to fling back at her predecessor and did what he had told her to.

'Needing your breakfast, wee mannie?' Frank lifted Jamie and delicately sniffed the air around him. 'A change o' nappy first, I'm thinking.' With the little boy in his arms he strode over to the range and pulled a large black pan forward on to the heat.

He did it all remarkably quickly, handing a clean Jamie, spoon and small bowl of porridge and milk to Ellie before they heard the footsteps trudging up the stone stairs on the other side of the door. 'Good job we're on the top floor,' he murmured as he walked across to open it. 'Gave us a wee bit o' time to compose ourselves.'

Trying to get some porridge inside rather than outside of Jamie – an endeavour in which the little boy, as usual, was proving to be no help at all – Ellie grimaced. 'I wouldn't go that far.'

One hand already on the doorknob, Frank turned and looked at her. 'I'm here with you,' he said. 'On your side, whatever you decide to do.' He swung the door open with a flourish that didn't bother to stop short of mockery. 'Welcome to my humble abode.'

Angela Tait came in first, closely followed by the Reverend Hunter. Ellie watched as their eyes travelled around the small room, wondering if they saw how ferociously clean and tidy it was or were noticing only its shabbiness and meanness. As they both looked from the rumpled bed to her, she realised only too well what thoughts were running through their heads.

Phoebe was the third person to enter Frank's home. Her eyes sought and found the one person she was interested in. Jamie beamed a porridgy smile when he saw his mother. Phoebe started forward, then checked the movement. Her blue eyes were overflowing with anxiety and longing.

'Eleanor,' Angela Tait said formally.

'Mrs Tait.' Ellie lifted her chin, determined to feel neither ashamed nor embarrassed. 'Mr Hunter,' she said, 'how are you?'

The man of God let out a long and dismayed breath. 'I'm fine, Eleanor. But I'm sorry to see you here.'

'Mixing with Catholics, you mean?' Frank interjected. 'Shameful, eh?' He was leaning against the wall next to the window, his hands stuffed into the pockets of his black trousers. ' "The Irish Menace",' he said. 'Isn't that how your lot refer to my lot?'

The minister looked gravely at him. 'That wasn't what I meant at all, young man.' He turned back to Ellie. 'We know you've been back in Temple since Friday night, Eleanor. Why did you not come to Mrs Hunter and myself for help?'

'But you've been away,' she protested.

'Mrs Hunter and I have been at home all weekend, Eleanor.' His face was full of reproach. 'It's clear you didn't even think of coming to the manse.'

Ellie's grasp on Jamie tightened. She had no time now to ponder why Rosalie Mitchell hated her quite so much. Besides, Angela Tait was speaking to her. 'May I hold my grandchild?'

It was like that sensation Ellie sometimes got of missing a step while she was lying peacefully in her bed. Frank walked over to the sink, cranked on the gleaming brass tap and ran a cloth under the trickle of water. He stepped across to the chair by the range, wiped Jamie's mouth free of porridge and handed him up to Angela.

Not old enough yet to be shy of strangers, he began

playing with the bow at the neck of her silk polka-dot dress. 'Definitely a family resemblance,' she said softly. 'As you said, Phoebe.'

'I've told Mother everything, Ellie,' her daughter said quickly. 'That I've been helping you and the baby, I mean. She knows you haven't heard from Evander and that he doesn't know anything about Jamie.'

Ellie was still taking all of that in when Angela Tait spoke again. 'I've come to make you an offer, Ellie. I'm willing to take the child and bring him up as part of the Tait family. That is where he belongs, after all.'

Ellie found her voice at last. 'May I ask what Mr Tait thinks about this?'

'I've put it to him that this child is our flesh and blood and that it's not right for him to be brought up here.' She looked around her without bothering to hide her distaste.

'I think I can understand that,' Frank said in an easy tone, which Ellie knew was designed to infuriate. 'If Catholics arenae good enough to work for him, they cannae be good enough to bring up his grandwean, can they now?'

If Ellie hadn't been so distressed she might have admired Angela Tait's coolness under fire. Not to mention how she went unerringly for the jugular. 'Do you really want the little boy to grow up here?' Her beautiful eyes flickered to Frank's scar, then back again to Ellie. 'We are, of course, prepared to compensate you for the child's loss.'

'Would you consider it, Ellie?' Phoebe blurted out. 'I promise you wee Jamie would be well looked after. I'd take care of him myself.'

As her mother sent her a warning look, Ellie wondered why she had ever thought Angela Tait wasn't very clever or perceptive. She was smart enough when it came to preserving what she really cared about: her own marriage, home and social position and her daughter's good name and happiness. She knew exactly what was going on here.

The minister and Frank didn't. The latter laid a warm hand on her shoulder. 'You do what you think is best. I'll back ye tae the hilt. Your choice, Ellie.'

'I need to speak to Phoebe. In private.'

They went out on to the landing, Frank closing the big wooden door behind them so no one inside that flat would be able to hear their conversation. There was no time to beat about any bushes.

'It's your father,' Ellie said. 'If he genuinely believes Jamie to be Evander's son, how do we know he won't treat him the same way he treated Evander?'

'I'm Jamie's mother, Ellie,' Phoebe said in a horrified whisper. 'D'you think I'd ever let anything remotely like that happen to him?'

'Swear you'll protect him, Phoebe. I need you to swear it before I agree to this.'

Phoebe didn't protest any further. She wanted her child back too much for that. She raised her right hand. 'Tell me what you want me to say, Ellie.'

Frank had his hand in the small of her back, bunched into a tight fist. 'You mentioned compensation,' he said coolly. She felt his fingers flex, open and slide round to grip her waist. They tightened painfully. Ellie took that for the warning it was.

'I was thinking of a hundred pounds,' Angela Tait said. Ignoring the minister's frown of disapproval, she was as cool as Frank was.

'Double that and we'll agree to what you're proposing.'

Eric Hunter gasped but Angela Tait didn't bother to argue. 'Will you take a cheque?'

Frank snorted in derision. 'Cash. You'll get the wee lad when we get the money. You can send Ellie's brother round wi' it just as soon as you like.'

Malcolm arrived within two hours, watching stolidly as Frank checked the money in the envelope he had handed over. 'Fine,' he said when he had finished counting it. 'I'll help ye doon the stairs wi' the pram.'

'There's still some stuff at Lesley Matheson's,' Ellie said, bringing up the rear with Jamie. 'I told her someone would collect it this week.'

Malcolm acknowledged that with a grunt. When they reached the close mouth he asked if she would walk to the end of the street with him. She agreed, thinking sadly that it would allow her a few moments more with Jamie in her arms.

'I'll wait for you here, Ellie.' Frank propped himself against the stone wall of the tenement and took out a packet of cigarettes.

Malcolm pushed the pram in silence until they reached the corner. 'You'd best put him in now.'

'Aye,' Ellie said, hardly trusting herself to say more. Jamie was sleepy and he was clinging to her, his solid little body warm against her breasts. Would he miss her when he woke up again and she wasn't there?

She pressed a kiss against his forehead, pulled back the covers and laid him down. Her hands were trembling as she tucked the blankets in around him. 'Goodbye, wee man,' she whispered. 'Maybe I'll see you again some time.'

'I shouldn't think so, Ellie.'

She straightened up and looked at her brother. 'I'm sorry,' she said. 'Frank should have refused the money.'

She let out a long breath. 'He certainly shouldn't have asked for more than Mrs Tait offered. I'll try and persuade him—'

'It's not the money, although that's bad enough.' Malcolm's voice was icy. 'That you're degrading yourself with *him* is so much worse.'

'*Degrading* myself?'

He moved a step or two away from the pram, gesturing to her to do likewise. 'What else would you call it, Ellie? How long do you think it'll be before he's back inside? What will you do then – take up his sister's trade?'

'What did you just say?'

'You heard what I said, Ellie.'

'I heard it but I don't believe it. How *dare* you say that to me?'

'How dare I?' He laughed harshly. 'How dare *you* behave the way you have done over this weekend? You've made me ashamed to call you my sister, Ellie.'

'Ashamed to call me your sister? Oh, Malcolm, that's a real cracker! Let me tell you something.' She waved wildly back towards Frank. 'That man with whom I'm *degrading* myself rescued me on Friday night. He was the only person prepared to give me and Jamie – your son, I should point out – a roof over our heads.'

'For God's sake, Ellie,' Malcolm hissed. 'Keep your voice down! If Frank Rafferty rescued you he also made you pay for the privilege.' His face set itself into a sneer. 'Although it looks to me from the way you're defending him that you went willingly enough into his bed.'

Ellie drew her breath in on a hiss. Then she lifted her hand and slapped her brother's face. Back along the street Frank threw away his cigarette and began to run towards them.

Malcolm stepped back from Ellie and gave himself an odd little shake. 'At least Phoebe only gave me a tongue-lashing,' he muttered. Recovering himself, he set his face once more into grim and condemning lines. 'One last chance, Ellie. Phoebe insists that we have to keep supporting you. I've agreed that we should do so for a limited period, until you find yourself a room and a respectable job. Then you stand on your own two feet.'

Rendered speechless by that last comment, Ellie could only stare at him as his eyes rose over her shoulder to Frank, approaching them at a rate of knots.

'But you have to walk away from him. And you have to do it now. I've persuaded Mrs Chisholm to let you stay for a couple of nights, Ellie. That wasn't easy. You've already earned yourself a bit of a reputation.'

'Ellie? You all right?'

'I'm fine now,' she managed, her whole body trembling with fury. 'Now that you're here.' She put a hand on Frank's shoulder and touched her mouth to his lips. Eyes as bright as emeralds, she turned to her brother. 'Goodbye, Malcolm.'

When they reached the top floor, Frank kicked the door shut with his foot and ushered her into the chair beside the range. 'It's for the best, hen,' he said, crouching down in front of her and taking her cold hands between his own two warm ones. 'Ye know that yourself. Otherwise ye wouldnae have let the wee laddie go.' The terrible scar creased as he smiled at her. 'We couldnae have him growing up like me, could we now?'

'I do know it's for the best, Frank. It's a relief too, such a huge relief . . . Oh,' she said as she saw his eyes narrow, 'you must think I'm a hard-hearted bitch.'

He shook his tawny head. 'No' you. I've spent the

last three months living wi' one o' those and it's no' hard to tell the difference.'

She looked at him. 'You don't love that girl?'

'She was using me as much as I was using her.' He grimaced in distaste. 'We both have a reputation for violence. It was kind of expected that we would get together. That's the way it works round here.' He lifted his chin, indicating the window in the wall behind him. 'There's wee boys down in that street who look up to me because I can handle myself in a fight.' His face was full of self-disgust. 'Because I've inflicted injuries on other men.' Low already, his voice grew lower still. 'And women.'

'One woman,' Ellie said.

'One's bad enough.'

'Tell me what happened, Frank.'

'She came at me,' he said, 'with a broken tumbler. She'd smashed it against the wall earlier. I saw her do it.'

'So she had a reputation for violence too?'

He shook his head again. 'She was still a lassie. I shouldnae have gone for her.' Ellie felt his grip on her hands tighten. 'I didnae mean to. I was fighting her boyfriend. She went round the back o' us and jabbed at me wi' the broken glass. I whirled round and lashed out.'

'Did you say all this in court?'

'Aye, but they didnae believe me. Why should they take the word of a Rafferty? And she's a rare wee actress, that girl. I thought the sheriff was gonnae bawl his eyes out when she told him her sad story. A wee touch less than the truth, of course,' he said bitterly, 'but it convinced the man in the wig.'

Frank rose to his feet and stood next to the range,

one elbow propped against the wall. 'I've heard she's actually quite proud o' her scar.' His generous mouth curved in a smile that was a lot more than rueful. 'Cannae quite understand that attitude myself. No' now.'

Ellie looked sadly up at him. Eyes downcast, he was studying the oilcloth on the floor beside the range. His head snapped up when someone knocked at the door. 'Who the hell's that now?'

Ellie blinked in surprise as the unexpected visitor came into the room. It was Willie Anderson, her father's old drinking partner. 'Mr Anderson?'

'I need to talk to you, hen.'

Hand still on the open door, Frank frowned at him. 'Now's maybe no' the best time. Can it wait?'

'No. It cannae.' Willie Anderson turned and spoke directly to Ellie. 'Alan Douglas,' he said tersely.

'My father,' Ellie replied.

'No, pet,' Willie replied. 'He wasnae.'

Chapter 26

'Your mother was aye fond o' a laugh, hen.' Willie Anderson's face lit up. 'Like my Mary. They were the best o' pals, that pair.'

'Mary?'

'My wife,' Willie explained. 'She died young. Her and the bairn wi' her.'

'I'm sorry, Mr Anderson,' Ellie said. 'I never even realised that you'd been married.'

'Water under the bridge, pet,' he said gruffly. 'It all happened a long time ago. She was a good lass though, was my Mary.' He coughed, then continued: 'There was no bad in Cathy either, but things werenae just going awful well between her and Alan. After they had your brother money was tighter than ever. I think that was the start o' it. No' enough spare cash even to go out to the dancing now and again. Cathy loved the dancing. The four o' us used to go together,' he said reminiscently. 'When we were all courting.'

'Did my father—' Out of the corner of her eyes, Ellie saw Frank grimace. She and Willie were in the two chairs in front of the range and he had positioned himself on the floor. Back propped against the wall beneath the window, he had his long legs drawn up in front of him. There was hardly room enough for him in the cramped room to stretch them out.

Ellie rephrased her question. 'Did he hit her? My mother, I mean.'

'Never laid a finger on her. He wasnae like that. Not back then.'

'But she had met someone else?' Frank prompted.

Willie nodded. 'A red-haired rogue o' a fisherman. Came from somewhere up north. Peterhead or Aberdeen or one o' those places. Every so often his boat used to come through thc canal. They stopped at various places to sell their catch. It was quite a regular run for a couple of years or so.'

'He was—' Ellie stopped again, not entirely sure what she was going to say. Once more Frank supplied the right words.

'A bit of a Casanova?' he suggested.

Willie smiled. 'Aye. That would be a good way of describing him. He was good-looking and a right smooth talker. Had all the lads laughing at his jokes and all the lassies running after him. Even that stuck-up Rosalie Mitchell fancied him. That was before she was married, like.'

'Only my mother *was* married,' Ellie said thoughtfully. 'That didn't bother the fisherman?'

'He was a rogue,' Willie said again. 'I think it was more serious as far as your ma was concerned. It started as a bit o' fun. Just talking and joking.'

'But it got more serious?'

Willie's face was very sombre. 'A lot more serious.'

'Did my father—' Once more she had to catch herself on. 'Did Alan Douglas know about the fisherman?'

'He found out when your wee sister was born. It was hard to deny it then. After Cathy and the wean died he just went to pieces.'

'Why did he keep me?' Ellie asked. 'Wouldn't the parish have taken me?'

Willie shifted uncomfortably in his seat, avoiding her eye. 'I persuaded him to keep you, hen. Told him none o' it was your fault, that he'd thought you were his up until then and that you were still Malcolm's sister – half-sister at least – and that it wasnae right for the two o' you to be separated.'

She surveyed him thoughtfully. 'Why are you telling me this, Mr Anderson? Do you want me to say that I forgive you?'

Willie looked up and met her gaze. 'Maybe, pet.'

'Well,' Ellie said as the door closed behind Willie Anderson twenty minutes later, 'that was fairly stunning.'

Frank shook his head as though he was trying to clear it. 'To find out that your father wasnae your father? I would say so.'

He put on the pan loaf. 'It has been a somewhat eventful couple of days, Miss Douglas. Would you not say so yourself?'

'I'm not Miss Douglas,' she pointed out. 'I'm Miss Nobody. Given that Willie Anderson can't remember the surname of this rogue of a fisherman.'

'Now there's a thought,' Frank said, tapping one finger against his lips. 'It *could* be possible to look on this as starting all over again wi' a clean slate.'

Ellie gave him a wan smile. 'Trust you to be philosophical about it.'

'Tell me something then, Miss Nobody.' He gave her his posh voice again. 'What exactly are your plans for the future?'

Ellie lifted her arms in a gesture of weary hopelessness. 'Oh, Frank! Right at this moment I have absolutely no idea. Right at this moment I have absolutely no idea about anything.'

'You can do better than that, Ellie.' Scrambling to his feet, he swung open the door of a cupboard beside the range and took out a claw hammer. Then he strode over to the opposite corner of the room, kneeled down and used it to prise up a loose floorboard. He brought out a biscuit tin. On his way back to where Ellie sat, bemusedly following his movements, he scooped up the envelope of money that Malcolm had brought. He laid both objects in her lap. 'There's three hundred pounds in that tin.'

She opened it and stared for a moment at its contents. 'How did you get this?' she asked at last.

Above her bowed head, Frank's voice was a mix of wryness and exasperation. 'How d'you think I got it, Ellie? I stole it. How else could someone like me get this much money together?'

Making her blink with the suddenness of the movement, he hunkered down in front of her. He put a finger under her chin, tilting her face up so she had to look him in the eye. 'I didnae take anything from anybody who couldnae afford it.'

'It's still dirty money.' She flicked one dismissive finger over the banknotes in the envelope. 'As dirty as this is.'

Frank gave her the oddest of smiles. 'I reckon you earned that money fair and square, Ellie. For services rendered to the Tait family. Especially,' he added carefully, studying her face, 'for services rendered to Phoebe Tait. Who's kept her good name while you've lost yours.'

'How did you know?' Ellie whispered.

His voice was very gentle. 'If that wee boy had really

been your son, you would never have let him go. That's how I know.' He took her two hands in his, lifting them on to the money. 'We could use this. Build something clean on top of it. You and me together.'

'I don't want any of it. You take it if you want.'

'Ach, Ellie, I'd only spend it on cigarettes and smart threads and flashy women!' Frank gripped the hands he held. 'I tried to get a decent job when I came out of prison, I really did. Nobody would take me on.'

'The scar?' she asked.

'That. And my name and my religion and my reputation and my background. I had no choices left.' His voice grew soft again. 'Just like you on Friday night.' He inclined his russet head towards the unimaginable sum of money sitting in her lap. 'This gives us a choice. And a chance. Come on, Ellie, what d'ye say?' His mobile mouth quirked. 'You'd be throwing your lot in wi' me, of course. That'll be your reputation completely shot tae hell!'

She extracted one hand from his grasp and raised it to his face. 'Funny how they're all prepared to believe the worst of me, isn't it?'

'Bugger the lot o' them, Ellie. That's what I say.'

She laughed. 'Bugger the lot o' them?'

'Aye. We know the truth. That's all that matters. Are we gonnae live our lives worrying what other folk think about us, Ellie? Worrying what hypocrites like your brother think?'

She was studying his face, searching for answers. His words helped her find them within herself. 'Are we hell. Let them all think what they want to think!'

'That's my girl,' Frank said.

'Aye,' she said softly, smiling into his eyes. 'That's exactly what I'll be.'

PART III

Chapter 27

1937

Thirty seconds after she walked through the door of The Minister's Cat, Frank Rafferty had the girl sized up. Even with only her back view to go on, he could tell she was somewhere in her mid-twenties, attractive, fashion-conscious and well-groomed. She wore a smart black costume belted round a trim waist and a georgette blouse. Its creamy frills sat neatly at her neck and tumbled artfully over her wrists.

She was a brunette, with short wavy hair topped by one of those daft hats with the small brim and tall crown which had always put him in mind of a chimney pot. He allowed his gaze to travel downwards, lazily enjoying the view.

It was pleasant enough, even if the girl's hips were a little too narrow and her legs a little too thin for Frank's taste. He himself was as long and lean as he'd always been, but he liked his women with a bit more flesh on their bones.

Unseen by the newcomer, he allowed himself a smile. Ellie was always going on about how she was becoming a typically plump cook. As far as Frank was concerned, Eleanor Douglas went in and out at all the right places, and he frequently told her so. Most certainly not fat, she had acquired a womanly softness and roundness.

He thought it suited her right down to the ground.

The broad and affectionate curve of Frank's lips tugged at the thin white line that ran across his face, stretching from the corner of his generous mouth almost to his ear. His scar had become part of his characteristic grin. Yet he knew how to use it to the opposite effect too.

Woe betide any supplier who tried to cheat them or any so-called gent popping in for a late-night supper after a night on the town who thought the lassies who waited on the tables in the evenings formed part of the menu. Over the last few years a fair few of those overamorous types had skulked home with a pervasive image in their mind's eye of Frank looming over them, followed by a rapid and humiliating ejection on to the slippery cobblestones of the lane that ran up the side of The Minister's Cat.

Dropping his pen, Frank lifted both hands from the accounts spread out on the table in front of him and draped his long and powerful arms along the honey-coloured wood of the window seat. If the restaurant was quiet enough to sit in that was the table he always chose. It was conveniently close to the door.

He always felt more comfortable near one that was open, or at the very least unlocked, as he always had to sit at the end of the row when he went to the pictures or the music hall. That was a legacy of his time in prison, an acquired personality quirk to which he had ruefully resigned himself.

That was odd. Despite her fashion-plate appearance, the young lady standing with her back to the table in the window was wearing very well-mended stockings and her shoes were quite literally down-at-heel. Frank filed the surprising incongruity away for possible future reference. You never knew when a seemingly irrelevant piece of information might come in handy.

She still hadn't spotted him, nor, it appeared, the electric buzzer fixed to the counter at the back of the restaurant. Press that and the morning waitress would come hurrying through, throwing off her apron and lifting the pad and pencil that hung from the waist of her pretty blue print dress. Currently helping out in the kitchen while the restaurant enjoyed its brief post-breakfast lull, she was the keen sort, bless her, earning some money to help her straitened family budget while her children were safely in school.

When they had refurbished The Minister's Cat back in the spring, Ellie and Frank had decided on tables and chairs in light wood, blue cushions and pale yellow tablecloths. The sprawling city outside their door was a great place, but its typical west coast climate could make it grey, wet and dismal. Whatever the weather outside, their customers would be able to step into a light, airy and welcoming space, a blue and white china cat with a grin as broad as Frank's beaming benignly down at them from a high shelf on one of the walls.

He had suggested extending the overall colour scheme to the waitresses' dresses. 'Give the lassies some freedom,' he had suggested. 'Tell the dressmaker what materials and shades we want but allow the girls themselves to choose between blue and yellow and the styles of their frocks.'

Both he, Ellie and the waitresses had been delighted with the results. So had the regular customers. One middle-aged bachelor, a commercial traveller from Manchester, had let out a sigh of satisfaction over his roast beef and Yorkshire pudding and said that coming into The Minister's Cat now was even better than it had been before: like going to your mother's or your sister's house for a home-cooked meal.

'Maybe no' to *my* sister's house,' Frank had muttered to Ellie as soon as they were out of earshot, a gleam of mischief in his eyes, 'but I know what he means.'

When they had first taken over the rundown and old-fashioned establishment on the corner of Buchanan Street and Sauchiehall Street it had been a gloomy place, situated in the middle of a parade of shops that included an ironmonger's, a pawnbroker's and a second-hand bookshop.

Though welcoming enough, the proprietors of those businesses hadn't held out much hope for the restaurant's survival. They had hardly bothered to hide their disbelief that a couple as young as Ellie and Frank would be able to make a go of it. The two of them had often had their own doubts. During the years of the Depression, when very few folk had money to spend on going out for meals, prices had been low, work had been hard and profits minimal.

Ellie and Frank had gritted their teeth, rolled up their sleeves and got on with it. They'd proved their neighbours wrong, and those neighbours had been big enough to admit that. Now the local businesses were some of The Minister's Cat's best advertisers. Many of their own customers came along to the restaurant after listening to enthusiastic reports of Ellie's cooking and the friendly atmosphere of the place.

The restaurant had become an integral part of the neighbourhood. It served business breakfasts to the dark-suited men and smart young women who toiled in the offices of Buchanan Street, morning coffee, luncheon and afternoon tea to the ladies who shopped in Sauchiehall Street, high teas to families out for a treat, and suppers before and after the show to theatre-goers.

Good honest food served with a smile, that was their motto. Ellie had another maxim: what the customer wants, when the customer wants it. From a culinary point of view the day had a definite rhythm but if someone came in at any hour in need of an omelette, a bowl of soup or some cheese on toast, that was what they would get.

She was a democratic boss, wearing the same print dresses as her waitresses and refusing absolutely to allow the praise for her cooking to go to her head. When, always reluctantly, she emerged from her kitchen because a customer wanted to present his compliments in person to the chef, she always shook her head at the designation, insisting she was a cook, not a chef.

As she had said to Frank on more than one occasion, 'I'm no' about to start throwing tantrums and pots about the place because I think I'm some sort of an *artist*.' She always pronounced that word with contempt, as she expressed herself scathingly on the airs and graces some chefs – almost invariably male – gave themselves.

'They think they're some sort o' high priests,' she'd said once, 'and that the rest of us should all bow down in front o' them. Know why they look down on traditional British cooking? Because it's always been women who've done it. Quietly, in their own kitchens and without making a big song and dance about it.'

The newcomer turned at last, and saw Frank. Most definitely too skinny for his taste. She was all geometry, sharp angles where there should have been curves. She was also in possession of an extremely determined chin. It rose haughtily as she surveyed him sitting there so expansive and relaxed on the blue cushions. The awareness that he must have been studying her for several minutes hung between them.

Feeling faintly ashamed of himself, Frank concentrated on that determined chin. Bred to command, he thought. Not happy that I didn't announce my presence earlier or that I haven't leaped to my feet and tugged my forelock like the bog-trotting Irish peasant that I am.

He saw cool grey eyes go to his scar and wondered with the familiar pang of disgust which type of posh lassie she was: the sort who was repelled by the violence his marked face represented or the sort who was excited by it.

'You must be Frank Rafferty.'

Her voice was lower-pitched than he had expected. If not exactly a warm west of Scotland brogue, you could at least tell that she was Scottish.

He didn't show his discomfiture. Keeping a poker face and your thoughts to yourself was something else he had learned in prison. And on the streets.

'Frank Rafferty?' she said again, her beautifully plucked eyebrows arching.

Frank flexed his shoulders, drew his long legs from under the table and stretched them out in front of him, between himself and the girl. 'Who wants to know?'

'I do,' she said. 'May I sit down?'

He didn't tell her that she could. She stepped round his legs and did it anyway, sliding in opposite him on the other end of the elongated horseshoe of the window seat. Unsmiling, Frank surveyed her over the pile of newspapers lying untidily in the middle of the table after the depredations of the breakfast customers. Busy with the accounts, he hadn't yet had time to fold them all up again neatly for any solitary morning coffee drinkers or lone lunchers.

Like the rest of her, the posh lassie's face was too thin. Despite the subtle and carefully applied make-up, it was also too pale. Frank's eyes narrowed.

'I've come about the job.'

'The job?' He repeated her abruptly uttered words, his thoughts following their own trail.

She untwisted the clasp of her handbag and fished out a newspaper cutting. 'In last night's *Evening Dispatch*,' she said, reaching over the pile of morning papers to lay the carefully cut-out advert on the yellow linen tablecloth. 'You're looking for a cook. I'm a cook.'

'Oh, aye?' Frank asked, his russet eyebrows rising in derision. 'You don't look much like one.' He glanced down at his own words.

> Versatile and hard-working cook
> required for busy restaurant.
> Knowledge of traditional dishes preferred.
> Enthusiasm essential.
> Apply Frank Rafferty,
> The Minister's Cat, Buchanan Street.

He could have put a card in the window but then Ellie would have discovered what he was up to. He didn't want her to know anything about this until he could present her with a *fait accompli*; even if he was taking the risk of her breaking the habit of a lifetime and hurling a few pots and pans at his head when she found out.

'We need someone who's prepared to work all the hours God sends,' he said briskly, 'no' some young lady wanting to play at being one o' the workers. So I'll wish you good morning.' He lifted the advert and handed it back to her, his eyes and his attention already on his next task of the morning. The dog's breakfast some folk could make of a newspaper after the simple act of reading it never ceased to amaze him.

Expecting a tug on his hand as the girl took her cutting back, he glanced up in surprise when he felt nothing. She didn't look like someone bred to command now. She looked like someone at the end of her rope. Unexpected, unanticipated and unwelcome, the tug came not on Frank's fingers but on his heartstrings.

He made a determined effort to resist the wordless pleas in those lovely grey eyes. That she was so down on her luck she couldn't even afford to get her shoes mended was hardly his fault. He'd had enough of all those waifs and strays whom Ellie's soft heart had been unable to withstand.

Oh, he'd had no objection to her organising a soup kitchen from the side door during the worst days of the Depression. Quite the reverse. He'd happily shouldered most of the running of that. Managing a queue full of hungry and desperate men had often called for a firm hand, and occasionally a firmer fist.

He'd understood too exactly why Ellie had kept a running total of how much money was spent on the soup kitchen. It wasn't that she was counting the cost of her charity; but she was determined to symbolically pay back the money with which they had started off, that money they had got from Angela Tait and from the fruits of his own nefarious past.

He had to admit that some of those he called Ellie's charity cases – like the morning waitress – had worked out fine. Alison Graham was fiercely loyal to Ellie, himself and The Minister's Cat. She was as flexible as her family commitments allowed her to be and she was keen to learn, ready and willing to cook simple dishes when required.

Some of the other charity cases had been disasters, like the sharp-faced middle-aged woman who had stayed only a week and then made off with the contents of the till one busy Friday afternoon.

Frank sighed. He most certainly wasn't going to take this girl on as a cook but he would send her on her way with a fuller belly than she'd come in with. That would salve his conscience.

'Stay here,' he said as he rose from the table. 'I'll get you a cup o' tea and something to eat.'

'No!'

Already halfway to the counter, he spun round. 'No?'

The well-spoken voice was flat and dull. 'I can't afford to pay you. And I won't take it for nothing.' She gave an odd little laugh, tossing her head in the daft wee hat. 'One has one's standards, after all. They're not nearly so high as they once were, but one still has them . . .' Her voice drifted off. So did her eyes, sliding past Frank to the scones and cakes that sat on the three-tiered glass display unit on top of the counter.

'Don't be so bloody stupid,' he said. 'If you havenae got the money to pay me, you're in no position to turn down an offer of food.' Fit and vigorous, his long legs sheathed in black trousers and his top half clothed in a smart blue-and-white-striped shirt, he cocked his auburn head to one side. 'You probably don't have the energy, either.'

He was at the counter and back again in a handful of long strides, hastily throwing two scones on to a plate. Feeding her before she upped and left had suddenly become a priority. 'Here,' he said, putting the scones in front of her. 'Get yourself outside o' these. I'll get you some butter and jam.'

It took him hardly any time to fetch those either, or

to fill a teapot from the urn behind the counter, but she had one dry scone eaten before he got back to the table. Remembering only too sharply the humiliation involved in going hungry for long periods of time, Frank said nothing. He simply poured her a cup of tea and pushed the milk jug and sugar bowl towards her.

'Better?' he queried a few moments later.

'Better. Thank you for your kindness.'

'Nothing to do wi' kindness. I don't want the bother o' you fainting to the floor, that's all. It'd be me who'd have to move you out of the way before the lunch rush.'

She gave him a cautious smile. 'Is there a lunch rush?'

'Oh, aye,' he said, leaning back and slipping his hands into the pockets of his trousers.

'You're doing well?'

Feeling just a little smug, the young man nodded his head. The girl leaned forward over the table. There was a tinge of natural colour in her cheeks now. 'That'll be why you advertised for a cook, then? Because you really need one?'

'You're persistent,' Frank said. 'I'll give you that. But I'm afraid you're wasting your breath. Now, I'd be obliged if you'd finish your scone, drink up your tea and go. I've got work to do.'

The grey eyes had been as soft as a wood-pigeon's wing. Now they glittered like gunmetal. The swiftness of the change made him want to laugh. This one *was* persistent. She dived once more into her handbag.

'What's this?' Frank asked, reluctantly taking hold of the small document roll being thrust at him. Judging by the steely gleam in those eyes, it was either that or take it in the chest like a spear.

'My qualifications,' the girl said. 'I have a Cook's Certificate from the Dough School.' She paused for a second, making sure the final card she had to play would land on the table with as much impact as possible. 'I was on the same course as Ellie and I'm not leaving without seeing her. This is her restaurant, isn't it?'

Dead on cue, the woman herself appeared. 'Soup of the day is lentil,' she announced, pushing open the swing door from the kitchen. 'And we're nearly out o' carrots as a result. Can you get me another bag when you go to the fruit market tomorrow, Frank? Oh!'

He turned in time to see the astonishment on her face. 'Lesley?' As though she needed its support, Ellie placed a hand on the solid wood of the counter and moved slowly round to stand in front of it. 'Lesley?' she asked again. 'Lesley Matheson?'

The skinny girl stood up. 'Hello, Ellie. How are you? I've come about the job.'

Frowning, Ellie took a step forward. 'What job?'

Frank had also risen to his feet. He was watching Ellie's face: seeing the painful memories. Forgetting all of those hard-learned lessons about keeping his own face poker straight and his innermost thoughts and feelings to himself, he closed the distance between himself and the girl to whom he'd just felt impelled to feed tea and scones.

'Lesley Matheson?' he yelled, his blue eyes blazing with the fury of a summer storm. 'The hard bloody bitch who threw Ellie and the bairn out on to the street to fend for themselves? Let's see how you like the same treatment!'

His hand shot out, gripping Lesley by the elbow. He pulled her in an arc around himself, shoving her towards the door. 'Get out,' he said through gritted teeth. 'And don't ever come back.'

Lesley looked in the direction of the counter. 'I'm so

sorry about all of that, Ellie. I'm really so sorry.' She gave a shaky laugh. 'I wasn't exactly at my best that day.'

Frank was having none of it. He seized her handbag from the table and held it out to her. 'Take this and get lost.'

Lesley's arms stayed where they were, hanging listlessly by her sides. 'Take it,' Frank bit out. When she still didn't respond, he slapped the bag angrily against her middle, trying to force her to accept it from him.

'Frank!' Ellie protested, starting forward. 'Don't! You'll hurt her!'

'I'm really so sorry,' Lesley mumbled. She turned her face up to Frank's. 'Please believe me, Mr Rafferty, please believe . . .' As though she were a puppet whose strings had been cut by an unseen hand, her head lolled forward.

'Frank!' Ellie yelled. 'She's going to faint!'

'Oh, for fuck's sake,' Frank muttered, but he had already dropped the handbag.

Lesley Matheson heard his curse. Strong, solid and warm, she also felt his arms come round her, knew it was only his strength and swift reactions that were stopping her from falling to the floor in a crumpled heap. He's dependable, she thought, he's very dependable. Pity he hates my guts.

Then she passed out.

Chapter 28

'Please don't say "Where am I?" ' admonished Ellie. 'It's *such* a cliché.'

That got her a wan smile. It wasn't much of one and the girl now lying flat on her back on the window seat was still as pale as paper but at least it was a reaction. To the considerable alarm of Ellie and Alison Graham, bustling through when she heard the commotion, Lesley Matheson had been out for the count for a full ten minutes. More if you added the time she'd spent in Frank's arms while the other two women hurriedly pulled the table out so he could walk forward to the window seat and carefully lay her down on it.

The focus of their attention bit into her lower lip. 'Give me a minute or two, Ellie. Then I'll leave you in peace. I had no right coming here in the first place.'

'You're not going anywhere until I get some more food inside you.' Sitting on a chair next to Lesley's head, Ellie looked up and over her shoulder into the concerned face of the waitress. 'Fetch Miss Matheson a bowl of lentil soup and some bread, would you, Alison?'

'Coming right up, Ellie.'

As Alison hurried through to the kitchen, Lesley tried another smile. Aware of Frank Rafferty as a brooding and silent presence somewhere outside her range of vision, she directed it squarely at Ellie. 'It's been a long time since anyone called me Miss Matheson.'

'Oops,' Ellie said. 'Sorry. You and Lachie are divorced, though, aren't you? I read about that.'

'Didn't everybody?' Lesley asked bitterly.

One-handed, Frank swung a chair round and straddled it, laying his forearms along its back. He looked Lesley straight in the eye. 'Quite a sensational business, I believe. Lots of grubby little details for the scandal sheets to get hold of. As I recall, you weren't exactly the innocent party.'

'Do you always believe everything you read in the papers?'

'No,' Ellie said, glaring at him, 'he most certainly doesn't. He also knows that old saying about people who live in glass houses.'

Lesley's eyes went to the bare fingers of Ellie's left hand. 'You two aren't married?'

'No, and we live together in the flat upstairs,' Frank snapped. 'Want to make something of it?'

'I wouldn't dream of it.' Bitterness once more threaded itself through the well-bred voice. 'How could a scarlet woman like me throw any stones either?'

Some instinct made Ellie reach for her hand. 'Want to talk about it, Lesley? Would it help?'

'Count me out,' Frank said roughly. 'I'm away to the lane for a smoke.'

Ellie found him there twenty minutes later, standing surrounded by the corpses of three or four half-smoked cigarettes, another one burning down unheeded in his right hand. One leg drawn up, the sole of his shoe flat against the stone wall of one of the tall tenements that bounded the lane, he had his head tilted back, gazing towards the chimneypots. She glanced up to see what else he could see.

' "That little tent of blue, Which prisoners call the sky," ' she quoted. 'Only it's grey today, not blue.'

Frank lowered his gaze and met her eyes. 'I'm sorry,' he said. 'I still hate her for what she did to you but I'm sorry I was so rough.' He took an absent-minded puff of his cigarette. 'I must have been gey heavy-handed to make her faint like that.'

'She fainted because she boiled her last egg for her tea two nights ago and she hasn't eaten anything since then. And because she's been going through a rough patch in a lot of other ways. She's still got the flat in Otago Street but otherwise she's completely skint. Since the divorce her friends have deserted her and her parents have virtually disowned her. She's been looking for work for weeks but her divorce and the way she speaks both work against her. The poor thing even had Douglas die on her last month.'

'Douglas?' Frank looked momentarily confused. 'A relative of yours?'

'Douglas the Dug. I'll tell you about him some other time.' Ellie laid a hand on his arm, feeling the soft cotton of his shirt and the strength of the arm beneath it. 'Sometimes living the way we do isn't easy. You lost your temper, that's all.'

The blue eyes brimmed with self-reproach. 'Och, Ellie! That's no excuse and you know it.'

'You're being too hard on yourself. You *were* only a bit rough, nothing more. You're not a violent man. Especially where women, children and small animals are concerned. It didn't take any of us long to work out why all the stray cats of the neighbourhood congregate around our side door.'

He gave her the wry smile she'd earned. They'd had this conversation a hundred times and more, as she had repeatedly asked him the question she now put to him. 'Are you going to blame yourself all your life for the things you did when you were a callow youth?'

'Listen to Grandma,' he said derisively. 'Her being all of twenty-four years old herself.'

'All the people you fought were fighting back, Frank. More than ready and more than willing. None of them were innocent parties, were they? Including that girl. You didn't even mean to hurt her. It was an accident.'

'It was no accident that I had a razor in my hand. And I was more an arrogant youth than a callow one. Thought I was Jack the Bloody Lad, didn't I?'

'You've made up for that since.' Ellie took his arm and gave it a shake. 'I think you should try to forgive yourself. Stop feeling so guilty about it all.'

'I'm a Catholic,' he said flatly. 'We go in for guilt in a big way.'

'I thought you confessed to the priest and sloughed your sins off like a snake shedding its skin,' she teased, trying to bring him out of the black mood.

'Ignorant Proddy heretic,' he muttered.

Ellie smiled. 'You and me have built something here, you know. Something we can both be proud of.'

'I am proud of it. Although you've always worked a lot harder than I have.'

She shook her head, denying that. 'You work just as hard.'

'I'm not stuck in that kitchen from six o'clock in the morning till after midnight. I manage to escape sometimes up into the hills. You bought that car last year and you hardly have the time to go out in it.'

'I get out in the Riley every Sunday afternoon. That

always does me good, you know it does. And I'm happy that you get away to the hills. I know how much you love it up there.'

Frank reached out a hand, gently rubbed the knuckles of his right hand down her cheek. 'I don't deserve you, Ellie Douglas.'

She gave him an impish smile. 'That's certainly true. Especially when you go about trying to hire another cook behind my back.'

'You could do with a break,' he said. 'A nice long break.'

'What would I do with it? I love to cook and I'm happy with my life.'

Frank addressed a bird that had fluttered on to a ledge above Ellie's head. 'You know, I used to know a lassie who told me – several times, as I recall – that one of her great ambitions in life was to make a culinary tour of Europe with her great friend Aileen, tasting the food, collecting the recipes. I seem to remember she also had this mad idea that one day when she thought she knew enough about the subject she might even try her hand at writing a cookery book celebrating the food of the British Isles. I wonder what happened to all those ideas, Mr Starling.'

'Aileen Drummond found true love with a raspberry grower from Blairgowrie. And the inhabitants of several of the countries I wanted to visit started either tearing great lumps out of each other or electing fascist dictators.'

'I'll give you that. Visiting Spain in particular might well be a spectacularly bad idea just at the moment. But by my reckoning you've got a wee bit of time before the rest of the place goes up like a powder keg.'

'You think it will?'

'Probably not this week,' Frank said, his flippancy belying his passionate interest in politics and his equally passionate hatred of the fascist dictators who dominated Europe. 'Maybe not even this year. But as I believe we've just been discussing, I was once a street-fighting man myself. I understand the psychology. Hitler and his jack-booted thugs won't be satisfied until the rest of us lie down and invite them to march all over us. If we've got enough backbone to resist that, sooner or later there's going to have to be a showdown.'

He adjusted his position, straightening his bent leg. 'Which is another reason for you to realise that there's more to life than work. If we could get someone we trusted enough to mind the shop, you and me could go travelling. You could make your culinary pilgrimage and I could make a religious one. I've aye wanted to stand in St Peter's Square in Rome and be blessed by the Holy Father. And kneel in the Sistine Chapel.'

'Never knew you were quite so pious. When did you last go to Mass, by the way?'

'Mind your own business. To return to the topic which initiated this discussion, if we had another cook you could also work shorter days and come out with me more than once in a blue moon. To the pictures, or the dancing.'

'I couldn't agree more,' Ellie responded, adopting a ludicrously wide-eyed expression. 'In fact, I agree so wholeheartedly that I've just *hired* another cook.'

Frank did a double take. 'You can't possibly mean what I think you mean.'

'She's ideal, Frank.'

'Huh,' he said, disgust driving him to throw away the cigarette that had burned down unnoticed in his hand,

and tap a fresh one out of the crumpled packet he extracted from his trouser pocket. 'She's down on her luck, you mean. And you feel sorry for her.'

'That's not a crime. Besides, she really is a good cook. Kept her hand in at it too.' Ellie grimaced. 'When she could afford the ingredients.'

'After what she did to you, Ellie?' Frank lit the cigarette and put it to his lips. 'I don't understand.'

'She's explained it all to me. Apparently things were starting to go wrong between her and Lachie even then – that day when they came back and found me at Otago Street.'

'What is the story about her divorce then?'

Ellie raised her eyebrows at him. 'I thought you weren't interested.'

'I'm not,' he said. 'Hey!'

For Ellie had plucked the cigarette out of his mouth, dropped it on the ground and ground it out with her foot. 'You never smoke half of the foul, disgusting things anyway. And I've got a starving woman to build up – and the lunch rush to deal with.'

He was grumbling as he followed her back inside. 'You're odd, you know. Practically everyone smokes. Next thing we know you'll be trying to stop the customers from doing it.'

Ellie threw him a smile over her shoulder. 'I'm working on that one!'

When they went back into The Minister's Cat they found their new cook sitting up in front of an empty bowl of soup.

'She's had two,' Alison whispered to Ellie, studying Lesley with the benign look she might give one of her children when they had eaten up all their vegetables. 'I'll get away back to the kitchen now.'

'Better, Lesley?' Ellie asked, sliding in beside her on the window seat.

This time Lesley's smile was genuine. 'Much better.'

Frank cut through the politeness, laying it on the line. 'You'll be paid a fair wage and you'll work your hours to suit us and you'll do so for a three-month trial period. If we don't like you or you don't like us by the end of it, we go our separate ways with no recriminations on either side. Got it?'

Lesley swallowed. 'Got it, Mr Rafferty.'

'As I believe I've already mentioned, Ellie and me live in the flat above the restaurant.' He fixed her with a gimlet stare. 'You don't come up there and you don't interfere with or comment on the way she and I are choosing to live our lives. The wee boy now lives with his grandparents at Bellevue and she doesn't like to talk about that either. Got that too?'

'Yes, Mr Rafferty, I have. I'm a hard worker, I really am. You won't regret this, Mr Rafferty, I promise you won't.'

Frank snorted. 'Frank,' he said. 'We're all on first-name terms here. If you're going to be working with us you'd better call me Frank.'

Chapter 29

'So what age are you going to be on your next birthday?'

Jamie smoothed the hair back from his forehead in a gesture of charming exasperation. 'You know that, Auntie Ellie!'

She opened her eyes wide at him. 'Do I?'

'Of course you do, silly! What age was I the last time you asked me?'

'Let me see now,' she said, pretending to have to think about it. 'That would have been before Christmas last year and I think you were six. Would that be right?'

Jamie breathed an exaggerated and rather theatrical sigh of relief. As she felt beside her for the parcel she'd laid unobtrusively on the window seat, Ellie allowed herself a brief moment of wistfulness. Fair-haired like both his parents, and blue-eyed like his mother, there were nevertheless one or two things about this bright and cheerful child that occasionally reminded her of his long-lost uncle.

'Yes,' he said, 'I was six. I still am six.' He beamed at her. 'So next week I'm going to be s-e-v-e-n.' He stretched the word out for emphasis, his hands wide apart as though he were holding a large ball.

'So you are,' she said, handing the colourfully wrapped present across the table to him. 'Don't open this till your birthday. And eat another cake.' She lifted the three-tiered stand and set it closer to him.

'Och, Ellie,' Phoebe scolded as Jamie wasted no time in obeying his aunt's instruction, 'you shouldn't have.'

She said that every year, as Ellie always said the same thing in reply. 'It's just a wee thing, Phoebe.'

This year's present was a small but rather nice box of paints and a pad of artists' paper. Jamie's doting mother and equally doting aunt were convinced that the little boy was beginning to show artistic talent.

Ellie didn't get many opportunities to spoil her nephew. Phoebe brought him to visit twice a year, before Christmas and before his birthday. Malcolm knew she did it, disapproved, but knew better than to try to stop her. The girl he had married five years ago was becoming a woman of considerable backbone. The birth of a baby daughter eighteen months before seemed to have contributed to that development.

Ellie knew that Angela Tait was aware of the visits her daughter and grandson made to The Minister's Cat but chose to pretend she wasn't, hence the need for an unobtrusive present, which didn't need to be explained away to Jamie's grandfather. Ellie had never asked Phoebe if James Tait still believed the little boy to be her and Evander's child. She didn't much care whether he did or not. As long as Jamie was happy and confident and secure of his place in the world and at Bellevue, as he apparently was, Ellie was happy too.

Officially an adopted child and unrelated to the Tait family – whatever the gossip might be – this version of events had been kept from Jamie himself.

He addressed Malcolm and Phoebe as 'Mummy' and 'Daddy' and was to all intents and purposes part of the

Douglas family. He was a very proud big brother into the bargain.

'How's wee Fiona?' Ellie asked. 'Can she say any more words yet?'

'She can say my name.' He wrinkled his small nose and wrestled with his conscience. Honesty triumphed. 'Well, sort of, anyway.'

'He's helping her get it right, Auntie Ellie. Teaching her lots of other words too.'

Ellie returned Phoebe's smile. 'And how's Malcolm?'

That question was usually the prelude to another ritual exchange. Phoebe would tell Ellie that Malcolm was fine and Ellie would ask Phoebe to give him her best. It was sad that it no longer seemed appropriate to send her brother her love. Sometimes she thought it was only for Phoebe's sake that she continued to enquire after her brother's health and wellbeing: mere politeness, nothing more.

She narrowed her eyes all the same when her sister-in-law didn't give her the stock response. 'Malcolm's fine in himself,' Phoebe said slowly, 'but he's a bit worried about the business.'

'I thought shipbuilding had picked up again.' Ellie grimaced. 'That race we're having with the Germans.'

'That's the point. Shipbuilding might have picked up but boatbuilding hasn't. We're hardly going to send puffers to war, are we? Plus everybody's prophesying gloom and doom for the future of the canal anyway. People want to move goods fast these days and that means the roads or the railways.'

Phoebe ruffled her son's hair. Having satisfied the inner man, he was now busy with the drawing pad and coloured pencils that Ellie kept for him and any junior members of her clientele who might be interested in them. She slanted a smile at his bowed head and noted the air of fierce concentration. She was sure he was going to love his paints.

'But what about the other companies within Tait's?' she asked, looking back up again at Jamie's mother. 'Aren't they doing well?'

Phoebe swallowed hard. 'What other companies?'

'They've been sold?' Ellie stared at Phoebe and added an incredulous, 'All of them?'

'The final four are on the market,' Phoebe admitted. 'We're having to sell them so as to be able to feed money into the boatyard. It's always been Father's pride and joy. Unfortunately it's been running at a loss for quite some time now.' She bit her lip. 'Malcolm says we should have faced up to that ages ago, sold it and kept some of the other businesses. Especially those ones which aren't tied up with the canal and its uncertain future. He's really worried about it all.'

'I'm sorry,' Ellie said awkwardly. 'I really am. I don't suppose Malcolm would want my sympathy but you might want to tell him I send it anyway. I'll leave it up to you, Phoebe.'

'Actually,' Phoebe said, 'I was wondering if you might agree to—' She stopped and shook her head. 'No, I can't ask you. It's not fair.'

Ellie groaned. 'You're not allowed to do that, Phoebe. Tell me what it is you were wondering if I might agree to.'

Phoebe took a deep breath. 'Meeting Malcolm.'

Ellie gave her a very level look. 'Does he want to meet me? Or are you planning on twisting his arm behind his back?'

Glancing at Jamie to make sure he was still engrossed

in his drawing, Phoebe leaned forward over the table. 'He is your brother, Ellie.'

'I think it was him who forgot that,' Ellie said sadly. 'About seven years ago.'

'That was an emotional time for all of us. Didn't we all do and say things that were maybe a bit stupid? Some of us might even have cut our noses off to spite our faces.'

'If you're referring to Frank and me and the way we live . . .'

'Would I dare?' Phoebe said, a smile lurking around the corners of her mouth. 'Perhaps I'm only suggesting that stubbornness isn't the prerogative of only one member of the Douglas family. Please say you'll meet Malcolm, Ellie. Please. I'm hoping that a reconciliation with you might perk him up a bit.'

'All right,' Ellie said reluctantly. 'But he comes here, accepts me as I am and meets me on my own territory.'

'Whatever you say.' Phoebe eyed up the cake stand. 'I think I'll succumb to another one. They're absolutely delicious, Ellie. Thank God we're finally getting rid of Mrs Rogerson. Once she retires we might get a cook who can make decent cakes.'

Jamie looked up from his drawing, an expression of disgust on his small face. 'Hers are horrible. I've been thanking God that we're getting rid of her too.' The disgust transformed itself into a look of ferocious seriousness. 'I've been thanking Him *very, very much*.'

Phoebe and Ellie looked at one another and burst out laughing.

'Can I get you a cup of tea before I start work, Ellie?'

Sitting at the round table in the part of the kitchen that served as an office, Ellie lifted her head from the afternoon mail delivery. Frank was next to her, muttering to himself as he checked through the accounts.

'Thanks, Lesley, but I'm awash with the stuff. Phoebe and Jamie were here for afternoon tea.'

'Phoebe and Jamie?' In the act of shrugging out of her jacket, Lesley paused. 'Oh,' she said. 'Phoebe and Jamie, of course. I didn't realise you still saw the little boy.'

'Now and again,' Ellie said. 'Not as often as I'd like. He's always grown so much each time I do see him.' Becoming aware that she was staring into space, she smiled apologetically at Lesley.

Having hung up her jacket, she fetched a fresh apron from the cupboard where the clean linen was kept. She slipped it over her sleek head and walked back to the table, tying the waist strings as she came. 'It can't be easy for you, Ellie.'

Frank's mutterings ceased abruptly. He raised his eyes to Lesley's face, the warning note in his deep voice unmistakable. 'Drop the subject, Miss Matheson. None o' your business, remember?'

Lesley paled. Stammering out an apology to Ellie, she took herself off to investigate the pots and pans simmering away at the other end of the kitchen.

'What's up wi' you?'

Ellie took her eyes off Lesley's too-rigid back and turned to meet Frank's gaze. 'Did I say a word?'

'When you look at me like that you don't have to.'

Since Lesley was safely out of earshot, Ellie let him have it. 'So you're aware that what you did there was bloody rude? Not to mention extremely unkind?'

'We're running a business here,' he snapped, 'no' a charm school.'

'Just as well,' Ellie murmured. 'Right at this moment you'd never be able to pass yourself off as a graduate o' one of those. Lesley's three-month trial period was up last week. Is she to be given her cards?'

Frank frowned. 'Of course not.'

'You agree she's an excellent cook and a hard worker? That she's already introduced new dishes which are proving popular with the customers?' Ellie smiled impishly. 'That you personally adore that Spanish potato omelette she makes?'

He scowled at her. 'Jesus, Mary and Joseph, Ellie. You know damn' well that I agree with all of that. I don't see what it has to do with anything. You're making a mountain out of a molehill anyway. What I said the now will no' bother a girl like yon too much.'

Ellie was studying Lesley's back again. 'Do you think that because she talks posh she hasn't got any feelings? We've all got feelings, Frank.'

'You don't say,' he said flatly. 'Now you're giving me your more-in-sorrow-than-in-anger look. Give up, Ellie.'

'Not until I get you to be nicer to Lesley. You told her to call you Frank but you keep calling her Miss Matheson. That's no' very friendly.'

'She's an employee,' he growled. 'I need to pay her wages on time, no' be nice to her.'

'You're nice to all the other employees. You pay them when they're off sick and you've been known to send folk home with food parcels when times are hard.' Ellie batted her eyelashes at him. 'The way Alison talks about you, you're Father Christmas and several saints rolled into one. The Blessed Francis Rafferty, that's you.'

'I'll have to snarl at Alison a bit more often, then. Can't have folk saying those sort of things about me. I've got my reputation to consider.' He couldn't keep the scowl up any longer.

Laughing as his face relaxed into its more customary

grin, Ellie raised her hand and ruffled his auburn locks much as Phoebe had done to Jamie earlier. 'My big bear with a sore head,' she teased. 'You'd really like Lesley if you got to know her, you know. The two of you have a lot in common.'

'Like what?'

'Politics for a start. The terrible state this world of ours is in. She's as interested in all that sort of stuff as you are.'

'I'll take your word for it.' His eyes drifted down the kitchen to where Lesley stood. 'What age would she be?'

'Twenty-eight, I think. Maybe twenty-nine. Why?'

'Nothing. She looks younger, that's all.' He gestured towards the post Ellie had been sorting through. 'Anything interesting?'

'Letter from Aileen, asking me up again.'

'Why don't you go, Ellie? You haven't seen her for ages and it would do you good to have a wee break.' It was his turn to bat his eyelashes at her. 'Since we do now have Miss Matheson you could go for a decent length of time. A week or even a fortnight.'

'I suppose I could,' Ellie said thoughtfully. 'I have to admit the prospect does appeal.' An imp of mischief crept into her green eyes. 'Maybe it's the chance of getting away from you.'

'You're a right cheeky wee bisom, d'ye know that?' He slid his arm around her shoulders, his eyes warm and his mouth curving affectionately.

Ellie placed her hand on his chest. 'Right, is that you back in a good mood?'

His eyes narrowed. 'What do you want?'

'What a nasty suspicious nature you've got, Frank Rafferty.'

'What do you want?' he asked again.

'For you to make yourself scarce for a wee while when Malcolm comes to lunch on Wednesday of the week after next.'

'Ah,' Frank said. He studied her face. 'You're sure that's a good idea?'

'I'm not sure at all, but maybe it's time I did my bit to try to heal the rift. Phoebe says he's prepared to meet me halfway.'

'Helluva bloody big of him. You think having to contend with me as well as you might be a bit much for him to cope with, given that you and me living together is apparently so offensive to his sense of moral decency?' Frank adopted a very arch expression. 'Him always having been such a pillar o' rectitude himself.'

'I know, I know,' Ellie said. 'He doesn't know the half of it.'

'You could try telling him.'

'He could try giving me the benefit of the doubt.'

Frank cocked one eyebrow. 'I can see that this reunion is gonnae be a great success!'

He fell in with Ellie's wishes all the same, as she had known he would. When the day of the lunch arrived, he announced ostentatiously at about half-past eleven in the morning that he had some business to attend to elsewhere in the city. 'I expect to be back around two o'clock. Will that suit you, madam?'

'Down to the ground,' Ellie said.

He leaned forward and kissed her on the cheek. 'I'll stay if you want me to. Skulk at the back of the kitchen.'

Ellie patted his shoulder. 'No. On you go. Wish me luck as you wave me goodbye.'

Once he had done that and disappeared, Ellie walked through to the restaurant. She'd asked the cleaner to give everything a bit of an extra polish this morning. The whole place shone. She had already reserved the table at which she, Malcolm and Phoebe would sit. In one of the corners for privacy, it had plenty of space around it. That way no one would feel trapped.

Ellie checked for the umpteenth time that she had remembered to put a selection of what she remembered as Malcolm's favourite dishes on the menu. Then she waited for him and Phoebe to arrive.

They were dead on time. Phoebe greeted Ellie with her usual kiss and hug, Malcolm standing back while the two young women said their hellos. Brother and sister had never been demonstrative, but Ellie was a little disappointed all the same when he made no move towards her.

'Malcolm,' she said. 'It's good to see you.'

'You're looking well, Ellie,' he responded gravely. 'Doing well too, I hear.'

He himself was looking rather tired. Wondering if the lines furrowing his brow were to do with Tait's current business difficulties or trepidation about his visit to The Minister's Cat, Ellie ushered Phoebe and him to the table in the corner.

Ordering the meal took up a few minutes, as did Ellie's enquiries into how the children were doing. As they waited for Alison to bring them their soup, she looked across the table at Malcolm. 'It's been a long time.'

'Yes,' he agreed.

'You don't look very different from how I remember you.'

'Don't I?'

'A little more mature, surely,' Phoebe put in nervously. 'I think he's starting to look rather distinguished.'

'Yes,' Ellie agreed, taking in the understated elegance

and fine wool of Malcolm's grey suit. She tried a smile. 'D'you remember when you could only afford to buy smart clothes by paying them up every week?'

As soon as the words were out of her mouth she realised that it had been the wrong thing to say. The look on his face made it clear that he didn't want to be reminded of those times.

Phoebe stepped into the breach. 'Don't you think the décor's lovely in here, Malcolm? Ellie and Frank did their renovations about a year ago now, didn't you, Ellie? It still looks so fresh.'

'We chose good quality materials,' Ellie said, irritated by the unmistakable *frisson* of disapproval she'd felt coming from Malcolm when Phoebe had mentioned Frank.

'Nice to be able to afford them,' he said. 'Still, I suppose you started off with a fair amount of capital.'

She fixed him with a very level look. 'We ploughed all that into the restaurant during the first year. Didn't get much profit out for the first five years. Not like these people who think a commercial venture is first and foremost about supplying them with the means to live lavishly. Frank and I worked bloody hard. Now we're beginning to reap the benefit.'

'Going to offer me some business advice, Ellie?'

'I wouldn't dream of it.' She sent up a silent prayer of thanks when Alison appeared at her elbow with soup and rolls. That kept them legitimately silent for a while.

'Delicious soup, Ellie,' Phoebe said while they were waiting for thc plates to be cleared and the next course brought. 'Don't you think so, Malcolm?'

She turned to Ellie as though she were sharing a great secret with her. 'Scotch broth is one of his favourites. But you know that already, Ellie, of course you do. I expect that's why you put it on the menu today. Wasn't that kind of her, Malcolm?'

'The soup was fine,' he said briefly.

'Did you make it yourself, Ellie?' Phoebe asked, still battling valiantly to keep the conversation going.

'Actually Lesley made it today.'

'Lesley?' Malcolm repeated. 'Lesley Matheson?'

'Yes,' Ellie said pleasantly. 'She's been working here for a few months now. Did Phoebe tell you?'

'She did.' His voice was once more clipped and terse. 'I can't say that I exactly approve of Lesley Matheson.'

Ellie leaned forward. 'You don't *approve* of her? Would you care to expand on what you mean by that?'

'Isn't it obvious? She's gone the wrong way.'

' "Gone the wrong way"?' Ellie repeated. 'I'm sorry, Malcolm, you'll have to explain that to me.'

'Oh, look,' Phoebe said desperately, 'here comes our main course—'

Ellie cut her off, as she put a hand out to stop Alison. 'Explain what you meant, Malcolm.'

Her brother sat back in his chair and thrust his hands into his trouser pockets. 'You know what it means, Ellie. Lesley Matheson started life at the top – born with every advantage imaginable. Now she's at the bottom. And she took herself there by her own actions and her own choices. Funny how some women seem to naturally gravitate towards the gutter, isn't it?'

Behind her, Ellie heard a sharp intake of breath. Out of the corner of her eye, she saw Alison set down her tray on the neighbouring table. Malcolm was still sitting back in an apparently relaxed pose, looking at his sister. 'You still with him?'

'Yes,' Ellie said. 'I'm still with him.'

'Run out on you today, though. Left you to cope with

me on your own. I suppose he doesn't have the same sort of commitment towards you that a husband would.'

'Frank and I are totally committed to each other,' Ellie said tightly. 'He's not here because I asked him not to be. He agreed to that because he's a gentleman.'

'Frank Rafferty a gentleman? Don't make me laugh, Ellie.' Dimly aware of Alison's bristling indignation, Ellie watched as her brother looked her in the eye and came out with a devastating avalanche of words. 'On our way here today Phoebe told me that I ought to be proud of you for what you've achieved, Ellie. Well, I'd like to know how exactly I'm supposed to be proud of a sister who's got such little self-respect that she's proud of living in sin with a scar-faced Irish Catholic gaol bird? You're no better than a fiddler's bitch, Ellie.'

She stared at him for a moment. Then she rose to her feet. 'Goodbye, Phoebe,' she said. 'Give my love to Jamie and Fiona. I'll see you at Christmas.'

She walked through to her kitchen without another word, Alison scuttling behind her. Lesley Matheson took one look at Ellie's face and followed the two of them to the table at the back of the room. As Alison pushed Ellie gently down into a chair, Lesley crouched down at her feet.

'Your hands are cold,' she said as she took them between her own. 'Shall one of us get you a cup of tea?'

'I will,' Alison said, adding grimly. 'I'll see that horrible man off the premises too. Oh! Here comes Mrs Douglas.'

Phoebe was pale, her face a picture of contrition. She too kneeled down in front of Ellie. 'I'm so sorry,' she said. 'Can you ever forgive me for bringing him here?'

'You meant well, Phoebe,' Ellie said, bestirring herself a little. 'I know that.'

'He's so worried about the business,' Phoebe said. 'Just not himself at the moment.'

Alison was looking unusually fierce. 'Whether he's himself or not he had no call to be saying what he did, Mrs Douglas. No call whatsoever.'

Phoebe looked up at her, biting her lip. 'You're absolutely right.' She rose to her feet. 'I'd better go to him all the same. He's not himself,' she repeated. 'Will you be all right, Ellie?'

Ellie managed a smile for her, and for Lesley and Alison. 'I'm in good hands, Phoebe. Don't blame yourself.'

'I'll bring both the children at Christmas. I promise.'

'That'll be lovely,' Ellie said. As soon as Phoebe had left the kitchen, she put her elbows on to the table and buried her face in her hands. She was still sitting like that when Frank came back at two o'clock.

'Ellie's meeting with her brother didn't go too well,' Lesley said.

'That's obvious. I'll take her upstairs with me for a bit.'

It was several hours before they came back down again. 'We're going out,' Frank announced unnecessarily as they walked into the kitchen. Both he and Ellie were clearly dressed for the evening.

'You look really lovely, Ellie,' Alison said admiringly.

Ellie was a little pale but her smile was genuine and unforced. Her dark green velvet dress was deceptively simple, its only ornamentation a sweetheart neckline. Short-sleeved and beautifully cut, it fitted snugly over her shapely breasts. From the waist the skirt flowed down to mid-calf, flaring out when she moved. With it she wore the string of pearls that had been Frank's birthday gift to her the previous year.

'Aye,' he said now, looking her up and down with a

grin on his face, 'half the time she goes round looking like a toerag but I'd have to admit she scrubs up well.'

'She was born to wear that dress,' Lesley agreed. She was standing at the main preparation area, a whisk in her right hand and a mixing bowl full of eggs in the crook of her left arm.

'You look very nice too, Frank.' Alison cocked her head to one side, taking in the picture he presented. 'I think it's the colour of your hair against the dark evening clothes,' she pronounced. 'Makes you look very debonair.' She swung round to the preparation area. 'D'you not think so, Lesley?'

It was Frank himself who saved Lesley from having to respond to that innocent question. He lifted a hand to his face, his mobile mouth quirking with amusement. 'Not sure if I can pass this off as my Heidelberg duelling scar, though. Good night, all. We're going out for a dinner not cooked by Miss Douglas and then we're going dancing. We intend to be home *very* late.'

'Och,' Alison said after the door had closed behind Frank and Ellie, 'they're such a nice couple.' Her pleasant face grew troubled. 'I can never understand why they *don't* get married. Surely that would make things easier between Ellie and her brother.'

Lesley had wondered about that too. She would have run a million miles rather than raise the topic, especially after how clear Frank Rafferty had made it that it was none of her business. She walked over to the hotplate to get on with her potato omelette, setting her bowl down and tipping a small plate of pre-cooked potato pieces into a pan already sizzling on the heat.

'Her brother doesn't approve of Frank, though, to put it mildly. I'm not sure he'd be much happier if Ellie were to marry him.'

'That doesn't explain why she doesn't.' Alison moved too, in her case to start assembling plates of biscuits and cheese. 'You would think all women wanted to get married, wouldn't you?'

'I'm not so sure about that,' Lesley said. 'It's the last thing I want to do again.'

Silence greeted that observation. Pouring her egg mixture in on top of the potato pieces, Lesley thought wryly that for decent working-class people like Alison, divorce was something completely outwith their experience, as shocking as a couple choosing to live together without getting married first.

Ellie and Frank had probably been together long enough to be considered married by habit and repute – as the legal phrase had it – but in most people's eyes that wasn't the same at all. One outraged father had recently terminated his daughter's employment as a waitress at The Minister's Cat when he had discovered that the joint proprietors weren't officially man and wife.

Lesley frowned as she watched the omelette form. Ellie and Frank had come a long way but in their values and outlook they too were still decent working-class people. She drew her round-bladed knife around the edge of the pan to loosen the edges of the omelette and wondered why it disturbed her so much to think that Ellie's reluctance to marry Frank might be because she still hoped for a reunion between her, Evander and their child. That was part of the story Lesley suspected Alison didn't know.

She remembered the awkward conversation she'd had with Angela and Phoebe Tait shortly before the latter had wed Ellie's brother. The two Tait women had asked if they could rely on her discretion as to young Jamie's real origins. She had assured him that they could, agreeing that it was in the child's best interests to believe himself to be Phoebe and Malcolm's son.

Lesley's doubts as to who exactly had fathered Ellie's child had evaporated within a few days of her coming to work at The Minister's Cat. Frank Rafferty was the last man in the world to part with his own son. It was blindingly obvious how fiercely loyal he was to everyone he cared about. It was blindingly obvious that he adored Ellie.

It was equally clear that Ellie cared deeply for Frank and that she loved young Jamie too much to ever want to uproot him from the only home and family he could remember. Ellie was the practical type too, surely far too sensible to still be carrying a torch for Evander Tait after all these years.

Lesley glanced up and saw Alison heading for the swing door into the restaurant carrying her tray of biscuits and cheese. She went into reverse gear, ready to push the door open with her bottom. 'Are you about to do the omelette?'

Lesley grinned at her, reached for a plate and placed it over the pan. She put a folded cloth above the plate and rested her left hand firmly on top of both items. Seizing the pan with her right hand, she lifted it away from the heat and swiftly turned the whole thing upside down. She lifted the pan off the omelette, put it back onto the heat and neatly slid the omelette back into it to brown its other side.

'Eh *voilà*, Madame Graham,' she said in her best French accent.

'Oh,' Alison breathed as she left the kitchen. 'I just love watching you do that!' Lesley laughed, shook the omelette pan and gave up the conundrum of why Ellie and Frank didn't make their relationship legal.

I'm happy, she thought. For the first time in years I'm really happy.

She laughed again at the strangeness of the emotion. There had been weeks and months of misery, one awful day when she had seriously contemplated taking her own life. There had been self-disgust in that too, after she had taken the despair-driven decision to try to beat Lachie at his own game.

It had been only the thought of the distress she would cause to Douglas that had stayed her hand that day. She had laughed then too but it had been hysteria, the realisation that the only living creature who really cared whether she lived or died was a dog.

So here she was working her socks off in a boiling-hot restaurant kitchen with only a weekly wage between herself and poverty. She was friendly with people her mother would consider beneath even the lowliest of her own servants. One of the people she worked for couldn't stand her. And she was happy.

It made Lesley feel she could do anything she set her mind to. Maybe she could even win Old Scarface round. It would be nice to be on the receiving end of one of his smiles instead of all those glowers. She supposed there had to be some good in him: otherwise a girl like Ellie wouldn't love him so much as she obviously did.

Handing over the *tortilla de patatas* to Alison – one of these days she'd convince Ellie that foreign languages on the menu weren't *necessarily* pretentious – Lesley started on the next order. Honesty compelled her to admit that she could see a lot of good in Frank Rafferty. He and she clashed, that was all. Some people did.

Frank and Ellie weren't the sort of couple who embarrassed other people by pawing one another in public. Quite the reverse. There was a delicacy and restraint there that Lesley found enormously attractive. She had never seen them give each other more than an affectionate kiss on the cheek. She presumed it was quite different when they were alone together.

She gave a little shudder of distaste, remembering cocktail parties full of supposedly sophisticated and brittle people where Lachie had embarrassed her by making it clear that she was his property. She had felt like the latest type of fast car, having its owner run his hand possessively along the bodywork. Then he had traded her in for a newer model: several of them.

Lachie had married her for her father's money. She could see that now. Oh, he'd been attracted to her as well and at the beginning there had been real passion. It had been lust, she supposed, the slaking of two healthy young appetites. They had never been friends – not the way Ellie and Frank were.

She found that aspect of their relationship rather touching. She liked the way they talked to each other too, the teasing and affectionate banter that so often flew between them. It must be nice to have that with the man you slept with. She'd never had it with any of them.

She had a sudden memory of walking along Great Western Road with Ellie, seeing her to the tram stop. They'd been talking about how ill-divided the world was. 'I don't begrudge you having what you've got.' That was what Ellie had said.

Well, she didn't begrudge Ellie having what she had, either. It was nice. Maybe one day she might find someone who loved her as Frank Rafferty loved Ellie. Lesley laughed again. If that wasn't the triumph of optimism over experience she didn't know what was.

Chapter 30

'More bad news from Spain?' Ellie asked, glimpsing a headline as Frank sorted through the newspapers. He nodded and handed her the *Bulletin*. She laid aside the envelope she was about to open and studied the photograph on the front cover.

'Oh God,' she said, feeling cold shivers run up and down her spine, 'not *more* bombing from the air. Wasn't what they did in Guernica last month enough?'

'I expect that only gave them the taste for it,' Frank said grimly. 'After all, from their point of view it worked beautifully. They killed and wounded thousands in one fell swoop and laid waste a whole town, demoralising those people who did survive. There was minimal risk to the airmen of the Condor Legion and they've terrorised not only the Republicans but the rest of the world. We're all scared of aerial bombardment now. *And* we all know how good the Germans are at doing it.'

Lesley was moving about the restaurant checking the flowers on each table, replacing those that needed freshening up. 'The Germans and the Italians are using Spain as a practice ground,' she put in, 'demonstrating what's in store for the rest of us if we're not happy to let Hitler tear up the map of Europe and redraw it to suit himself.'

'Aye,' Frank agreed, 'and with all that firepower weighing in on Franco's side, you wonder how much longer the Republicans can hang on. It might help if all the socialists and communists and anarchists didnae all fight so much among themselves,' he added gloomily.

'The odds are stacked against them anyway,' Lesley said, coming over to check the two jugs of flowers on the big table in the window, 'what with our government and the other democracies refusing to intervene. They seem incapable of comprehending that each time another country falls to fascism it's like a rising tide threatening to engulf us all.'

'You're dead right there,' Frank said with some warmth. 'And being a collection o' offshore islands doesnae mean the wave cannae reach us. Chamberlain seems to think that if we give Hitler a bit o' what he wants, that'll satisfy him. That man won't be satisfied until he's stamped the swastika all over Europe.'

Ellie shivered again. 'The things you hear about what's happening to the German and Austrian Jews . . .'

'Oh, I know,' Lesley said, laying a comforting hand briefly on her shoulder. 'I remember Vienna as such a beautiful city: Baroque buildings and music and wonderful coffee houses. Now I have different pictures in my head. It's horrible, really horrible. Are those flowers next to you all right, Frank?'

He gave them the once-over. 'They're fine . . . Lesley.'

Ellie lowered her head to the mail. Despite the sombre nature of their conversation, that 'Lesley' had made her smile. Frank might have added it on as a bit of an afterthought but at least he was making the effort. If he would only give her a chance Ellie was sure the two of them could become good friends. When it came to politics they certainly had a meeting of minds.

She'd left the one personal letter in among the business ones till last. His newspapers all tidied up to his satisfaction, Frank looked up and saw her taking it out of the hand-written envelope. He squinted at the postmark. 'Is that Aileen asking you to go up again? You didn't go last year, did you?'

'She'd only just married Hugh.' Ellie's eyes sparkled with mischief as she looked up at him. 'I had no desire to play gooseberry.'

Frank groaned. 'You've cracked that joke one too many times, Ellie.'

'Hugh grows berries in Blairgowrie,' Ellie explained when Lesley looked quizzically at her. 'Once the picking season starts she claims she's going to be not a *merry* widow but a *berry* widow. Says she's also in dire need of some civilised company, which she defines as anybody who's not obsessed with soft fruit and what the rain might or might not do to it.'

'She doesn't help out when they harvest it?' Lesley asked.

'Only by making several hundred pounds of jam,' Ellie said with a laugh. 'Hugh's got plenty of pickers.'

'The tinker folk do it,' Frank said. 'Plus whole families from Glasgow and Dundee. It's a big thing every year, going to the berries at Blair.'

'So, Ellie,' Lesley asked, 'are you going to visit Mrs Drummond?'

'Mrs Robertson now,' Ellie corrected. She tapped Aileen's letter against her lips. 'I'm tempted,' she said. 'I have to admit that I'm tempted. Especially at this time of year.'

'The lochs and the rivers,' Lesley offered. 'The wild flowers by the side of the road.'

'The deid rabbits *on* the road,' Frank put in, giving Ellie a dirty look. 'Especially when the racing driver here thinks she's whizzing round the circuit at Brooklands.'

'I swerve to avoid each and every one of them,' she said indignantly.

'Thanks for telling me that. Now I'll worry even more about you.' Ready to move on to his next task, he stood up but stayed for a moment looking down at her. 'Go on, Ellie. It would do you good.'

'You need a break too,' she said. 'Why don't you head for the hills?'

'We can't both be away at the same time.'

'Yes, we can. Lesley can hold the fort now.'

He muttered something incomprehensible and took himself off to the kitchen. Ellie looked over at Lesley. 'Sorry,' she said.

Lesley shrugged.

Ellie was standing in front of her wardrobe mirror that evening when Frank sauntered in.

'Not like you to be admiring yourself.' He cupped her shoulders with his big hands. 'Are you wondering what Aileen Robertson's going to see after the two-year gap?'

Ellie smiled at him in the mirror. 'You know me too well, Francis Rafferty.'

'You're not plump,' he said. 'You're womanly.'

'So you keep telling me,' murmured Ellie.

'Believe it,' Frank responded. 'You're a very attractive young lady, Miss Douglas. Speaking of your single status . . .'

'Yes?' Ellie said, lifting her chin as though in anticipation of a fight.

Frank smiled. 'I was only going to ask if you think she'll have a go at you about it. The big question, I mean.'

'If she does,' Ellie said decisively, 'I shall tell her to mind her own business, jump in the Riley and drive home as fast as I can.'

He planted a soft kiss on the top of her head. 'Do the first one but not the second. And certainly not the third. You need some good fresh countryside air to put the roses back into your cheeks.'

'Don't you need that too, Frank?'

'I'm fine. You go off to Pitlochry and relax. I don't suppose I can persuade you to go for a fortnight?'

'Too bloody right you can't. After a week of all that peace and fresh air I'll be desperate to get back to Glasgow. You could go, you know,' she said, refusing to leave the subject. 'We can trust Lesley to look after things here.'

His hands moved on her shoulders but he said nothing.

'Give her a chance, Frank,' Ellie said softly, studying his unsmiling face in the mirror. 'She's an asset to The Cat, plus she's had a really hard time over the past few years. Be nice to her – for my sake, if nothing else. Because it would make me happy if you did.'

His hands stopped moving. 'Don't do that coaxing thing,' he growled.

'All right,' Ellie said, dimpling at him. 'Promise me you'll at least make an effort. Like you did today when you called Lesley by her first name. I was really pleased when I heard you do that.'

'Dammit, Ellie, now you're being the mammy rewarding the wee boy wi' a sweetie for being good.'

Ellie shrugged off his hands and turned round to face him, putting her own hands on her hips. 'Francis Rafferty, you're not playing the game! Men are supposed to allow women to wind them round their little fingers. That's how it works.'

'No' between us,' he said. 'Didn't we agree on honesty when we started out on this adventure together?'

'We did,' Ellie said. 'Just promise me one thing, then.'

'Tell me what it is first.'

She grinned at him. 'That I won't come back and find blood on the walls.'

'Are you warm enough, Ellie? Don't want to go in yet?'

'I'm lovely and warm,' Ellie said, turning as Aileen came out of her cottage on to the wooden veranda at the back of it. 'Especially with this travelling rug over my feet. You're spoiling me. Oh, you're doing it again. Thanks.' Feet stretched out on the cushions that topped the slatted steamer chair, she reached up to take a china beaker of tea out of Aileen's hands. 'I love the light nights, don't you?'

'They're wonderful. Except they mean Hugh can be out in the fields until midnight. Something sweet to go with your tea?'

'The land o' cakes,' Ellie murmured as she pondered the delights being offered to her. 'As it says in F. Marian McNeill's book.'

Aileen nodded. 'It's an old, old name for Scotland. We've always been known for our sweet tooth.'

They sat for a while sipping their tea and nibbling on their cakes. Having been chatting non-stop since Ellie's arrival the day before, it was nice to enjoy some companionable silence. Besides, Ellie was feasting her eyes on the scene before her, gazing down the long garden of tussocky green grass bordered by gorse and rhododendron bushes to the peaty and tumbling burn at the foot of it. Shaggy red Highland cattle grazed in a field on the opposite bank. Behind them the land climbed up into the hills. She drew a sigh of deep contentment.

'I must say, I envy you this view, Aileen.'

'I never thought you were much of a country person, Ellie.'

'I do love the city.' She put her empty beaker down and laced her hands together behind her neck. 'But I wouldn't mind a wee bolt hole somewhere. So would Frank. We talk about buying somewhere now and again. Loch Lomondside, maybe.'

She had deliberately introduced his name into the conversation. Her hostess had spent the last twenty-four hours scrupulously avoiding it. Ellie looked across at her, a wry smile twisting her mouth. 'Why don't we get the question out of the way now, Aileen, so I can enjoy the next few days without worrying when it's going to come up?'

Aileen gave her something approaching one of the glowers Ellie remembered from her early days at Bellevue. 'What question would that be?'

'The one as to why the whole world wonders why Frank doesn't make an honest woman of me.' Ellie brought her intertwined fingers up over the back of her head, ruffling her auburn hair. 'I wonder why there's no male equivalent of that expression?'

'That's easy to answer,' Aileen said darkly. 'It's the woman who earns herself the bad reputation. The man in question is looked on as a bit of a lad – envied by other men because he's having his cake and eating it. I'm sorry to put it so crudely, Ellie, but that is the way most people look at it. I really don't understand why you don't sort things out. Do you have some Bohemian horror of being respectable?'

It was on the tip of Ellie's tongue to ask Aileen how respectable she thought James and Angela Tait's marriage had been when she herself had been the third partner in that particular relationship, but that would have been cruel. She contented herself with a marginally less barbed question.

'What is it about happily married people that makes them want the whole world to live the same way they do? Pipes and slippers and a bungalow in Bearsden.'

'Hugh and I aren't like that at all,' Aileen retorted. 'We've both kept our own houses, I've stayed in my job and we really only see one another at the weekends. We both get sick of the sight of that road over thc Moulin Muir between here and Blair but I'm determined to keep my job and my independence. I learned that lesson the hard way.'

Ellie looked at her. 'I'm sorry, Aileen. You've been through some stormy waters in your life. I know that.'

'I'm in a safe harbour now. That's what Hugh has done for me. He knows about James Tait and he's forgiven me for it. I'll always be grateful to him for that.'

Ellie returned her gaze to the Highland cattle. One of them had a calf. With its curly coat and its cute little face, it reminded her of a teddy bear. Staring at the little beast, she was wondering if it was Hugh Robertson – a humorous and kindly man – or his wife who felt she needed to be forgiven for something that had happened long before they had met one another.

'I'm sorry,' she said, turning once more to Aileen. 'I'm a bit prickly on the subject.'

'Which might explain why you tell me to ask the question and then craftily manage to avoid answering it.'

Ellic smiled into her eyes. 'Damn,' she said. 'I was hoping you wouldn't have noticed that.'

'Go on,' Aileen said. 'Get *your* question out of the way. Then I can enjoy the next few days too.'

'I never have asked you.'

'No, and I appreciate the delicacy. But I think you've been curious.'

'I have,' Ellie agreed. 'Do you still think about him?'

'Sometimes.'

'But you love Hugh.'

'Yes,' Aileen said, 'I love Hugh. Maybe it's not the grand passion I felt for James Tait,' she laughed softly, 'not like it is in the romantic novels. But it's comfortable. More than comfortable.'

'I'm comfortable with Frank,' Ellie said. 'The way we are. We're both really comfortable with that.'

Aileen gave her a speaking look, then posed another question. 'Do you still think about Evander?'

'Sometimes.' She smiled at her interrogator. 'He's a fond memory. We were both so young and it was all so terribly romantic. Including the fact that it was *doomed*.' She emphasised the word and opened her eyes wide as she said it, making fun of it. 'The son of the house and the kitchenmaid. Like something out of a novel by one of the Brontë sisters.' She was silent for a moment or two, remembering it all. 'I think of him sometimes and hope that he's happy. Wherever he is. He's probably living on the other side of the world with a wife and six children.'

'But you're happy with Frank? The way things are?'

'Yes,' Ellie said firmly. 'To both of those.'

'You're so stubborn, Ellie. Since I'm obviously getting nowhere here, I suppose I might as well tell you my big news.'

Ellie laughed. 'I thought we'd exhausted every possible piece of that.'

'I've been saving the best till last.' Aileen's hand went protectively to her still flat stomach.

Ellie's eyes opened wide. 'Oh, Aileen,' she breathed. 'Oh, Aileen, that's wonderful news!'

Chapter 31

Delivering her pay to one of the waitresses who was off work with a heavy cold, Lesley came down the stairs of the red sandstone tenement in Garnethill where the girl lived and scowled at the torrential rain that was sweeping along the street. July in Glasgow. The monsoon season.

There was no point in raising her brolly. It would only get blown inside out. Or possibly lift her up right up into the air and set her down again somewhere about Falkirk. The wind was blowing a fearsome westerly.

Pausing for a moment in the close mouth, Lesley reconnoitred her route back to The Minister's Cat. There was an office building on the corner of the next street with an extravagant polished pink granite portico. Once she had reached its shelter she plucked her hat off her head and looked at it in disgust. The force of the rain had knocked its brim completely out of shape and the little feather that adorned it was broken in half. She squashed it, stuck it into the pocket of her raincoat, and made another mad dash for the Roman Catholic church on the next corner.

She shook herself when she got there, reminding herself of Douglas the Dug after he'd emerged from an illicit swim in a boating lake or duck pond. As one of the inner double doors of the church swung open behind her, Lesley stepped out of the way of whoever was coming out. 'Horizontal rain, eh?' she said cheerfully.

'It's bloody wet whichever way it falls.' Frank Rafferty turned his collar up and extracted a pack of cigarettes from the pocket of his trench coat.

Blinking in surprise at seeing him, Lesley spoke without thinking. 'Been in there seeking forgiveness for your sins?'

He stopped in the act of putting the cigarette to his mouth. 'If I was, it's no concern of yours. D'you think you could maybe mind your own business for once, Miss Matheson?'

She didn't say anything. She simply looked at him and went back out into the rain. Frank stared after her for a few seconds before muttering, 'Oh, bloody hell,' and returning his unlit cigarette to the packet. Running along the street, he fell into step beside her. He noticed that she was wearing flat shoes, was almost exactly the same height as him and walked like a sportswoman – one who seemed intent on reaching her own personal finishing line in record-breaking time.

'Look,' he said, putting one hand out to grab her arm, 'I'm sorry if I snapped at you back there.'

She shook him off and kept on walking. 'You never do anything else but snap at me, Mr Rafferty.'

'I'm trying to apologise—'

'Well, you're not very good at it!' Lesley howled, stopping in the middle of the pavement and whirling round to face him. Her dark hair had gone into sodden ringlets and rivulets of water were dripping down her face. Frank's eyes narrowed. Was that only rain he could see running down her cheeks?

'You're completely drookit, woman. Let's run.' He

reached for her hand but she leaped back from him as though a coal had fallen out of a fire. A droplet of water collected on the end of her nose and she wiped it away with the back of her hand. 'Leave me alone, would you? Just leave me alone!'

For the second time in as many minutes, she left him staring blankly after her. He followed her to the restaurant, keeping well back and allowing her to go on ahead of him. Even so, when he got there she was still taking off her coat, standing in the middle of the kitchen, staring into space.

Thinking savagely that there was no accounting for the strangeness of women, Frank strode over to the linen cupboard and pulled out two towels, flinging one across to Lesley. 'Here. Dry your hair. You look like a drowned rat.'

'Thank you for those few kind words,' she murmured.

That was the last full sentence he heard from her all afternoon. She had clearly decided to give him the silent treatment, speaking to him only when it was strictly necessary and rejecting all his attempts to be friendly. By the early evening Frank's nerves were jangling like a box of knives.

It didn't help that the woman herself seemed suddenly to have become accident prone. Frank wasn't at all convinced that the dropping of pans and bowls and wooden spoons – one of those fell out of Lesley's hand and skited from one side of the kitchen to the other, smearing a sticky trail in its wake – wasn't deliberate, designed to annoy him.

Why did women have to be so bloody irrational? Ellie had asked him to give Lesley Matheson a chance. He'd been trying to do that for several hours now and getting absolutely nowhere. Why the Honourable Miss Matheson couldn't meet him halfway he didn't know.

After the early evening rush was over he went through to the kitchen, determined to have it out with her.

He hit the swing door with far too much force. Ladling soup into two plates on Alison's tray, Lesley looked up, a startled expression on her face. Her hand jerked, spilling the ladleful of soup over the tray and on to the floor. 'Do you have to come in like a bull in a china shop?' she demanded.

'For God's sake! What a bloody mess! Can't you be more careful?'

'It was an accident,' Alison put in anxiously. 'Lesley got a fright when you came in.'

'It was clumsiness,' Frank snapped back. 'If it's the wrong time of the month or something maybe Miss Matheson should go home.'

Alison blushed, a deep rosy-red suffusing her face and throat. Tight-lipped, Lesley wiped her tray, took down another plate from the shelf above her and filled it with soup. 'On you go, Alison,' she said. 'Can't keep the customers waiting. I'll clear up the rest of it.'

She reached for a floor cloth and rinsed it out under the tap. She crouched down and mopped up the mess on the floor. Only once she had bobbed back to her feet did she look at Frank. 'That remark was totally unnecessary.' She raised her beautifully arched eyebrows. 'Also inaccurate. You're three weeks out. Which is neither relevant nor any of your business.'

Absurdly, now Frank himself was feeling the beginnings of a blush. Lesley hadn't finished with him yet. 'More importantly, it was absolutely unforgivable to come out with something like that in front of Alison. You embarrassed her.'

Only too aware of that, Frank glowered ferociously at her. 'Not you?'

'Oh,' Lesley said, rinsing out the dirty floor cloth. 'It takes a lot to embarrass me, Mr Rafferty.' Now she was wringing the scrap of material between her two hands with the sort of force he imagined she really wanted to apply to his neck.

'I'm sure it does,' he flung back. 'You're not exactly a shrinking violet, are you?' He regretted the words the moment they were out of his mouth, especially when he saw Lesley's busy hands still. 'Go home,' he said roughly. 'Alison can take over from now. You're obviously not in the mood tonight.'

Lesley's determined chin flew up. 'I'm a professional cook,' she said, the grey eyes glittering like gunmetal as they always did when she got angry. 'I've got to be in the mood every night. Kindly get out of my kitchen.'

'Your kitchen?' he spluttered.

'I'm the cook,' she said. 'You're front of house. So go out there and flash your scar at all those respectable ladies who come here to get a cheap thrill from ogling it.'

He stared at her for five unforgiving seconds. Then the only evidence that he'd been there was the sound and the motion of the swing door moving violently backwards and forwards.

'Last customers gone?'

'That's why I'm pulling the shutters down.' Completing the job, Frank turned and ran a tired hand through his hair. Like Lesley, courtesy of the rain that had soaked both of them earlier in the day, he had a head of curls tonight. He sighed heavily. 'I'm sorry. That was another unnecessary remark. Start again?'

Lesley looked at him. 'Did Ellie ask you to be nice to me?'

'Can't you tell by how charming I've been to you all day?'

There was something lurking about her mouth which might have been the makings of a smile. Frank took a deep breath. 'You were quite right. What I said earlier *was* unforgivable. I did apologise to Alison, by the way.'

'Who undoubtedly forgave you. You can do no wrong in her eyes.'

'Will *you* forgive me?' he asked. 'For that other unforgivable comment I made?'

Lesley shrugged. 'You only said what a lot of people think about me. That I'm a bit shop-soiled.'

Frank winced. 'Horrible expression to use about yourself.'

'It was Lachie's lawyer who used it first. In open court with everybody listening in. "Are you really trying to convince us that you came to your marriage an untouched virgin, Mrs Hamilton-Stewart? Wouldn't it be more accurate to say that my client found himself cruelly deceived and that he had in fact taken on a rather shop-soiled bride?" I can still see him in my mind's eye, all superior and condescending in his wig and gown.'

'Tell me where to find the bastard and I'll go round and punch his lights out.'

The smile broke through. 'You would too, wouldn't you? If someone insulted Ellie in any way. Or anyone else you cared about.'

'Like the proverbial shot,' Frank said. 'Look, it's a foul night. The rain's stoating off the pavements. Let's sit down together for ten minutes; have a bowl of soup or something.'

'If I haven't thrown it all over the floor?'

'Aye.' He grinned. 'Afterwards I'll call for a cab to take you home.'

'All right,' she said, responding to his grin and his invitation with a shy dip of the head which was as intriguing as it was unexpected, 'we'll do that.'

They sat at the table in the window. Frank walked round beforehand, turning off most of the lights. 'We don't want any late-night revellers seeing a wee glint through the shutters and thinking we're still open for business. This is nice,' he said as he joined her at the big table. 'Maybe we ought to start serving candle-lit suppers on Saturday nights.'

The shadows around them cast his face into stark relief, highlighting its strong planes. Something else was highlighted too. Lesley's eyes went to the thin line that snaked across his right cheek. 'I have to apologise too,' she said. 'For that remark I made about your scar.'

He shrugged. 'Your observation was accurate enough. My problem is that I can never get rid of it. You know? It colours people's opinion of me.' He applied himself to his soup.

'There are some things I don't think I'm ever going to be able to get rid of either,' Lesley said wryly. 'My notorious reputation for a start.'

He tore a bread roll in two and handed her half of it. 'Want to talk about it?'

She took the bread from him and drank two spoonfuls of soup. Then, eyes downcast, she began to talk. 'I did have affairs after I got married. Lots of them.'

'Why?'

That brought her eyes back to his face. 'Why?'

'Presumably you married the toff with the name that sounds like half the entire line-up o' the Kingussie shinty team because you loved him. It could hardly have been for the money. You came frae money.'

Lesley raised her left hand to her hair, teasing out some of the rain-set curls. 'It was the other way round. Lachie wanted my father's money and my family wanted their daughter to marry into the more ancient echelons of aristocracy.'

'And when your father's money dried up during the Depression?'

'Lachie consoled himself by keeping company with several members of the opposite sex. Lots of members of the opposite sex.'

'Could you no' have divorced him for that? Then he could have married some other poor lassie for her father's dough.'

Lesley raised her eyebrows at that 'poor lassie'. 'He refused to co-operate. Said he came from one of Scotland's most ancient and noble families and that the shame of divorce had never yet besmirched their escutcheon.'

Frank's grin flashed briefly. 'That's easy for you to say. I'll no' attempt it myself. I suppose his lot murdered their spouses if they wanted rid o' them.' He chewed a morsel of bread. 'When they werenae too busy having their wicked way with half the women on their estates or evicting folk to make way for sheep.'

Lesley smiled at him. 'You should see what goes on at house parties too.'

'Really?' Frank sat up straighter in his chair. 'So it's true what they say about folk creeping about the corridors in the middle o' the night?'

'Yes. But I'm not going to give you any salacious details.'

'Spoilsport.' He spooned up what remained of his

soup and tore off another wedge of bread to wipe the plate. 'The rest of the story?'

'My parents didn't want me to get divorced either.'

'Because it would besmirch the Matheson thingumajig?'

She nodded. 'In the end I thought that if I couldn't beat Lachie, I would join him. I started having affairs all over the place, with the most unsuitable of people, the sort who would blab to their friends and to the scandal sheets.'

'So he would divorce you?'

'I think I also wanted to punish myself in some way for having been such a fool as to marry the dreadful cad in the first place. Maybe for having been daft enough to fall in love.'

'How many men did you sleep with? Apart from the cad, I mean?'

Lesley drew her breath in.

'I want to know for a reason,' Frank said gravely. 'I'm no' asking out o' prurient interest. A hundred?' he suggested.

'Nothing like a hundred!'

'How many then? Twenty? Ten? Two?'

'Four,' she said at last.

'Four?' Frank repeated. '*Four?* Christ, lassie, in my book that makes you more or less as pure as the driven snow. I must have slept with—' He caught himself on. 'Well, a lot more than four. An awful lot more. No' that I've ever counted the scalps, so to speak.'

Lesley frowned. 'Are you telling me that you've been unfaithful to Ellie?'

Frank sat back in his chair and smiled a smile of heart-melting warmth. 'I could never be unfaithful to Ellie.'

She visibly relaxed, although she was still frowning at him. 'You must have been extremely precocious in your youth, then.'

Frank rose from the table. 'If I knew what that meant I might agree wi' ye,' he said cheerfully.

Lesley looked up at him. 'Why do you so often pretend to be stupid when you're anything but?'

'Because it catches folk off balance.'

'You really do love Ellie, don't you?'

'She's like a part of me,' he said softly. 'The better part of me. Come on, it's time we were getting you home. You take the rest of the stuff and I'll bring the plates. It's a bit dark in here,' he said when they reached the kitchen. 'Put some lights on, would you?'

He stood to one side of the swing door, holding the plates and waiting for her to do as he'd asked. The only area that was illuminated was the section at the other end of the room, which they used as an office. Standing in the shadows in front of him, Lesley made no move toward the bank of switches on the other side of the door.

Frank's brain was once more registering the fact that she was the same height as him when she suddenly leaned forward and planted a kiss on his cheek. He felt himself freeze into immobility. 'What was that for?'

'To thank you for being nice to me like Ellie asked you to. You're a sweet man.'

'I've been called a lot o' things in my life but the word "sweet" has very seldom figured.' As his mouth curved he saw Lesley's eyes go to his scar.

'Did it hurt terribly when you were slashed?'

'No' at the time. Too much adrenalin flowing then. Afterwards, yes. Especially when the young doctor was stitching it. It hurt like buggery then.'

She had raised her hand to his face, was tracing the scar with her fingertips. 'Like a road in the moonlight,' she whispered.

Frank's russet eyelashes fluttered and closed. When she reached the end of that moonlit road and lifted those indescribably gentle fingers away from his face he opened his eyes and made one simple request. 'Do that again.'

Lesley drew her breath in: a gasp of horror at what she had done. 'No. I shouldn't have touched it in the first place. I'm sorry. I don't know what came over me. Please forgive me.' She stepped back, putting distance between them. Retreating from him.

The man who liked everything neat and tidy and who abhorred mess of any kind simply dropped the plates he was holding on to the floor. His hands were cupping her face before they even hit it. He didn't hear them crack and break.

'Why did you touch my scar, Lesley Matheson?'

Her fingers were on his wrists, trying to pull his hands away. Her voice was a tortured whisper. 'I don't know. *I don't know!*'

'Yes you do.' Frank bent his head forward and kissed her gently on the mouth. He felt the electrifying pleasure of that contact. He felt Lesley's shock at what he had done. He took advantage of that to kiss her again, his lips more urgent and more passionate. When she melted against him and met his mouth with a passion that equalled his own, a fierce joy coursed through his veins.

When it was over he rested his arms loosely on her shoulders. 'I've been fighting that since you first walked in here,' he confessed, 'that day you fainted into my arms.'

Lesley began to struggle, pulling herself out of his embrace. 'We can't do this to Ellie. We can't!' She ran to the side door, snatching her coat from the pegs beside it.

Frank reached it seconds later, one strong arm across the door to bar her way. 'Lesley . . . please . . .'

'Don't say anything. Please don't say anything. Let me go.' She looked at him out of wild and despairing eyes. 'Please let me go.'

'Of course I'll let you go.' He dropped his arm, stunned that she would think him capable of using his superior strength to stop her from leaving. Then again, hadn't he proved himself capable of much worse towards defenceless females?

Lesley flung herself out into the lane, the door banging behind her. Frank slid down to the tiled floor of the kitchen. He sat as he had done as a boy, knees drawn up and his head lowered down on to them.

He looked up eventually, reaching up to the coat hooks for the cigarettes in the pocket of his trench coat. Then he began to smoke his way through the entire packet.

The following morning Lesley marched in and flung a white envelope down in front of him where he sat at the table in the office area.

'What's this?' He sounded like a grizzly bear with a sore throat. Small wonder when his mouth felt as rough and as dry as a gravel pit.

'My resignation.' The words were beautifully enunciated, her voice calm and level.

Frank locked eyes with her, tore her letter neatly in two and dropped it into the waste-paper bin at his feet. 'Your resignation is not accepted. We need to talk.'

'There's nothing to talk about. I'm handing in my notice. I'd like to leave as soon as possible, if that's all right with you.'

He glared at her. 'No, it bloody well isn't all right with me.'

When she gripped the edge of the table he saw that she wasn't calm at all. 'I can't stay here with you!'

'Lesley . . .' He reached forward, wanting only to cover those whitening fingers with his own; wanting only to comfort her. She snatched her hands away.

'There's things I need to tell you,' he said. 'Important things.'

'I don't want to hear them.'

'All right,' he said. 'I'll go away for a few days, give us both some breathing space. When I get back we'll talk.'

Running upstairs to the flat, he threw some things into his rucksack. He needed fresh air and wide open spaces. He needed to walk and he needed to think.

Ellie came breezing into the kitchen a few hours later, changing immediately into her print dress and cook's apron. She'd be ready for action as soon as she'd finished the sandwich and cup of tea Alison had set down in front of her. 'When did Frank say he'd be back?'

'He didn't,' Alison replied. 'Said we've to look for him when we see him coming.'

'Very helpful.' Ellie took a healthy bite of her sandwich and riffled through the letters lying in the middle of the table. 'Looks like he only got halfway through this morning's mail before he decided to head for the hills. That's not like him.' She lifted one envelope, slit it open and unfolded the letter inside. As she scanned down it she began to frown.

'Something wrong?' Alison asked.

'It's from the new landlords of this building.' Ellie's frown deepened. 'I didn't know that we had new landlords. I'm sure Frank paid last quarter's rent to the factors' office in Bath Street where we've always paid it.'

'Where's that letter come from?'

'Somewhere up in Port Dundas. It seems a funny place for this sort of a company.' She looked up. 'Lochaber Holdings. Ever heard of them?'

Alison shook her head. 'Lesley might know.'

'What might I know?' Turning around from the store cupboard in front of which she was standing, Lesley had a rather odd look on her face: as though she'd been caught doing something she shouldn't be rather than simply taking out a fresh wooden spoon. Ellie repeated the name at the top of the letter.

'There was an article in the paper last week about this company that has only recently moved into Glasgow and seems to be buying up an awful lot of property. I think that might have been your Lochaber Holdings.'

'What do they want with us?' asked Alison.

'To put the rent up,' Ellie said in dismay. 'After first congratulating us on how well we're doing – as evidenced by the recent article in the *Glasgow Evening Dispatch*—'

'The one Josie wrote after she and Roddy were here the last time,' Lesley said. 'It was great publicity. Brought us lots of new business.'

Ellie's voice was very dry. 'Not enough to justify putting the rent up to three times what it is now.'

'Oh, that's not fair!' Alison breathed.

Ellie scanned down the page to find the signature. It was indecipherable. The only thing typed beneath it were the block capitals of 'LOCHABER HOLDINGS.'

'Right,' she said, standing up and shoving her chair back. 'Whoever Lochaber Holdings are they aren't going to know what's hit them by the time I finish with them.'

Within seconds she was heading through the restaurant and out to the Riley, parked at the kerb in front of it.

'Sometimes you remember that she's got red hair, eh?' Alison looked at Lesley, still standing in front of the store cupboard clutching the new wooden spoon. 'Are you all right?'

Lesley flashed her a brilliant smile. 'I'm fine.'

'Speak to my superior?' The young man in the smart double-breasted suit gave her a pitying smile. 'I'm afraid Mr Cameron never speaks to individual tenants, dear.'

Gritting her teeth at that 'dear', Ellie leaned forward over the counter. Her temper hadn't been improved by the time it had taken her to find the offices of Lochaber Holdings. Parking the car near Spiers Warf, she'd had to ask six different people before she found anyone who'd ever heard of them.

Discovering them eventually at the top of a rickety outside staircase at the end of a large stone building, she had entered their premises to be surprised by how modern and up-to-date their fixtures and fittings were. This certainly wasn't the kind of business you expected to find in an industrial complex like Port Dundas.

'Mr Cameron is going to have to make an exception in my case,' she said sweetly, 'because I'm not leaving here until he does. He is in, I take it?'

The young man wasn't as clever as he thought he was. His gaze drifted across to a door that obviously led into an inner office. Before he had realised what she was up to, Ellie dodged behind the counter. The three other young men and the two girls sitting at typewriters or speaking into telephones gawped in amazement as she strode past them.

He was sitting in a very modern black leather chair with his back to the door. All she could see was an arm and hand holding a phone and a glimpse of thick dark hair. The cuffs of what looked like a silk shirt were undone and an expensive watch was sliding down his fine-boned wrist.

'Could somebody please do something about this infernal racket? I'm making an important phone call here.' The leather chair swung round. 'Ah,' said the man sitting in it. He spoke into the phone. 'Forgive me, I'll have to get back to you later.'

He uncoiled himself from the luxurious chair and stood up. He was as tall and as dark-haired as he had been the last time she had seen him. His shoulders were wider and his face stronger, its features more defined and more masculine. His nose was a little broader than she remembered. Then again, it would be.

'It's all right,' he said to the cocky lad who'd pursued Ellie into the office. 'I'll attend to this lady.'

Evander walked round a desk littered with documents. 'You must have a lot of questions, Ellie. Shall we go outside and I'll try to answer at least some of them?'

Chapter 32

He stood back politely to allow her to precede him down the rickety wooden stairs. Waiting at the bottom, Ellie watched him descend the last few steps. 'Round to the *Gipsy Queen*'s berth?' he suggested. 'Although she'll not be there now. She still does the Craigmarloch run.'

They walked in silence through the busy wharfs, steering a course between lorries, horse-drawn carts and men shouldering bags of coal or delivering materials and machinery to the engineering workshops and boat repair yards that covered the area. At Spiers Warf itself a group of men were unloading a grain scow. Moving past them to a quieter corner, Ellic stopped and turned to face him, taking a step or two back so that his height wouldn't give him quite such an advantage over her.

'You've still got freckles,' Evander murmured.

'What?'

'Nothing. You must have some more questions. You look like you've seen a ghost.'

'I have. What the hell are you doing here?'

'Running a business,' he said smoothly. 'The same as you, so I hcar. I understand you're doing very well. Lots of regular customers. With the added bonus that you've recently become fashionable with the smart set.' His lips twitched. 'I'm glad to see that you yourself still go in for the tempestuous petticoat look.'

Coming out in such a rush that she'd forgotten even to put her hat back on, Ellie was still wearing her cook's apron under her jacket. She might be a highly successful restaurateur but she must look like a typical wee Glasgow housewife. In his elegant dark suit Evander looked every inch the successful young businessman.

'How did you know what I was doing?'

'The name of that restaurant you and Frank Rafferty run is a bit of a giveaway, don't you think?'

'Whereas the name you've adopted is intended to conceal?'

He shrugged. 'I didn't much care for the name I had, so I took one belonging to a man I admired.'

'Your grandfather.'

'Well remembered.'

'I presume it also means that your family doesn't know you're back in Glasgow.'

'I bloody hope not.' Evander thrust his hands into his trouser pockets, pushing back the edges of his unbuttoned jacket. 'That would spoil my plan.'

'You have a plan?'

'Doesn't everybody?'

'And you're a property speculator?'

He gave her a reproachful look. 'Don't say it like that, Ellie. I don't deal in slum housing and I don't foreclose on any widows and orphans. I specialise in commercial property. You'd be surprised how many people have been paying more or less the same rent since Queen Victoria was a girl. If their businesses are doing well they should be paying more.'

'You drive a hard bargain?'

'Of course I do. In a couple of years' time all these buildings I buy and sell and sometimes lease back out may well be bombed to smithereens by our German friends. With all the confusion and uncertainty about that, now is the ideal time to drive hard bargains. I'm trying to accumulate as much capital as possible in as short a time as possible.'

This wasn't the dreamy and idealistic boy she had known. The disappointment sent a harsh question to Ellie's lips. 'Like father, like son?'

'Ouch.' Evander reached into his inside pocket but his hand came out empty. 'I keep forgetting that I've given up smoking. A filthy habit. As you always used to say back at Bellevue.'

The disappointment was as bitter as vinegar now: that relaxed reaction to her comparing him with his father, the equally relaxed reference to Bellevue and his earlier crack about her 'tempestuous petticoat'. She had thought that poem would have been a precious memory for both of them, not something to be bandied about in casual conversation.

Now he appeared to be extending a cosy invitation to share their joint memories of the time they had spent together at Bellevue. Ellie's head went up. Oh, she didn't think so!

If he was all about business these days then that was what he would get. Her voice was very cool. 'I'm prepared to discuss a reasonable increase in rent but tripling it at one fell swoop is completely unreasonable.'

'I agree. I only set that figure on it because I had a hunch that such patent unfairness would send you racing up here like a Valkyrie.'

She stared at him. 'How long have you been back in Glasgow?'

'Three weeks. I have offices in London and Manchester and I sent a team up to open this one a couple of months ago. I thought I'd come up and see how they're doing.'

She had heard only that 'three weeks'. She repeated the words, her voice rising. 'Three weeks? And in all that time, and seemingly knowing exactly where I was, you didn't think of simply walking through the door of The Cat? I don't understand. Why play this stupid game with the rent?'

'Perhaps I thought your . . . *partner* . . . might object to my presence,' he said, pronouncing the ambiguous word in a silky tone of voice that reminded her horribly of his father. 'You and Frank Rafferty do work *and* live together, don't you, Ellie,' he paused, 'the latter activity being in what you might call the Biblical sense?'

Ellie's green eyes blazed. 'Eight years,' she said, her voice shaky with anger. 'Eight years without a single word. Not a card or a letter to even let me know that you were still alive.'

'You worried about me?'

'Worried about you?' she howled. '*Worried about you?* How dare you, Evander Tait?' She waved one hand wildly in the air. 'Or Evander *Cameron* or whatever the hell it is you call yourself these days. You disappear off the face of the Earth eight years ago. Now you *sneak* into Glasgow like a thief in the night, breenge back into my life and have the unmitigated gall to *judge* me? Let me tell you something, Mr Evander Cameron, you don't understand a *thing* about Frank and me!'

'I understand that the two of you started your business on money you got from selling your child to my parents,' he said calmly. 'Fooled them into believing I was his father. Can't really understand why they would have wanted him on that basis but I suppose that's a question I'll have to put to them. Oh, by the way,' he said, casually folding his arms across his chest, 'remind me to return that money you gave me when you put me on the *Torosay*. I'll try to get it as thirty pieces of silver, shall I?'

Ellie's eyes narrowed. 'What?'

'I'll try to get it—'

'I heard you,' she said tightly. 'Got it all worked out, have you?'

'Actually I can't work out any of it. I can't understand why the Ellie I remember would have given up her own child. I can't understand how in God's name she could have chosen to put a little boy into that house.'

Suddenly not calm at all, he stepped forward. Two impassioned questions were rattled out inches from her face. 'How do you know he's not suffering as I suffered? Is your business success worth a small child's happiness?'

'Jamie's not suffering! Phoebe wouldn't let that happen!'

'My sister?' Evander responded, incredulity written all over his face. 'You're relying on my sister to protect him?'

'Phoebe's changed,' Ellie yelled back. 'People do.'

'So it would appear.'

For a moment they simply looked at one another. He was the first to recover his composure.

'Shall I phone for a taxi to take you back down the road?'

'I have my own car.' Ellie gestured angrily towards it. Watching him as he took in the gleaming dark green paintwork of the sporty little tourer, she saw his brows rise.

'I'm not a kitchenmaid any more,' she snapped.

'Pity,' he said. 'I rather liked the kitchenmaid.' His dark eyes returned to her face. 'There was a time when I even fancied myself in love with her.'

* * *

'Mr Cameron, could you look at—'

'Later. All right?' He was in his office, slamming the door behind him with a vigour that shook the surrounding walls.

The employees of Lochaber Holdings exchanged glances. 'Meeting with the old flame didn't go too well?' suggested one of the girls.

'D'you think that's who the redhead was?' asked the lad sitting at the next desk.

'She didn't look his usual type.' Speaking in the same carefully low tones, the young man who'd tried to stop Ellie from entering the inner office walked over to join his colleagues. 'Besides, in the two years I've been working for him Mr Sophisticated has never struck me as the type who dreams of settling down with one woman for the rest of his life.'

The girl batted her eyelashes at him. 'Maybe that's because the redhead broke his heart when he was a young and sensitive lad.'

The trio of young people jumped apart like guilty lovers when the door to the inner office was flung open again.

'I'm going out,' snapped their boss.

'When will you be back, sir?'

'When I get here,' he snarled.

'Any of the tables which are free, sir. None of them is reserved for another hour. We're usually fairly quiet in the early evening,' the waitress confided.

'I want to see Miss Douglas,' he said, 'and I want to see her right now. Kindly inform her that Mr Evander Cameron is here.'

'Will you take a seat while you're waiting, sir?'

'No.' He propped himself against the wall, folded his arms across his chest and scowled at the china cat on the shelf on the opposite wall.

'There's a Mr Somebody Cameron out here asking to see you.' The waitress pulled a face. '*Demanding* to see you might be a better way of putting it.'

'Tell him the cook never speaks to her diners.'

'But that's no' true, Ellie—'

'Then tell him to clear off. If he tries to object, inform him that the management reserves the right no' to serve any customers it damn' well doesnae want to.' Ellie shook her head. 'No, it's no' fair to ask you to do it.' She marched towards the swing door but Lesley ran after her.

'Let me see if I can sort this out.' She laid a calming hand on Ellie's shoulder. 'We don't want a scene in front of the customers, do we?'

Although she hadn't seen him since he was a boy, Evander bore enough of a resemblance to his father for Lesley Matheson to recognise him immediately. Heathcliff in a business suit, she thought. Or maybe Lord Byron at his most passionate. She recalled what else people had said about the poet. 'Mad, bad and dangerous to know.'

'Well,' she said brightly, 'you handled that really well, didn't you?'

'I beg your pardon?' His tone was icy.

'Your reunion with Ellie,' Lesley said, deliberately using the sort of tone you might employ if you were teaching a small child how to perform a simple task like telling the time. 'After eight years of her having no idea whether you were alive or dead, you spring out of the secret door in the wainscoting and accuse her of being a cross between Lucrezia Borgia and a female King

Herod. She's been banging and crashing pots together for hours. Ever since she came back down the hill from Port Dundas. As you may possibly recall, that's not her style at all.'

'Do I know you?' The ice had grown several inches thicker: as dense and opaque as the surface of Bingham's Pond in a good winter for skaters.

Lesley's voice was an amused murmur. 'Nice to know I'm so forgettable.'

Recognition dawned on Evander's face. 'Miss Lesley Matheson. Mrs Hamilton-Stewart as was. Messy divorce, I believe.'

She raised her eyebrows. 'Make it our business to know everything, do we? I suppose it's a prerequisite for ruthless capitalists.'

'I want to see Ellie,' he said stiffly. 'I *insist* on seeing Ellie.'

'You're in no position to insist on anything, my friend.' She gave him a withering look. 'Thirty pieces of silver? Whatever the circumstances and whatever the rights and wrongs of it, don't you think that particular comment was a bit much? A little melodramatic too, I'd say. Have you any idea how much you've upset her?'

The thaw was as complete as it was unexpected. Evander found his way to the window seat and sank down on to it. 'You're quite right. Even by my admittedly rather puerile standards, it was extremely melodramatic.' He rubbed a hand over his face. 'Not to mention unforgivable.'

Lesley had followed him to the table. 'Yes, well. There's been lots of that going on around here lately.'

He hadn't heard her. 'Would you do something for me?' He extracted a business card and a fountain pen from the inside pocket of his jacket. Throwing the card on to the table, he leaned over and wrote a number on the back of it. 'Please tell her that if she ever feels like speaking to me again she can reach me on either of these numbers – my office and the hotel I'm staying at.'

He stood up, gave her the card and headed for the door out to Buchanan Street. Lesley made a grab for his sleeve. 'Come with me. You may have to be prepared to duck.'

Ellie was standing in the middle of the kitchen with a large pot in either hand. 'What do you want?'

Evander smiled a weary smile. 'What I would like at this precise moment is some food. I haven't had anything since breakfast and I didn't eat much then.' He eyed up the pans she held. 'I dare say what I'm going to get is bashed about the head with assorted cookware.'

'You realise that's what you deserve?'

'I do. I'm sorry, Ellie. I apologise unreservedly. You're quite right. I have absolutely no right to judge you.'

She grunted, and set down her pans. 'Sit there,' she said, pointing to the table. A minute later she put a plate of stovies in front of him. 'You'll take a glass of milk with these and like it.'

'The only possible accompaniment,' he murmured, looking gravely up at her. 'Will you sit down with me while I eat?'

'No.' She set a fork on the table. 'If you were hungry why didn't you eat your dinner earlier?'

'Because I've spent the last few hours walking all over Glasgow. I couldn't seem to stop walking. Even when I began to get really tired.'

'Bloody stupid thing to do.'

'Yes,' he agreed. He lifted the fork. She let him get a few mouthfuls in before her next question.

'Why didn't you have much to eat at breakfast?'

'Because I thought I'd probably see you today and I was nervous about it.'

She raised her eyebrows at that. 'At least you were forewarned. How d'you think I felt when I walked in and saw you sitting there?'

'Shocked, I suppose. A bit surprised.'

'A *bit* surprised? You're a master of understatement.'

'Look,' he said, 'can we start again?'

'Why would we do that?'

'Because we were good friends once.'

Ellie folded her arms. 'Such good friends that you never wrote me a letter to tell me whether you were alive or dead.'

'I wrote you scores of letters. Just never posted any.' He glanced around the kitchen. 'Have you noticed how carefully everyone in here isn't looking in our direction? Will you come to my hotel for a drink so we can talk a bit more privately?'

Ellie shook her head. 'No. I'm tired.'

'Is that my fault?'

'Don't flatter yourself.'

'Come out with me tomorrow afternoon, then, when we're both fresh. We could go for a run in your car. Or would Frank Rafferty not let you do that?'

'Let me?' Ellie snorted in derision. 'Frank knows that I make my own decisions. He's not here at the moment anyway. I'll pick you up from your office at two o'clock tomorrow afternoon.' She narrowed her eyes at him. 'Have I just been outmanoeuvred?'

'Possibly.' He gave her a suspiciously bland smile. 'May I have some more stovies?'

Chapter 33

Picking him up as arranged the following afternoon, Ellie laid down her ground rules. 'I want you to know that I'm doing this against my better judgement. I was going to change my mind about it but Lesley Matheson persuaded me not to.'

'I'm grateful to her then,' Evander said lightly.

'I won't tolerate any more recriminations or accusations.'

'I won't make any. I also promise not to comment on your driving.'

Ellie shot him a sideways glance as they pulled away from the kerb. 'I might have known the humble act wouldn't last long. I'll have you know I've just driven up and down to Pitlochry. I've got to deliver something to a place in Ingram Street before we go anywhere. All right?'

'You're the driver. What's at Pitlochry?'

'Who,' Ellie corrected. 'Aileen Robertson. You knew her as Aileen Drummond. She and I became good friends. After you'd left Bellevue.'

That silenced him for a while. Not for long. 'You know,' he said as they bowled across the top of George Square. 'I think she was probably more sinned against than sinning.'

'Wasn't what you used to say.'

'Maybe I've grown up a bit since then. People change, you know. As you reminded me yesterday. Look out for that cart!'

'I saw it from about a mile back,' Ellie said scornfully, pulling out to overtake the horse-drawn brewer's dray.

'Don't you think you're driving a bit fast?'

'I'm slowing right down now.' She had pulled into the kerb. 'Back in two minutes.' She was back in less than that, tucking herself in behind the steering wheel. 'We'll go up Montrose Street.'

'You're the driver,' he said again. He'd been studying a map. He lowered it from his face and looked at her. 'Montrose Street,' he said. 'Quite possibly one of the steepest streets in a city of steep streets.'

'It's all right if you take a run at it,' she said coolly. 'Hang on to your hat.'

'Sometimes I wish I was a Catholic,' Evander muttered as they shot up the hill. 'At moments like this I could do with praying to a whole raft of saints.' He began to enumerate them on his long fingers, the map lying crumpled in his lap. 'St Christopher, for obvious reasons. St Jude for the lost cause of getting up this hill in one piece. Ellie, there's a motorbike and sidecar heading straight for us!'

'He's only overtaking that parked car. All we've got to do is slow down a wee bit to let him back in. It'll probably call for a swift bit of double-declutching but I've never found that to be a problem.' She was very cool, reacting only with the slightest of starts when the man beside her suddenly started shouting in German.

'*Gott im Himmel!* End zis torture by motor vehicle, I beg you, *Du verdammtably* beautiful British spy. I vill tell you vare I haf concealed ze secret plans for ze new German submarine. If only to avoid ending my days squashed between zose two ruddy great trams vich are rumbling past on ze Cathedral Street.'

She didn't react, not even glancing at him as she sat hunched over the steering wheel, waiting for the said trams to pass.

'Thank you, St Jude,' Evander murmured. 'Looks like we're not going to end up in the Ca-shew-ality, as I believe the members of the local tribe refer to the Accident and Emergency department along at the Royal.' He gave a nod of his dark head in the direction of the hospital in question. 'Can we go along that way?'

Not seeing any immediate gap in the traffic, Ellie turned and looked at him. Like her, he was casually dressed today, wearing linen trousers and an open-necked shirt with a sleeveless Fair Isle pullover over the top of it. 'What are we doing?' she asked.

'Sitting waiting to turn right into Cathedral Street.'

'You know what I mean.'

He gave her an odd little smile. 'You've just been showing off your driving skills and I've just been trying to make you laugh. Unsuccessfully, it would appear.'

She was frowning a little. 'I liked the "*verdammtably*".'

'Good,' he said lightly. 'That's a start. I think you've got a space now.'

She pulled out into Cathedral Street and drove along it at a rather more sedate pace than she had tackled Montrose Street. 'Does it hurt your masculine pride to be driven by a woman?'

'Can't say that it does,' he said easily. 'You wouldn't let me drive this car anyway. It's your pride and joy. Am I right?'

'You're right. Beautifully made, a smooth runner and reliable. "As old as the industry . . . as modern as the hour" – that's what they say about Rileys. Would you like me to tell you all the technical details about her engine? In case the conversation flags,' she added sarcastically.

'Ellie,' he said, 'you *know* me. D'you think I'm the sort of man who has even the vaguest idea of, or remotest interest in, what goes on under the bonnet of a car? Besides, we've got lots to talk about.'

'Have we?' she queried, thinking about that 'you know me'. 'I should have thought someone who went to sea might have been interested in engines.'

'Aye, but I swabbed decks and painted interminable lengths of riveted iron to protect them from the salt sea spray. I didnae drive the bloody boat. Can we turn left at the Royal, please?' he asked as they approached the looming grey bulk of the huge Victorian hospital. Both of them checking the traffic in Castle Street, Evander turned his head to the right at the same time as Ellie turned hers to the left. '*Now* you're smiling. Why's that?'

'It's your Glasgow accent. It's stronger than when you lived here. Could you please explain to me why you're the one giving the directions?'

'I sailed with quite a few Glaswegians during my years on the ocean wave. The accent rubs off on you. How did you know that I went to sea?'

'Captain MacLean told me.'

'So you did have some news of me,' he murmured. 'I'm giving the directions because I'm the one with the nice new map of Glasgow and environs. Best quality linen-backed, price three shillings and sixpence. And because men are better at navigating,' he added, losing all the points he had earned by his relaxed attitude to being driven by a female. 'It's a proven scientific fact.'

Ellie made a rude noise. 'Says who? Frank cannae

navigate his way out of a paper bag. It's a minor miracle each time he finds his way home from the hills.'

'Is that where he is now? Hill-walking? Keep going up here. We should be passing Sighthill Cemetery on the left and the St Rollox locomotive works on the right.'

'Don't look so smug,' Ellie said as he was swiftly proved right. As they continued to climb up out of the city he let out an exclamation. 'Oh, look at the Campsies!'

'They'rc beautiful,' Ellie agreed, her eyes also on the green and verdant hills.

'Stunning,' he said. 'I love the way the light falls on them. Has Frank gone up there?'

'No idea. He'd left before I got back from Pitlochry. What was going to sea like?'

'Character building,' he said succinctly.

'Fist fights on foggy wharfs with grim-faced locals in Montevideo and Vladivostok, and that was only the women?'

'Good Lord, you must have been there yourself, Miss Douglas. The weather was often pretty ferocious too.'

'Were you scared?' she asked curiously.

'Sometimes. I did one trip as a steward. When you were told to wet the tablecloths in the officers' mess so the plates wouldn't slide off you realised that a storm was about to catch up with the ship. You always knew you were *really* heading for trouble when the cook stopped serving soup.'

'Not a problem we have in The Cat.'

'I'm sure. When you round the Cape of Good Hope you sail through the Cape Rollers, these hugely powerful waves which rock you from side to side.' Evander lifted one hand from the map, spreading out his fingers and demonstrating the extent of the motion. 'That could be frightening and soothing at the same time. Like being lulled to sleep in a giant cradle.'

'You miss some of it?'

'Some of it,' he agreed. 'Like leaning on the handrail of an evening watching Albert Ross. The sailor's name for the albatross,' he explained when Ellie sent him a swift glance of incomprehension. 'They're wonderful birds. So graceful in the air, with a huge wingspan. They'll stay with a ship for days, like a flying escort. According to the old hands they're the ghosts of departed seafarers.'

'Lovely idea.' Her eyes were once more on the road ahead. 'Which way at this next junction?'

'Straight through Springburn and on up to Bishopbriggs. I wrote a poem about the albatrosses.' He laughed. 'You're the first living soul to whom I've ever confessed that. Some of my former shipmates regarded even the reading of poetry as a somewhat suspect activity.'

'Did you conform to the more traditional picture of seafaring behaviour by having a girl in every port?'

'Ask me no questions and I'll tell you no lies.' He sounded amused. 'Why would you be interested in the history of my love life, anyway? I thought you were happily settled with Frank. Keep going straight.'

Ellie negotiated the next crossroads before she spoke. 'Given that you've only been back in Glasgow for three weeks, why is it that you assume he and I are more than simply business partners?' She glanced over at him. 'Been listening to gossip?'

'I've known about you and Frank for almost four years. One of the Glaswegians I sailed with had ambitions to come ashore and set himself up as a private detective. I gave him his first commission. Keep your eyes on the road,' he said as Ellie turned and stared at him. 'I'm too young and handsome to die.'

She managed that, just. 'You *spied* on us?'

'I got him to make some enquiries,' he said defensively. 'It was hardly spying.'

Ellie decided to let that one go for the moment. 'And you found out what, exactly?'

'About the baby,' Evander said carefully. 'That apparently kept the Temple gossips busy for quite some time. I also found out that you and Frank were a couple. Not much point in sending you letters then, was there?'

She decided to let that one go for the moment too, driving in silence through Kirkintilloch and Kilsyth.

'Here,' Evander said, not long after they had driven out of the latter, 'we turn right here.' Ellie applied the brakes and read the name: '*Craigmarloch*'.

There was a car coming in the opposite direction. She couldn't turn until it had passed them.

'Different when you come by road, isn't it?' He folded the map away. 'It shouldn't be far from here. You can go now, Ellie. There's nothing coming.'

When they had descended a winding hill and reached the canal she parked but didn't turn off the engine.

'Something the matter?'

She drummed her fingers on the steering wheel, not looking at him. 'I'm not sure that this is a very good idea.'

'A walk along the towpath. That's all I'm asking for.'

'Evander . . .'

'For old times' sake,' he said. 'For an old friendship's sake.'

Ellie switched off the engine and peeled off her driving gloves.

As they strolled by the canal a few moments later he commented on the profusion of hawthorns that grew all along the towpath. 'The blossom's glorious, isn't it? Although I suppose the perfume must remind you of hiding from your father the morning he died.'

'I'm surprised you remember that story.'

'I remember a lot of things, Ellie. Do you still think about your father and how badly he treated you?'

'Very seldom.' She hesitated briefly, then decided to tell him. 'He wasn't actually my father, you know.'

'What?' Evander came to a halt, turning to stare at her.

'Keep walking and I'll tell you the tale.'

He shook his head in amazement when she had finished. 'When did you find all this out?'

'Oh, quite a long time back. A friend of my father's took it upon himself to tell me.'

'Nice thing to spring on you.'

'Willie Anderson meant well. He'd always kept it from me before. Circumstances changed and he felt it was something I needed to know.'

'You're sure he was telling you the truth?'

'Oh, aye. Captain MacLean confirmed it all later.'

Evander was pondering what she had said. She could see the cogs turning. 'Did it make it any easier when you thought about how your father had treated you?'

'It made it harder at first,' she said thoughtfully. 'Thinking that I might have grown up in a very different kind of family. Then again, by all accounts my real father was a bit of a ladies' man. The captain also told me that he took a long walk off a short pier one night about fifteen years ago when he'd had one too many. So maybe he wouldn't have been any better than Alan Douglas. Probably wouldn't have wanted the responsibility in any case.'

'You're not curious about him? This "red-haired rogue of a fisherman",' he added, quoting back at her the description which had originally been Willie Anderson's.

Ellie shrugged. 'Not particularly. Don't know how I would find out anything about him, anyway. Neither Willie nor Captain MacLean could remember his surname, only that his first name was Sandy and that his boat sailed out of Aberdeen or Peterhead.' She smiled wryly. 'Or possibly even one of the other fishing ports up there.'

'You could try looking for his family. Go up to the north-east and ask around.'

She looked pityingly at him. 'Evander, do you have any idea how many fishing boats sail out of those harbours? Plus I'd be looking for a red-haired man called Sandy. In Scotland.'

'Good point.' He frowned. 'Didn't you have a little sister who died? Stella, wasn't it?'

'Yes,' Ellie said, once more surprised that he should remember something she had told him so long ago. 'What of it?'

'There are names fishermen traditionally like to give their boats. One of them is *Stella Maris*: the star of the sea. Perhaps your sister was named for her father's boat.'

'It's a possibility, I suppose,' Ellie said, responding to the greeting being thrown across at them from a man sailing past on a lighter piled high with timber.

'But it still doesn't make you want to go and see if you can find your father's family? Maybe you've got other siblings somewhere.'

Ellie smiled. 'Maybe I have.'

He stopped again, surveying her as though she were some exotic laboratory specimen. 'So you're not interested in finding out anything about your real father? You don't think that's always going to be a loose end in your life?'

'I'm happy to live in the here and now. I think looking back to the past was what ruined the life of the man I knew as my father. Alan Douglas never got over my mother's betrayal of him. He took his bitterness out on me. And on Malcolm too,' she added, thinking sadly about her brother, 'who was his own child. I don't want to look back and think about what might have been. I'm content with my life as it is.'

'And happy with Frank.'

'He and I are very comfortable together.'

Evander folded his arms and extended one long leg a little to the side. 'Aren't you a bit young to be settling for content and comfortable?'

'Aren't you a bit young to be making nostalgic journeys back to the past?'

'Is that what you think I'm doing?'

'I think you're like a lot of people nowadays. I think you're wondering what the future holds and I think you're feeling the need to sort things out: tie up those loose ends you were talking about a moment ago.'

Evander unfolded his arms and turned to look at a pair of swans gliding regally by. 'I am at a crossroads in my life,' he admitted.

'Being a property speculator isn't giving you a warm glow of satisfaction and achievement?'

He swung back round. 'Don't be so superior. It's given me a very healthy bank balance. It's often very exciting: when you're about to close a deal and when you get what you want at the price you want to pay for it.'

'You started the business with the money you got from your grandparents' will?'

'That certainly helped,' he said consideringly, 'but I actually bought my first properties before I got my inheritance – which wasn't huge, anyway. When you leave a ship you're paid off, get all the money you've earned in one lump sum. I used some of those to start my business and I'm rather proud of that – that my business grew on top of money I earned by the sweat of my own brow. Oh,' he said, 'please don't think there's a criticism of you in there.'

'How kind of you to say so,' Ellie said drily. 'You think there hasn't been a lot of sweating of brows in building up The Minister's Cat?'

'I can see there has.'

'I take it,' she went on, still smarting at the memory of what he had said to her the day before, 'that you're also proud of yourself for having proved you're as good a businessman as your father? Without having had the advantage of marrying the boss's daughter like he did?'

Evander shot her a look from under his brows. 'What a very shrewd observation.'

'And now you've proved that, you want to move on to something else?'

'Possibly,' he admitted. 'It might help if I knew what that something else was.'

'All that money in your healthy bank balance and no idea what to do with it?'

'I have some ideas. Principally that I want to buy an old house somewhere and make a home for myself. I'm fed up of living in hotels and out of suitcases.'

'Re-create Gowanlea,' she said.

He shook his head. 'Not possible. But I would want my house to have the same sort of feel that Gowanlea did. The same sort of spirit.'

'Deep window seats and funny little corners and comfortable old furniture,' Ellie said softly. 'A garden with flowers in every colour in the rainbow and where the daisies are allowed to grow.'

'So you haven't entirely forgotten the past, Ellie. You remember things too.'

His gaze travelled over her shoulder. 'Do you remember that old horse chestnut tree along there? And the boy and girl who stood under it eight years ago?' His eyes had come back to her face.

'Coming through!' called a loud female voice.

A cacophony of bicycle bells ensued. Jumping apart like guilty lovers, Ellie and Evander found themselves separated by a troupe of cyclists. She counted fifteen young women, all in divided skirts and short-sleeved tops. The badge sewn on to those flashed at her as they passed: 'Kirkintilloch Lady Cyclists' Club'.

'Well,' Evander said lightly after the last one had pedalled her cheeky and cheerful way through, 'the Kirky lady cyclists rather destroyed the moment, didn't they?'

'It's probably just as well.'

He turned to her, his dark eyes alert and watchful. 'You think so?'

'Don't you?' Ellie countered. 'You know what I remember about that boy and girl from eight years ago, Evander? That they were very young and that they were very good friends.'

'Nothing more than that?'

'That was a lot. That friendship meant so much to both of them.'

For a moment he said nothing. Then he nodded. 'Your friendship saved my life, Ellie. And my sanity. I'm sorry I didn't appear to be very grateful when we met yesterday. Has the way I behaved ruined any chances of us becoming friends again?'

Ellie folded her arms across her breasts and surveyed him thoughtfully. 'Is that what you'd like? For us to be friends again?'

He raised his right hand to his head and ran his fingers through his hair. 'Yes,' he said at last. 'That's what I'd like.'

'So let's try to do that.' She smiled brightly at him before allowing her gaze to drift away to their surroundings. Too many ghosts here, she thought. Too many ghosts.

'Ellie?' Evander asked. 'Are you all right?'

She flashed him another dazzling smile. 'I'm fine. Shall we go back to the car now?'

Chapter 34

'I'm going to attend to one particular loose end tomorrow,' he said as they got back into the Riley. 'I wonder if I might come and see you afterwards.'

'Where's your loose end?'

'Anniesland,' he said softly. 'Since last week I own a parcel of companies there. More specifically, one of them is in Temple.'

'The boatyard's up for sale?' she breathed. 'Phoebe told me things were bad. I didn't realise they were quite *that* bad.'

'The boatyard's more or less sold,' Evander corrected. 'To me, and along with the other remnants of the Tait empire. "Lochaber Holdings" is calling on James Tait and his son-in-law tomorrow to discuss what happens about the company's debts.'

'What does that mean?'

'That I could call them in. I now have it within my power to ruin my father completely, maybe even force him to sell Bellevue.'

'And are you going to do that?' Ellie asked as they turned back on to the main road.

'I have no idea what I'm going to do. *May* I come and see you when I get back from Bellevue tomorrow?'

'You're nervous about going there?'

'I'm absolutely bloody terrified.'

'But they don't know that you're Lochaber Holdings?'

'No.'

'No need to be nervous then,' Ellie said. 'Surely you're holding all the cards.'

'Yes,' Evander said. 'This time I'm holding all the cards.'

'How was your afternoon?' Lesley asked as Ellie walked into the kitchen of The Minister's Cat two hours later.

'Interesting,' Ellie said vaguely. 'Give me five minutes to change and I'll let you get off home.' She blinked as Lesley stepped forward to bar her way to the stairs that led up the flat.

'Are you seeing him again?'

'He's coming tomorrow. After he's been to Bellevue.'

Lesley frowned. 'Bellevue? Why is he going there?' The frown deepened as she listened to the answer to her question.

'Ellie, do you really think it's wise to get involved with him again?'

'I don't know if it's wise, Lesley.' Biting her lip, Ellie watched as the other girl stepped back and took off her apron. 'He asked if he could come and see me tomorrow afternoon and I said yes. Going to Bellevue is going to be quite an ordeal for him. He's got some dreadful memories to contend with there.'

'And is that your concern?' Walking over to the laundry hamper that stood in the back corner of the kitchen, Lesley dropped her discarded apron into it. Feeling unaccountably on the defensive, Ellie blurted out some more information. 'He told me this afternoon that he'd like us to be friends again.'

'Doesn't he want more than that?'

'I don't think so.'

'You sound upset.'

'Do I?'

'Ellie,' Lesley said, coming back to stand in front of her, 'what about Frank?'

Ellie lifted her arm in a gesture of helplessness. 'What *about* Frank?'

'He loves you, Ellie! He loves you so much. If I were in your shoes I would think very carefully about jeopardising what you've got with Frank for the sake of some dream from the past. Sometimes I think you don't realise how lucky you are—' She stopped herself. 'This is none of my business.'

'Lesley?' Ellie said, following her as she lifted down her jacket from the hooks by the door. 'Are you all right? Stay for a minute.'

'I can't,' Lesley said wildly. 'I have to go home now. I'll see you tomorrow.'

'Lesley!'

She was speaking to fresh air.

Evander didn't recognise the neat parlourmaid who opened the door to him.

'May I take your hat, sir?'

'Thank you,' he said, smiling at her as he handed it over. 'Where are the family?'

'In the dining room, sir. I'll show you there now.'

'No need,' he said politely. 'I know my way.'

The girl stood for a moment staring after him. Small wonder. His looks were his own but the similarity to his father was strong enough for him to understand why she might be a touch confused.

As he walked across the black and white tiles of the hall he felt a flood of remembered images assail him. They and the emotions they brought with them were strong enough to make him pause. Himself when young. Not to mention beaten, bloody and broken.

He remembered the girl who'd been Ellie too, rescuing him and seeing him safe with no thought at all of what the repercussions to herself might be. He thought of the woman she was now, and felt emotion of an entirely different sort flood his senses. Taking a deep breath, he walked over and opened the dining-room door.

'Good afternoon, Father. Mother.' Standing a few feet from the dining table, he spun round on his heels. 'Phoebe,' he said. 'How are you? Malcolm. It's been a long time.' He could feel their shock. It made him want to laugh out loud.

At the head of the table James Tait was rising to his feet. 'You,' he breathed. 'Get out of my house!'

Evander raised his dark eyebrows. 'Not a very nice welcome to a son from a father. Or from a debtor to a creditor.'

James Tait slammed the palms of his hands on the table but his wife gripped his arm. 'I think we're meeting Mr Cameron,' she said quietly.

'You're Lochaber Holdings?' Malcolm asked.

Evander inclined his head in acknowledgement of that fact.

'Come to see your bastard as well?' blustered James Tait. 'The one your mother and your sister unaccountably felt we had to take in?'

Phoebe rose to her feet, pale but composed. 'Father, please don't talk about your grandson like that.'

'I've nothing against the lad himself,' James Tait said shortly, throwing a glance up at his daughter. 'You know how fond I am of him.'

'But you don't know the truth about him,' she said. 'I

think it's time you heard it. I think it's time we all heard it.' She pushed away the hand her husband was reaching up towards her. 'No, Malcolm, this has gone on for long enough.' She glanced out of the window to where Jamie and his sister played in the garden with their nursemaid. 'There have been too many secrets in this house. Far too many secrets.'

She looked at her brother. 'Is it all right with you if I speak first, Evander?'

'Go ahead, Phoebe,' he said. 'You say your piece and then I'll say mine.' He looked at his father, still standing at the head of the table. 'Sit down, Father. After Phoebe's had her say we'll discuss what we're going to do about your business difficulties.'

'You've come to crow, I suppose,' James Tait said bitterly.

Evander studied his father and felt one emotion. Not anger, nor a desire for revenge. Only pity. 'Sit down, Father,' he said again.

His father sat down.

'You gave it all back to him? The boatyard *and* the other four businesses?'

'I did,' he said. 'I threw the papers down on the table in front of him and recommended he should listen more to his son-in-law in the future.' A gleam of mischief crept into Evander's eyes. 'Close your mouth, Ellie. You'll catch flies.'

She shook her head. 'I'm just so amazed at what you've done.'

'What were you expecting? Did you think I'd come home to wreak my revenge on all those who'd wronged me?' He smiled, rueful but relaxed. 'Bit too *Count of Monte Cristo*, don't you think?'

'I might have expected it from the boy I put on the *Torosay* eight years ago.'

'God, yes. I was so *intense*, wasn't I? Against all the odds, I seem to have grown up into a reasonably well-balanced human being.' He sounded faintly surprised.

'I admire you for it. You've survived your father and you haven't let him turn you into the angry and embittered man that he is. Did you know you were going to give him back the businesses when you went in there?'

'I wasn't sure what I was going to do. When it came to the crunch I simply didn't feel the need to triumph over him.' The wicked gleam stole back into his eyes. 'Or maybe only a little. Much more satisfaction in being Evander the Magnanimous.'

'Are you saying that you forgive him for what he did to you?'

Evander hooked one arm over the back of his chair. 'I'm not that bloody noble. I think maybe I understand *why* he reacted to me the way he did. It didn't help that I was a pompous little prig who went out of my way to provoke him.'

'You only did that after he had already started to mistreat you,' Ellie protested.

'Maybe. I do think that when he looked at me it must have been like looking at himself.' He pulled a face. 'All those aspects of his character which he least liked and which he saw as weaknesses. He and I are very alike in many ways.'

'You know,' Ellie said, 'Phoebe said something very similar to me once and I fell out with her over it.'

'My sister has changed. Wonder if she and I might get the chance to get to know one another again?'

'I hope so.'

'How about you and Malcolm?' he asked. 'Phoebe told me about her attempt to reconcile the two of you. Will you try again?'

'Maybe in another seven years,' Ellie said wryly. 'If only for the sake of Phoebe and the children.'

'She introduced me to them both, by the way. Nice infants.' His gaze drifted down the kitchen to where Lesley was concentrating ferociously on her cooking. 'Your friend seems to be in a bit of a bad mood today.'

'Yes,' Ellie said, knowing she'd have to tackle Lesley's distress sooner rather than later. 'I'm glad the children don't have to leave Bellevue. I know from what Phoebe tells me that they love the place. They bring a lot of happiness to it too. Why are you smiling at me like that?'

'Because you're a very remarkable woman, Eleanor Douglas.'

'Am I?'

'You are indeed. You know, it seems to me that young Jamie shares some characteristics with his auntie.'

'Does he?'

'Uh-huh. Great sense of humour for one thing. He doesn't have red hair and freckles, of course,' Evander said carefully. 'That's one way in which he differs from her.'

Ellie had been leaning forward over the table. These comments thrust her back into her chair and brought three flat words out of her mouth.

'Phoebe told you.'

'She told everyone. Almost upstaged me,' he said lazily, sounding not at all concerned about that. 'You're a very remarkable woman,' he said again.

Ellie shrugged. 'I did what had to be done.'

'You shouldered a burden which wasn't yours.' He thought about that for a moment. 'Like you shouldered the burden of being my friend when I was that intense and unhappy boy who used to live at Bellevue. I must have been bloody hard work. Looking back on it I can see that you did all of the giving and I did all of the taking.'

'You gave me so much!'

He looked startled. 'Name one thing.'

'There are loads of them. Encouraging me to read, for a start. Do you know how important that was? And talking to me about all sorts of things and playing all those word games with me. Practically everyone else in my life had told me I was stupid. It was you who made me realise I wasn't. That gave me belief in myself, allowed me to feel I could do anything I set my mind to. I don't think I'd be sitting here today if I hadn't known you. Oh, Evander,' she said again, 'you mustn't say that you didn't give me anything! It's not true! You've been so important in my life!'

By the end of this impassioned little speech both Evander's casual slouch and the nonchalant expression on his face had undergone a dramatic transformation. Sitting rigidly upright, he reached across the table for her hand. 'Ellie,' he began urgently, 'yesterday at Craigmarloch—'

A madman burst into the kitchen. He was wearing brown corduroy trousers, a soft checked shirt and he had a rucksack on his back. He threw that off, and headed off down the kitchen as though he were a soldier marching to a battle which only he could see. Ellie stood up and intercepted him.

'Are you all right, Frank? What on earth's the matter?'

He gripped her shoulders. 'Ellie,' he said. 'I've got something to do and I've got to do it right now.' He spotted Evander behind her and registered only mild surprise. 'I'll deal wi' you later,' he promised.

When he reached Lesley he pulled her away from her pots and pans and propelled her back to the office area, sparing one hand to pull out an upright chair and spin it round. He pushed her down into it and crouched at her feet.

'I love you,' he blurted out. 'I have to say it. I love you, Lesley Matheson.'

Lesley looked wildly at him. Then she looked up at Ellie. Frank pulled on her hands to bring her attention back to him. 'Ellie'll no' mind. Don't you worry about that. Look,' he said, 'I know I'm maybe no' very much o' a catch. I smoke too much and I'm bad-tempered sometimes and I've got the scar and I'm a Catholic and you're no', and I'm a couple of years younger than you are.'

'How very gallant of him to point that out to a lady,' murmured Evander.

Mesmerised by the drama unfolding in front of them, Ellie shushed him furiously. Frank was still pouring his heart out.

'I can understand that you might no' be very keen on getting married again. But I'm asking you to think about it. Or at the very least take a chance on me. You and me could be happy together, Lesley. I know we could. What d'ye say?'

Lesley opened her mouth. Nothing came out. She looked up at Ellie again. Ellie's eyes were sparkling. 'Give the poor fool an answer, Lesley. Put him out of his misery. I expect he'd also appreciate a kiss.'

'But, Ellie,' Lesley said, 'do you really not mind?'

Evander was looking backwards and forwards from Ellie to Frank. 'Of course,' he muttered, 'that red-haired rogue of a fisherman!'

Ellie beamed at him, then directed a smiling question at Lesley. 'Why on earth should I mind if my dearest friend and my brother want to kiss each other?'

Chapter 35

'We should have realised from the hair,' Lesley said ten minutes later. 'I suppose it was just too obvious.' The four of them were upstairs in the flat, Ellie and Frank giving the others a conducted tour of the place.

'This is my bedroom,' Ellie said, flinging open the door of it. 'Next door you have the bathroom.'

'Which is also exclusively her ladyship's domain,' Frank put in. 'Since she likes to soak in there for several hours at a time, I decided a couple of years ago to install a shower and another toilet down my end of the flat. That way I can get clean without having to wait hours for the privilege.' He pretended to glower at Ellie.

Lesley smiled. 'You always knew you were brother and sister?'

Ellie shook her head. 'Not until Willie Anderson told us. When I went back to Temple with Jamie and ended up going to stay with Frank, he came round to see us. He was concerned that we might be living together in what might be called the Biblical sense.'

Evander coughed and studied his feet.

'He needn't have worried,' Frank confided. 'Ellie and I have always been really close but we've never had those sort of feelings for each other.' He grinned at his half-sister. 'I once had to kiss her on the mouth and it damn' near turned my stomach.'

'The feeling was entirely mutual, brother dear,' Ellie said cheerfully. 'It was a bit of an emergency, as I recall.'

'It must have been a shock to find out the truth all the same,' Lesley said.

Standing in the corridor with one arm draped about her shoulders, Frank dropped a kiss on her nose. Then he blushed like a schoolboy. 'Shame and disgrace, more like,' he said, recovering his manly poise. 'My real father was a bloody Scotsman, and probably a flaming Presbyterian heretic to boot. Might even have been a Wee Free,' he added in accents of horror.

Evander propped himself against the wall of the corridor. 'What I don't understand is why you kept it a secret for so long.' He looked accusingly at Frank. 'Especially when the two of you living together had such a devastating effect on Ellie's reputation. Not to mention her relationship with Malcolm.'

'It was Ellie who chose to keep it a secret.'

'Really?' Evander asked. 'I find that a little hard to believe. I seem to remember that Ellie's reputation was always very important to her.'

'Really,' Frank repeated stolidly. 'As you may possibly also remember, she's always had a bit of a stubborn streak too. Malcolm had believed the worst of her with absolutely no justification for that belief. So she dug her heels in. Plus it was all tied in with not telling anyone who wee Jamie's real parents were. She had made a solemn promise to your sister about that. I guessed the truth. As did her pal Aileen.' He threw a smile across to Ellie. 'Any secret is safe with Miss Douglas. It's one of her sterling qualities. Of which she has many.'

'Well,' Evander said coolly. 'We can agree on that.'

Now it was Ellie who was studying her feet, listening to Frank giving the rest of the explanation.

'It also wasn't long till we realised that it might no' be very wise to let the cat out o' the bag. When we were wee we both had to put up wi' folk making nasty comments about our respective mothers. Ironically enough, my sister Marie was known for leaping to the defence of hers and mine. And I don't mean only with words.'

'Is that still a worry?' Lesley asked anxiously.

Ellie lifted her head and hastened to reassure her. 'It's faded into the background. Neither Frank nor I have seen Marie in years.'

Frank grimaced. 'We don't exactly move in the same circles.'

'No,' Ellie agreed. 'I suppose I always had this thing about Malcolm too.'

'Being stubborn about it like Frank said?'

'That,' Ellie said. 'But I knew how much it would upset him too, to find out that the stories about our mother did have some basis in reality.'

'Still thinking about his feelings, Ellie?' Lesley asked sympathetically.

Ellie grimaced. 'Perhaps I was just being a martyr. I think Frank and I also got locked into the story. It suited us both. He's never really thought he was entitled to love and marriage and that sort of happiness. Guilt about his misspent youth.'

'How did you know that?' Frank growled.

Ellie smiled at Lesley. 'Sort him out, will you?'

Lesley laughed. 'I'll do my best.'

Something was brewing behind Evander's eyes. 'So practically everybody except Phoebe and Malcolm and Aileen Drummond – I beg her pardon – Robertson thought young Jamie belonged to Ellie and me.'

'Aye, well,' Frank said. 'It seemed a logical enough assumption.'

'Logical?' Evander queried.

Lesley laughed again. 'Biology,' she said. 'Love, desire and all that sort of thing.'

Evander shook his head. 'Whilst I'm happy to admit that "love, desire and all that sort of thing" figured large in my feelings towards Ellie, it was all terribly innocent really. Passionate,' he said reminiscently, 'but very innocent. You were always so terribly moral, Ellie.'

'She still is,' Frank said. 'All the time her and me have been living together as brother and sister, there havenae been any other men in her life. No' in the romantic sense, anyway.'

Like guns mounted on the deck of a battleship, three pairs of interested and speculative eyes swivelled round to train themselves on Ellie.

'Oh great,' she said, 'discuss the most intimate details of my private life in front of everybody, why don't you? And why are you looking at me like that, Evander Cameron? If you've got something to say, spit it out.'

He swallowed hard. 'I'm scared to. I don't suppose you'd understand that,' he added a little wistfully. 'You who's never been scared of anything in your entire life.'

'Never been scared of anything in my entire life? Is that what you think?' She walked forward and poked him in the chest. 'Would you like to hear what I'm scared of? *Would you?*' she demanded.

'Ellie—'

'Shut up,' she said. 'I'm going to tell you whether you want to hear or not. I'm scared of hundreds o' things. I'm scared there's going to be another war and I'm scared of what's going to become of everyone I care about if that happens. I'm scared we'll get bombed from the air. I'm scared the restaurant will get flattened.

I'm scared of the fact that while I bear absolutely no malice towards your six children, I have enough venom in me to quite happily shove your wife off the nearest available cliff.'

'Eh?' Evander looked baffled. 'I don't have a wife or six children. Ellie, I don't have any—'

She jabbed her finger in his chest again. 'I'm scared of the fact that you've been back in my life for a mere three days but already you've managed to turn it completely upside down. I'm scared of how I felt when I walked into your office on Thursday and saw you again for the first time in eight years. Those are just a few of the things I'm scared of, Evander Cameron. What have you got to say to that?'

He grabbed her hand. 'How *did* you feel when you walked into my office on Thursday?'

'Terrified. I've been sailing along on waters as peaceful as the canal on a summer's day. I have my work, my business, my home—'

The corners of his mouth were lifting. 'Don't forget your car.'

'I wasn't going to. Now I feel as if my nice comfortable life is about to steer itself into uncharted seas, full steam ahead to those Cape Rollers of yours.'

He was still holding her hand. Now he cocked one eyebrow. 'Oh. Why would that be?'

'Why d'you think, you great numpty? Because I'm scared that I'm still in love with you!'

She felt his fingers tighten convulsively on hers, saw the dawning amusement flee his face as completely as if it had never been there in the first place. Yet he responded to the statement she'd thrown at him without missing a beat, his voice cool and crisp. 'I was scared that I was still in love with you. Until Thursday.'

'What happened on Thursday?' Her angry shout had subsided to a whisper.

'Thirty seconds after you burst into my office like an avenging fury I realised that I am still in love with you. No doubt about it.' He took advantage of the stunned silence around him to keep on talking. 'Which is undoubtedly why I behaved like a complete and utter boor. Jealousy, you see. Nothing but jealousy.' He glanced briefly at Frank. It was obvious that he was poised to intervene. An admonishing hand on his arm, it was equally obvious that Lesley wasn't going to let him. Evander turned his attention back to Ellie.

'Even before I found out the truth about you and Frank I realised that I didn't care about any of what I *had* believed to be the truth. And although I had no reason to doubt that you and he were together as a couple I still found it impossible to forget you. That's why I came home.' His voice grew gentle. 'Because you weren't actually married to him I suppose I was hoping that there might still be a chance. For you and me, I mean.'

Ellie's eyes were scouring his face. 'Why didn't you tell me any of this yesterday at Craigmarloch?'

'Blame the lady cyclists.' A faint smile once more lightened his face. 'They gave me the time to get scared again. I'm scared now. Of what you might be going to say.' He adjusted his grip on her hand. 'Please say something, Ellie. Let me know if there's any hope at all.'

She looked up at him. 'But Evander, this doesn't make any sense, does it?'

'It makes perfect sense as long as we both want it to.'

'We don't know each other any more. Not as we are now.'

'Then we'll get to know each other.'

Ellie stared at him for a moment. 'Och, I don't know!' she blurted out, wrenching her fingers out of his grasp. 'I'm confused and scared and—' She stopped, took a deep breath and spoke more calmly, 'I need time to think about this. Can we do that?'

'Sensible Ellie,' he murmured. 'Always so sensible.' He recaptured her hand, only to bestow the lightest of kisses on her fingertips and immediately release it again. 'Of course we can do that.' He looked past her towards Frank and Lesley. 'I get the distinct impression that you two would like to be alone together. Why don't you give yourselves the evening off?'

'It's Saturday night,' Lesley said, looking longingly at Frank. 'Our busiest.'

He was looking as longingly at her. 'We're short-handed too. One o' the waitresses is off sick. I should take her place.'

'I'll do it,' Evander said.

'It's no' a job that just anybody can do,' Frank protested.

'I know that,' came the calm response. 'I have done it before. And in a room which rocked from side to side. I don't think I'll find it difficult to wait on tables which don't have to be bolted to the floor. You two take the night off. Ellie and I will have our evening off tomorrow. Won't we, Ellie?'

'Will we?' she asked faintly.

'Yes.' Evander looked over at Frank. 'Can you lend me a suitably masculine apron? I don't think I'd look very good in frills.'

A little over twenty-four hours later it was Ellie's appearance which was provoking one of Frank's best glowers. 'You're wearing your green velvet dress.'

She tossed her auburn waves. 'You have some objection to that?'

'If I wasn't your brother *I'd* fancy you in it. That's my objection.' He pointed a warning finger at Evander. 'You'd better have her back home by midnight, pal.'

Ellie and Lesley caught one another's eye, then had to look swiftly away. Evander took a more direct approach, offering Frank his hand. 'Try to be friends?' He inclined his dark head towards the girls. 'For their sakes?'

Frank looked at that outstretched hand, his own arms now folded resolutely over his chest. 'You serious about her?' His gaze fixed on Evander's face, he indicated Ellie with a lift of his chin.

'I'm serious about her.' Evander had uttered the words with quiet but unmistakable sincerity. Frank still wasn't giving an inch.

'Planning on sticking around this time?'

'I'm planning on becoming a permanent fixture in her life. If she agrees.'

'And if she gives you your marching orders?'

'Then I have to accept them.' Evander inhaled sharply. 'Though they're the last words I want to hear!'

Frank thrust out his right hand, his face slowly breaking into its characteristically broad smile. 'Put it there, Evander. And good luck!'

Ellie and Evander walked down Buchanan Street in the warm evening air, heading for a new and very cxclusive restaurant that had recently opened in Royal Exchange Place. She had chosen it, muttering darkly that they would be a lot more private there than in The Minister's Cat.

'Though I give it less than twenty-four hours till the tongues are wagging about all of us,' Lesley said cheerfully as she waved them off. 'Glasgow's a village, you know!'

'Right,' Evander said after they had sat down, accepted menus from the hovering waiter and ordered. 'Let's get some things sorted out. Do you want to speak first or shall I?'

'You go first. Start with all those letters you never posted to me.'

'I'm sorry about that,' he said quietly. 'It simply didn't occur to me how much you would worry if you didn't hear from me. Obsessed with myself and my own problems as usual. I hope I've matured a bit since then. Although I suppose I did have some sort of an excuse at the beginning. I really wasn't fit to write.'

He nodded when Ellie's eyes went to his nose. 'Hurt like hell for weeks and weeks and by that time I was well into my first voyage. Shouted and sworn at and taunted for my posh accent and worked like a dog every day. I fell into my bunk every night and went out like the proverbial light. Oh, don't look so worried!' he exclaimed. 'By the time we made our first landfall in South America I'd hardened up quite a bit.' He sat back in his chair. 'Here comes our wine.'

Once that had been tasted, pronounced satisfactory and their two glasses filled he looked questioningly at her. 'A toast?'

'Not yet. Go on with your story. Did you harden up enough for people to stop treating you badly?'

'Oh, yes. There are always petty tyrants in confined communities like ships, of course, but I began to stand up to the bullies among my crewmates, give back as good as I got.'

'Verbally and physically?'

'The latter only when completely unavoidable. I

became rather adept at talking my way out of trouble. But it was the lack of letters you were asking about. Once I'd got into a routine where I could fit in some spare time between working and sleeping I found I also had time to think. Chiefly about how much of a liability I must always have been to you.'

He dropped his eyes to the white linen tablecloth. 'I managed to convince myself that you'd be much better off without me, that you hadn't really been in love with me, only ever felt sorry for me. You never actually said the words, you know.' His gaze came back to her face, his mouth curving in a faint smile when she gave him no response to that statement.

'You could have written a letter telling me all of that.'

'I did. Several times. All those epistles I wasn't brave enough to send. Your turn to speak,' he said brightly. 'Raise all of your objections so that I can demolish them with my faultless logic.'

'You'd like to settle down and make that home for yourself,' Ellie began. 'Probably up in the wilds of the Highlands somewhere. My life is here. In Glasgow and in The Minister's Cat. And I love everything about it. Nor have I been sitting here pining for the last eight years waiting for you to ride home on your white charger and rescue me.'

He was watching her intently. 'I'm well aware of that.'

'I'd also like to do some travelling. See Europe while it's still possible. You've obviously travelled enough to last you a lifetime.'

'I could stand to do some more. I've seen the ports of the world, that's all. And this home I want to make doesn't have to be miles away from Glasgow. Somewhere like Loch Lomond would be fine. More than fine. Lots of wild little corners up there. I wouldn't dream of asking you to change your life either. I'm quite happy to fit in wherever you'll let me.'

Ellie snorted. 'Want a job as a waiter?'

'Actually I've had an even crazier idea. You know how the owner of that bookshop a couple of doors along from you wants to sell up and retire? I thought I might take it over. Personally, I mean.'

'Sell second-hand books for a living? I shouldn't have thought there's much profit in that.'

'I don't need a huge profit.' He lifted his wine glass. 'Shall we drink? To the pleasure to be found between the covers of a good book, if nothing else. I take it that's one thing we can both still agree on?'

'Absolutely,' Ellie said, clinking glasses with him and taking a sip of her wine. 'Are you serious about the bookshop idea?'

He set his own glass down again. 'Can't you see me in the role? I'll get one of those little embroidered velvet hats with a tassel and a pair of half-moon specs, and you can crochet me a shawl to wear over the shoulders of my moth-eaten smoking jacket. When you're not popping along with nutritious bowls of soup, that is. Unless you do want to offer me a job as a waiter. You'd have to admit that I did well last night.'

'You did well,' she admitted, laughing at the picture he had drawn of himself as a bookseller. 'Charmed everybody, so I'm told. Staff and customers.' She thought back to the previous evening, recalling Alison Graham coming into the kitchen with a broader smile on her face each time as she sang the praises of the tall, dark and handsome stranger currently working the tables with her.

Before she had gone home for the night Ellie had taken her aside and told her the details of the day's developments. Alison's eyes had grown wider and wider and, at the end of the recital, it had been as clear as crystal that her loyalty to The Minister's Cat, its owners and friends was as fierce and as unswerving as ever. Ellie looked curiously at Evander.

'Why *did* you volunteer to help out last night? Because Frank and Lesley needed that time along together?'

'That would be the noble reason. The less noble one was that I could see you also needed some breathing space.' He took another swig of wine before surveying her over the rim of the glass. 'Had enough of that yet? I do love you, you know.'

Her smile was swift and a little wistful. 'Sure you're not in love with that kitchenmaid you knew?'

'Isn't she sitting opposite me?'

'I've come a long way since those days. So have you.'

'We're still the same people where it matters. In our hearts.' He struck his chest with his free hand. The typically theatrical gesture made her smile.

'You were always such a romantic, Evander.'

'And you were always the opposite. Sensible Ellie, who's so happy with her life, who doesn't need anything or anybody to make it better. I envy you.' His voice was carefully light, but as he set his glass down again she noticed that his hand wasn't quite steady. The base of the glass wobbled enough before it came to rest for a drop of wine to spill out on to the tablecloth.

Ellie stared at it for a second or two, thinking that at least both wine and cloth were white. Easier to get the stain out than it would be with red.

Feeling all at once a little dizzy, her eyes travelled from the tiny spot of wine to Evander's fingers, then up his arm to his face. He was still trying for nonchalance. 'Service could be quicker, don't you think?'

'Good things are worth waiting for,' she said slowly. Something was happening deep inside her, provoked by that small betrayal of the depth of his feelings. It was like the opening of a set of lock-gates, the pent-up water emerging first as a trickle, soon to be a rushing waterfall. She could feel it.

'Would you like to know how sensible I really am, Evander?' She didn't wait for a reply. She simply laid her hands flat on the tablecloth and took a run at it.

'I'm so sensible that I still keep a book rendered unreadable by virtue of being dropped in the bath almost a decade ago. I'm so sensible that I still keep a tattered old poster of a cat. I'm so sensible that I still keep a black velvet waistcoat which is far too big for me and which never belonged to me in the first place. I'm so sensible that I carried those things around with me wherever I went. However impractical that was at the time.' She skidded to a halt, enough breath left only for one last quick question. 'What do you have to say to that?'

His hands slid forward over the white linen. 'I suppose I'd have to ask *why* you kept all of those things.'

'And if I told you that I'd be stepping off the edge of a waterfall!'

'Step off,' he urged. 'Let the water carry you safely down. I'm waiting at the bottom to catch you. Look, I've already got hold of you.'

'I'd noticed,' she said shyly, glancing down at their newly entwined fingers.

'Does it feel nice?'

'More than nice.'

'Then tell me why you kept my things.'

'Because I could never forget you. Because I could never stop hoping that one day you'd come home. Like you said you would before you climbed aboard the *Torosay*. Naïve, eh?'

'Not naïve at all. I have come back.' There was a smile on his face, spreading out all over it. 'Welcome to the bottom of the waterfall, Ellie.'

She shook her head. 'I'm not there yet. There's more I want to say. More I *have* to say. That night you left? I can still see myself sitting on my bed trying to decide whether or not to come down the stairs to you. Knowing what a risk I could be taking in doing that.'

'And what did you decide?'

'Why do you think I was walking past Aileen's door long after we'd got back from Craigmarloch? I was on my way to the stairs. To come to you.'

Evander's eyelids fluttered briefly closed. 'Oh,' he said, 'that thought is very—'

'Be careful which adjective you use,' she warned.

He opened his eyes again. 'They're all wonderful ones.'

'Have you considered the fact,' Ellie asked, her own eyes growing troubled, 'that if I hadn't made the decision to come downstairs that night, the sequence of events which followed wouldn't have been triggered? You might have stayed at home and gone to university like you always wanted to and had a much more comfortable life.'

Now it was him who was shaking his head. 'My father and I would have had that confrontation sooner or later. And I like the life I've had. The only thing that's been wrong with it is that you weren't in it.'

Ellie's face was still full of doubt. 'Evander, after you went away on the *Torosay*, there were weeks and months when I thought I was never going to be happy again. Adrift on an endless sea of tears in a rudderless boat with no charts to help me find my way across it. No stars to look up to for guidance. They might have been there but for a long time I couldn't see them. Once I began to recover I knew that I never wanted to feel like that again. Not ever.'

'Nor will you if I have any say in the matter.'

'But other people will have a say too,' she said sadly. 'If the war comes – *when* the war comes – they'll call you up, more than likely put you in the Navy. And you'll go willingly.'

'Yes,' he agreed, thinking about it. 'I probably will. I still think war is the great obscenity. But this is one war that does need to be fought.'

'So I could lose you all over again.'

'Or I could lose you.' He flexed his fingers, pulling her halfway out of her seat. 'Or we could both step out of this restaurant tonight and get mowed down by a runaway tram. Or the chef here might have mistakenly bought poisonous mushrooms today and we could die writhing in agony before the dawn comes up tomorrow.'

'Evander,' she hissed. 'People are beginning to look at us!'

'Let 'em look.' He was rising up out of his own chair to meet her. He pulled his fingers out of hers, only to use both of his hands to cup her face. The words were rattled out. 'Take a chance on us, Ellie. Make the only possible response to this terrifying world we live in. Seize happiness wherever and whenever you find it and live life to the full for as long as it's humanly possible to do so. Oh, please take a chance on us, Ellie!'

She looked at him. He looked at her. At his elbow their waiter gave a discreet cough. Ellie took her eyes off

Evander's face long enough to bestow a dazzling smile on the man. 'We'll be ready for our entrée just as soon as I've kissed this gentleman.'

'Very good, madam. Would you like me to come back in five minutes?'

'Not at all,' Ellie said. 'This will be short and sweet. I don't really believe in canoodling in public. I'm only doing it now because this is a special occasion. I'm in love with him, you see.'

The impeccable manner crumbled along with the impeccable accent. 'Is that right, hen? On ye go, then. I promise I'll no' look.'

'Thank you,' Ellie said gravely, turning back to Evander with her green eyes sparkling. He could hardly kiss her for laughing.

By the time they walked out into Buchanan Street an hour or so later the streetlights had come on and a few stars were twinkling overhead. They strolled up the road hand in hand, not speaking until they were almost at The Minister's Cat. Evander brought them to a halt under a hazy yellow streetlight, turning to gaze up and down the slope they had climbed. 'It's deserted at this end of the street. Still too early for the dance halls to be kicking out, I suppose.'

'Was there some point to that announcement?'

He took her by the lapels of her coat. 'I was just wondering if you believed in canoodling in private, that's all. Or if you knew how to French kiss.'

She stirred the soft night air with her finger. 'Correct me if I'm wrong, but didn't we have some discussion about an hour ago about taking this slowly?'

Evander removed his hands from her lapels and slid them in under her open coat to rest on the waist of her green velvet dress. 'We don't have time. The world's going to hell in a handcart. Besides, it would be in the nature of an experiment. That kiss over the table was extremely enjoyable—'

'Not to mention reminiscent of our very first kiss,' Ellie put in.

'Indeed. But it wasn't perhaps the sort of kiss by which we can measure if the spark's still there.'

'You think we need to check on that, professor?'

'I'm convinced of the need for it. Oh,' he moaned, 'let's stop talking.'

'Well,' Ellie said after a rather prolonged silence, 'I think we'd have to agree that the spark's still there. Wouldn't you say?'

'Impossible to tell without further experimentation. Several more tests are urgently required.'

They carried out those tests, passing through tenderness to passion and back again to tenderness. Afterwards he held her loosely in his arms, her hands lying flat on his chest under the lapels of his evening jacket. 'Has there really never been anyone else?'

'No one,' she admitted, gazing up at him out of a face glowing with a mixture of shyness and excitement. 'I'm not going to apologise for that either.'

'No reason why you should.' His mouth quirked. 'Quite the reverse.' He whooped with laughter at her response to that comment. 'The fishwife glare! How perfectly charming to see it again.'

Ellie narrowed her eyes at him. 'You wouldn't possibly be casting yourself as the experienced but reformed rake who's fallen for the innocent maiden and is about to initiate her into the arts of love, would you?'

'I see you still read romantic novels, Miss Douglas.'

'Yes, and I still have high moral standards.'

'I'm delighted to hear it. Will you marry me?'

'Because that's the only way you'll get round my high moral standards?'

'Because I love you and want to spend the rest of my life with you. *Will* you marry me?'

'Maybe. Ask me again in a month.'

'I'll ask you again in a week,' he promised. 'And every other week after that until you say yes.'

'What shall we do about the world going to hell in a handcart? How can we find our way through all of that?'

Once more he cupped her face in his hands. 'We'll steer by the stars, of course. If we're together in our hearts we'll always be able to see them and they'll always bring us safely home. You do love me, Ellie?'

'Oh yes,' she said. 'I love you.'

'We'll take it from there then, shall we?'

'Yes,' she said again, losing herself in the warm depths of his loving eyes. 'We'll take it from there.'

The Bird Flies High

Maggie Craig

Glasgow, 1920s. Grinding poverty and violence are an everyday part of Josie Collins' life. Her mother's death has left her alone with an abusive stepfather, struggling to bring up her younger brother and sister. Sadly, the children are taken away and only Josie's secret ambition – to become a reporter on one of Glasgow's newspapers – provides any hope for the future. Geographically it's not a big move but socially it's a million miles away.

Disaster strikes when Josie is sixteen. A tragic love affair leaves her alone and pregnant. Forced to give up her baby, Josie starts a new life under a different name. With renewed determination, she eventually achieves her dream, even enjoying a close friendship with a male colleague. But, although Josie finally begins to enjoy her new happiness, she also realises that she must come to terms with her own past, even if it threatens to destroy everything she's worked so hard to build.

Praise for Maggie Craig's sagas:

'Craig seems to fully inhabit her fictional world in a manner reminiscent of Daphne Du Maurier and provides a sensorial feast for the reader' *Scotsman*

'Few writers evoke the senses quite so strongly' *Scots Magazine*

'Maggie Craig, one of the most promising writers of romantic fiction, has all the answers in this spell-binding new book' *Middlesbrough Evening Gazette*

0 7472 6392 2

headline

The Long Journey Home

Wendy Robertson

As the Second World War progresses and the Japanese Army edges ever closer to Singapore, mass evacuation seems inevitable. Ten-year-old Sylvie Sambuck is heartbroken – Singapore is the only home she's ever known. So, when her mother and younger brother board a ship leaving the island, Sylvie slips away, seeking refuge with her old governess, Virginia Chen.

Sylvie's presence puts Virginia and her Chinese family constantly at risk. As the war progresses, it seems increasingly unlikely they'll escape the Japanese internment camps, where the beautiful Virgina must pay the ultimate price for her beloved Sylvie.

A vibrant, heart-stopping tale of the friendship, love and laughter which sustain people during the deprivation and hardship of war.

Praise for Wendy Robertson:

'A powerful writer' *Mail on Sunday*

'A blend of accessibility and total sincerity' Pat Barker

'A great storyteller whose strength lies in her characters – from the exotic to the loveable ordinary' *Northern Echo*

0 7472 6601 8

headline